Addicted to Love

ALSO BY LORI WILDE

Addicted to Love

Lori Wilde

FOREVER

NEW YORK   BOSTON

Book design by TexTech International

Forever
Hachette Book Group USA
237 Park Avenue
New York, NY 10017

Forever is an imprint of Grand Central Publishing.
The Forever name and logo is a trademark of Hachette Book Group USA, Inc.

ISBN 978-1-60751-052-9

Printed in the United States of America

In memory of Frederick Shawn Blalock

1967–2007

Be at peace, my brother.

Acknowledgment

While Valentine, Texas, is a real place, the town of Valentine depicted in the pages of this book is completely fictional. I've taken literary license for story purposes.

Rachael's Story

Chapter One

The last thing Sheriff Brody Carlton expected to find when he wheeled his state-issued white-and-black Crown Victoria patrol cruiser past the WELCOME TO VALENTINE, TEXAS, ROMANCE CAPITAL OF THE USA billboard was a woman in a sequined wedding dress dangling from the town's mascot—a pair of the most garish, oversized, scarlet puckered-up-for-a-kiss lips ever poured in fiberglass.

She swayed forty feet off the ground in the early Sunday morning summer breeze, one arm wrapped around the sensuous curve of the full bottom lip, her other arm wielding a paintbrush dipped in black paint, her white satin ballet-slippered toes skimming the billboard's weathered wooden platform.

The billboard had been vandalized before, but never, to Brody's knowledge, by a disgruntled bride. He contemplated hitting the siren to warn her off, but feared she'd startle and end up breaking her silly neck. Instead, he whipped over onto the shoulder of the road, rolled down the passenger-side window, slid his Maui Jim sunglasses to the end of his nose, and craned his neck for a better look.

The delinquent bride had her bottom lip tucked up between her teeth. She was concentrating on desecrating the billboard. It had been a staple in Valentine's history for as long as Brody could remember. Her blonde hair, done up in one of those twisty braided hairdos, was partially obscured by the intricate lace of a floor-length wedding veil. When the sunlight hit the veil's lace just right it shimmered a phosphorescent pattern of white butterflies that looked as if they were about to rise up and flutter away.

She was oblivious to anything except splashing angry black brushstrokes across the hot, sexy mouth.

Brody exhaled an irritated snort, threw the Crown Vic into park, stuck the Maui Jims in his front shirt pocket, and climbed out. Warily, he eyed the gravel. Loose rocks. His sworn enemy. Then he remembered his new bionic Power Knee and relaxed. He'd worn the innovative prosthetic for only six weeks, but it had already changed his life. Because of the greater ease of movement and balance the computerized leg afforded, it was almost impossible for the casual observer to guess he was an amputee.

He walked directly underneath the sign, cocked his tan Stetson back on his head, and looked up.

As far as he knew—and he knew most everything that went on in Valentine, population 1,987—there'd been no weddings scheduled in town that weekend. So where had the bride come from?

Brody cleared his throat.

She went right on painting.

He cleared his throat again, louder this time.

Nothing.

"Ma'am," he called up to her.

"Go away. Can't you see I'm busy?"

Dots of black paint spattered the sand around him. She'd almost obliterated the left-hand corner of the upper lip, transforming the Marilyn Monroe sexpot pout into Marilyn Manson gothic rot.

The cynic inside him grinned. Brody had always hated those tacky red lips. Still, it was a Valentine icon and he was sworn to uphold the law.

He glanced around and spied the lollipop pink VW Bug parked between two old abandoned railway cars rusting alongside the train tracks that ran parallel to the highway. He could see a red-and-pink beaded heart necklace dangling from the rearview mirror, and a sticker on the chrome bumper proclaimed I HEART ROMANCE.

All rightee then.

"If you don't cease and desist, I'll have to arrest you," he explained.

She stopped long enough to balance the brush on the paint can and glower down at him. "On what charges?"

"Destruction of private property. The billboard is on Kelvin Wentworth's land."

"I'm doing this town a much-needed community service," she growled.

"Oh, yeah?"

"This," she said, sweeping a hand at the billboard, "is false advertising. It perpetuates a dangerous myth. I'm getting rid of it before it can suck in more impressionable young girls."

"What myth is that?"

"That there's such things as true love and romance, magic and soul mates. Rubbish. All those fairy tales are complete and utter rubbish and I fell for it, hook, line, and sinker."

"Truth in advertising *is* an oxymoron."

"Exactly. And I'm pulling the plug."

You'll get no argument from me, he thought, but vandalism was vandalism and he was the sheriff, even if he agreed with her in theory. In practice, he was the law. "Wanna talk about it?"

She glared. "To a man? You've gotta be kidding me."

"Judging from your unorthodox attire and your displeasure with the billboard in particular and men in general, I'm gonna go out on a limb here and guess that you were jilted at the altar."

"Perceptive," she said sarcastically.

"Another woman?"

She didn't respond immediately and he was about to repeat the question when she muttered, "The Chicago Bears."

"The Bears?"

"Football."

Brody sank his hands onto his hips. "The guy jilted you over football?"

"Bastard." She was back at it again, slinging paint.

"He sounds like a dumbass."

"He's Trace Hoolihan."

Brody shrugged. "Is that supposed to mean something?"

"You don't know who he is?"

"Nope."

"Hallelujah," the bride-that-wasn't said. "I've found the one man in Texas who's not ate up with football."

It wasn't that he didn't like football, but the last couple of years his life had been preoccupied with adjusting to losing his leg in Iraq, getting over a wife who'd left him for another man, helping his wayward sister raise her young daughter, and settling into his job as sheriff. He hadn't had much time for leisurely pursuits.

"How'd you get up there?" Brody asked.

"With my white sequined magical jet pack."

"You've got a lot of anger built up inside."

"You think?"

"I know you're heartbroken and all," he drawled, "but I'm gonna have to ask you to stop painting the Valentine kisser."

"This isn't the first time, you know," she said without breaking stride. *Swish, swish, swish* went the paintbrush.

"You've vandalized a sign before?"

"I've been stood up at the altar before."

"No kidding?"

"Last year. The ratfink never showed up. Left me standing in the church for over an hour while my wilting orchid bouquet attracted bees."

"And still, you were willing to try again."

"I know. I'm an idiot. Or at least I was. But I'm turning over a new leaf. Joining the skeptics."

"Well, if you don't stop painting the sign, you're going to be joining the ranks of the inmates at the Jeff Davis County Jail."

"You've got prisoners?"

"Figure of speech." How did she know the jail was empty fifty percent of the time? Brody squinted suspiciously. He didn't recognize her, at least not from this distance. "You from Valentine?"

"I live in Houston now."

That was as far as the conversation got because the mayor's fat, honking Cadillac bumped to a stop behind Brody's cruiser.

Kelvin P. Wentworth IV flung the car door open and wrestled his hefty frame from behind the wheel. Merle Haggard belted from the radio, wailing a thirty-year-old country-and-western song about boozing and chasing women.

"What the hell's going on here," Kelvin boomed and lumbered toward Brody.

The mayor tilted his head up, scowling darkly at the billboard bride. Kelvin prided himself on shopping only in Valentine. He refused to even order off the Internet. He was big and bald and on the back side of his forties. His seersucker suit clung to him like leeches on a water buffalo. Kelvin was under the mistaken impression he was still as good-looking as the day he'd scored the winning touchdown that took Valentine to state in 1977, the year Brody was born. It was the first and last time the town had been in the playoffs.

Brody suppressed the urge to roll his eyes. He knew what was coming. Kelvin was a true believer in the Church of Valentine and the jilted bride had just committed the highest form of blasphemy. "I've got it under control, Mayor."

"My ass." Kelvin waved an angry hand. "She's up there defacin' and disgracin' our hometown heritage and you're standing here with your thumb up your butt, Carlton."

"She's distraught. Her fiancé dumped her at the altar."

"Rachael Renee Henderson," Kelvin thundered up at her. "Is that you?"

"Go away, Mayor. This is something that's gotta be done," she called back.

"You get yourself down off that billboard right now, or I'm gonna call your daddy."

Rachael Henderson.

The name brought an instant association into Brody's mind. He saw an image of long blonde pigtails, gap-toothed grin, and freckles across the bridge of an upturned pixie nose. Rachael Henderson, the next-door neighbor who'd followed him around like a puppy dog until he'd moved to Midland with his mother and his sister after their father went to Kuwait when Brody was twelve. From what he recalled, Rachael was sweet as honeysuckle, certainly not the type to graffiti a beloved town landmark.

People change.

He thought of Belinda and shook his head to clear away thoughts of his ex-wife.

"My daddy is partly to blame for this," she said. "Last time I saw him he was in Houston breaking my mother's heart. Go ahead and call him. Would you like his cell phone number?"

"What's she talking about?" Kelvin swung his gaze to Brody.

Brody shrugged. "Apparently she's got some personal issues to work out."

"Well, she can't work them out on my billboard."

"I'm getting the impression the billboard is a symbol of her personal issues."

"I don't give a damn. Get 'er down."

"How do you propose I do that?"

Kelvin squinted at the billboard. "How'd she get up there?"

"Big mystery. But why don't we just let her have at it? She's bound to run out of steam soon enough in this heat."

"Are you nuts? Hell, man, she's already blacked out the top lip." Kelvin anxiously shifted his weight, bunched his hands into fists. "I won't stand for this. Find a way to get her down. Now!"

"What do you want me to do? Shoot her?"

"It's a thought," Kelvin muttered.

"Commanding the sheriff to shoot a jilted bride won't help you get reelected."

"It ain't gonna help my reelection bid if she falls off that billboard and breaks her fool neck because I didn't stop her."

"Granted."

Kelvin cursed up a blue streak and swiped a meaty hand across his sweaty forehead. "I was supposed to be getting doughnuts so me and Marianne could have a nice, quiet breakfast before church, but hell no, I gotta deal with this stupid crap." Kelvin, a self-proclaimed playboy, had never married. Marianne was his one hundred and twenty pound bullmastiff.

"Go get your doughnuts, Mayor," Brody said. "I've got this under control."

Kelvin shot him a withering look and pulled his cell phone from his pocket. Brody listened to the one-sided conversation, his eyes on Rachael, who showed no signs of slowing her assault on the vampish pout.

"Rex," Kelvin barked to his personal assistant. "Go over to Audie's, have him open the hardware store up for you, get a twenty-five-foot ladder, and bring it out to the Valentine billboard."

There was a pause from Kelvin as Rex responded.

"I don't care if you stayed up 'til three a.m. playing video games with your geeky online buddies. Just do it."

With a savage slash of his thumb on the keypad, Kelvin hung up and muttered under his breath, "I'm surrounded by morons."

Brody tried not to take offense at the comment. Kelvin liked his drama as much as he liked ordering people around.

Fifteen minutes later, Rex showed up with a collapsible yellow ladder roped to his pickup truck. He was barely twenty-five, redheaded as rhubarb, and had a voice deep as Barry White's, with an Adam's apple that protruded like a submarine ready to break the surface. Brody often wondered if the prominent Adam's apple had anything to do with the kid's smooth, dark, ebony voice.

Up on the billboard, Rachael was almost finished with the mouth. She had slashes of angry black paint smeared across the front of her wedding gown. While waiting on Rex to show up with the ladder, Kelvin had spent the time trying to convince her to come down, but she was a zealot on a mission and she wouldn't even talk to him.

"I want her arrested," Kelvin snapped. "I'm pressing charges."

"You might want to reconsider that," Brody advised. "Since the election is just a little more than three months away and Giada Vito is gaining favor in the polls."

The polls being the gossip at Higgy's Diner. He knew the mayor was grandstanding. For the first time in Kelvin's three-term stint, he was running opposed. Giada Vito had moved to Valentine from Italy and she'd gotten her American citizenship as soon as the law allowed. She was a dyed-in-the-wool Democrat, the principal of Valentine High, drove a vintage Fiat, and didn't mince her words. Especially when it came to the topic of Valentine's favored son, Kelvin P. Wentworth IV.

"Hey, you leave the legal and political machinations to me. You just do your job," said Kelvin.

Brody blew out his breath and went to help Rex untie the ladder. What he wanted to do was tell Kelvin to shove it. But the truth was the woman needed to come down before she got hurt. More than likely, the wooden billboard decking was riddled with termites.

He and Rex got the ladder loose and carried it over to prop it against the back of the billboard. It extended just long enough to reach the ladder rungs that were attached to the billboard itself.

Kelvin gave Brody a pointed look. "Up you go."

Brody ignored him. "Rachael, we've got a ladder in place. You need to come down now."

"Don't ask her, tell her," Kelvin hissed to Brody, then said to Rachael, "Missy, get your ass down here this instant."

"Get bent," Rachael sang out.

"That was effective," Brody muttered.

Rex snorted back a laugh. Kelvin shot him a withering glance and then raised his eyebrows at Brody and jerked his head toward the billboard. "You're the sheriff. Do your job."

Brody looked up at the ladder and then tried his best not to glance down at his leg. He didn't want to show the slightest sign of weakness, especially in front of Kelvin. But while his Power Knee was pretty well the most awesome thing that had happened to him since his rehabilitation, he'd never tested it by climbing a ladder, particularly a thin, wobbly, collapsible one.

Shit. If he fell off, it was going to hurt. He might even break something.

Kelvin was staring expectantly, arms crossed over his bearish chest, the sleeves of his seersucker suit straining against his bulky forearms. The door to the Cadillac was still hanging open and from the radio Merle Haggard had given it up to Tammy Wynette, who was beseeching women to stand by their man.

Brody was the sheriff. This was his job. And he never shirked his duty, even when it was the last thing on earth he wanted to do. Gritting his teeth, he gathered his courage, wrapped both hands around the ladder just above his head, and planted his prosthetic leg on the bottom rung.

His gut squeezed.

Come on, you can do this.

He attacked the project the same way he'd attacked physical therapy, going at it with dogged determination to walk again, to come home, if not whole, at least proud to be a man. Of course Belinda had shattered all that.

Don't think about Belinda. Get up the ladder. Get the girl down.

He placed his good leg on the second rung.

The ladder trembled under his weight.

Brody swallowed back the fear and pulled his prosthesis up the next step. Hands clinging tightly to the ladder above him, he raised his head and counted the steps.

Twenty-five of them on the ladder and seventeen on the back of the billboard.

Three down, thirty-nine left to go.

He remembered an old movie called *The Thirty-Nine Steps*. Suddenly, those three words held a weighted significance. It wasn't just thirty-nine more steps. It was also forty-two more back down with Rachael Henderson in tow.

Better get climbing.

Thirty-eight steps.

Thirty-seven.

Thirty-six.

The higher he went, the more the ladder quivered.

Halfway up vertigo took solid hold of him. He'd never had a fear of heights before, but now, staring down at

Kelvin and Rex, who were staring up at him, Brody's head swam and his stomach pitched. He bit his bottom lip, closed his eyes, and took another step up.

In the quiet of the higher air, he could hear the soft whispery sound of his computerized leg working as he took another step. Kelvin's country music sounded tinny and far away. With his eyes closed and his hands skimming over the cool aluminum ladder, he could also hear the sound of brushstrokes growing faster and more frantic the closer he came to the bottom of the billboard.

Rachael was still furiously painting, trying to get in as many licks as she could.

When Brody finally reached the top of the first ladder, he opened his eyes.

"You're doing great," Kelvin called up to him. "Keep going. You're almost there."

Yeah, almost there. This was the hardest part of all, covering the gap between the ladder from Audie's Hardware and the thin metal footholds welded to the back of the billboard.

He took a deep breath. He had to stretch to reach the bottom step. He grabbed hold of it with both hands, and took his Power Knee off the aluminum ladder.

For a moment, he hung there, twenty-five feet off the ground, fighting gravity and the bile rising in his throat, wondering why he hadn't told Kelvin to go straight to hell. Wondering why he hadn't just called the volunteer fire department to come and get Rachael down.

It was a matter of pride and he knew it. Stupid, egotistical pride. He'd wanted to prove he could handle anything that came with the job. Wanted to show the town he'd earned their vote. That he hadn't just stumbled into the office because he was an injured war hero.

Pride goes before a fall, his Gramma Carlton used to say. Now, for the first time, he fully understood what she meant.

Arms trembling with the effort, he dragged himself up with his biceps, his real leg tiptoed on the collapsible ladder, his bionic leg searching blindly for the rung.

Just when he thought he wouldn't be able to hold on a second longer, he found the toehold and then brought his good leg up against the billboard ladder to join the bionic one.

He'd made it.

Brody clung there, breathing hard, thanking God for letting him get this far and wondering just how in the hell he was going to get back down without killing them both, when he heard the soft sounds of muffled female sobs.

Rachael was crying.

The hero in him forgot that his limbs were quivering, forgot that he was forty feet in the air, forgot that somehow he was going to have to get back down. The only thing in his mind was the woman.

Was she all right?

As quickly as he could, Brody scaled the remaining rungs and then gingerly settled his legs on the billboard decking. He ducked under the bottom of the sign and peered around it.

She sat, knees drawn to her chest, head down, looking completely incongruous in that wedding dress smeared with black paint and the butterfly wedding veil floating around her head. Miraculously, the veil seemed to have escaped the paint.

"You okay?"

She raised her head. "Of course I'm not okay."

Up close, he saw tear tracks had run a gully through the makeup on her cheeks and mascara had pooled underneath her eyes. She looked like a quarrelsome raccoon caught in a coyote trap, all piss and vinegar, but visibly hurting.

He had the strangest, and most uncharacteristic, urge to pull her into his arms, hold her to his chest, kiss the top of her head the way he did his six-year-old niece, Maisy, and tell her everything was going to be all right.

Mentally, he stomped the impulse. He didn't need any damsel-in-distress hassle.

The expression in her eyes told him anger had propelled her up here, but now, her rage spent, she was afraid to come back down. That fear he understood loud and clear.

Calmly, he held out a hand to her. "Rachael, it's time to go."

"I thought I'd feel better," she said in a despondent little voice as she stared at his outstretched hand. "I don't feel better. I was supposed to feel better. That was the plan. Why don't I feel better?"

"Destruction rarely makes you feel good." His missing leg gave a twinge. "Come on, give me your hand and let's get back on the ground."

"You look familiar. Are you married?" she asked.

He opened his mouth to answer, but she didn't give him a chance before launching into a fast-paced monologue. "I hope you're married, because if you're not married, you need to get someone else to help me down from here."

"Huh?" Had the sun baked her brain or had getting stood up at the altar made her crazy?

"If you're not married, then this is a cute meet. I'm a sucker for meeting cute."

"Huh?" he said again.

"My first fiancé?" she chattered, her glossolalia revealing her emotional distress. "I met Robert in a hot-air balloon. He was the pilot. I wanted a romantic adventure. The balloon hung up in a pecan tree and the fire department had to rescue us. It was terribly cute."

"Sounds like it," he said, simply to appease her. Mentally, he was planning their trip off the billboard.

"And Trace? I met him when he came to the kindergarten class where I taught. On career day. He was tossing a football around as he gave his speech. He lost control of it and accidentally beaned me in the head. He literally knocked me off my feet. He caught me just before I hit the ground and there I was, trapped in his big strong arms, staring up into his big blue eyes. I just melted. So you see I succumb to the cute meet. I've got to break the cycle and these romantic notions I have about love and marriage and dating and men. But I can't do it if I go around meeting cute. There's no way I can let you rescue me if you're not married."

The woman, Brody decided, was officially bonkers.

"Sorry." He shrugged. "I'm divorced."

She grimaced. "Oh, no."

"But this isn't a cute meet."

She glanced over at the fiberglass billboard lips, then peered down at her paint-spotted wedding dress and finally drilled him with almond-shaped green eyes, the only exotic thing about her.

The rest of her was round and smooth and welcoming, from her cherubic cheeks to her petite curves to the full bow of her supple pink mouth. She was as soft-focus as a Monet. Just looking at her made him think of springtime and flowers and fuzzy baby chicks.

Except for those disconcerting bedroom eyes. They called up unwanted X-rated images in his mind.

"I dunno," she said, "this seems dangerously cute to me."

"It can't be a cute meet," he explained, struggling to follow her disjointed train of thought, "because we've already met."

She tilted her head. "We have?"

"Yep."

"I thought you looked familiar."

"So no cute meet. Now give me your hand."

Reluctantly, she placed her hand in his. "Where did we meet?"

"Right here in Valentine." He spoke with a soothing voice. Her hand was warm and damp with perspiration. He drew her toward him.

She didn't resist. She was tired and emotionally exhausted.

"That's it," he coaxed.

"You do look familiar."

"Watch your head," he said as he led her underneath the billboard, toward the ladder.

She paused at the ladder and stared at the ground. "It's a long way down."

Tell me about it.

"I'm here, I'll go first. I'll be there to catch you if you lose your balance."

"Will you keep your hand on my waist? To steady me?"

"Sure," he promised recklessly, placing chivalry over common sense.

He started down the ladder ahead of her, found secure footing, wrapped his left hand around the rung, and reached up to hold on to her waist with his right hand as she started down.

Touching her brought an unexpected knot of emotion

to his chest. Half desire, half tenderness, he didn't know what to call it, but he knew one thing. The feeling was damned dangerous.

"I'm scared," she whimpered.

"You're doing great." He guided her down until her sweet little rump was directly in his face. Any other time he would have enjoyed this position, but not under these circumstances.

"I'm going down another couple of steps," he explained. "I'm going to have to let go of you for a minute, so hold on tight."

The long train of her wedding veil floated in the air between them, a gauzy pain in the ass. In order to see where he was going, he had to keep batting it back. He took up his position several rungs below her and called to her to come down. As he'd promised, he put a hand at her waist to guide her.

They went on like that, painstaking step by painstaking step, until they were past the gap, off the billboard, and onto the collapsible aluminum ladder. In that regard, coming down was much easier than going up.

"You're certain I already know you?" she asked. "Because seriously, this has all the makings of a meet cute."

"You know me."

"How?"

"I'm from Valentine, just like you. Moved away, came back," he said.

Only four feet off the ground now. His legs felt flimsy as spindly garden sprouts.

"Oh my gosh," she gasped and whipped her head around quickly.

Too quickly.

Somehow, in the breeze and the movement, the infernal wedding veil wrapped around his prosthetic leg. He tried to kick it off but the material clung stubbornly.

"I know who you are," she said and then right there on the ladder, she turned around to glare at him. "You're Brody Carlton."

He didn't have a chance to answer. The ladder swayed and the veil snatched his leg out from under him.

He lost his balance.

The next thing he knew, he was lying on his back on the ground, and Rachael Henderson, his one-time next-door-neighbor-turned-jilted-psycho-bride, was on top of him. They were both breathing hard and trembling.

Her eyes locked on his.

His eyes locked on her lips.

Brody should have been thinking about his leg. He was surprised he wasn't thinking about his leg. What he was thinking about was the fact that he was being straddled by a woman in a wedding dress and it was the closest he'd come to having sex in over two years.

"You! You're the one."

"The one?" he asked.

"You're the root cause of all my problems," she exclaimed, fire in her eyes, at the same time Brody found himself thinking, *Where have you been all my life?*

But that was not what he said.

What he said was, "Rachael Renee Henderson, you have the right to remain silent..."

Chapter Two

Kelvin Wentworth was so steamed he couldn't enjoy his crullers. He tossed the half-eaten pastry to Marianne and dusted his sticky fingers against this thigh. The bullmastiff snarfed it up with a smack of her lips, and then eyed him to see if more was forthcoming. When she realized it wasn't, she settled back down on her plush pillow.

"Dammit, Marianne," he complained. "This couldn't have happened at a worse time. You should see what that foolish Henderson girl did to our billboard."

The dog made a huffing noise and covered her nose with her paws.

"I know!" Kelvin pushed himself up out of his chair and paced the generous length of the study that had been his daddy's and his granddaddy's and his great-granddaddy's before that.

Three generations of Wentworths had been born and raised in this house. All their portraits and photographs of their accomplishments hung on the wall. There was Great-Granddaddy, Kelvin Wentworth I, covered in crude oil and grinning like an opossum as his first well came in. Next was a snapshot of Granddaddy Kelvin Wentworth II breaking ground on Wentworth Novelties. Beside that was a picture of Kelvin's daddy, Kelvin Wentworth III, shaking hands with LBJ at the dedication of his man-made, heart-shaped Lake Valentine.

A wall of fame. An illustrious heritage.

"Maybe I should've gotten married," he mused. "Had kids."

Marianne didn't offer an opinion.

"I had plenty of chances. I just never expected to get this old, this quick. I always thought I'd have time. Sow some wild oats before I settled down. Then again, how could I get married when I had a town to run? Valentine depended on me. Needed me. Especially after Daddy died."

He stopped pacing in front of his own photograph in the lineup. In the picture he was being hoisted up on the shoulders of his teammates, all the while tightly clutching the Texas State High School Championship football trophy. Back then he'd had a full head of hair, a lean body, and a thousand-watt smile. "Where'd the years go?"

Marianne sighed.

"This Amusement Corp deal is the only legacy I have to leave behind," he said. "Other than the championship win. It's gotta go through. The Amusement Corp representatives can't show up in town on Wednesday and see that billboard in the shape it's in."

Marianne barked.

"You're right. I'm probably overreacting about the billboard. I can get it cleaned up in time. But it's not just the billboard. It's that damned Giada Vito and the back-to-nature concepts she's kicking up. What the hell is wrong with the woman? She has no idea what's best for this town. She's a foreigner for crissake."

But Kelvin knew what was best. His family had founded Valentine.

He walked over to the pool table in the center of the room that held a mock-up of his vision for Valentine's future. His plans had been a decade in the making and were finally coming to fruition.

Squatting down to eye level, he admired the replica of a theme park the likes of which had never before been conceived. Valentine Land. The ultimate destination for fun-loving honeymooners. He flicked a switch on the plywood foundation and everything sprang to life.

The *Gone With the Wind* roller coaster started up the incline. The *My Fair Lady* Tilt-a-Whirl twirled. The *Pride and Prejudice* waterslide gurgled. Strobe lights flashed in the *It Happened One Night* Tunnel of Love while the *Camelot* Carousel went round and round.

And along with the theme park would come the Wentworth Airport, Wentworth Resort Hotels, and Wentworth Restaurants.

Excitement coursed through Kelvin's veins. Great-Granddaddy had found oil and built this house. Granddaddy had constructed Wentworth Novelties and groomed it into the world's largest supplier of Valentine's Day novelties outside of China. Daddy had created Valentine Lake and started the annual Fish-A-Thon tournament to supply the local food bank.

And now it was his turn.

Kelvin was going down in history as the man who brought true prosperity to Valentine. He had Walt Disney dreams, and with Amusement Corp's backing, he could make it happen.

The telephone rang.

Irritated at being interrupted, Kelvin straightened and went for the phone. The caller ID told him it was the sheriff. "What you want, Carlton?" he grunted.

"Are you really serious about pressing charges against Rachael Henderson?"

"Hell, yes, I am." He had to nip her insurrection in the bud. He couldn't have anti-romance sentiment floating round while trying to sell the town on Valentine Land.

"Couldn't she just agree to clean it up and let it go at that? There's no reason to take this to court."

"My sign was vandalized, Sheriff. Do your job."

"Judge Pruitt is out of town until tomorrow. If you insist on pressing charges, Rachael is going to have to spend the night in jail."

"Boo hoo. Tough luck. She should have thought about that before she went and painted up my billboard."

"You're being a hard-ass for no reason."

"She defaced a local landmark."

"It's not like it's the first time someone's taken a pot-shot at the sign."

"She's a negative influence. I'd think you'd be more concerned about her disrespect for our hometown."

"Okay, Mayor, you have every legal right to press charges, but I want to go on record here. I think you're being a jackass."

"Thanks for your opinion. Now why don't you take it and a buck fifty and head on over to Higgy's Diner and buy yourself a cup of coffee. I'll drop by to file an official complaint right after church."

BRODY SLAMMED THE phone down on his desk and muttered an oath under his breath.

His only full-time deputy Zeke Frisco's wife had given birth last night to their first child. The baby was five weeks early, putting Brody at a disadvantage. His two part-time deputies had taken their summer vacations together in order to be off when Zeke went on paternity leave. The dispatcher, Jamie Johnston, was a single mom who worked nine to three Monday through Friday so she could take her kids to school and pick them up afterward without having to hire a babysitter.

Damn Kelvin and his insistence on pressing charges. If the Wentworths hadn't owned the land where the sign was erected, he would have told the mayor he could stuff it.

As it was, he'd had no choice but to arrest Rachael.

Hands down, the hardest part of his job was putting up with the mayor. There wasn't much crime in Valentine. Occasionally one of the regulars at Leroy's Bar on the outskirts of town would kick up a fuss and Brody would have to lock him in the drunk tank overnight. Or he'd have to haul someone in on a warrant for child support violations or unpaid traffic tickets. Once in a rare while there would be a few petty thefts or shoplifting incidents or he'd catch some high school kid selling weed from the trunk of his car. But most of the time things were pretty peaceful in his hometown and that's the way he liked it. He'd had enough excitement in Iraq to last a lifetime.

Kelvin was the only thing that got under his skin. That and his insecurities over his leg. He was determined to be a good sheriff in spite of his handicap.

Don't let Wentworth get to you.

Good advice. Now if he could just heed it.

Of course, the real source of his problem was the woman in the wedding gown sitting in lockup.

Inexplicably, his gut tightened as he remembered just how good it had felt to have her firm thighs wrapped around his waist. He still couldn't believe she was the same kid who used to live next door to him all those years ago.

Nor could he believe the way his body had responded to her. He hadn't felt much in the way of sexual interest since Belinda had taken off with another man. It had been over two years and while he'd gotten over her betrayal, he knew he still wasn't ready to lay his heart open again.

Lay your heart open? Hell, you're just horny. That's all it is.

But deep down inside, he feared that wasn't true. He was lonely and he missed the good parts about being married. The long talks, the intimacy, the fun times.

Love's not worth the risk.

He took a deep breath and pushed his hands through his hair. If he tilted his head, he could see through his open door to the jail beyond. Rachael sat behind bars, her head cradled in her palms.

Sympathy kicked him. He hated this but he had no choice. He had to go tell her she'd be spending the night in jail.

"How you holding up?"

Rachael sat on the cement jail slab amid the billowy taffeta of her paint-smeared wedding dress. She raised her chin to see Brody Carlton walk over to stand in front of her jail cell, his leather shoes creaking against the cement, his hands on his hips just above the holster of his gun. He looked amused.

"You think this is funny?" she snapped.

"I didn't say that."

"You're smirking."

"I'm not smirking."

"You are."

"Okay, maybe I am a little," he said, "but you've got to admit, it's sort of funny."

She glared. "It's not the least bit funny."

He wiped the smile from his mouth, but not from his eyes. "Can't say I've ever seen a bride behind bars."

"What's the matter with you," she scolded, "enjoying the tragedy of another?"

"You call this a tragedy?" he growled, the expression in his eyes suddenly flashing from teasing tolerance to borderline anger. "Princess, come down out of your ivory tower. You have no idea what real tragedy is."

She remembered something her mother had told her about him in passing. Brody had been sent to Iraq. He'd been wounded and won some kind of medal for bravery. But that's all she knew about him. She hadn't even known he was the new sheriff. She hadn't paid much attention to Selina's gossip about Valentine in the years after she'd moved away. She'd been too busy repeatedly falling in love with all the wrong guys. And she hadn't been back home for a long time. Usually her parents came to see her in Houston, or they all gathered at her younger sister's home in San Antonio. Hannah was married and had two babies.

Humiliation burned in her chest over what she'd just said to him. The man was a war hero. He'd seen real tragedy.

Oh God, she was so selfish.

"You're right," Rachael admitted, shamefaced. "It was

a stupid thing to say. I was just feeling sorry for myself. I know this is a problem of my own making."

"You're upset."

He'd come closer and was now leaning against the bars with his hands on his hips, elbows thrust out, studying her like an anthropologist in the Outback. As if she were some curious creature who'd caught his attention. But it was a clinical, controlled interest devoid of personal feelings.

He's learned how to step outside himself, she realized. To detach from whatever emotionally chaotic situation he found going on around him. A handy skill. One she'd do well to emulate.

But instead of emulating his calm, cool manner, she found herself remembering what it had felt like straddling his hard, muscular body after they'd fallen from the ladder together. She recalled the tumble and the disconcerting thrill that had shot through her. The same thrill that—whenever she experienced it—had always signaled potential romance.

She'd managed to ignore it at the time, to thrust it from her mind. But now, looking at Brody's hard, lean frame, she was finding it very difficult to forget. He reminded her of the actor Matthew Fox. He played the character of Jack Shepard on the television show *Lost*: moral, principled, self-contained, not to mention a stone-cold hottie.

Rachael couldn't stop her gaze from drifting over him. She could smell his scent from here. Manly—all leather and gunpowder overlaying the aroma of clean soap. Stupidly, she found herself wondering if he tasted as masculine as he smelled. He possessed a strong, stubborn jaw and dark enigmatic eyes. The look he gave her seemed to say, *I know all your secrets; you can't hide anything from me.*

Rachael gulped. Not that she'd ever been any good at hiding her feelings.

He was tall. Well over six feet. A tower compared to her own five-foot-three inches. His dark brown hair was clipped short. Not quite a military cut, but not much longer. His tan uniform fit him to perfection. The sleeves of his shirt and the creases of his pants were crisply starched. Even in the muted jail lighting, the badge on his chest gleamed smartly. Give the man a black mask and a white horse, and he could pass for the Lone Ranger.

Involuntarily, Rachael licked her lips.

He was as tempting to her as a double scotch on the rocks was to a boozehound. Just looking at him had her spinning happily-ever-after daydreams.

Stop it!

She had a very serious problem. Fantasizing about a new guy the day after the old guy had stood her up at the altar.

Warped. She was warped.

Brody's not new. He's the very first guy you ever spun romantic fantasies about.

Yeah, and look where that had gotten her.

"Um," she said, "I need to use the bathroom and I have the most awful feeling that hole in the floor is where I'm expected to go."

A look of pity crossed his face. That irritated her more than his amusement. She didn't need his pity.

"I'll let you use my private restroom," he said, taking the jail keys from his pocket and opening the door. "And I've brought you a sandwich from Higgy's."

Her mouth watered but she wasn't going to let him know she appreciated his kindness. "Don't do me any favors," she muttered.

He arched an eyebrow. "You want to use the hole?"

"No, no."

The amusement was back on his lips.

Okay, he was officially making it easy for her to swear off men forever.

"This way." He took her elbow and guided her out of the cell. His fingers were calloused. His grip strong. Rachael felt something twist inside her. Something she couldn't name curled against the wall of her chest. She caught her breath, suddenly afraid to breathe.

Brody led her through the main lobby and back into his office. His shoulder brushed against hers. Rachael's skin tingled beneath his touch. Unnerved by the sensation, she felt her muscles coil up tight. This was ridiculous.

He shut the door behind them, indicated a second door on the other side of the room. "Don't get any ideas about escaping."

"You think I could shimmy out a window in this getup?" she asked, fluffing the skirts of her wedding gown.

"You climbed up on a billboard in it."

"You've got a point," she said and went into the bathroom.

A few minutes later, she emerged to find him lounging against the desk, arms folded across his chest. The thought that he'd overheard her in the bathroom made her cheeks burn.

"Eat your sandwich," he said, kicking a rolling chair over for her.

Rachael sat down on the other side of his desk, grateful

for the ham-and-cheese sandwich on a plate covered with plastic wrap, along with a pickle and a scoop of potato salad. There was also a plastic glass filled to the brim with ice-cold sweet tea.

She was starving. She couldn't remember the last time she'd eaten. After Trace had left her at the altar, she'd taken off without thinking, without changing clothes, without even stopping for food. She'd hopped in her VW Bug and driven the four hundred miles from Houston to Valentine through the dark of night — with only a slight detour to Wal-Mart for the black paint — bent on annihilating that damned billboard because it represented a decade of bad dates, broken hearts, and shattered dreams.

She tore into the sandwich and Brody sat down opposite her. "So," she said between bites, "how long you been sheriff?"

"A few months. Ever since Mel Hartly got sick and I was elected his replacement."

"Aren't you kind of young to be a sheriff?"

He shrugged.

"It's the war vet thing, right?"

"I don't like to talk about it."

She studied him over the rim of her glass. "I heard you got some kind of a medal."

"That's talking about it."

"It might help if you discussed it."

"Does talking about getting dumped at the altar help you?"

He had her there. "No."

"Glad we settled that."

Rachael polished off the rest of her sandwich. "Hey, you remember that time we climbed the chinaberry tree in your front yard and I got stuck and you had to help me down?"

"Vaguely," he said.

"Seems like you're making a habit of helping me climb down when I get myself up a tree. I wanted to say thanks for getting me off that billboard in one piece. Thanks for the chinaberry tree, too."

He grinned. "Don't mention it."

She dusted off her fingertips. "So when can I get out of here?"

"Not until tomorrow morning. Judge Abigail's out of town. She'll be back to arraign you at ten."

Panic took hold of her then. "What? I'm going to have to spend the night here? Just for painting the billboard?"

"I couldn't talk the mayor out of pressing charges."

Her eyes stung. She swallowed hard. "Don't I get a phone call?"

"You do."

"Can I make it now?"

He nodded, plucked the receiver from the phone on his desk, and extended it toward her.

Rachael started to reach for the phone, but stopped midway. Who was she going to call? She was furious at her parents. Trace was on his way to Chicago. She certainly wasn't going to alarm her sister, Hannah. Immediately, she thought of her three best friends, all of whom had been at the wedding: Delaney, Tish, and Jillian. But Delaney and Tish both had little kids. She couldn't ask them to drive four hundred miles to bail her out of jail. And Jillian, well, much as she loved her, Jillian was such a cynic when it came to love she would probably get a huge kick out of the whole thing.

But what choice did she have? It was either Jillian or her parents and she wasn't speaking to them.

Taking in a deep breath, she spun around in the swivel chair until her back was to Brody and placed the call, all the while extremely aware of the heat of his gaze burning the nape of her neck.

"Samuels." Jillian answered the phone on the second ring in her usual clipped, no-nonsense style.

"Jilly?" She was alarmed to hear her voice sounding so shaky. "It's Rachael."

"Rach! Where are you? Everyone is worried sick. You just took off without a word to anyone. Your parents are frantic. Have you called them?"

"No! And don't you tell them that I called you."

"Rachael," Jillian chided gently. "It's not like you to be so inconsiderate."

Well, it wasn't like Jillian—who often wore steel-toed army boots when it came to other people's feelings—to scold Rachael for being insensitive. That hurt.

"I'm sick of it, Jilly. My parents, my town, the media, advertising. Force-feeding me romance for twenty-six years when it's all just a load of bull..." Rachael paused to take a deep breath.

"Hey, you'll get no argument from me. I'm anti-romance. Always have been, always will be."

"I used to think you were coldhearted when it came to male-female relationships," Rachael said. "But I see now you were right and everyone else is off their rocker."

"I wouldn't go that far."

"Men suck."

Behind her, Brody cleared his throat.

Well, too darn bad if he got his feelings hurt. Men did

suck. They pursued you like gangbusters, promising you the moon and the stars and happily-ever-after. Promises they had absolutely no intention of keeping once you succumbed to their pursuit and gave them your heart. Cruel bastards. Every last one of them.

"Listen, Jilly, I desperately need your help."

"Anything; you know that."

"I need you to come bail me out of the Jeff Davis County Jail."

"What?" Jillian sounded stunned. "You? You're in jail?"

"I got arrested."

"What for?"

"Vandalizing gigantic lips."

"Excuse me?"

"You'll see what I'm talking about when you get here."

"Get where? Where is Jeff Davis County?"

"Valentine."

"Your hometown?"

"Yes."

"Where is that, exactly?"

"This is the part that makes the favor really huge. Valentine is seriously in the middle of nowhere. Over four hundred miles from Houston. It's the only town in Jeff Davis County. We don't have a real airport, just a private airstrip. You'll have to drive. I'm being arraigned at ten in the morning."

Her friend hesitated but only for a fraction of a second. "I'll have to rearrange my schedule, but I'll be there. It sounds like you could use a good lawyer." Jillian was an ace Houston prosecutor. She'd rip the mayor's case to shreds and have Rachael out of there in no time.

"Thank you so much; you have no idea how much I appreciate this. I know what an imposition it—"

"Hush. What are friends for?"

"You're the best," she whispered.

"Now, are you sure you don't want me to let your parents at least know you're okay?"

Rachael paused, guilt warring with anger. "You can tell them you heard from me and that I'm all right, but please, Jilly, whatever you do, don't tell them I'm in Valentine. Don't tell them I got arrested. I need time to think this all through and figure out what I'm going to do next."

"I can respect that."

"Thank you," Rachael whispered.

"I'll be there in time for your court appearance," Jillian replied, then said good-bye and hung up.

Rachael cradled the telephone receiver then turned in the swivel chair to meet Brody's eyes. He was watching her the way a cat would watch a caged bird. Did they teach those unnerving looks in sheriff school? Or was this something he'd picked up on his own? A dubious gift from Baghdad, perhaps?

His gaze drilled into hers and a radiant wave of energy zapped from him to her. Fanciful, she told herself, struggling to deny the heat simmering inside her. She'd had these feelings before, mistaken them for something more than sexual attraction. She wasn't going to make that mistake again. She would admit it. She was sexually attracted to him.

Big deal. That's all it was. Hormones. Chemistry. It meant absolutely nothing. She was not going to start imagining the cute little cottage and the white picket fence and two kids in the yard.

She'd be much better served to imagine them naked, rolling around in his bed, having hot, sweaty sex. After that, she'd visualize herself getting up, getting dressed, and walking away without a backward glance.

WHILE RACHAEL WAS cooling her heels in the Jeff Davis County Jail, Selina Henderson paced her hotel room at the Houston Four Seasons, trying for the fiftieth time to contact her daughter's cell phone. But just as it had the other forty-nine times, the call went to voice mail. Instead of issuing yet another plea for Rachael to call her back, Selina hung up and threw the phone across the room.

"Dammit all," she screamed and knotted her fingernails into her palms.

Anger had replaced guilt and concern. She was mad. Furious, in fact. Yes, Rachael had been hurt. She understood that. But this refusal to answer her phone or call her mother back was bordering on childishness.

However, the real object of Selina's fury wasn't her erstwhile daughter, but rather her soon-to-be ex-husband. She gritted her teeth. How could Michael have let it slip that they were getting divorced not ten minutes before that ridiculous Trace Hoolihan ran out on his wedding to Rachael?

She and Michael had driven to Houston together, agreeing not to tell Rachael about their split until she'd returned from her honeymoon. Agreeing for this one day to put up a united front. Selina had been so disgusted with Michael for going back on their agreement that she hadn't even been able to talk to him about their daughter.

So here she was on the verge of ending a twenty-seven-year marriage. All alone in a hotel room in a big city where she knew no one, and she had absolutely no idea where her daughter might have gone after being dumped at the altar on her wedding day.

Love, romance, marriage. Bah—*fucking*—humbug.

She flung herself across the bed she hadn't slept in. She'd been awake all night, thinking, planning, worrying, regretting, hating, loving, and hurting. The urge to cry was there, but honestly, she was cried out. Exhaustion permeated her bones. She was tired of fighting. Tired of pretending. Tired of trying to convince herself there was such a thing as happily-ever-after.

It was a myth.

Selina stared up at the ceiling textured with arty swirls. Forty-five years old, almost single and starting all over again. How had this happened? Once upon a time she'd loved Michael with an emotion so strong and fierce and true it scared her. Where had that foolish, lovesick girl gone?

It was a rhetorical question. She knew the answer.

The first tiny piece of doubt had taken root on her own wedding day when she'd discovered that her new husband had spent the night before their wedding with another woman. Her flaw had been that she'd loved him so much she'd chosen to believe his story that nothing had happened. That he'd gone out with his high school sweetheart, Vivian Cole, for old time's sake and nothing more.

God, she'd been such an idiot.

Selina closed her eyes. The swirly ceiling patterns were making her dizzy. Purposefully, she pushed away thoughts of Michael and the failure of her marriage. Her time had come and gone. This was about Rachael. What was she going to do about her daughter?

She wished she could hold Rachael in her arms and tell

her not to grieve too hard over losing Trace. Tell her she'd been lucky to dodge a bullet. But she knew none of that would comfort her. As much as she might want to protect her daughter, she knew this was ultimately something she had to work out for herself.

And that thought left Selina feeling lonelier than ever.

Her stomach grumbled and she realized she hadn't eaten anything since the morning before. Food might be the last thing on her mind, but the hunger pains were annoying.

She reached for the telephone to call room service, but simply didn't have the energy to punch the button. Slumping back against the pillow, she pondered her next move.

Where did she go from here?

She'd been born and raised in Valentine. She was a small-town girl with roots that stretched across the Texas-Mexico border. She was simple, earthy. She'd liked gardening and raising her babies and cooking hearty comfort foods and taking care of Michael.

Scratch that last part.

Michael was no longer her concern.

And her kids were grown. No one to cook for anymore.

A sudden, frightening realization took hold of Selina. She didn't know who she was, now that she was no longer the mother of young children or the wife of one of Valentine's most prominent and wealthiest citizens. She had no purpose.

It was a horrifying feeling, this sense of uselessness.

A tiny terrified part of her whispered, *Go back to Michael, tell him you made a mistake. Tell him you forgive him for Vivian.*

But that would be so easy to do. She'd been tamping it

down, denying her feelings, denying the truth of twenty-seven years. She simply couldn't do it any longer.

So these were her choices? Continue to live a lie or fade away into old age all alone?

No!

Another part of her, a stronger part of her, the part of her she'd hidden away the day she married Michael, protested. Enough was enough. She would find a way out of this. She was only forty-five. There was still time left to decide who she was going to be for the rest of her life.

She was on the verge of something monumental. She could feel it. The only thing holding her back right now was Rachael. Once she knew where her daughter was, that she was safe and going to be okay, then Selina could let go.

Until then, her daughter was her main concern.

After that, all bets were off.

The thought made her feel better. *Deal with Rachael first, pick up the pieces of my life second.* It sounded like a plan. Selina liked plans.

There was a knock at the door.

Startled, Selina sat up in bed. "Who is it?" she called out.

"Room Service."

"I didn't order room service."

"This is room 321."

"Yes, but I didn't order room service."

"Someone ordered it for you."

Oh bother, Selina thought and got out of bed. She padded to the door and looked out through the peephole at the young man in a Four Seasons uniform, holding something clutched behind his back. She put the chain on and opened the door. "What is it? What are you holding behind your back?"

"These, ma'am." The young man revealed a slender vase filled with three pink roses in full bloom.

Immediately, she knew who they were from. She didn't want to take them, but the kid was already thrusting them at her.

From the time they were married, whenever Michael sent her flowers — which had been surprisingly often — he sent three pink roses in full bloom, never buds. Pink, he said, for the purity of her soul. Three because it was his lucky number and she was the luckiest thing that had ever happened to him. Full bloom to show how full his heart was with love for her.

She used to find the gesture exceedingly romantic. Now, in light of everything that had happened between them, she found it hopelessly corny and manipulative.

Even so, she couldn't seem to stop herself from taking the chain off the door and reaching for the flowers. The young man scooted away and Selina took the roses inside her room. She shut the door, set the roses on the table, and perched on a chair beside them.

She stared at the roses. The cloying scent filled her nostrils and caused her head to ache. She thought about her husband and how she'd suppressed her fears, doubts, and emotions. Recalled how foolish she'd been over the years. Remembered all the dumb things she had taught her daughters about love and romance.

Then slowly, petal by petal, Selina disassembled the roses and ate them.

Chapter Three

From the CD player, the Rolling Stones were telling Michael Henderson that he couldn't always get what he wanted as he drove the Porsche he'd purchased that morning down the lonely stretch of highway leading west toward Valentine. Michael certainly didn't need Mick Jagger's advice on that score. Not only had he not gotten what he thought he wanted, he'd screwed up the thing he needed most.

His marriage.

He'd lost Selina for good.

After Vivian had shown up at Rachael's wedding yesterday, he was certain he had no chance of winning his wife back. Selina hadn't acknowledged the roses he'd sent to her hotel room that morning. But he really hadn't expected her to. Over the years, the romantic gestures he'd doled out had impressed her less and less. It seemed there was nothing he could do to convince his wife he loved her. Had always loved her. In spite of the fact he could be a stupid ass sometimes.

So why are you going home? Why not stay in Houston and fight for her? whispered a voice at the back of his mind.

"Because sometimes a man just gets tired of being

discounted and disregarded," Michael muttered. No matter how hard he tried to make up for the past, it never seemed to be enough for Selina.

After twenty-seven years of marriage, was he finally done trying to please her?

The thought caused his heart to skip a couple of beats. No, he wasn't ready to throw in the towel. He just needed a break. Needed some time to think, to adopt a whole new life strategy.

Just as his daughter did.

He knew Rachael was okay. She was just pissed off at him and her mother and hurt over Trace Hoolihan's betrayal. He understood. She needed her space. Selina, on the other hand, didn't get it.

Overall, Michael wasn't a worrier, and while Rachael wasn't particularly sensible, she was a good girl. Other than her numerous failed love relationships, she'd never given him and Selina a moment's worry.

Michael tightened his fingers around the steering wheel and pressed harder on the accelerator. When had he first begun losing his wife?

After Rachael was born he'd noticed a change. From wife to mother, he'd told himself. It was inevitable. Hadn't his own father warned him that's what happened to a marriage? Kids took over.

He'd tried his damnedest to keep the romance going. Flowers sent simply because he loved her. Jewelry slipped unexpectedly into the pocket of her housecoat. He'd arranged impromptu getaways just for the two of them. Nannies hired, housekeepers retained, all to cut down on her workload so they'd have more time together. He'd given her an unlimited expense account, encouraged her to pamper herself with spa dates and nights out with her friends. But no matter how hard he tried, she hadn't seemed to appreciate a bit of it. In fact, the more he gave her, the more distant she became.

He'd thought things would improve when the girls went off to college, when the nest was empty and they had the house to themselves. He imagined them golfing together, taking a trip around the world, maybe even building a get-away cottage on the Gulf of Mexico. But that wasn't the way it turned out.

She hated golfing, didn't want to travel, and she was afraid of hurricanes. No matter what he suggested, she nixed it. Gradually, he ended up hanging out with his friends and she hung out with hers, until it seemed there wasn't any point in staying married. Except he still loved her desperately.

Truth was he'd been lonely. Starved for attention from his wife and hungry for her company. Was it any wonder that he'd answered flirtatious Vivian's e-mail in kind the fateful day it appeared in his in-box?

From the corner of his eye he caught a flash of red in his rearview mirror. A low-slung crimson Jaguar came out of nowhere, zipping into the passing lane.

In this part of the country it was rare enough to see an expensive foreign-made sports car. Most of the vehicles on the road to Valentine were farm trucks or pickups, with an occasional SUV, minivan, or compact car thrown into the mix. There was Giada Vito's green Fiat, but this powerful machine was no Fiat.

Jeff Davis County was not a particularly wealthy part of Texas, although once upon a time, in his granddaddy's day, there'd been a cache of oil hidden in the ground. But those days were long gone. There were only a handful of people in town who could afford an expensive sports car, and thanks to his granddaddy's planning, foresight, and wise investing, and the fact that they'd found plenty of Texas crude beneath the Hendersons' peanut farm, Michael was one of them.

The Jaguar pulled alongside the Porsche.

His masculine competitive streak had Michael speeding up for no good reason other than that he liked the singing strum of adrenaline racing through his veins.

The Jaguar sped up, too.

He peered into the driver's-side mirror, trying to see the face of his challenger, but the windows were tinted so darkly he couldn't even make out if the driver was young or old, male or female.

It's probably some other middle-aged fart going through a life crisis.

The Jag blew past him and eased back into the lane in front of him, jauntily tooting its horn in the process.

"Oh, so that's how it's going to be." He jammed his right foot all the way to the floor.

The Porsche, happy to be given the gas, leaped forward so fast Michael's head thumped back against the headrest.

The race was on.

His heart pumped faster than it had pumped in years. His pulse throbbed in his throat. In his ears. In his groin. His gaze was glued to the Jag's taillights as he slipped into the passing lane.

"Upstart," he yelled, shooting past the Jag.

On the radio, "You Can't Always Get What You Want" had reached a crescendo. The guitars were wailing and

Mick was singing and Michael was driving like he'd never driven before.

He felt utterly, completely alive.

And the Valentine city limits lay just ahead.

His hometown. The place where he'd been born, grown up, married the love of his life, raised two daughters. The place where he would most likely die.

The bleakness of that thought hit him all at once and he suddenly felt like the oldest fool on the planet. What the hell was he doing drag-racing a stranger on the highway? Someone could get hurt. Killed.

He let off the accelerator.

The Jag passed him again.

Michael let it go, his attention snagged by the WELCOME TO VALENTINE, TEXAS, ROMANCE CAPITAL OF THE USA sign. The sign that had been erected back in the 1950s after the oil had dried up and the town was desperate for revenue. Turning Valentine into a tourist destination had seemed foolhardy to many at the time, but it had been the brainchild of Kelvin Wentworth II and his scheme had unexpectedly saved the town.

But what socked Michael in the gut was the sight of those bright scarlet lips—they had dominated the Valentine landscape for his entire life—gone all dark and gothic black.

His mouth dangled open in shock. He slowed the Porsche to a crawl. What the hell? During his three-day absence in Houston, someone had vandalized the Valentine sign.

He hadn't expected to feel personally insulted, but he did.

By the time he drove down Main Street, he'd almost

forgotten about the Jag. Until he spied it parked at the Exxon pumps.

He pulled in next to it.

The Jag's door opened and out stepped Vivian Cole, dressed all in black and looking like she'd walked off the pages of the glossy New York fashion magazine she edited. Still thin, still attractive, still hotter than a firecracker in July, even after twenty-seven years.

Blood pumping, engine running, radio blaring, Michael slung open his door, stood up, and looked over the hood of the Porsche at her.

Vivian slipped off her designer sunglasses and nailed him with a brilliant, seductive smile. "Hello, Michael."

"V ... V ... Vivian," he stammered. "What in the hell are you doing here?"

"Why, didn't I get a chance to tell you at Rachael's wedding?" She smiled slyly and shifted her weight so that her breasts thrust out prominently. "The divorce is final. I'm moving back home to Valentine."

Michael's heart skipped three beats this time and his mouth went stone-cold dry as one last time Mick Jagger assured him emphatically that while he might not be able to get what he wanted, if he tried hard enough, he just might be able to get what he needed.

BRODY WATCHED RACHAEL over the surveillance camera as she sat huddled on the cement bench, arms clasped to her chest. She looked so forlorn.

Stop feeling sorry for her. She got herself into this mess.

That's what his head told him, but his heart said something else entirely. He knew all too well how losing the person you loved most could make you do crazy things. Hadn't he volunteered to go to Fallujah for a second tour after he'd learned Belinda had left him? He closed his eyes briefly, remembering how that mistake had ended in a bloody battle where he'd lost his leg.

He shook his head. The past was over. He lived in the now.

It was almost six p.m. and he'd been on the job since six a.m. And because it was Sunday and Judge Pruitt was out of town, Rachael was stuck in jail overnight.

There was no way around it. He couldn't leave her locked up here alone. He was going to have to spend the night in the jail.

Unless...

He took her home with him.

Right. And Kelvin would have his hide if she ran off in the middle of the night.

You could always handcuff her to your bed.

Unexpected erotic images bloomed in his mind. A freeze-frame montage of Rachael splayed out naked across his bed, her wrists cuffed to the headboard, her blonde hair fanned over his white sheets, her almond-shaped green eyes drilling him with a "come hither" gaze.

Ridiculously, Brody felt sweat bead his brow and his groin tightened.

Now this was just plain wrong.

It's only because you haven't had sex in going on three years. That's all. Don't read any more into it than that.

Maybe he shouldn't, but the images were disturbing as hell and he couldn't seem to shake them. It was as if he had X-ray vision and could see right through that wedding gown. In his mind's eye she had on a lacy white bustier, white lace thong panties, thigh-high stockings ringed with blue flowered garters. He imagined himself undressing her with his teeth.

Dammit. What was it about her that stirred the heaviness in his loins? How was she different from any of the other women he met in the course of his day? Why her? Why now?

As if Rachael Henderson, great-granddaughter of one of Valentine's founding fathers, daughter of the wealthiest man in town, would have anything to do with a gimp. She'd been engaged to a football player for the Chicago Bears. How was he supposed to compete with that?

Good God, why would you even want to compete for her? The woman is a head case, not to mention a royal pain in the ass.

But a very cute pain in the ass.

He thought about the chinaberry tree incident when they were kids and it brought up a few other memories. He recalled one summer when their families had celebrated the Fourth of July together. They'd shot off bottle rockets together. He and Rachael; his sister, Deana; and her sister, Hannah. As the memory drifted over him he could smell the gunpowdery scent of exploded Black Cats, taste watermelon on his tongue, see Rachael's face grinning in the glow of the porch light. How innocent and carefree they'd both been, unaware of the twists and turns the future held.

"Make your move, Carlton," Brody mumbled under his breath. "The past is past. Either take her home with you or call Deana and have her bring over a cot."

He weighed his options. Smart money said he should just stay here.

As he watched the monitor, Rachael reached up to

swipe away a tear sliding down her cheek. His heart knotted up. Damn. He couldn't leave her in the cell overnight.

What a sap.

He might be a sap but he'd seen too many cruel and hurtful things. After he'd left Iraq he'd sworn to himself he'd do his best to ameliorate suffering whenever he had the chance. Cooling one's heels in the Jeff Davis County slammer might not be a big deal to him, but it was to her.

And that's what mattered. Even if he didn't trust himself around her.

Brody got up and headed back into the holding cell. He'd left her alone most of the afternoon to think things through. The minute he appeared in the doorway, she straightened, sniffled, and blinked hard, trying to hide the fact she'd been crying.

"You ready to go?"

Rachael hopped off the bench, her eyes hopeful, her fingers laced together. "You're letting me out? What about the mayor? I thought he was pressing charges."

"He is and I can't turn you loose until tomorrow when Judge Pruitt arraigns you, but that doesn't mean I can't put you under house arrest."

"You mean wear one of those little tracking monitor thingies on my leg?"

"I don't think that will be necessary in light of the fact the county doesn't own one of those devices."

"Oh," she said. "Are you just going to let me go home and come back tomorrow? Because in all honesty I'd rather stay here than go to my parents' house."

"Really?" He eyed her.

She waved a hand. "Long, miserable story."

"Actually," he said, "I was thinking I'd take you home with me. It's either that or I spend the night here with you."

"You don't have to stay with me. I'll be fine. Go home."

"Can't. My deputy's wife had her baby earlier than planned and both my jailers are off on vacation. I can't leave you locked up in here alone. What if there's a fire?"

"Good point."

"Besides, you look like you could use a home-cooked meal and a change of clothes."

"You're going to cook for me?" She sounded skeptical.

"Not that I couldn't," he said. "But we'll leave the cooking to my sister, Deana. She and her six-year-old daughter, Maisy, are living with me for a while."

"I see. So we won't be all alone at your house."

Brody had the strangest feeling Rachael was disappointed by the news, but he had no idea as to why that would be the case. *You're imagining things. You're wanting her to want you because you want her.*

"No," he said, denying his thoughts out loud as much as answering her question.

He opened the cell door and Rachael thrust out both arms toward him, wrists pressed together.

"What's that all about?" he asked.

"Aren't you going to cuff me?"

"I don't think that's necessary. It's not like you wouldn't be easy to track in that getup and I live just down the block."

"Like it's even necessary for you to arrest me in the first place."

"Seriously, Rachael, did you think you could just waltz into town, deface the most beloved icon in Valentine, and waltz back out again without any consequences?"

She shrugged.

"What does that mean?"

"I wasn't thinking."

"Clearly not."

"I suppose you're always rational and in complete control of your actions," she said.

"I try."

"Have you ever had your heart broken, Brody Carlton?"

He paused a long moment. "As a matter of fact, I have."

"Didn't anger and grief ever make you do something totally stupid?" she asked.

He thought of his ex-wife and swallowed hard. "We're not talking about me," he said, shutting the cell door behind her. "I'm not the one who gave the Valentine sign an unflattering makeover."

"So what did you do?" She tilted her head up at him. "When you got your heart broken?"

"I joined the Army."

"What was her name?"

"9/11," he said, not knowing why he was telling her this. He never talked about it. Was it to make her feel better about her life? Or to make himself look like a hero in her eyes? He didn't like the thought of that last motivation. He needed to get out of this conversation ASAP. He'd made a big mistake bringing it up.

She looked puzzled. "9/11?"

"I was in the Twin Towers that day."

She gasped. "Oh, no, Brody."

"Oh, yes."

"Wh . . . what were you doing there?"

"I was going to school at NYU, working on a degree in political science; my roommate and I were there on a class project."

"I can't imagine how horrible that must have been."

"There's no words. I lost my best friend."

"Your roommate died?"

He nodded. "Joe was trapped under a collapsed rafter. I stayed with him until the cops arrived, but his injuries were too great. He didn't survive."

Rachael shuddered. "I can't imagine the horror of it."

"Be grateful for that. I quit college and joined the Army. My life had changed forever and I knew I would never be the same again."

The sudden silence was as significant as a gunshot.

"Oh, Brody," she whispered. "I didn't know."

"Why would you?" he said, latching his fingers around her elbow and guiding her toward the front door, turning out lights along the way. "I don't tell many people. My family hadn't lived in Valentine for years and my paternal grandparents had already passed away by then."

She reached up and touched his shoulder. Gently, he shook her off. "Come on, let's go."

Rachael must have seen something in his eyes that warned her off because she didn't press for more details and she injected a teasing note into her voice. "You broke my heart, you know."

Brody let go of her elbow in the foyer to activate the alarm system, then he ushered her over the threshold and locked the door behind them. "When did I do that?"

"The very first time my heart got broken, you were the culprit."

"You're kidding."

"No."

He stared at her. "What are you talking about?"

"I was seven, you were twelve. I gave you a Valentine

card on Valentine's Day. Not only did you not give me one in return, but you called me a baby, tore up the card, and told me to go away."

Her words took him aback. "I did that?"

"You did."

"I don't remember it."

"Of course not. I meant nothing to you."

He didn't know why he was feeling guilty for something he didn't even remember. "For crying out loud, Rachael, cut me some slack. I was a kid. Kids do dumb things."

"Well, I did make the mistake of giving you the Valentine in front of your buddies," she admitted. "In retrospect it was thoughtless of me."

All at once, the memory came rushing at him. He and his buddies had been in his driveway shooting hoops when pigtailed, gap-toothed Rachael had cut across her lawn, clutching a big pink heart-shaped envelope in her hands. He'd barely noticed her until she came to stand underneath the basket, her green-eyed gaze fixed on him, her hand outstretched with her little fingers wrapped around the card. His name was written on it in a childish scrawl of blue crayon.

"Hey, Brody," one of his buddies had said. "I think you've got a secret admirer."

He didn't know why that comment had embarrassed him, but he felt it again now as he had then, the blaze of heat rising to his cheeks, the knot of denial that had the same one-two punch as anger.

"For you," Rachael had said, smiling. "Be my Valentine."

"Brody's got a girlfriend," his other buddy had chanted.

"Brody and Rachael sitting in a tree..." singsonged his first friend. "K...I...S...S...I...N...G..."

Shamefully, he recalled snatching the envelope from her hand, ripping it into two pieces, and handing it back to her. "I don't take Valentine cards from babies," he'd said gruffly, even as his guilty heart had nosedived into his stomach at the shattered expression on her face. "Go home."

She burst into tears as she turned and ran sobbing back to her house. If Brody listened hard enough to the past, he could still hear the sound of her front door slamming.

"Bet I can shoot a free throw from across the street," he'd said to his friends, using bragging and action to douse the bad feelings over what he'd said to hurt the sweet little girl next door. The truth was he liked Rachael and he had a Valentine for her up in his room, but he was horrified to think that his friends might discover his secret.

He considered telling her about the Valentine's Day card he'd made for her. Thought about apologizing for his behavior all those years ago, but what would be the point? Most likely, she wouldn't believe him anyway.

"Let's go," he said.

"Where to?"

"White house on the right at the end of the street."

"You bought the old McClusky place," she said.

"I did."

"When was that?"

"Two and a half years ago, when I got back from Iraq."

"I heard you got injured over there," she said as he hustled her down the sidewalk. Neighbors were standing on their porches and on their lawns gawking at the sight of Brody escorting a woman decked out in full wedding regalia toward his house.

"I'm sorry," she said, her voice full of sympathy. "For all your suffering."

Her kindness triggered his anger. "Don't," he growled.
"Don't what?"

"Don't you dare feel sorry for me. I don't need your pity."

Her muscles tensed beneath his fingers and Rachael
fell silent.

Brody glanced over. Her head was tossed back, shoulders straight, jaw clenched, gaze beaded straight ahead.
But she was blinking rapidly as if trying to hold back tears.

Aw, hell. What was the matter with him? Why was he
lashing out at her?

They'd reached his house. The screen door flew open
and his niece, Maisy, came barreling headlong down the
front steps.

"Unca Brody, Unca Brody," she cried, but stopped
abruptly when she saw he wasn't alone. She looked at
Rachael the way only one female jealous of another could
look. "Who are you?"

"My name's Rachael. What's yours?" she asked.

Maisy scowled at Rachael then swung her gaze to
Brody. "What's she doing here?"

Rachael winced and he could see the hurt in her eyes.
This weekend was clearly not good for her ego. Jilted at
the altar, arrested for vandalizing the town's icon, and
disrespected by a six-year-old.

"Rachael's going to be spending the night with us," he
explained.

Maisy sank her hands onto her hips and glowered at
Rachael. "Why?"

"Because I'm your uncle's prisoner," Rachael said.

Brody hadn't planned on telling Maisy that.

"Prisoner?" Maisy's eyes widened with increased
interest. "Did you rob a bank?"

"No."

"Whadya do?"

"I put black lipstick on the Valentine billboard."

Maisy turned to Brody. "That's bad?"

"According to your uncle, it is," Rachael supplied before he could answer.

"How come you're wearing a wedding dress?" Maisy looked her up and down. Brody could just see his niece's little six-year-old brain cogs whirling and turning as she tried to figure this all out.

"I was at a wedding," Rachael explained.

"Were you the one on top of the cake?"

Rachael smiled. "Something like that."

Maisy's gaze shifted to Brody and she looked alarmed. "Is he the boy on top of the cake?"

"No, no," Rachael assured her. "The boy on top of the cake ran away."

"How come?"

"He decided he didn't want to get married after all."

"He didn't like you anymore?" Maisy asked.

"Not so much." Rachael shook her head and the wedding veil bobbed like a field of white butterflies.

"Let's go inside," Brody said, out of his element with this conversation. He could feel the pressure of the neighbors' gazes, knew they were being stared at. "What are we having for dinner?"

"It's taco night," Maisy said and slipped her little palm into his to lead him up the porch.

They went inside, Maisy pulling him by the hand, Brody tugging Rachael along by the elbow. The smell of chili powder, garlic, and onions hung in the air. From the kitchen, they could hear Deana humming a Faith Hill tune.

"Dee," he called out as Maisy escorted them into the kitchen. "We're here."

Deana turned from the stove, wiping her hands on a cup towel. She took one look at Rachael and her mouth dropped open.

It was then that Brody realized he should have given his sister a heads-up that he was bringing a prisoner home for dinner. And not just any prisoner, but a wilted bride-that-wasn't.

"What's all this, then, baby brother? If you tell me that you eloped, I'll clobber you." Menacingly, she waved a spatula.

"Rachael's in custody," Brody explained. "Zeke's with Mia and the baby and my jailers are out of town. I couldn't leave her locked up alone."

"You," Deana said to Rachael. "You're the one who defaced the Valentine billboard."

"Guilty as charged," Rachael said proudly.

"The whole town's buzzing about it. Some old-timers even want to hang you, but I want to shake your hand." Deana thrust out her palm to Rachael. "I've wanted to take an ax to that damned billboard for years. You go, girl. Down with romance."

Brody noticed Rachael's checks flushed pink with pleasure as she shook his sister's hand.

"Don't encourage her," Brody growled to Deana. "She broke the law."

Deana eyed Rachael's wedding dress. "I'm guessing there were extenuating circumstances."

"Dumped at the altar," Rachael said.

"Hey, consider yourself blessed you narrowly escaped," Deana said. "I'm going through a wicked divorce and Maisy's the only good thing to have come out of that mess."

"I'm sorry to hear about your divorce," Rachael said. "My parents are getting divorced. After twenty-seven years."

"You're Michael and Selina Henderson's daughter, right? You used to live next door to us on Downey Street," Deana said. "I babysat you and your sister, Hannah, a time or two before we moved to Midland."

"Uh-huh." Rachael nodded.

"You wanna get out of that dress?"

"I don't have anything else to put on. I left Houston without my bags."

"Don't worry," Deana said. "We're about the same size. I've probably got something you can wear."

"That'd be wonderful."

"Here." Deana shoved the spatula into Brody's hand. "Don't let the hamburger meat burn."

He stepped to the stove to scramble the browning hamburger meat around in the pan as Deana took Rachael's arm and led her from the kitchen, Maisy trailing in their wake.

Fifteen minutes later, they trooped back downstairs. Brody had already set the taco meat in the middle of the dining room table along with toasted corn tortilla shells, diced tomatoes, shredded lettuce, and grated cheese.

He looked up to see Rachael dressed in a pair of his sister's skintight blue-jean shorts, a skimpy, navel-baring sleeveless T-shirt, and a pair of white mules that showed off her toenails, painted a racy shade of scarlet. He could tell from the way she was tugging at the hem of the shorts that she wasn't accustomed to wearing the sort of daring clothes Deana preferred. His sister didn't own anything conservative and Rachael was stuck with the sexy outfit. And right now, Brody was glad. Rachael had also brushed her hair and it lay in smooth, gentle curls around her shoulders.

Wow! His libido lunged like a pit bull on a chain, desperate to be unleashed. Just looking at her was an exquisite form of torment.

She caught his eye and her cheeks pinked. That's when Brody realized he'd been staring. Openly. Hungrily.

Quickly, she looked away.

He sank down at the head of the dinner table and Rachael sat at the opposite end. He said grace, and everyone ducked their heads, except Brody. He didn't look down and he didn't close his eyes. Irreverently, he watched Rachael when his mind should have been on the prayer.

In the wedding dress, she'd been safe, untouchable — a bride on her wedding day. He'd felt the first burst of sexual attraction when she'd ended up straddling him at the bottom of the ladder, but mostly his feelings had alternated between pity, amusement, and minor irritation.

But what he was feeling now was a horse of a different color.

Her arms were bare and her legs were bare, her creamy skin exposed. He saw too much sweet flesh. The blood surging through his body told him this was a dangerous thing.

So was the sudden fire burning inside his groin as he watched her tilt her head, lift a taco to her mouth, and crunch into it with ladylike gusto.

The sight of her sweet, pink tongue unraveled something inside him. Something he'd kept wound up tight for a very long time. Something he feared he might never feel again.

Flaming hot lust.

Brody didn't like what he was feeling, but it was too damned strong to deny.

Chapter Four

Giada Vito was taking her evening power walk around Valentine Lake with one-pound dumbbells clutched in her hands when a man stepped out of the shadows of a hundred-year-old pecan tree.

"Aren't you skinny enough?"

She startled at the sound of the deep, threatening masculine voice that accompanied the hulking figure suddenly looming on the path in front of her. The weights could double as a weapon and she had pepper spray clipped to her belt. She'd lived in Valentine for fifteen years, but she'd been born in Rome, Italy. You'd never catch Giada leaving her doors unlocked or her keys in the car or her pepper spray in a drawer.

Raising her left hand, she cocked the dumbbell, ready to fling it if he gave her cause. Dropping the weight in her right hand, she went for the pepper spray on her hip, like a gunslinger at the O.K. Corral going for his six-gun.

He was the size of a bodybuilder, big and menacing, with an oversized cowboy hat tilted back on his slick, shaved head and a shark's deadly blue-eyed stare. He was dressed in a blue seersucker suit and he stood with the arrogant air of the privileged.

She recognized him then, but that didn't make her

lower the weight or put the pepper spray back into her belt: Kelvin Wentworth in all his cocky, strutting glory.

"You shouldn't push yourself so hard. Anyone ever tell you that men like women with a few curves?"

"Anyone ever tell you to go screw yourself?" she replied tartly.

Kelvin laughed.

"What are you doing here?" She sniffed, pretending a courage she didn't feel. "You don't look like you've taken up power walking."

"I came to see you." He smiled and the smile scared her more than a frown.

"What for?" she asked suspiciously.

"Wanna set that weight down? I have a feeling you're just waiting for an excuse to bean me."

"My mother always said to trust your instincts," she replied. "And my instincts are telling me you're up to something."

He laughed again. "Sharp cookie. That's one thing I like about you, Vito."

"Hmm," she said. "Too bad that I don't like anything about you, Wentworth."

"How did this feud between us ever get started?"

"Feud?" She feigned ignorance.

"Come on. We both know you're only running for mayor to piss me off. What I don't know is why."

"Is it working?" She batted her eyelashes. "Am I pissing you off?"

"I find you . . ." His gaze raked over her body in a look so intimidating, Giada almost shivered. "Amusing."

"Would this little visit have anything to do with the fact that I am beating the pants off you in the polls?"

She arched an eyebrow and wondered why she was hav-ing trouble catching her breath. She could walk a mile in twelve minutes. Her lung capacity was that of a highly trained marathon runner. She had no reason to feel breathless.

"Beating my pants off? Only in your dreams."

Fury burned her cheeks.

"Come on. Let's sit down and have a civilized discus-sion." Kelvin reached out and took hold of her arm, pull-ing her toward a wrought-iron picnic bench positioned beneath the pecan tree.

"Hands off," Giada exclaimed and swung at him with the dumbbell.

But Kelvin ducked and the weight swished harmlessly through the air. The big man was quicker than he looked. He clamped a hand around her wrist and wrenched the dumbbell away from her. "Settle down a minute, Spitfire."

"Hmph. I show you spitfire," she said, struggling against him, the English she'd perfected slipping in the heat of the moment.

"I just wanna talk." He maneuvered her toward the pic-nic bench. "And if you depress the nozzle on that pepper spray, believe me, you're going to live to regret it. But be a good girl and maybe you and I can cut a deal."

She stopped fighting and slid a glance at him from the corner of her eye. Her interest was piqued. This sounded like a man on the ropes and desperate to get back on his feet before the bell rang. Curiosity got the better of her and she followed him to the bench.

He dusted leaves and errant pecan hulls off the seat with a sweep of his hand. She hadn't expected such a chivalrous gesture, but then he had to go and ruin it all by commanding, "Sit."

The contrary part of her wanted to argue, but common sense told her to pick her battles. She sat.

"Now isn't this much better?" he said, plopping down beside her. "Two politicians sitting down for a nice chat."

"A scenario that strikes terror in the hearts of voters," Giada observed archly.

He grinned. "Water?" He surprised her by pulling a small bottle of Evian out of his jacket pocket. "It's important to stay well-hydrated."

"I have my own," she said, determined not to take anything from him. She fished an identical bottle of water from her fanny pack.

He held his water bottle up and nodded.

In unison they twisted off the tops of their respective water bottles and drank. It was almost like a perverse toast. She found the idea unsettling.

To be honest, she found Kelvin Wentworth unsettling.

"So Giada..." He paused. "Is it okay if I call you Giada?"

"I prefer Ms. Vito." She straightened her back. It wouldn't do to let him get too familiar.

"Of course you do, Giada," he continued, his eyes narrowing. "Just what in the hell is your beef with me?"

"Other than the fact you're a narcissistic drama king who thinks the entire town revolves around him?"

"That wounds me deeply," he said, and splayed a hand over his chest, but the expression on his face told her he had the hide of a rhino. "Everything I do is for the benefit of this town."

"Ah," she said. "A self-delusional, narcissistic drama king."

Kelvin surprised her by throwing back his head and letting out a roar of laughter.

"What's so damned funny?" She glared.

"You," he said. "You look so feisty with your hands cocked and your knees bent like you're gonna take a swing at me."

"That's funny?"

"I'm more than twice your size."

"And that's something to brag about? You should look into Lean Cuisine. The baked chicken is quite tasty."

"I'm big all over." He wriggled his eyebrows, his innuendo clear.

Refusing to rise to the bait, Giada bit down on her tongue.

"You know," he said, "you and I could become friends."

"Not in this lifetime."

"Or we could skip the friendship and go straight to lovers." His eyes drilled into hers. There was no missing the sexual interest.

"I'd rather poke my eyes out with a rusty knife."

"You say that now," he said, getting to his feet, "but that's only because I haven't kissed you yet."

He moved toward her.

Giada reached for the pepper spray again but was dismayed to find it was not housed in the clip at her waist.

"Looking for this?" He waggled the small spray can in front of her.

"Bastard," she said through gritted teeth.

"You're going to have to do a lot better than that if you're hoping to rile me up," he said.

Giada glared and tried to stare him down, but he wasn't going along with it. Instead, he was grinning at her like one of her unruly students. His gaze slid over her warm as hot fudge over homemade vanilla ice cream.

An edgy warm sensation, thrilling and unexpected, rolled through her. She snatched the pepper spray from his hand, stuffed it into the clip, grabbed up her dumb-bells, and walked away as fast as she could, while the sound of his wickedly sexual chuckle rang in her ears.

FOLLOWING A DINNER filled with an undercurrent of sexual tension that Rachael hoped no one else could detect, she helped Deana wash dishes. Brody was a handsome man, no doubt. But she wasn't in any position to be thinking romantic thoughts. In fact, ridiculous romantic thoughts were the very things that had landed her in this mess.

Once she and Deana had finished cleaning the kitchen, Maisy begged the three adults to play Chutes and Ladders with her at the dining room table.

When she had been Maisy's age, Chutes and Ladders had been Rachael's favorite board game. Her parents had dubbed Sunday family game night when she and her sister, Hannah, were growing up. It was a tradition she'd hoped to continue with her own children. The children she'd dreamed of having with Trace.

Dreams died hard.

Misery pushed into Rachael's throat and she swal-lowed back the bitter taste of it as her game piece ended up on a chute and she slid all the way down, landing at the beginning square.

"Ha!" Maisy gloated. "Start over!"

"Maisy," her mother chided. "Don't be rude."

"What?" The child shrugged and tried to look innocent, but ultimately, she was unable to hide her mischievous grin.

"It's not nice to take joy in the misfortune of others, Missy. Next turn you might be right at the bottom of the chute alongside Rachael."

That's me, bottom of the chute. Starting over yet again.

Roll the dice. Take a chance. End up right back where you started. Story of her life. From now on she was finished with rolling the dice, taking chances, starting over. She was tired, discouraged, and fed up with romance.

"Your turn," Brody said.

"Huh?" She was so wrapped up in thinking about how sexy his forearms looked with the sleeves of his shirt rolled up she hadn't heard what he said.

She felt the heat of his gaze on her face and her cheeks heated. She rolled the dice without looking over at him, but her cheeks stayed strangely warm. One thing you could say about being back at the beginning, you couldn't fall down any more chutes. Not until you ventured out from home base, put your heart on the line all over again.

But she was done with putting her heart on the line. It hurt too damned much to have your hopes dashed again and again.

Maisy ended up winning the game. Brody came in second, Deana third, and Rachael a distant fourth. But of course. She'd landed on twice as many chutes as ladders.

Maisy interlaced her fingers, raised her arms, and walked around the room shaking her clasped hands over her head like a cocky, triumphant prizefighter.

Deana rolled her eyes. "Sorry for the poor sportsman-like conduct," she apologized to Rachael. "When it comes to competition, Maisy takes after her father."

"No need to apologize. She's just passionate about the game," Rachael said.

"Let's play again." Maisy hopped up and down beside the table.

"No way," her mother replied and tickled her under the rib cage. "The competition is too stiff."

Maisy giggled.

"Come on, Muffin." Deana ruffled her daughter's hair. "It's time for bed."

"Aw, Mom, can we please play just one more game?" Maisy pleaded.

"Well," Brody said and stretched out his long arms. "I've had enough ladder climbing for one day."

Rachael raised her head.

He caught her eye and winked. An inside joke. He was sharing an inside joke with her. A clutch of something dangerous hooked somewhere in the general vicinity of her heart.

Stop it.

But no matter how much she scolded herself, Rachael couldn't prevent her gaze from taking him in. Brody Carlton wasn't a man you could easily ignore. She was so busy staring at him, in fact, she barely noticed when Maisy said good night as Deana led her upstairs for her bedtime rituals.

Brody was still dressed in his sheriff's uniform, looking every inch the public servant, except for the turned-up sleeves. He watched her. She could see him sizing her up in that calculating, sheriff-y way of his.

A shaft of light slanting in from the kitchen threw a shadow over his profile. His hair was the color of maple syrup, his eyes equally as dark. He looked serious, dutiful, manly. On alert, forever on guard.

Rachael's heart fluttered and she had to dig her fingernails into her palms to remind herself where she was and how she'd gotten here.

He consulted his watch. "It's nine-thirty. You ready for bed?"

Those words, spoken in his rich, deep, masculine voice, sent perilous mental pictures clicking through her brain. She imagined him leading her upstairs to his bedroom and kissing her with those hot, firm lips as his nimble fingers undressed her. She thought about peeling his shirt over his head, exposing his bare chest, running her fingers along the taut muscular ridges.

"Who, me?" she squeaked.

"It's a little early, I know," he said. "But I get up at five every morning."

"So go on to bed." She waved a hand. "I'm a night owl."

"That's not going to work. You're my prisoner."

"And that means..."

"You sleep when I sleep, wake up when I wake up."

"You've gotta be kidding me."

"Not at all."

"Seriously?"

"Yep." He gave her a look that sent all the blood rushing to her pelvis.

"Where will I be sleeping?"

"In my bed."

"What?" The word flew out of Rachael's mouth in a breathless gasp.

"Don't look so panic-stricken." An amused smile curled his lips. He was enjoying teasing her. "I'll be sleeping on the floor."

She felt her heart slip and slide right down into her shoes. "No. No way."

"Those are the rules," he said. "You're in my custody. Unless you'd rather go back to the jail."

"I can't let you sleep on the floor in your own home," she said. "I'll take the floor."

"Hey, when I was in Iraq I dreamed of sleeping on my own floor. It's a privilege."

Was he teasing her again?

Part of her—the stupid, starry-eyed part—almost told him they could share the bed *It Happened One Night*-style. Just the thought of reenacting the classic movie made her heart race with romantic notions. Rachael pressed a hand to her forehead. God, she was a hard case. Totally brainwashed by fairy tales and lippy billboards and the fanciful mush of moonlight and violins and grand gestures.

Lies. It was all a pack of lies.

And yet, she yearned for those fairy tales.

What she needed was a support group. Like alcoholics had. Or overeaters or gamblers. She needed help to talk herself out of these crazy romantic cravings.

Brody got up from the table, moving a little stiffly. "My bedroom's downstairs. You can use the adjoining bathroom. I'll put out one of my T-shirts for you to sleep in and I keep a new toothbrush in the middle drawer, just in case of unexpected visitors."

Rachael wondered what that meant. Did he have a lot of unexpected, overnight guests?

What do you care?

Right. She didn't care. His overnight guests were none of her business.

Thirty minutes later, she emerged from his bathroom, scrubbed clean after her unsavory day in jail. Tomorrow was a new day, an opportunity for a fresh start.

While she'd been in the shower, Brody had made a pallet on the floor near the door, boxing her in. If she had the urge to make an escape, she'd have to do it through the window. But she had no inclination to run. She might as well be here as anywhere. She'd vandalized the sign. She'd take whatever lumps the judge dished out when she was arraigned. She just hoped Jillian would get to Valentine in time to stand in as her lawyer. She didn't mind facing the music. She just didn't want to do it alone.

Brody was sitting up with his back against the door. Apparently he'd used another bathroom. His hair looked slightly damp from his shower and he had on a pair of pajamas that thankfully revealed very little of the hard body she knew lurked beneath. Knew because she'd felt his muscles when she'd straddled him after they'd fallen off the ladder together.

She was standing in the doorway between the bedroom and the bathroom wearing his University of Texas T-shirt, the hem skimming just above her knees. She watched his gaze drift slowly over her and she realized the light from the bathroom was shining through the material of the thin cotton shirt. He could see straight through it to the outline of her body beneath.

He moistened his lips.

Rachael gulped. Quickly, she reached back and flipped off the bathroom light. Brody let out an audible breath.

The bedcovers were turned back. He'd done that.

For her.

The thought made her go all soft and squishy inside.

Stop it!

She slid into bed, pulled the sheets up to her neck. Listened to the blood strumming through her ears.

"Lights out," he said and flicked off the overhead lamp, dousing them in darkness. In the silence, in the inky black of night, she could hear him breathing. It was a rough, deliciously masculine sound that sent chill bumps up her spine.

The bedside clock ticked, counting off the seconds until dawn. The pillow smelled of fabric softener, Egyptian cotton, and Brody. The mattress was neither too soft nor too firm. It was just right. She rolled over onto her side. The box springs squeaked.

Brody coughed.

Was he as aware of her as she was of him?

The silence elongated. Awareness stretched from her to him and back again. Then quietly, unexpectedly, he said, "I have a question for you."

"What's that?"

She couldn't help wondering if he was going to ask her about Trace. Why she'd been foolish enough to get engaged to a man who obviously did not love her. She hoped he didn't ask that. She didn't have an answer for it other than she'd been swept away on fairy-tale promises and foolish romantic ideals.

"How'd you get on top of the billboard?"

"Oh, that." Rachael laughed, relieved he hadn't asked her about Trace. "I climbed on top of the boxcar."

"How'd you get on top of the boxcar?"

"I climbed on the roof of my VW."

"The boxcar is parked that close to the sign?"

"I had to do a bit of jumping," she admitted.

"In a wedding dress?"

"I was pretty determined," she said.

"Carrying a can of black paint?"

"The paint can was on the ground attached to a rope. I had the other end of the rope in my hand. When I got to the billboard, I just hauled the paint up."

"You'd thought it out."

"I had a four-hundred-mile drive to put it all together."

"You were determined." Was that admiration she heard in his voice?

"That sign represents all that's wrong with Valentine." She rolled onto her back again, tucked her palms underneath her head, and stared up at the ceiling. "It symbolizes the wreck I've made of my life due to all the wrong values and starry-eyed beliefs this town instilled in me."

"You sure this isn't just a stress reaction to getting dumped and finding out your parents are getting divorced?"

"It's more than that."

"How are you feeling about your parents' divorce?"

Rachael took a deep breath. Good question. What was she feeling? She lay there letting the emotions flow over her—betrayal, sadness, guilt. Yes, guilt. She couldn't help thinking that somehow this was all her fault. She should have recognized that all was not right in her parents' marriage. She should have done something, said something. She should have been more aware of what was going on, not been so self-absorbed.

"Don't you think you're throwing the baby out with the bathwater?" Brody asked. "Romance is what kept this town alive after the oil dried up. There wouldn't be a Valentine without it."

"It might have been a bit rash," she admitted. "But a bold statement needed to be made. Someone has to take a stand. A balance must be struck."

"Is this the argument you're going to present to Judge Pruitt in the morning?"

"Yes."

"Good luck with that."

"What do you mean?"

"Judge Pruitt is as much in love with Valentine as Kelvin Wentworth. She's going to throw the book at you."

That provoked a knot of worry inside her. "Exactly what does having the book thrown at you entail?"

"Hours of community service."

"Seriously?" The thought panicked her. "How am I going to do hours of community service? I live in Houston. Or at least I did. Before I gave up my apartment to move in with Trace."

"Plus you'll be expected to repair the damage you did to the sign. And there will probably be a hefty fine."

"How hefty?" Maybe she should have given a bit more thought to her vandalism spree.

"Depends on what kind of mood the judge is in. You better hope she had a good vacation."

Rachael blew out her breath in relief. "I've got a sharp lawyer on the way."

"That's good."

They fell silent again.

"Brody," she said after a long moment.

"Uh-huh?"

"Thank you."

"For what?"

"This."

"This what?"

"Bringing me home with you. Not leaving me in jail. I know you're probably violating all kinds of rules and regulations."

"Not too many. Besides, I'm the sheriff. Up to a point I can bend the rules," he said.

"I had fun tonight, eating tacos and playing Chutes and Ladders with you and Deana and Maisy."

She'd forgotten how much fun it was, spending time with a loving family. She thought of her parents and bit down on her bottom lip. She still couldn't believe they were getting divorced. Were all the memories of her happy childhood really such a lie? Had she romanticized even that?

"Hey," Brody said, interrupting her thoughts. "Don't thank me. My motives were purely selfish. I didn't want to sleep on a cot in the jail."

"It couldn't be any worse than the floor."

"The floor's not so bad."

"You could get up on the bed. It's king-sized and I don't thrash around much." She didn't make the offer out of some movieland fantasy. She simply asked because he'd been so nice and she hated the thought of him waking up in the morning all stiff and achy simply because of her.

"I'm good right here," he said.

"Well," she said, "just in case you wake up in the middle of the night and change your mind, the offer stands. I trust you to be a gentleman."

Then Brody said something that took her totally by surprise. "Rachael, you've got to stop trusting people so easily."

*   *   *

BRODY LAY ON the pallet for hours, listening to the sound of her soft breathing and imagining himself doing all kinds of unprofessional things. Talk about breaking rules and regulations. If a man could be locked up for his sexy thoughts, he'd be in prison for the rest of his life.

Finally, just when he'd managed to stop thinking about how damned much he wanted to kiss her, touch her, make love to her, and was almost asleep, Rachael bolted upright in bed.

"Brody, get up!"

His soldier's training kicked in and he was instantly alert. "What is it? What's wrong?" He grappled for his bionic leg in the dark, feeling intensely vulnerable without it on.

"You have to take me back to the jail right this minute."

He fumbled with the leg attachment. All he could see of her in the dark bedroom was the pale glow of the white T-shirt she wore. He wanted to get the leg back on before she turned on the light. "What for?"

"This can't be happening."

"Tell me what's happening so I can fix it."

"You can't fix it. *You're* what's happening."

Was she talking in her sleep? Puzzled, Brody got his Power Knee in place and hoisted himself to his feet. "Rachael, are you awake?"

"Wide awake. I haven't been asleep."

Me, either.

The clock on the bedside table read 11:57. Almost midnight.

He snapped on the lamp next to the clock and sat down

on the mattress beside her. It was all he could do to keep from taking her in his arms. What was with this illogical protectiveness? Sure, his natural male instinct prompted him to take care of a woman in need. But this was something different. Something more.

He was a sheriff; she'd been booked on vandalism. He could not allow himself to touch her in any way except in the course of duty. Cradling her to vanquish night terrors didn't come under that heading.

But dammit, he wanted to touch her. He wanted her to rest her head on his shoulder. He longed to trace his fingers over her throat, then trail lower to the curve of her breast and the flat of her belly and that soft, sweet spot between her legs.

Silently, he cursed himself. Good old-fashioned chemistry had knocked the wind out of him with this one.

She stared at him.

Brody saw panic in her eyes.

"I gotta get out of here," she said, throwing back the covers.

"Shh, settle down. Tell me what's wrong."

"You. You're what's wrong."

"I'm not following your reasoning."

"You. Me. This."

"Is it that meeting cute thing again?"

"No, no." She shook her head. "This is much worse. This is the romantic equation."

"Romantic equation?" Could people talk in their sleep with their eyes open?

"You know. It's like in *Sleepless in Seattle* where Sam has lost his beloved wife and he believes lightning doesn't strike twice. That he'll never love again. Meanwhile

Annie is looking for lightning. It's the romantic equation between the two of them. They both lack something that only the other can provide. They balance each other out. Meg Ryan's character can give Tom Hanks's character back his belief in love and Tom can give Meg the lightning she's been searching for."

"I didn't see the movie."

Rachael looked at him as if he'd suddenly sprouted a second nose. "You never saw *Sleepless in Seattle*?"

"Is that a sin?"

"It's just the best romantic movie ever made. I've seen it twenty-seven times," she said.

He struggled not to notice that her nipples were poking right through the thin fabric of her T-shirt. Or how much she smelled like his sandalwood soap and minty toothpaste. "I can tell."

"Omigod." She splayed a palm to her forehead. "I'm doing it again, aren't I? Acting as if movie romances are real."

"Yep."

She took a deep breath and met his eyes. "I'm sorry I panicked and woke you up over something as silly as a romantic equation. You're right. We don't have a romantic equation. How could we? That's the movies, this is real life. Right?"

"You're thinking we have one of these romantic equations?"

"No. Not anymore. You set me straight. Thanks."

"So theoretically, if we were in a movie and we did have one of these romantic equations, what would ours be?" It was a dumb thing to ask, but he couldn't seem to stop himself.

"I'm lacking a hero in my life and you're a real hero. While you, on the other hand, are lacking a romantic soul and I'm romantic clean through to my bones."

"I suppose you had a romantic equation with those other guys who left you at the altar." It bothered Brody to think about those other guys.

"Actually, no. Maybe that's what was wrong with my other relationships. Maybe they were Bellamys."

"What are Bellamys?"

"In the romantic comedies of the forties and fifties there was an actor named Ralph Bellamy. He seemed like the right guy for the heroine. At least on the surface. But really he wasn't a match for her and she couldn't see it until the hero came into her life."

"You're doing it again," he said.

"Doing what?"

"Mixing up movies with real life."

Rachael looked chagrined. "I am, aren't I."

"You have no worries where I'm concerned," Brody said. "I'm not your man. I'm a complete cynic when it comes to love. Now go back to sleep. You've got a judge to face in the morning."

Then just as he had settled back down on his pallet, he heard her whisper, "But Brody, what if being a cynic is your half of our romantic equation?"

Chapter Five

By six the next morning, Rachael was back in her jail cell and in her paint-stained wedding gown waiting for her audience with the judge. Brody had cooked them fried-egg sandwiches for breakfast while Deana and Maisy slept.

He never brought up what they'd discussed in the middle of the night. For that, she was grateful and she prayed he hadn't heard that extra little bit she'd whispered to him in the dark.

The wedding veil lay folded neatly on the cement-slab bench beside her. Lightly, she picked up the fragile veil and fingered it, remembering the day she and her three friends had found it in that strange little consignment shop in Houston.

It was a floor-length mantilla style made of delicate rose pointe lace that had captivated Delaney. She'd been on the verge of marrying the wrong man when she found it. Both Tish and Jillian had been skeptical of the veil. But Rachael had been as enraptured by its romantic legend as Delaney.

According to the lore, long ago in Ireland there had lived a beautiful young witch named Morag who possessed a great talent for tatting incredible lace. People came from far and wide to buy the lovely wedding veils she created, but there were other women in the community who were envious of Morag's beauty and talent.

These women lied and told the magistrate that Morag was casting spells on the men of the village. The magistrate arrested Morag, but found himself falling madly in love with her. Convinced that she must have cast a spell upon him as well, he moved to have her tried for practicing witchcraft. If found guilty, she would be burned at the stake. But in the end, the magistrate could not resist the power of true love.

On the eve before Morag was to stand trial, he kidnapped her from the jail in the dead of night and spirited her away to America, giving up everything he knew for her. To prove that she had not cast a spell over him, Morag promised never to use magic again. As her final act of witchcraft, she made one last wedding veil, investing it with the power to grant the deepest wish of the wearer's soul. She wore the veil on her own wedding day, wishing for true and lasting love. Morag and the magistrate were blessed with many children and much happiness. They lived to a ripe old age and died in each other's arms.

"Baloney, rubbish, crap," Rachael muttered underneath her breath, although her heart still ached to believe in the magic of the wedding veil.

Delaney had wished on the veil to get out of marrying the wrong man and in the end, she'd found her heart's desire in her soul mate, Nick Vinetti.

Then Delaney had passed the veil on to Tish.

Tish wished to get out of debt, and the granting of that wish had brought her back together with the husband she'd lost but had never stopped loving.

And Tish had passed the veil on to Rachael.

And there, the fairy tales had ended.

On Saturday, the day she was to marry Trace Hoolihan, Rachael hadn't wished on the veil because she thought she didn't need it. Everything was already perfect. She'd been such an idiot.

She snorted and glared at the veil. Look how things had turned out. The very opposite of perfection. A punch of sorrow and regret pummeled her stomach and she drew her knees up to her chest. Not only had the day been horrible, but her life had gone distinctly downhill ever since.

Now, here she was, all alone, awaiting criminal mischief charges, and she was guilty as sin.

Tears welled up in her eyes. She dropped her forehead in her hands. She would not cry. She refused to cry. Trace was not worth her tears.

Her fingers tingled against the lace. What if she were to wish on the veil? Would anything happen?

Resolutely, she swung her legs off the bench, sat up straight, and settled the veil over her head. "I wish," she murmured, "to be cured of my need for romance. I wish to stop believing in true love and soul mates and happily-ever-after. I want a calm life free of the exciting adrenaline rush of first lust. I want to stop having crushes and spinning fantasies. I wish this love monkey off my back."

The minute she made the wish, something strange happened. Her scalp tingled until her entire head throbbed with a vibrant, pulsating energy.

Her pulse quickened. Her breath hung in her lungs. Her vision suddenly blurred.

Whoa!

And then there he was in the doorway of the holding

cell. Gun strapped on his hip, badge glistening in the harsh fluorescent lighting, Stetson cocked back on his head. He looked strong and big and in control. The kind of man you could count on in an emergency. A guy who wouldn't run away at the first sign of trouble.

Brody Carlton.

"Rachael," Brody called her name and broke the spell.

The tingling in her head vanished, leaving her breathless and gawking at him as if he were a stalwart knight lifted from the pages of *Grimm's Fairy Tales*.

There you go with the romantic fantasies. Knock it off.

Clearly, the stupid wedding veil had malfunctioned.

"Yes?" she said, startled to find that her voice came out little more than a whisper.

"You have visitors."

She jumped off the bench, ran to the bars. "Visitors?"

"One of them says she's your lawyer."

"There's more than one?" Her hopes soared.

"Three to be exact and they aren't real happy with me."

Relief and happiness and a sweet sense of belonging washed over her. All three of her friends had come. She had true friends. Why on earth had she ever thought she needed a man?

"Against my better judgment," he said, "I'm going to let them all come back to see you. Mainly because your lawyer keeps making threats."

"You'll have to forgive Jillian," Rachael said. "She's a bit intense."

"A bit?"

"Okay, a lot intense. But she has a heart of gold."

He looked like he wasn't going to take her word on

that. He left the room and returned moments later with Delaney, Tish, and Jillian following behind him.

"Oh, you guys," Rachael said as Brody unlocked the cell door and let them inside. The bars clanged closed behind her friends and Brody stepped back into his office to give them privacy. "Thank you so much for coming to my rescue. I love you all!"

"The first time our sweet little Rachael gets into real trouble?" Tish said and enveloped her in a hug. "I wouldn't miss it for the world."

"How's Shane and the baby?" Rachael asked about Tish's husband and new infant son.

"Fine, fine." Tish nodded and tucked a dark auburn corkscrew curl behind an ear studded with multiple earrings. She was dressed in a bohemian-style peasant blouse and stonewashed blue jeans. "Max is cutting his first tooth and Shane sends his love."

Delaney hugged her next, her baby bump pressing into Rachael's side as she squeezed her so tightly it almost took her breath. "Sweetie, we know you're hurting. We're here for you."

"How are Nick and Audra?" Rachael asked, changing the subject by referring to Delaney's police detective husband and their toddler daughter.

"Great. Although Audra's deep into the terrible twos." Delaney turned to Tish. "Just wait until Max gets there. You'll think a demon has possessed your darling child."

"Do you know what sex the new baby is?" Rachael asked.

Delaney encircled her belly with her arms and her eyes lit up. "It's twin boys."

"Twins!" Tish exclaimed. "You didn't tell me that."

"We just found out on Friday. Twins run in Nick's family," Delaney explained.

Delaney and Tish started talking about babies. Rachael looked past them to see Jillian standing to one side, cool and slightly aloof as always. Watching everyone closely, not missing a beat.

Jillian possessed exotic looks with her ebony hair and dark eyes. She had the kind of curvy body that drove men wild and a Mensa IQ. She was dressed in an expensively tailored business suit and three-inch stilettos that sent her towering to over six feet. In her hands she held a leather briefcase. No doubt about it. Jillian was a force to be reckoned with.

As far as Rachael knew, Jillian had never had a serious romantic relationship. She'd snared every man she'd ever set her sights on, but then she dumped them just as easily as she collected them.

The four friends had all met at Rice University where they'd been sorority suitemates. Over the years, Rachael and Jillian had had their differences. A natural clash of romantic versus cynic. But now, for the first time, Rachael totally *got* where Jillian was coming from. And amid the bubbly new mothers, they had a new alliance. Women who weren't besotted by babies.

Plus, while she appreciated both Delaney and Tish for leaving their families to come all this way to show their support, Jillian was the only one who could really help her.

"We saw the billboard," Tish said.

"We still can't believe you did that," Delaney added. "You? Miss Romantic?"

"Not anymore," Rachael muttered. "I'm done with romance. Jillian had it right all along. Love stinks."

Delaney and Tish shared that knowing look of women lucky enough to have found true love. Then they glanced at Rachael with pity in their eyes.

A tinge of envy, mixed with anger, took hold of her. Why couldn't she have found that kind of happiness, too? And so what if she never found true love? She could still have a happy, productive, fulfilling life. She didn't need a man for that. Look at Jillian.

"Could you guys give us a moment alone?" Jillian asked Delaney and Tish. "I need to go over her defense."

"I don't need a defense," Rachael said. "I'm guilty."

Jillian shook her fingers. "Not so fast. I'm going to prove there were extenuating circumstances that drove you to rash action."

"That's certainly true."

"Sheriff," Jillian called out to Brody. "Could you please open the door?"

Brody returned to let Delaney and Tish out and he escorted them back to his office, leaving Jillian alone with Rachael.

Jillian took Rachael's hand and pulled her down on the cement bench. "Tell me everything."

Rachael told her what had happened from the moment she'd fled the chapel in her wedding dress and driven straight to Valentine, stopping only to buy the bucket of black paint.

"You were pushed to the limits of your endurance," Jillian said.

"Uh-huh."

"You snapped."

Rachael nodded.

"Anyone who's ever been in love and been dumped will sympathize with what you've been through."

"Judge Pruitt married her high school sweetheart. The only man she ever loved," Rachael said.

"You forget, I live for challenges." Jillian's eyes gleamed. "First order of business, we've got to get you out of that wedding dress. The evidence against you is smeared all over it."

"I've got nothing to wear. My wedding trousseau is in the trunk of Trace's car."

"Trust you to say trousseau." Jillian shook her head. "Only a die-hard romantic."

"Hey," Rachael said. "I'm through with being a romantic. Painting the Valentine sign was my emancipation proclamation."

"Don't worry about the clothes. I've got you covered." Jillian snapped open her briefcase and took out a simple blue suit skirt with matching jacket and white silk blouse.

The conservative outfit was as far a cry from Rachael's style as Deana's flashy clothes. She preferred flowing, feminine garments in floral prints and pastels, dresses to pants, empire waistlines to form-fitting sheaths. But she accepted the suit without comment. Beggars couldn't be choosers and after all, Jillian knew what she was doing.

"Thank you," Rachael said. She reached over to pick up the wedding veil lying beside her on the bench and handed it to her friend. "I want you to have this."

Jillian shook her head. "I have no use for that thing."

"Delaney and Tish don't need it anymore and it didn't work for me. You might as well have it."

Jillian took the wedding veil, holding it gingerly, as if she feared it might give her some dread virus. "I'll hang on to it for you," she said and slid it into her briefcase. "Just in case you change your mind."

"I won't be needing it," Rachael said stubbornly. "I'm finished with romance."

"You say that now—"

"This time I mean it."

"Rachael, a leopard doesn't change its spots. You are who you are. You can't change by graffitiing a billboard with black paint and declaring you're done with love. You're a starry-eyed romantic optimist. It's your essential nature. It's one of the things we love most about you."

"You're wrong," she said fiercely, struggling to deny that Jillian was right. "I can change and I will. I'm going to become a hard-boiled cynic, just like you."

"No, Rachael, no," Jillian whispered. "You don't want to be just like me."

"Yes, I do. You're smart and successful and you don't kowtow to anyone. You don't lose your focus when a man comes into your life. You're strong and powerful and brave."

"And lonely. Don't forget lonely."

Rachael blinked. "You're lonely?"

Jillian's nod was almost imperceptible.

"But you have Delaney and Tish and me."

"And you were all in love, all involved with your men." Jillian held up a hand. "Don't get me wrong. I'm not complaining. My work is rewarding. It's just sort of sad to have nothing but a briefcase to curl up with on a cold, winter night."

"Curling up with someone is overrated," Rachael muttered, trying to convince herself. She needed Jillian's cynicism to keep her on track. To prevent her from embracing her romanticism and letting it drag her down.

"This from a person who's never gone without someone to curl up next to," Jillian observed.

It was true. From the time she was sixteen years old, Rachael had always had a boyfriend. Whenever she was briefly without one, she felt lost, adrift, as if she had no real purpose, no identity if she wasn't part of a happy couple. This grasping need for romance had stunted her emotional growth, held her back.

How could she have shortchanged herself for so long? How could she have been so blind?

"Take the veil," she insisted, pushing it toward her friend. "I don't want it."

Jillian pushed the veil back toward her. "Neither do I."

"Then just take it and get rid of it for me, please? Sell it on eBay and keep the money. Give it to a bum on the street. I don't care, just make it disappear." *Before I change my mind*.

"You're sure?"

"Absolutely."

Jillian nodded. "Okay, I'll take it, but it's not for me. I'm holding on to it for your wedding."

"I'm never getting engaged again."

"You say that now—"

"I mean it!" she shouted.

She shouldn't have shouted. She knew that, but she was denying it out loud to convince herself as much as Jillian. This was tough. Battling lifetime indoctrination in the myth of Prince Charming and happily-ever-after. She was tired of wearing glass slippers.

It was way past time to lace up the combat boots.

*　　*　　*

BRODY LEANED AGAINST the wall of his office, sipping a cup of black coffee while Rachael used his restroom to change into her court outfit. She'd been in there for about fifteen minutes with the water running full blast. To hide the sound of her tears? He hated to think she was crying. Or—his cop instincts couldn't help wondering—the sound of her escaping out the window?

He discounted the idea as soon as it popped into his head. One, Rachael had never resisted taking responsibility for the consequences of her actions. As sheriff he'd learned most of those he arrested couldn't wait to blame someone else for their predicament, but not Rachael. And two, the window was really small. Even someone as petite as Rachael was bound to get stuck if they tried to shimmy out of it.

Belinda would have tried to go out the window.

The thought gouged him. Belinda's modus operandi was to run away or to blame her problems on other people. He hadn't known that about her before they married. They'd gotten engaged two weeks before September 11, 2001, because she'd thought she was pregnant. She'd been against his enlisting in the Army and initially, she'd wanted to back out of the engagement. He should have let her. But under the circumstances, he'd lobbied hard for the marriage and in the end they'd moved up the wedding and got hitched the day before he shipped overseas.

The same day she got her period.

Brody was almost grateful when the cell phone in his back pocket buzzed, breaking into his glum thoughts. He pulled it out, flipped it open. "Carlton here."

"Brody, it's Audie Gaston."

"What's up?"

"Someone broke into my store last night and stole a couple of gallons of black paint."

"They take anything else?"

Audie paused. Brody could almost see him looking around his cluttered hardware store.

"I'll have to double-check."

"How'd they get in?"

"Jimmied the back lock."

"Your alarm didn't go off?"

"I didn't switch it on." Audie sounded sheepish.

Why would someone steal black paint? He thought of the billboard, but he knew it wasn't Rachael. Not only had she been in custody since yesterday morning, but when he'd processed her, he'd found the Wal-Mart receipt for a gallon of black paint in her purse. What he feared was that her desecration of the billboard had spurred a copycat vandal.

Great. That was all he needed. People going all over town painting anti-romance slogans.

Maybe this has nothing to do with that. Maybe it's just a coincidence.

Except that Brody didn't believe in coincidences. "I've got to go to court this morning," he told Audie, "but I'll be over there as soon as I can."

"Thanks." Audie grunted. "See you then."

Brody hung up, then rapped on the bathroom door. "Come on, Rachael. Get a move on. Justice waits for no one."

JUDGE ABIGAIL PRUITT was not only the first African American to sit on the bench in Jeff Davis County. She was also the first woman. That made her something of a local legend.

"If you work hard and stay out of trouble you could be the next Abigail Pruitt," Valentine mothers told their daughters. "If she can be a judge, you can, too."

What they often failed to take into account was Abigail's razor-sharp mind, keen observation skills, and a dogged determination to excel, no matter how tough things got. Most people, whether male or female, simply weren't made of such stern stuff.

Judge Pruitt was closing in on sixty. She had a short shock of kinky gray hair, dark intelligent eyes, and a habit of stroking her chin with her thumb and index finger when she was deep in thought. She also possessed an ironclad sense of right and wrong and once she'd made a decision, she was not inclined to change her mind.

At nine a.m. on the nose, Brody led Rachael into the one-hundred-year-old courtroom, Jillian right at their heels. Delaney and Tish followed at a safe distance before slipping into the gallery seating.

Brody pushed through the swinging door separating the gallery from the bench. The aged wooden floors creaked beneath his feet. The building smelled musty and punitive. Rachael found herself wondering how many lives had been forever altered here. She knew hers was about to be one of them and she welcomed the change with open arms.

Judge Pruitt was already behind the bench. She set aside the papers she was reviewing, slid her reading glasses down on her nose, and stared unblinkingly at Rachael over the top of them.

Rachael tried a smile, but the judge remained stony-faced. No charming this woman. She wasn't accustomed to people ignoring her smile and it unsettled her.

"Intimidation tactics," Jillian whispered in her ear, anticipating Rachael's anxiety. "Let it roll right off your back."

Easy for her to say. Jillian was used to swimming in the shark-infested waters of the state legal system.

On the complainant's side of the courtroom, Mayor Wentworth stood with Jeff Davis County's lone full-time prosecutor, Purdy Maculroy. Brody guided Rachael to the defense stand and then stepped back to let Jillian take his place beside Rachael. The minute Brody's body heat was gone, she missed him. Something about his unflappable presence calmed her.

He gave her an encouraging wink that lifted her spirits. Why hadn't she met him before Trace?

You did. He rejected you.

He was twelve. She was seven. It didn't count.

Stop it! You're about to be sentenced in a court of law and you're going gaga over some guy?

But quitting just wasn't that easy. Looking for love in all the wrong places had unwittingly become her modus operandi.

The judge went through the usual housekeeping of proper courtroom procedure, and then she fixed Rachael with a strict glare. "You're charged with vandalizing the Valentine billboard."

"I'm an eyewitness, Judge," Kelvin Wentworth said, "to the destruction of our beloved town landmark."

Judge Pruitt addressed Purdy Maculroy. "Counselor, please remind your client he cannot speak out of turn in my courtroom."

"Yes, Your Honor." Maculroy nudged Kelvin in the ribs.

Everyone in town knew the one thing Judge Pruitt and Kelvin Wentworth had in common was their mutual adoration of Valentine. Other than that, they pretty well hated each other's guts. He was from the good-old-boy network and Judge Pruitt was anything but a good old boy.

"How do you plead, Miss Henderson?" Judge Pruitt asked.

"Guilty as charged," Rachael sang out.

Jillian stepped forward. "With extenuating circumstances, Your Honor."

Judge Pruitt steepled her fingers. "I'm listening, Ms. . . ."

"Samuels. And I intend to show how the town of Valentine drove my client to her rash and unlawful actions."

"Valentine made her do it?" Judge Pruitt arched a skeptical eyebrow. "That's your defense?"

"In a manner of speaking. If Your Honor would just hear me out," Jillian pressed.

Judge Pruitt waved a hand. "You may proceed."

"By nature, my client, Miss Rachael Henderson, is prone to fanciful romantic ideations."

"Meaning?" Judge Pruitt asked.

"She sees the world through rose-colored glasses, and she's easily swayed by love."

Gosh, when Jillian put it like that she sounded like a ditzy nutcase. Rachael sneaked a glance over at Brody to see how he was responding to this evaluation of her character, but the man was a rock, revealing nothing.

He must have been an exemplary soldier, to control his feelings so well. She tilted her head, studied his profile, but he gave away nothing. His eyes were focused on

Judge Pruitt. He stood with a straight stance. She could see the preparedness in the way his hand rested on his hip just above his duty weapon. A hero. The other half of her romantic equation.

If she were in the market for another love —

You're not! Jeez, what are you? A glutton for punishment?

"Is that true?" Judge Pruitt asked.

Chagrined, Rachael realized her mind had wandered as her gaze had slid to Brody's rump and she hadn't heard the question. "Ma'am?"

"If you'd quit staring at Sheriff Carlton's butt long enough to discuss your fate, I'd appreciate it."

At Judge Pruitt's comment, Brody swung his gaze her way and their eyes met.

Rachael's cheeks flamed and she ducked her head. How embarrassing to be caught ogling Brody's backside. "Yes, ma'am."

"I asked if your lawyer's assertions were true. Did you learn that your parents were divorcing on the same day your fiancé jilted you at the altar?"

"Yes, Your Honor, that's true."

"Those are extenuating circumstances."

"Objection!" Kelvin shouted. "She's just trying to weasel out of what she did to our sign."

"You don't get to object." Judge Pruitt scowled at the mayor. "Please control yourself or I'll have you escorted from the courtroom." The judge swung her gaze back to Rachael. "Miss Henderson, I'm a firm believer the punishment should fit the crime. You have pled guilty. Your lawyer has laid out the extenuating circumstances that led

to your lapse in judgment and I have taken that into consideration. A lapse that I trust was temporary."

"Yes, Your Honor." As satisfying as painting those lips
had been, it wasn't worth this.

"Then I sentence you to clean the graffiti from Mr.
Wentworth's sign, to commit one hundred and sixty hours
of community service to the town of Valentine, and to pay
two thousand dollars in restitution." Judge Pruitt banged
her gavel.

"One hundred and sixty hours!" Jillian exclaimed.
"Your Honor, that is excessive. My client lives in Houston. How can she be expected to spend a month out of her
life working for Valentine?"

"She should have thought about that before she painted
the sign," Judge Pruitt said archly.

"She has a job, a—"

"She's a kindergarten teacher. It's summer. School's
out. Her parents live here in town. The sentence stands."
Judge Pruitt banged her gavel again for emphasis. "You
can make arrangements to pay your fine with Becky, the
county clerk. And see Sheriff Carlton about scheduling
your community service hours."

"Yes, ma'am," Rachael mumbled.

"Come on, let's get the hell out of this kangaroo court."
Jillian hustled her out the heavy wooden doors. They
stepped into the hot July morning. Rachael blinked against
the blinding sunlight. Her eyes hadn't even adjusted before
someone shoved a microphone in her face.

"Leesie Stringer, KRTE News, Del Rio," the woman
said in a crisp, professional manner. Del Rio was the closest town with a television station. Beside the reporter, a

cameraman was filming Rachael as she descended the courthouse steps. "Are you the woman that the Chicago Bears' new wide receiver, Trace Hoolihan, jilted at the altar?"

It was the ultimate humiliation. Ambushed by the media after being sentenced for something she'd done in reaction to being dumped on her wedding day. Rachael opened her mouth to respond but no words came out.

Jillian raised an arm to shield her face from the camera. "My client has no comment."

"Miss, miss," the reporter insisted, staying right at her elbow, keeping the microphone thrust in Rachael's face. "How does it feel to be thrown over for a professional football team?"

Rachael was about to offer a smart-assed retort, something completely unsuitable for the noon news, when suddenly Brody was there, getting between her and the reporter.

"You heard the lawyer. Miss Henderson has no comment and if you don't stop harassing her, I'll be happy to show you the inside of the Jeff Davis County Jail, Ms. Stringer."

The next thing she knew, Brody's arm was around Rachael's waist and he was escorting her to his patrol car.

"Miss Henderson, Miss Henderson," the reporter called out as Brody opened the door and helped Rachael into the passenger seat. "Did you know Trace Hoolihan is giving an interview to *Entertainment Weekly* and he's going to discuss why he jilted you at the altar?"

AFTER BRODY DROPPED Rachael off at Higgy's Diner for lunch with her friends, he drove to Audie's Hardware, which was just down the block. He parked in the alley and went in through the back entrance so he could get a look at the jimmied door.

He squatted to examine the pry marks. Big flat-head screwdriver, he surmised. The kind that was in every tool box in the county.

Audie must have heard him because he came to the back, winding his way past shelves of merchandise. "What do you think?"

Brody stood and pushed his sunglasses up on his head. "I think you need to start setting your alarm."

"You wanna see where they took the cans?"

"Sure." Brody followed Audie over to the paint section where he kept the premixed colors. They stood staring at the shelf where two cans of paint used to sit.

"You gonna dust for prints?"

Audie had been watching too much *CSI*. "I'll dust the back door for prints, but this is a public place. And I know the local builders come to your back door. Plus, these shelves are littered with fingerprints. There'll be no way of knowing who was the thief and who was thumbing through the paint cans or coming through your back door."

"I guess you got a point." Audie stuffed his hands in his pockets. "Oh, by the way, after I talked to you, I discovered something else was missing."

"What's that?"

"A pipe cutter."

"Hmm," Brody mused, stroking his chin with his thumb and index finger as he puzzled out what a thief would want with two gallons of black paint and a pipe cutter. Criminal mischief was clearly in the offing.

"You suppose this has got anything to do with Rachael Henderson vandalizing the billboard?"

"Maybe." Brody was staying tight-lipped. He didn't want any rumors getting started.

"You know that paint is for outdoor use. Oil-based. It don't come off easy."

"I'm sure that's what your thief was angling for. If he or she wants to make a statement, they'll want something that's hard to remove."

Audie sighed. "Thanks for coming by."

"No problem. And remember to turn on the alarm."

"Will do. Hey, I was just headed over to Higgy's for the blue plate special. You wanna join me?"

Brody shook his head. "With Zeke out, Jamie is the only one at the station," he said. "Enjoy your lunch."

After he dusted the back door for prints and came up with more than two dozen possible suspects, he knew he didn't have much chance of solving the break-in until the thief used the paint or he happened upon another clue. As Brody headed back to his office to file the police report, he couldn't help thinking that Rachael's little Valentine insurrection was already having unintended consequences.

And he had a sneaking suspicion things were just gearing up.

Chapter Six

Rachael and her friends were inside Higgy's Diner, seated at a pink vinyl booth with heart-shaped seat backs and a matching pink Formica tabletop. The waitress, a bosomy woman named April Tritt who'd altered her uniform to show both more leg and cleavage, handed them heart-shaped menus.

Rachael didn't need a menu. She knew Higgy's food offerings by heart. She'd worked here for two summers when she was in high school. At the time, she'd thought it was the sweetest job in the world. It had been ten years since she'd schlepped meat loaf on thick blue glassware plates, but the menu hadn't changed.

"Wow," Tish said. "Is this place for real? I feel like I've stepped into a thirteen-year-old girl's romantic fantasies."

Rachael glanced around the diner, seeing it through her friends' eyes. On the back wall was an elaborate mural of unicorns and rainbows along with the slogan ALL YOU NEED IS LOVE written in spindly neon pink script. The mural on the right side was a field of sunflowers, butterflies, and bumblebees. This slogan read: LOVE BLOOMS IN VALENTINE, TEXAS. The tackiest mural was the one on the wall where they sat. It featured hearts painted with a 3-D optical illusion effect that made the hearts appear as if they were beating. The slogan: WITHOUT LOVE THE HEART DOESN'T BEAT.

The remaining wall was filled with movie posters from such romantic classics as *It Happened One Night, Tootsie, Dirty Dancing, The Big Easy, While You Were Sleeping,* and *When Harry Met Sally.* And of course, Rachael's all-time favorite, *Sleepless in Seattle,* was also featured.

Shelves running along the wall were chock-full of romance-oriented memorabilia: motion-sensitive, dancing flowers that twirled and played "I Can't Help Myself" whenever anyone walked past; heart-shaped, rhinestone-studded, Elton John–style sunglasses circa 1974; velvet, heart-shaped ring boxes. Teddy bears embracing. Magnetic, lip-locking Raggedy Ann and Andy. Nesting white turtledoves. Scarlet, heart-shaped Mardi Gras beads. Pink feather boas. Heart-shaped candles in various sizes and colors. A figurine of a sloe-eyed girl with her arms stretched out as wide as she could open them and on the base were carved the words: *I Love You This Much.* Everything was manufactured by Wentworth Novelties.

For the first time, Rachael saw the truth. What she'd always thought of as kitschy, cute, and sweetly romantic was corny, cheesy, and incredibly tasteless.

What a load of hooey.

"Or," Tish went on, "the die-hard romantic's version of the Hard Rock Café. They should rename this place Hard-Core Romance Café."

"Um, the ambience is certainly original," said Delaney, always the diplomatic one.

"It looks like the creators of Hello Kitty dropped acid in here," Jillian observed, shrugging out of her jacket.

"Girls, girls," Delaney chided. "Rachael needs our support, not our criticism of her hometown."

"Seriously, though." Tish reached across the table to lay her hand on Rachael's. "I see why you snapped and went after that lippy billboard."

"You think this is bad?" Rachael waved a hand at their surroundings. "You should see the rest of the town."

"It's all like this?" Delaney sounded horrified in spite of herself.

"You didn't notice the heart-shaped parking meters when we drove up?" Jillian asked. "Or the heart and arrow in the cement sidewalk outside with 'Bill + Laurie 4 Ever' carved into it when we came through the front door?"

"There are hearts and names of prominent local couples on every sidewalk square on Main Street," Rachael explained. "Like the Hollywood Walk of Fame. Except they call it the Valentine Walk of Flames."

"Seriously?" Tish arched an eyebrow.

"I saw the 'Bill + Laurie' one," Delaney said. "But I didn't realize it was a pattern."

Rachael shrugged apologetically. "It's for the tourists. Tourism is Valentine's main industry."

"I did you a grave disservice, Rachael," Jillian said. "I should have argued more stringently with Judge Pruitt. I understand you so much better now. Clearly, you have been brainwashed from birth."

"You think?" Tish said, but it wasn't a question.

"One hundred and sixty community hours and two thousand dollars is too much to pay when you've been set up your whole life to take a fall."

"Two thousand dollars." Rachael moaned. "Where am

I going to get two thousand dollars, much less the money to pay Jillian's fee and court costs?"

"Don't be silly," Jillian said. "You're not paying me a penny. We're friends. And don't worry about coming up with the money all at once. They'll let you make arrangements to pay it off. Which, by the way, we need to go see the county clerk about after lunch."

Rachael placed a hand against her stomach to soothe the twisting ache of anxiety. "I have six hundred and thirty-seven dollars in my savings account. How am I ever going to pay it all?"

"We'll find a way," Jillian said. "You interested in suing Trace for breach of contract?"

"Can I do that?" Rachael asked.

"Y'all ready to order?" April Tritt had wandered back over to their table with four glasses of ice water and set them down on the table.

Jillian frowned at the menu. "You have anything that isn't too heavy or deep-fried?"

"Nope," April said cheerfully. "We specialize in home-style country cooking."

"Take my advice," Rachael said. "At Higgy's, stick with the blue plate special."

"I don't like meat loaf," Jillian said.

"Menu surf at your own risk," Rachael warned.

"Blue plate," Tish ordered quickly.

"Me as well," Delaney said. "Meat loaf sounds like a nice comfort food."

"This fish you have on the menu..." Jillian pointed.

"The fried catfish fillets?"

"Could you ask the cook to blacken it?"

"Sure." April took their menus and sashayed off, rolling her generous hips for the benefit of the men in the diner.

"I hope," Rachael said, "the cook knows to prepare your fish with blackened seasoning at a high heat and doesn't literally blacken it in the deep fryer."

Jillian looked alarmed. "Is that a possibility?"

Rachael shrugged. "Look around. This is Valentine."

"Excuse me, miss." Jillian hopped up and scurried after the waitress. "I've changed my mind. I'll have the blue plate special."

Tish giggled. "You were yanking her chain, right?"

Rachael smiled. "Sometimes Jillian needs to come down off her high horse a little."

TEN MILES OUTSIDE of Valentine, Selina had to pull over to have a good long cry. Early that morning Jillian had called to tell her Rachael had been arrested for vandalizing the Valentine billboard. On top of everything else, it was almost more than Selina could bear.

But she was first and foremost a mom. Rachael needed her—even if she might believe she didn't want to see her—and Selina was determined to be there for her. She'd lost her marriage; she'd be damned if she was going to lose her daughter as well.

She'd driven fifteen miles over the speed limit to make the drive from Houston to Valentine, at a personal record of four hours and forty-seven minutes. Rachael was supposed to have been arraigned at ten this morning, so she knew she was too late for that, but she wasn't too late to help her pick up the pieces of her life.

However, now that she was within hugging range of

her eldest daughter, her composure flew out the window. After a hard, five-minute cry, she wiped her face, blew her nose on a Kleenex, and reapplied her makeup.

"Stiff upper lip," she told herself and got back on the highway.

A few minutes later, she rolled past the WELCOME TO VALENTINE, TEXAS, ROMANCE CAPITAL OF THE USA billboard.

Seeing the lips painted startlingly black and knowing her daughter was responsible caused her to feel both shocked and irreverently amused. The child had more spunk than Selina had given her credit for.

More spunk than me.

Good. It was wonderful that Rachael was fighting back. If Selina had stood up for herself twenty-seven years ago, she wouldn't be in this mess now.

She took a deep breath. Okay, maybe she was twenty-seven years too late, but she'd finally worked up her gumption. She was filing for divorce, moving out of Michael's ancestral family home. She'd already rented a furnished house in town and her friend Giada Vito had already promised her a job as a teacher's aide.

But now that she was here, where was she supposed to go? What should she do first?

Find Rachael.

She thought about calling her daughter's cell phone, but she'd been doing that for two days. Rachael wasn't taking her calls or returning her messages. It was eleven-thirty and she seriously doubted Rachael would still be at the courthouse, especially since her friends were in town. Selina didn't want to go home and deal with Michael, although he was probably at the country club playing golf.

Home.

The second-biggest house in town — Mayor Kelvin Wentworth owned the biggest — was no longer her home. Selina was going to have to get used to the idea. It shouldn't be too hard. Not when she was feeling so betrayed. Not when she'd already rented a house in town.

Honestly, it had never really seemed like her home.

She remembered arriving there as a new bride, filled with silly ideas of happily-ever-after, awed by her wealthy young husband, slavishly in love with him, but terrified he'd married her only because of the new life growing in her womb. It had been tough, living there with his parents. After the girls were born she'd convinced him to buy a quiet modest house in the middle of town. They'd lived there ten years before Michael's father had a stroke and they'd been forced to move back into the mansion. She couldn't help thinking those ten years had been the best of her life.

Fresh tears hovered at the back of her eyelids, but resolutely she shoved them away. What was done was done. She couldn't rewrite history.

"Great, now you're giving yourself pep talks with platitudes," she muttered. "You have lived in Valentine too long."

What she needed was a plan. And first on her list was finding her daughter. It was almost lunchtime. The chances of her being at Higgy's Diner were good.

As was usual for the Monday blue plate lunch special — meat loaf, garlic mashed potatoes, garden-harvested corn on the cob, buttered biscuits, sweet tea, and peach cobbler; all for just six dollars and ninety-five cents — the parking spaces up and down both sides of Main Street were filled to capacity.

Hoping someone was only running a fast errand inside the Mercantile Bank and would be pulling out soon,

Selina steered the Caddy around the next block. And just happened to glance down the alley behind Higgy's.

Two people, a man and a woman, were sneaking out the back door like illicit lovers. The woman went left, the man went right, headed in Selina's direction.

She did a double take and slammed on the brakes.

The man was Michael.

And the woman was that hussy Vivian Cole.

Anger and hurt and the aching need for vengeance slapped her like a wet rubber glove across the face. It was one thing to suspect your husband was having an affair with his high school prom-queen ex-sweetheart.

It was quite another to have it so blatantly confirmed.

Twenty-seven years of doubts about a marriage she'd pretended was perfect coalesced into one stunning moment of utter betrayal. Her deepest, darkest fear had just come to pass.

Michael had never truly loved her. He'd just married her because she was pregnant with Rachael. And he'd spent almost three decades lying and pretending. Before she had time to fully think her actions through, Selina shoved the Caddy into reverse and stomped the accelerator. The tires squealed like mating bobcats as she whipped the car around.

Michael spotted her. He stood frozen in the middle of the alley, eyes wide, mouth falling open in disbelief.

Vivian was long gone.

Selina glowered through the windshield at her husband.

Michael raised his palms.

Twenty-seven years of loving him with all her heart, fearing, dreading that he did not love her the way she loved him, robbed her of any rational thought.

Without a moment's hesitation, Selina gunned the engine and aimed her Cadillac straight toward her rat bastard, soon-to-be ex-husband.

THE FOUR FRIENDS were deep into their meat loaf when a loud, booming impact sounded behind the diner and shook the building.

Rachael's head jerked up, her fork halfway to her mouth. *What was that?*

It sounded like a car wreck.

Immediately half the people in the diner were on their feet and headed for the rear entrance. The first one out the door was Audie Gaston.

"What's going on?" Delaney asked.

Rachael tensed as a weird feeling of impending doom came over her. "I don't know."

"Hey!" Audie yelled. "Someone call 911. Selina Henderson just smacked the hell out of Higgy's Dumpster with her Caddy and she's bleeding all over the air bag."

HEART THUMPING SO fast he thought it might pound right out of his chest, Michael yanked open the passenger-side door of his wife's car. A minute ago, she had been aiming to run him down, but at the last second she'd swerved and demolished Higgy's Dumpster.

The air bags had deployed and he couldn't get to her via that route, so he pivoted and wrenched open the back door. He crawled in and leaned over the seat. "Selina, sweetheart, speak to me!"

From behind the wheel of the crunched Caddy, Selina

could barely turn her head to look at him. "Fuck off, Michael."

Startled, he drew back. Never once in twenty-seven years had he heard his wife use such language.

Okay, she was seriously mad. He could respect that but he wasn't going to let her anger stop him from checking on her.

"Are you hurt?" he asked.

"That's none of your damned business."

She had a cut on her forehead and blood was slowly oozing down the left side of her face. People came pouring out of Higgy's Diner, but Michael had eyes only for his wife. He reached out a hand.

"Touch me," she said, "and the next time I try to run you down, I won't swerve."

"You don't mean that."

"You think I'm blind?" she shrieked. "I saw you with Vivian."

"It's not what you think."

"That's what you said on our wedding day. And you know what? I believe it is *exactly* what I thought it was. I think you've been lying to me for twenty-seven years." She grimaced.

He didn't know how badly she'd injured herself in the accident, but he knew her real pain was emotional. And he knew he was the cause. What in the hell was wrong with him? Why had he been having lunch with Vivian?

In public, in front of the whole town.

Well, because it was in front of the whole town. No one would think they were having an affair if they were out in broad daylight together.

We aren't having an affair.

Maybe not yet, but his thoughts had been running along dangerous lines. Why else had he sneaked out the back door when he realized Rachael and her friends had come into the restaurant?

He'd been hiding from his daughter.

Shame flamed in Michael's chest. What in the hell had he been thinking? He'd had a great marriage, an unbelievably wonderful wife, and he'd pissed it all away by flirting with Vivian in those damnable e-mails she'd sent him after she'd separated from her husband. It was stupid. It was a middle-aged man looking back down the road of his life, wondering what might have been. And it had been a grave mistake.

Fool. He was an utter fool.

"Selina, honey," he said, his voice cracking with emotion. "You're bleeding."

He tried to reach for her again, but Audie Gaston was wrenching open the driver's-side door and diner patrons were spilling out of Higgy's and encircling the car. The squealing sound of the siren atop what passed as an ambulance in Valentine—a refurbished old World War II Red Cross vehicle—vibrated the air.

And then he saw Rachael in the crowd, pushing forward to get to her mother.

"Let me through, let me through," she said.

Michael backed out of the car.

"Daddy?" Rachael's eyes widened when she spotted him. "What happened?"

"Your mother…" He shook his head, unable to trust his voice.

"Tried to run down your father." Selina finished his

sentence just as the ambulance pulled into the alley behind them.

The EMT rushed forward.

"I'm okay, I'm all right. I don't need an ambulance." Selina struggled to get out of the car around the air bag. Audie was holding out a hand to help her up and Rachael was standing beside her, nervously shifting from foot to foot.

Michael ducked his head back into the car. "Honey, you hit your head. You need stitches."

"You don't get to call me honey," Selina snapped and got to her feet.

"Mom," Rachael cautioned. "Be careful."

"I'm okay, I'm fine, really—"

Selina swayed and her knees buckled. The EMT caught her before she hit the ground. Michael raced around the back of the Caddy to help the man get her onto the gurney, but Audie Gaston was already there, filling in his role.

"I'm riding in the ambulance with you," Michael said as Audie and the EMT loaded her into the back of the ambulance.

"No, you're not," Selina said. "You gave up your right to do that when you took up with Vivian again."

"I didn't take up with her, I—"

"Daddy," Rachael said, muscling past him to get to her mother and shooting him a darkly accusing glance. "I think you've done enough damage for one day."

"Me? I…I…" he stammered, trying to think up a defense but realizing he had none.

Rachael climbed into the ambulance beside her mother and the EMT shut the doors.

Hurt and bewildered, Michael stood there watching

his family drive away, and it hit him like a sucker punch to the jaw. Selina was serious. She wasn't going to try to work things out. There would be no counseling, no couples therapy, no relationship-enhancing retreat.

Clearly, in her mind, their marriage was over.

VALENTINE HOSPITAL BOASTED only twenty beds, fifteen full-time nurses, one under-equipped operating room, and two doctors on staff: Dr. John Edison Sr. and Dr. John Edison Jr. The ambulance pulled up outside the emergency room — such as it was — at the same time as the sheriff's cruiser.

The minute Rachael spied Brody she felt both relieved and anxious. Her heart punched strangely against her chest. She was so happy to have him here. She didn't know how to handle the fact that her mother had tried to run her father down.

"What are you doing here?" she asked as he came over to help the EMT unload the gurney.

"Checking on your mother."

She raised a hand to her heart and wondered what it meant that he was checking on her mother. *He's the sheriff. Your mother smacked her car into a Dumpster. He's just doing his job. It's got nothing to do with you.*

"Are you all right?" he asked.

Rachael shrugged and tried to appear nonchalant. "Sure, fine, why wouldn't I be?"

"You've had an eventful weekend." His eyes darkened with concern.

"Hello, Brody." Selina smiled at him. "You look handsome today."

"You flirting with me, Mrs. Henderson?" he asked, pushing his Stetson back on his forehead as he and the EMT wheeled her into the emergency room.

"Well, if my daughter won't do it..." she said. "You know I'm single now."

"So I heard."

"Mother!"

"Settle down, Rachael. Brody knows I'm just teasing." Her mother said his name like they were the best of friends.

Brody's gaze met Rachael's, his eyes crinkled up at the corners. A slight smile tipped his lips. It was a knowing smile, a smug smile, and for some reason it bugged the hell out of her. She didn't like what his smile insinuated.

Why did it feel as if he knew her mother better than she did?

She'd been so clueless about her parents' marital problems. Probably the entire town of Valentine knew more than she did. She'd believed they were so happy and now she'd found out they'd been miserable enough to consider divorce. How was that possible? It made her reconsider everything she'd always believed about her family, and that tore her up inside. She felt betrayed by her own expectations and foolish to have accepted a fantasy as reality.

"Mom's going to be okay," Rachael said, struggling to fight her attraction to the man standing beside her. "So you can go now."

"I'll stick around," he said. "I don't have anything else to do. Besides, it'll give us a chance to set up your community service hours while the doctor examines your mother."

"Community service?" Selina asked. "What's he talking about?"

"I'll explain later," she said to her mother.

A nurse came into the room. "Hey, Selina, is it true you tried to run Michael over?"

"I tried," her mother said. "But I chickened out at the last minute and swerved."

"Didn't want to get blood on the Caddy's grille?" the nurse joked.

"Something like that."

Rachael hated hearing her mother talk this way. "Mom..."

"Brody," her mother said, "would you take Rachael out to the waiting room?"

Brody put a hand on her shoulder, but she twisted away from him. "I'd rather stay."

"Well, I would rather you would have stayed in Houston and talked things out with me," Selina said. "But you didn't."

Guilt grabbed hold of her and shook hard. This was all her fault. If she hadn't gotten so upset, hadn't run away, maybe her mother wouldn't have tried to run her father down. Rachael raised her palms. "Okay, fine. I'll be outside if you need me."

"Take care of her, Brody. She's fragile right now."

"I'm not fragile," Rachael muttered. And she damn well didn't need any man looking out for her, especially one as tempting as Brody. She gave in to temptation way too easily and her emotional wounds were raw. Her mother was right. She *was* fragile.

Crap.

"Can I offer you some advice?" Brody asked when they were sitting side by side in the waiting room.

"No."

"Don't blame what's going on in your own life on your parents," he said.

"You don't listen so well, do you?"

His grin widened. "I have a hard time keeping quiet when I see someone headed for trouble."

"I'm not headed for trouble."

"You're letting your emotions color your perspective. You can't make rational decisions when you're under the influence of powerful emotions."

"I'm beginning to get that. Thanks for your sage advice." She stepped away from him. Who was he to tell her how to run her life?

Brody trod closer, closing the gap of space she'd just opened, his gaze assessing her. The corners of his mouth curled up, his arms crossed over his chest. He was close. Too close. If she raised her hand, she would graze his upper arm.

He had such broad, straight shoulders. His uniform fit like it had been tailor-made and Department of Public Safety tan was definitely his color. He looked sharp, smart, and in control.

Not to mention his mouth. Her gaze hung on his lips. He looked like he would be a great kisser. His mouth was just the right size. Not too large, not too small. And to think that she'd slept in the same room with this potent, masculine male. Involuntarily, she swallowed against the memory. She'd also acted a little irrational and she didn't want to remember that, either.

"Do you want to talk about your community service schedule?"

"No."

"It's court ordered. Plus, you've got to scrub down

the Valentine sign and repaint it. That's not going to be a cakewalk."

"I'll get started on it tomorrow. That soon enough for you?"

"Why are you mad at me?"

Because, she thought. *You epitomize everything I've ever wanted in a man and I know I can't have you. I shouldn't even want you, after all I've been through. And yet I do. And I know it's all just a symptom of my affliction.*

She had a serious problem. She couldn't stay away from thoughts of romance no matter how hard she tried.

Rachael didn't answer him. Instead, she plopped down in an uncomfortable metal chair and picked up a well-thumbed copy of *Texas Monthly.* Brody settled in beside her.

She heard a faint whirring sound. Like gears turning. "What's that noise?"

He paused a long moment, then said, "My leg."

"Your leg?"

"It's computerized."

"Your leg has a computer chip in it?"

"My prosthesis, to be exact."

"Your prosthesis?" She sounded like a parrot.

He looked at her. "You didn't know?"

"I knew you were hurt in Iraq. I didn't know you'd..." She dropped her gaze to his knees.

"Lost a leg." He said it so matter-of-factly.

"But how? I mean...you climbed a ladder after me yesterday."

"Courtesy of the Power Knee. It's state-of-the-art. I'm part of a special test group. I couldn't afford the thing otherwise."

"I didn't see it when I slept in your room. Even when you got up in the middle of the night to reassure me."

"Because I didn't want you to see it."

"Are you ashamed?"

"No."

"Self-conscious?"

"A little, maybe. I don't want people thinking I can't do my job just because I'm an amputee. I don't want people judging me, lauding me. Or feeling sorry for me because of it."

"It must have been horrible. In Iraq." She shuddered. She could not imagine the awful things he'd seen, done.

"After the Twin Towers, it was nothing. It was what I had to do in order to justify what happened to Joe."

"Joe was your friend that got killed?"

"Yeah."

"But going to Iraq cost you your leg."

"Small price to pay for freedom."

A strange feeling came over her. Sadness, wistfulness, and an odd aching sensation that made no sense. She didn't know what else to say to him, so she said nothing at all.

She was supposed to be in Fiji on her honeymoon sipping mai tais and making love to Trace. Not sitting here in the hospital emergency waiting room in Valentine, Texas, beside a sexy Iraq War vet with an artificial computerized leg, waiting for her mother to get stitches after a car smashup in which she'd tried to run down Rachael's father.

So much for best-laid plans.

A laundry cart laden with freshly folded sheets squeaked as a member of the housekeeping staff wheeled it from the laundry room; the smell of bleach, fabric softener, and the slightly singed odor of overheated cotton trailing the corridor.

"Is that why you're divorced?" she dared to ask. "Did your wife leave because of the leg?"

He got up without answering, heading for the coffeepot and Styrofoam cups on a stand in the corner. "You want a cup of coffee?"

She shrugged, but inside she felt weirdly disturbed. Was he still so hung up on his ex-wife he couldn't even talk about her? "Sure."

"How do you take it?"

"Lots of cream and three sugars."

"Sweet tooth," he commented, tapping three packets of sugar into the coffee and two spoonfuls of creamer. He dropped a red plastic stir stick into her cup and handed it to her. He sat back down, took a long sip of the coffee, and then said, "Belinda left before the leg. While I was still stationed in Iraq."

It took a second before she realized he was finally answering her question.

"Another man?"

He nodded.

"That sucks."

"Can't argue."

"At one time, were you guys ever truly madly in love?"

"I'm not exactly known for my romantic soul."

She sat up straighter, took a sip of her coffee. Perfect. Exactly how she liked it. "Really? Why not?"

"Couple of reasons, I suppose." He stared off into space.

"So what are the reasons?" she prompted.

"Huh?"

That's when she realized he'd been staring at her legs. The way she was sitting — still wearing the suit Jillian had brought her — the skirt had risen up high on her thighs. She lifted her butt off the seat, tugged the skirt hem down.

"Aw," he complained. "I was enjoying the view. You've got world-class legs."

That made her feel pleased, and feeling pleased made her feel put out with herself. "I thought you said you didn't have a romantic soul."

"Peaches," he said, his grin wolfish, "what the sight of your legs stirs in my soul is anything but romantic."

"Peaches?" she asked, latching on to anything to keep the excitement jumping inside her at bay. "What does that mean?"

He shook his head. "I have peach trees. You remind me of the peaches. Ripe and rounded and sun-kissed and juicy."

She didn't know what to say to that. One part of her wanted to enjoy the compliments, another part wanted to accuse him of sexual harassment. But she'd started this whole line of conversation.

"Rachael?"

Startled, she looked up to see Dr. Edison Jr. standing in the doorway. Her pulse quickened. She got to her feet. "Yes?"

"Your mother is going to be just fine. I had to give her a couple of stitches for the wound on her forehead but it shouldn't leave much of a scar."

Rachael splayed a palm to her chest and let out a pent-up breath. "Oh, thank heavens."

"She'll be ready to go in just a minute."

"Thank you, Doctor."

The junior Edison had no sooner disappeared than

Selina came around the corner. Her color was pale and she had a small rectangular bandage taped just above her eye, but other than that she looked fine.

"Rachael," she said. "Take me home."

Rachael hesitated. "You mean take you home to Daddy's house?"

"No," she said. "Take me to my new home."

"You have a new home?"

"I moved in last week."

Distressed, Rachael sank her hands onto her hips. "Why didn't you tell me?"

"You were so busy getting ready for your wedding, I didn't want to spoil your big day."

"No worries there," she said. "Trace is the one who spoiled it."

"Along with your father and I. He shouldn't have sprung the news of our separation on you like that."

"It's okay. I'll adjust," Rachael said coolly, even though she was feeling anything but cool. She had a million questions for her mother about the divorce, yet she had no idea where to start. "Where are you staying?"

"Didn't Brody tell you?" Selina looked over at Brody, who'd also gotten to his feet.

"Tell me what?"

"I'm renting Mrs. Potter's place. She broke her hip and had to move into Shady Hills Manor and her son's letting me stay there while it's on the market."

Mrs. Potter had been the old high school principal before Giada Vito took over the job. The very same Mrs. Potter who lived right across the street from Brody.

"Hey," Brody said. "I can give you a lift home."

Chapter Seven

Rachael called Delaney, Tish, and Jillian to let them know what was going on. She'd been so unnerved, she'd forgotten about her friends. They rallied around and came over to offer moral support as she got Selina ensconced in her new place.

Not long after her friends arrived, the local florist's delivery driver showed up with a bouquet of twenty-seven pink roses in full bloom. "Delivery for Selina Henderson," he said when Rachael answered the door.

Rachael tipped the guy and took the bouquet into the living room where Selina was propped up on the couch, watching the evening news and drinking a glass of Shiraz. Jillian had shown up with the bottle of wine and a corkscrew. Delaney, being pregnant, was the designated driver back to Houston. Everyone else was having a glass to take the edge off the day.

Selina took one look at the roses and waved them away. "Get rid of them."

"What?" Rachael stared at her mother.

"Throw them in the trash."

"Don't you want to know who they're from?" Rachael held up the little white envelope that had come with the flowers.

"I know who they're from. Pink. In full bloom. How many are there? Twenty-seven, I'm guessing. For the number of years we've been married. Plus it's nine bouquets of three. I'm sure your father enjoyed the symmetry. Pitch them."

"It might not be from Daddy. Would you like for me to read the card?"

"No." Selina hardened her cheek and acted as if she were paying extra attention to the television sportscaster.

Rachael read the card anyway. "Selina, my darling, words cannot express the depth of my sorrow and shame for the hurt I've caused you. Please forgive me. Love, Michael."

"I told you not to read it."

"Aw, Mom. Come on, it sounds like he's really sorry. Can't you give him another chance?"

Selina raised her hand. "This is between me and your father. He thinks roses and an apology can fix everything. Well, it can't. I've spent twenty-seven years trying to convince myself romance was enough, but it's not. What matters is real intimacy. And that's the one thing he's never given me."

Rachael didn't know what to say. Deep down inside she kept thinking it was all her fault. If her mother hadn't gotten pregnant with her, her parents wouldn't have gotten married. Her father would have gone to Harvard the way his family had wanted. Her mother could have followed her dreams of being a chef. Instead she'd been stuck. Forced into pretending she was happy because she was a mom and had no choice. Guilt gnawed on Rachael. She hated thinking she'd held her parents back from what they had truly wanted in life.

"Please." Selina's voice was brittle, fragile. "Just get the flowers out of the house."

"We'll take them with us when we leave," Delaney said.

"Thank you," Selina whispered.

Just then Rachael's cell phone rang from inside her purse, lying on the floor beside the front door. She put the roses on the coffee table and noticed that her mother turned her head away so she couldn't see them. She went for her phone.

Her father's number flashed on the caller ID. She didn't want to take the call in front of Selina, so she ducked into the kitchen. "Hello, Daddy."

"Rach, are you with your mother?"

"Yes."

"Did she get the flowers?"

"She got them."

"Did she read the card?"

"I read it to her."

"What'd she say?"

"She's not impressed."

He blew out his breath. Rachael could almost see the dejected expression in his eyes. He was probably pulling a palm down his face the way he did whenever he felt defeated. "Have I lost her for good?"

"I've never seen her like this, Daddy. She looks so hopeless." Rachael wanted to ask her father what had happened between them to cause such a rift. She didn't dare ask if he'd had an affair. She couldn't bear to hear the answer. If her father couldn't be true to the woman he loved, how could she ever hope to find a man that could stay faithful to her?

Forget about finding a man. Find yourself.

"I love her so much…" His voice tightened and he paused.

Was her father crying?

Gut wrenching, Rachael found her own eyes tearing up and her throat constricting. Were all her happy childhood memories really a lie? She thought about the family vacations. The adventures the four of them had together. The kisses their parents had bestowed upon her and Hannah. The love they'd shown each other. It couldn't all be a lie. Could it?

She remembered waking up early one Christmas morning to find her parents sitting in the middle of the living room floor putting together a pink bicycle. Selina would read the instructions, then pass her father the appropriate tools. They'd worked as a precision team, except for when they'd taken a break to smooch and giggle. Surely, that gentle moment had been real.

Rachael thought of other happy moments and her chest knotted with emotion. Playing Marco Polo in the pool at Corpus Christi during spring break when she was nine. She on Daddy's shoulders, Hannah on Mom's. Getting lost on a trip to Carlsbad Caverns, Selina saving the day by having four Mars Bars and a pocket compass stashed in her fanny pack. Watching her parents dance together at Hannah's wedding to "Can't Help Falling in Love," her mother's head resting on her father's shoulder.

Sadness, regret, nostalgia, tenderness, and a flicker of hope mingled inside her. There was love there. Something like that couldn't be faked. Clearly, her parents had just lost their way. They could find their way back to each other. She desperately needed to believe that.

"How are you holding up, Princess?" he asked, his tone stronger.

She sniffled. "I'm okay."

"I should have smashed Hoolihan's teeth in and made him marry you."

That made her smile briefly. "I don't want a man who doesn't want me."

"Who wouldn't want you, Princess? You're smart and gorgeous and kind—"

"And something of a flake."

"No, you're not. But sometimes your trusting nature and your need to be liked lead you astray. You got that from me."

Her father had always been her hero. She'd had an idyllic childhood. Or at least she'd perceived it that way. Parents who loved each other. A younger sister she happily squabbled with over Barbies. A great hometown. She'd had everything she'd ever needed. The Henderson name opened a lot of doors. She'd been privileged and pampered, but never spoiled.

She had so many wonderful memories of her father. She remembered how he would perch on the edge of his daughters' little girl–sized chairs, his knees bent up to his chin, and pretend to sip imaginary tea when she and Hannah invited him to their tea parties. She remembered the piggyback rides and the bedtime stories and the way he would wrap ice in a cup towel and smash it with a hammer to make ice chips for her when she was home from school sick with the flu. She thought of how he would sneak her copies of teenybopper magazines her mother didn't want her to read. How he taught her to whistle and play chess and fish.

He was a good man. A kind man. He was Rachael's blueprint for the way a man was supposed to be. What did her mother mean when she said their marriage had been empty of real intimacy? That picture conflicted with everything she knew about her dad.

No one knows what goes on inside a marriage except the two people who are in it. She'd heard that somewhere and she supposed it was true, but she found it unsettling to think the romantic front her parents had presented all these years had been a façade. So what had gone on? What was she missing? How could she be so misguided? Why couldn't she shake this need for happily-ever-after, not just in regard to herself, but to her parents as well?

Confusion clouded her mind, misery churned her stomach. She didn't know what to think.

"Are you going to stay there with your mother?" her father asked.

"Yes."

"That's good. Thank you."

"Maybe you just need to give her some time, Daddy. Stop sending flowers. Stop trying to win her back."

"You really think that's the best move?" He sounded unconvinced.

"Just a little breathing room. That might be all she needs. Can you give her that?"

"I'm afraid if I back off, I'll lose her forever."

"I'm afraid if you keep on trying to woo her with romantic gestures, you'll lose her."

"I don't know what to do."

Stay away from Vivian Cole, she wanted to say, but she didn't have the guts to voice the words.

"Rachael," Tish called from the living room, her tone urgent. "You gotta get in here. You've gotta see this."

"I have to go, Daddy," she said. "But hang in there. I'll see if I can talk to Mom."

"I love you, Rachael."

"I love you, too."

She hung up the phone and stepped into the living room. What she saw made her jaw drop.

DEANA AND MAISY were watching *Entertainment Tonight* when Brody walked into the house. He passed by the television set just as Deana flipped the channel.

"Hey, look," she said. "It's Rachael's ex-fiancé, Trace Hoolihan, being interviewed by Kimberly Quick."

Brody stopped halfway to the kitchen and backed up. Hoolihan was good-looking in a pretty-boy way. All blond hair and straight teeth. Although Brody thought he smiled like a horse. Involuntarily, he fisted his hands.

"Turn it up," he told Deana.

"So, Trace," asked *ET*'s newest coanchor. "Rumor has it that you left the chapel in the middle of your wedding when your agent interrupted the ceremony to tell you the Chicago Bears had picked up your contract. Is that true?"

"Kim." Trace eyed the reporter as if she were a juicy T-bone steak. He leaned forward, placed a hand on her wrist and lowered his voice. "May I call you Kim?"

The anchorwoman giggled. "Of course."

"Hey, hey," Deana protested and snapped her fingers at the television screen. "None of that nonsense, girly. Giggling isn't professional."

"He's putting the moves on the *ET* anchorwoman two days after he dumped Rach at the altar," Brody growled. "Jerkwad."

"Little pitchers." Deana covered Maisy's ears and glared at Brody.

"What's a jerkwad?" Maisy asked, pushing her mother's hands away.

"Never mind. And don't go around saying it."

"Kim, don't believe everything you hear," Trace continued. "Those reports are greatly exaggerated."

Brody crossed his arms over his chest and glowered at the television. "What a prince."

"I'd already decided to break off the engagement before I heard about the offer from the Bears," Trace went on.

Brody wanted to punch him on principle.

"And why is that?" Kim, the glossy, giggly anchorwoman asked.

"I'd come to realize my fiancée was simply too needy. She had the most unrealistic notions about love and marriage and romance," Trace said.

"For example…" Kim led him to his next comments.

"She expected me to call her three or four times a day to reassure her I loved her." Hoolihan was looking straight into the camera now. "She was always sending me these goofy little cards and gifts. And she liked for us to wear matching outfits. Can you believe that? Whenever we went out, I felt like Ken and Barbie."

Kim clicked her tongue in sympathy and stroked Trace's forearm. "So tell us how it feels to get picked up by the Chicago Bears after the Houston Texans cut you last season."

"Aw, hell," Brody muttered. He sure hoped Rachael wasn't watching this. But Valentine being the small town it was, he knew someone was bound to call and tell her to turn on the TV.

He headed for the front door.

"Hey," Deana said, "where you going? I'll have dinner on the table in twenty minutes."

"When I drove in I noticed the peaches on the Alberta needed picking. I'll be back inside in time for dinner."

"Tell Rachael Trace Hoolihan is a bonehead," she called after him.

Was he that transparent? How had she known he planned on going across the street?

He plucked a bushel of ripe peaches off his tree, then carried them across the street. Brody didn't know what motivated him to do it other than the fact that he'd seen enough suffering to last a lifetime. He understood first-hand the cruelties man could inflict on his fellow human beings. When he'd returned from Iraq, he'd vowed when-ever an opportunity presented itself to help someone, he'd make the effort.

Yeah, whispered a voice in the back of his head. *Keep telling yourself that's the reason you're going over there.*

Of course it was the reason he was here. Why else would he be on Mrs. Potter's front porch, ringing the bell, won-dering what he was going to say when Rachael answered the door?

Except Rachael didn't answer the door. Rather, it was her sharp-eyed lawyer. "What do you want?" Jillian greeted him.

"I brought Rachael some peaches," he said.

"Thank you." She held out her hands. "I'll take them."

"I'd like to give them to her myself if you don't mind."

"Look, Sheriff," she said. "You seem like a decent enough guy and all, but Rachael really isn't interested in talking to anyone of the masculine persuasion right this minute.

Could you come back later?" She started to shut the door, but he stuck his Power Knee inside before she could get it all the way closed.

"You're not getting rid of me that easily, Counselor," Brody said, giving the woman his most determined stare. "I'm not leaving until I see Rachael."

Jillian studied him a long moment, then she squared her shoulders, tossed her head, and came to a decision. "Okay, hang on. I'll ask her if she'll see you. But she's very vulnerable right now, so don't give her any crap about community service."

"This isn't about that."

"What's it about?"

"Anyone ever call you a bulldog?" he asked.

Jillian beamed. "Why, thank you, Sheriff. I will accept that as a compliment."

He allowed her to shut the door this time and he was left standing there with a basket of peaches in his arms, wondering why he'd felt the need to challenge Jillian. If Rachael didn't want to see anyone, why was he insisting?

Because his gut told him this was the right thing to do and he'd made a policy of always listening to his instincts. His gut had saved the lives of his men in Iraq. He wasn't ignoring it now.

He set the peaches beside the welcome mat. A minute later Rachael appeared. She stepped out onto the front porch, pulled the door closed behind her, and crossed her arms over her chest. She wore a simple white cotton V-neck T-shirt, thin blue cotton drawstring pants, and a pair of white crew socks. Her hair was pulled up off her neck in a breezy ponytail and her face was scrubbed free of makeup.

He'd seen her in other outfits over the past couple of

days. From her spectacular wedding gown and white ballet slippers to the skimpy shorts set and mules she'd borrowed from his sister to the no-nonsense business suit and stilettos she'd worn in court today. But this outfit appealed to him most. Simple, honest, straightforward. She looked like the girl next door.

She is the girl next door, you bonehead.

Suddenly, he was hit with a memory. He and Rachael sitting on the curb on a hot summer afternoon, quarters clutched in their hands, waiting for the ice cream truck to come around the corner. He could hear the music chiming: "Pop Goes the Weasel." They'd been in her backyard swimming pool. He'd probably been about ten and he'd only gone over to their house to get cool. She couldn't have been more than five, sitting there in her bathing suit, blonde hair plastered to her head, grinning at him like he was the most wonderful thing on earth. She'd made him feel like a hero when she'd pressed her quarter into his palm and whispered through the gap in her front teeth, "Peese buy me a peach push-up."

Rachael smelled like the girl next door, too. Like olive oil and honey. Soothing and sweet.

"What is it?" she asked, crossing her arms tighter. Holding herself in or blocking him out, Brody didn't know which, but he could read the body language loud and clear—*Keep your distance, buster.*

"I'm sorry," he said. "I know that was brutal to hear on national television."

"You saw *Entertainment Tonight*." Rachael hit him with her vulnerable green-eyed gaze and his heart stumbled.

"Deana was watching. By the way, she sends her sympathy and a few negative comments about your ex."

That got a small grin out of her. The sight of her smile lightened his spirits. If she could find the humor in the situation, she was going to be all right.

Rachael blew out her breath, ducked her head, studied her socks. "You must think I'm a kook."

"When I look at you, 'kook' is not the word that comes to mind." The suggestive innuendo in his voice took Brody by surprise.

"No?" She raised her head, shot him a look, then quickly dropped her gaze again. "What word comes to mind?"

"Caring, expressive, a little overly passionate, maybe, but that's not a bad thing."

"It isn't?"

"No." He didn't know why, or what he intended to do when he got there, but Brody took a step toward her.

Rachael took two steps back, bumping her butt against the door. Her breathing quickened. He couldn't help noticing the rapid rise and fall of her breasts beneath the T-shirt. "Not even when that misplaced passion lands a girl in jail?"

His gut was telling him something else now. Something he needed to ignore no matter how much he ached to act on it. He had to be careful.

Kiss her.

Without meaning to, Brody propped one forearm against the doorframe above her, leaned in, and lowered his head. He heard her sharp inhalation of air, smelled the fruity scent of wine on her breath.

The sexual tension was so electric he could almost hear it snapping. Gut pulling him forward, he dipped his mouth lower.

And damn if Rachael didn't pucker her lips and close her eyes. She wanted him to kiss her!

Walk away. Your gut is losing it. Don't do something you'll regret. She's vulnerable. You're horny. It's a terrible combination.

Plus, there was the not-so-insignificant fact that he hadn't gotten naked with a woman since he'd lost his leg. He was the one who was vulnerable.

Common sense prevailed. He took his arm from the door, stepped back, struggled to get his breathing—and other bodily functions—under control.

Slowly, Rachael opened her eyes and lost the pucker. She looked wounded.

Aw, crap.

"For what it's worth," he said, trying to make amends, "I think Trace Hoolihan is a giant jackass and that's the polite way of putting it. Why were you engaged to this guy?"

"He didn't always act like an ass. He was pretty humble and contrite after he'd been dumped by the Houston Texans. He was charming. Very charming. And romantic. Gifts. Candlelight dinners. Long walks in the park holding my hand. Plus I jumped in too quickly. He asked me to marry him three weeks after we met. He had me snowed. He's great at being whatever he thinks people want him to be." Rachael shrugged. "And I fell for it. Story of my life."

"Hey, at least you dodged a bullet," Brody said, then cringed inwardly. He wanted to make her feel better, but he realized he was doing a terrible job of it. What he really wanted was to take her into his arms and kiss her so hard she forgot Trace Hoolihan ever existed.

"Yeah," she said forlornly, "there is that."

"Look, Rachael." He raised a hand as impulse spurred

him to reach out, cup her chin, and force her to meet his gaze, but he knew that would be overstepping boundaries. He craved feeling the curve of her soft cheek against his palm and he had to fist his hand at his side to keep from reaching out. "There's a million guys who would give anything to be with you."

And damn if I'm not one of them.

But of course he didn't say that. He couldn't say that. It was stupid to say that now and probably not even really true. He'd just been too long without sex and she was the first woman who'd stirred him this strongly in years.

"That's the problem."

"What?"

She lifted her head again and met his gaze, and this time didn't look away. "I've been putting my hopes and dreams and plans on a guy. Why? What's a guy going to give me that I don't have already?"

Brody arched an eyebrow. "I can think of one thing."

She raised a palm. "Okay, sex maybe, but I don't need a relationship for sex. I could trot on down to Leroy's Bar right now and get all the sex I wanted without any of the grief of a relationship."

Alarm spread through him. The thought of Rachael waltzing into Leroy's and picking up some random guy made him want to go right down there and suspend Leroy's liquor license. "You're not going to do it. Right?"

She didn't say anything, but a speculative look came into her eye as if she was honestly considering it.

"Right?" He ground out the word.

"Would it bother you if I did?"

Oh, hell yeah.

Back off. Calm down. Don't let her rattle you with idle

*threats. She doesn't mean it. She's just hurting. You of all
people should understand that.* "You can't let this Hoolihan character cause you to throw away your values."

"Why not?" she dared, anger sparking in her sea green
eyes. "Where have my values gotten me? Alone. Dumped
on my wedding day. Again. Arrested in my hometown.
Humiliated on national TV."

"You're just angry."

"Damn right I'm angry," Rachael said. "And I have
every right to be."

"Granted. Just don't go jumping into something you'll
regret later," he said, still worried like hell she was going
to saunter on down to Leroy's and make good her threat.

"I appreciate your concern, Sheriff. I really do, but I've
been listening to men's advice just a little bit too long."
She nodded fiercely and narrowed her eyes at him. "Now
if you'll excuse me, I have company."

She turned to go inside.

"Rachael?"

She hesitated, hand on the doorknob, and slightly
turned back to him. "Yes?"

"Don't forget your peaches." He handed her the basket.

She rewarded him with a smile that lit him up inside.
She clutched the basket of sweet-smelling peaches to her
chest. "Thank you."

"You will get through this," he said. "I promise."

"You're right." She lifted her chin proudly and tossed
her head. "In fact, I've already got a plan."

"Please tell me it doesn't have anything to do with
Leroy's Bar."

"Sheriff Carlton," she said, "I'm a big girl and I don't
owe you any explanation."

And with that, she turned and went back inside the house. Leaving him feeling frustrated, irritated, and worried like hell she was setting herself up for big trouble.

RACHAEL WENT BACK into the house with the basket of peaches to find her mother and her friends all staring at her.

"So what's up with the sheriff?" Jillian asked. "Anything I should know as your lawyer?"

"Honey?" her mother said. "Are you all right? You look pale."

"There's nothing going on with the sheriff. He just wanted to talk about scheduling my community service," she said, not knowing why she lied, other than the fact she didn't want to talk about what had happened on the porch.

What had happened on the porch?

She thought about the way he'd crowded her personal space, forcing her back against the door. How the look in his eyes had set her heart to thumping. How her stomach had gone all quivery with excitement. How she'd crazily, dizzily wished he'd kiss her until she couldn't breathe.

Dear God, she'd actually puckered her lips. For a moment, she'd been certain he was going to kiss her. She'd practically dared him to kiss her.

But he hadn't and she'd been sorely disappointed. And that disappointment disappointed her. What was wrong with her that she saw every handsome man as a potential love match? Why was she so desperate for love?

It was a question Rachael should have asked herself a long time ago.

"Ooh," Delaney said. "Peaches."

"Why don't you take some with you on your trip back to Houston?" Rachael offered.

"Thanks, we will. And speaking of heading back to Houston, it's almost a six-hour drive. You guys ready to hit the road?" Delaney asked Tish and Jillian. "I'd like to get home before midnight."

Rachael saw her friends out to their car and hugged them all before they left. It was good to see them again and she really appreciated the moral support, but it was tough having them witness her falling apart. Tish and Delaney had everything she'd ever wanted and she had to admit she was a little envious. Jillian, on the other hand, was an exemplary role model of a woman who didn't need a man to be a success in life. She should be more like Jillian.

Waving good-bye until their car disappeared from sight, she then turned and headed back inside the house, feeling even lonelier than she had before they'd arrived.

She found her mother at the kitchen sink, industriously peeling peaches. "What's up?"

"I needed something to keep my mind busy and these peaches are so ripe they'll go bad in a couple of days. We need to put them up. Would you go down to the cellar and get some of Mrs. Potter's Mason jars?"

"You're going to can them tonight?"

"*We're* going to can them. You need something to keep your mind off your problems, too." Her mother tossed her a red gingham apron. "Put this on."

Rachael retrieved the Mason jars from the cellar and washed them in the sink. She watched as her mother's fingers expertly skinned the peaches with a paring knife. Drying her hands on her apron, she reached for a plump, rosy peach and bit into it.

A burst of juicy peach flavor exploded in her mouth. "Mmm. Oh, this is so good," Rachael said. "If romance had a flavor, it would taste just like this. Sweet and lush and perfect."

"Romance," her mother scoffed, tossing pitted peaches into a large mixing bowl. "There's a reason it's sweet and lush and perfect. It isn't real."

Rachael grabbed a paper towel and dabbed at the peach juice dribbling down her chin.

"Romance is a fantasy. An ideal that doesn't exist." Selina took a potato masher from a drawer and started systematically smashing the pieces into pulp. "This is what happens to romance. This is what marriage does to you. Smashes and mashes until you're just flattened and there's nothing left of that sweet promise except carnage."

Whoa.

Rachael backed away from the peach nectar flying up from Selina's potato masher. "Mom? Are you okay?"

"Romance. It's just like this peach. It looks good at first. All tempting and tasty, but inside there might be worms or you could poke your gum with the sharp edge of the pit. And when peach juice gets on you, it leaves a permanent stain."

"Mom?" Tentatively, Rachael reached out to touch her mother's shoulder. Fear, concern, and genuine disaster gripped her. She'd never seen her mother so upset and she had no idea how to comfort her or what she could say to make things better.

Selina tossed the potato masher, dripping with mashed, stain-producing peach pulp, into the sink, dropped her face into her hands, and began to sob.

"It's going to be okay." Rachael slipped her arm around

her mother's waist. "Daddy still loves you, I know that he does." The words sounded empty, but she knew they were true. How could she convince her? Was love enough? She used to think so, but now she had no clue.

Selina raised her head, swiped at her eyes with both hands. "Rachael, please don't end up like me. Living your life for one man. You put everything into Trace and see how he treated you? Don't let that happen again. Be your own woman. Believe in yourself. Don't make romance the be-all, end-all of your existence. Promise me that."

The look in her mother's eyes rattled Rachael to the core. All the values and beliefs she'd held dear for twenty-six years were in question. "Okay. I promise."

"I think I better go to bed now." She touched her bandaged forehead. "My head is throbbing."

Rachael got her mother some aspirin and helped her to bed, then went back to the kitchen to clean up the peach mess. As she washed and wiped, she reflected on the events of the past few days. She thought about all the mistakes she'd made. All the old sweethearts, the crushed dreams, the broken hearts. She thought about Robert, the first fiancé who'd dumped her at the altar. Correction. Robert hadn't dumped her, he'd just never shown up. Cold feet, he'd told her later when he'd called to apologize. And then he'd gone on to tell her he wasn't good enough for her. That she deserved someone who could love her as much as she should be loved. The sentiment had sounded right and she'd agreed with him. She thought she'd found that someone with Trace. How wrong she'd been.

She recalled how Trace had just made a fool of her during his *Entertainment Tonight* interview. She thought about how her anger had landed her in jail and then into community service that would force her to stay in Valentine for the remainder of the summer.

And, she thought about her parents and the turbulence they were going through even if she didn't understand what it was all about. Her stomach ached for them. Tearing the fabric of twenty-seven years woven together couldn't be easy. Sorrow clogged her throat and she clenched her fists against the sadness of it all.

Her mother was right. Romance wasn't real. It was just an illusion, a nice fantasy but nothing more. She'd let the pursuit of a fantasy run her life.

No. Not just run her life, but dominate it.

She simply had to change.

But what had happened with Brody on the porch this evening told her it wouldn't be easy. She couldn't trust herself. She couldn't do this alone.

She needed help. She needed a twelve-step program. But nothing like that existed. They had programs for sex addicts, but she wasn't addicted to sex. When she went after a man, sex wasn't her main goal. It was flowers and gifts and long walks in the park holding hands. It was the fairy tale she wanted. The knight in shining armor. The feeling of being Cinderella at the ball. The lovely promise of happily-ever-after.

Life just didn't work that way, no matter what growing up in Valentine had promised. But how did she stop yearning for it? How did she put an end to her cravings when there was no support group for romanceaholics?

The answer came to her as clearly as if someone had spoken into her ear.

Start your own.

Chapter Eight

Early the next morning, Rachael was atop the Valentine billboard again, this time with turpentine and a scrub broom in her hands instead of a paintbrush. Cleaning up the sign wasn't as much fun as vandalizing it had been, but in a Zen-like way, it was almost as therapeutic.

As she mindlessly scoured the sign, her thoughts were on her new endeavor. The more she thought about Romanceaholics Anonymous, the more excited she got. This was her new mission in life. She'd seen the error of her ways and she was a convert. Now, to get other people on board.

She'd been working about an hour and she was already starting to sweat, even though it wasn't yet nine o'clock. The day promised to be another scorcher. Just when she was beginning to realize she should have brought water and sunscreen, Brody's Crown Vic motored by.

When he pulled to a stop on the shoulder of the road beneath the billboard, Rachael's heart started pounding erratically.

Looking resplendent in his uniform and sunglasses, he got out of the car.

Rachael set down the scrub broom and pushed back a strand of hair that had fallen from her ponytail and was trailing across her face. She glanced down at him.

Brody held a white paper sack in his hand. "Had breakfast yet?"

"Cereal bar this morning," she called back down. "But I've worked up an appetite."

He waggled the bag. "Come on down. You deserve a break."

He didn't have to ask twice. As fast as her legs could carry her, she was off the billboard and in the passenger seat of his car.

"Besides breakfast," he said, "I thought you might need a few other supplies." He handed her a second, bigger sack containing sunscreen, bottled water, a battery-powered fan, a straw hat, and a collapsible umbrella.

Something strange tugged inside her at his considerate gesture. "How did you know I needed all this?"

"I drove by earlier," he admitted. "I figured you'd forgotten how hot it can get in Valentine in late July."

He was right, she had forgotten.

"Egg McMuffin," he said, taking a breakfast sandwich wrapped in yellow paper from the other sack and passing it to her. "Hash browns and orange juice."

"Thanks so much." She hadn't known she was so ravenous until tempted with the aroma of food. She dug into the sandwich. They sat in the car, air conditioner running, eating in companionable silence.

They were halfway through breakfast when Brody's radio crackled.

"Sheriff?" came the young female voice over the bandwidth. "We've got trouble."

Brody stuck his Egg McMuffin back in the sack, dusted his hands on a napkin, and then reached for the radio. "What's up, Jamie?"

"You better get over to the courthouse. Mayor Wentworth is raisin' a ruckus."

Brody rolled his eyes and Rachael suppressed a giggle. "What's he got his shorts in a bunch over this time?"

"He's pitchin' such a bitch I'm not really sure, but he keeps saying something about parking meters."

"I'll check it out, Jamie. Thanks." Brody settled the radio back in place.

"I better get out"—Rachael reached for the door handle—"and let you do your job."

"Stay put," he said. "Finish your breakfast. This shouldn't take too long."

He put the patrol car in gear and headed over to the courthouse. They arrived to find Kelvin pacing the courthouse lawn, face florid, mopping his brow with a handkerchief, letting loose with a string of colorful curse words.

That's when Rachael saw the parking meters. She sucked in her breath as a mix of emotions surged through her. Shock, disbelief, and an odd, heady sense of glee.

She wasn't the only one in town disgruntled by Valentine's gaudy attachment to romantic symbolism. Someone else had taken a stand.

Because every last one of the sixteen heart-shaped parking meters in front of the courthouse had been neatly beheaded.

"CALM DOWN, KELVIN," Brody soothed.

"I will not calm down. Not only has this town been disrespected twice in one week, but you're consorting with the perpetrator." Kelvin glared at Rachael, who'd gotten out of the patrol car behind him. "She's the cause of it all. I want her arrested again."

Brody cast a glance at the parking meter heads that had been arranged in the middle of the courthouse lawn to form the letters "F.U." The poles stood impotently bare, no longer capable of extracting parking fees from courthouse patrons. The message was pretty succinct. Brody couldn't help wondering if Kelvin was the target of this latest vandalism and they were using Rachael's billboard scandal as a dodge. Or maybe it was just someone tired of paying to park.

"Rachael didn't cut the heads off the parking meters."

"How do you know?" Kelvin demanded.

"For one thing, I asked her and Rachael doesn't lie. For another thing, Rachael was in custody the night someone stole pipe cutters from Audie's Hardware."

"Yeah, but where was she last night?"

Brody looked at Rachael.

"I was at home with my mother," she said.

"There you go." Brody spread his palms.

"That doesn't mean she doesn't have an accomplice, and you're assuming someone used pipe cutters and that they were the same ones stolen from Audie's store. Hell, they could have used a Sawzall."

"Examined the tool marks." Brody waved at the markings on the posts. "It's a pipe cutter. Besides, a reciprocating saw would have made too much noise. Someone did this under cover of darkness and it took them most of the night."

"That's what I mean. It's someone with an anti-romance agenda like your girl there. It's a plot." Kelvin glowered.

"A plot?" Brody couldn't keep the amusement from his voice.

"And she's behind it." Kelvin jerked a thumb in Rachael's direction.

"So we're talking conspiracy theories here?" Brody pressed his lips together to keep from laughing. "Do you know how paranoid that sounds, Kelvin?"

"Someone's trying to sabotage my business deal. I have investors coming in tomorrow and someone is trying to make Valentine look bad."

Brody paused to consider what Kelvin was saying. The mayor was overly dramatic, it was true. But if Kelvin did have investors coming to town, there might be something to his paranoia. "What kind of investors?"

"I'm not prepared to discuss it with you."

"Then how am I supposed to explore your theory?"

"Just do your job and catch whoever did this."

"That's what I'm trying to do," Brody explained patiently.

Kelvin chuffed out his breath and ran a hand over the top of his bald pate. "How am I going to explain this to my investors? It's going to look bad."

"It doesn't have to."

Kelvin eyed him. "What do you mean?"

"You can say removing the parking meters was your idea. Wasn't it your daddy that got them installed in the first place? Free parking in front of the courthouse is a gesture of goodwill toward the town. It couldn't hurt you in the election."

Kelvin perked up. "That's not a bad idea, Carlton. Now get that woman back to the billboard so she can clean up her mess."

Brody snorted, knowing it was the best he could expect from the mayor. "So you don't want me to file a report. I mean, if you're having the parking meters removed, that's what you'd want appearing in the paper. Not that someone beheaded the parking meters in the middle of the night in the police blotter."

"Right, right."

Crisis averted.

Brody headed back to the car satisfied that he'd solved Kelvin's PR problem, but he couldn't help thinking this act of vandalism was just the start of something that could easily get out of hand.

And when he slid a glance over at Rachael, who was standing beside the patrol car looking so sweet and inno-cent, he couldn't help thinking that she was going to get caught in the cross fire.

"This is a call to order for the first ever meeting of Romanceaholics Anonymous. My name is Rachael Hen-derson, founder of the group, and I'm a romanceaholic."

The small group assembled in the meeting room of the Valentine Public Library consisted of her mother, Deana Carlton, Rex Brownleigh, Audie Gaston, and two old-maiden sisters, Enid and Astrid Pope, who were notorious for attending any and every social event in town. They all just blinked at her.

"You're supposed to say, 'Hello, Rachael,' " she schooled them from the podium. After spending two weeks boning up on twelve-step programs — in between serving some of her community service hours — she'd learned the basics. But tonight, their first time, they would be flying blind.

"Hello, Rachael," they greeted her in unison.

She beamed at them. "Very good."

They beamed back.

"Everything we say in here is confidential. It's like Vegas. What happens in Romanceaholics Anonymous stays in Romanceaholics Anonymous. Does everyone agree?"

Heads bobbed.

"The first step," she said, "is for us to admit we are powerless over romance and that our lives have become unmanageable because of our romantic ideations. I'll go first and tell you what led me to start this group."

Even though Rachael was fairly certain everyone in the room had already heard her story through the Valentine grapevine, she told it anyway. "After my ex-fiancé Trace Hoolihan appeared on *Entertainment Tonight*," she said, leaving out the part that minutes later she'd been on the verge of kissing Brody Carlton, "I realized I had a problem and I couldn't conquer my addiction alone. And being back in Valentine, with all its emphasis on romance, I realized other people might have the same problem. So who would like to go first? You don't have to share if you don't want to, but the sooner you admit you have a problem, the quicker you'll get on the road to clearheaded thinking."

Deana's hand shot up.

"Come on up, Deana," Rachael said and took a seat while Brody's sister claimed the podium.

"My name is Deana Carlton, and I'm a romanceaholic," she said.

"Hello, Deana," the group greeted her.

"As many of you may know, romantic notions about

happily ever after led me into an ill-fated marriage to a guy who turned out to be a con man. Because we had a daughter together, I stayed with him for seven years, pretending that everything was all right. My craving for the romantic gestures he dealt out when things were flush—lavish gifts, love notes pinned to my pillow, impromptu vacations—kept me hanging on. I never once questioned where he got the money for the extravagant gestures. I didn't want to know. Until government agents showed up on our doorstep to haul everything away."

Deana's voice cracked. She sniffled and a tear rolled down her cheek. Rachael hopped up to offer her a Kleenex. She was proud that she'd remembered to buy a brand-new box specifically for the meeting.

A murmur of sympathy ran through the collective.

"That's not even the worst of it," Deana said. "The bad part is that two days ago he called me and begged me to meet him in Costa Rica where he'd fled, but he said I'd have to leave Maisy behind." Deana cringed. "I'm ashamed to admit I actually bought the ticket. But then I heard about Rachael's meeting from the flyer she posted in the window at Higgy's and I knew I couldn't do this alone. I need help. To think I'd be willing to leave my child behind and go back to this guy because he made romantic promises I couldn't resist." She shuddered.

"Do you have the airplane ticket with you?" Rachael asked.

Deana nodded.

Rachael looked her in the eye. "I know this is hard for you, but I want you to tear that ticket up, right now."

Nervously, Deana licked her lips.

"You can do it," Rex Brownleigh called out.

Deana directed a shaky smile at the audience, reached in her purse, and took out the ticket. She tore it into little shreds.

"It's an e-ticket," Selina pointed out. "What's to keep her from going online and printing out another one?"

"The desire to get better," Rachael said. "Plus, Rex has his laptop with him. He can cancel Deana's ticket right now."

Rex opened his laptop.

"Do you want him to cancel the ticket, Deana?"

Deana, looking pale and shaky, nodded.

"Go sit beside Rex," Rachael instructed. "And give him the information so he can cancel the ticket for you."

Deana did as she was asked.

"What's to keep her from ordering another one when she gets home?" Enid Pope asked.

"We will."

"How's that?" asked her sister, Astrid. "Steal her computer? Lock her in leg irons?"

"We do it by offering her emotional support. Deana, whenever you feel tempted to fall back under the spell of your ex-husband, I want you to give any one of us a call. We'll talk you through it." She looked at Deana. "Okay?"

Deana nodded.

Rachael looked at her watch. "We've got time for one more declaration tonight. Anyone else want to admit that their life has become unmanageable because of romantic ideations?"

Rex raised his hand and Rachael waved him to the podium. He declared he was a romanceaholic and he was powerless to keep off Internet dating sites.

"I keep meeting women, falling in love with them,

pouring my heart and soul into the relationship, and they walk all over me," he said. "I've had my car stolen, my identity ripped off, and I contracted a nasty computer virus all because I can't say no to women." His deep voice boomed in the confines of the tiny room. "Growing up in Valentine a guy is taught to be chivalrous and help damsels in distress. It all sounds so romantic, but what happens is that when you're sweet to a woman, she thinks you're a wimp and walks all over you."

"That's not necessarily true," Rachael said. She loved it when men were sweet to her. Problem was, she fell for sweet talkers who never really meant their declarations of love. "I think this is the hardest thing about being a romanceaholic, knowing the difference between mere romance and true love. That's why we need each other. To help us sort it all out. Do we need a guest speaker on the topic?"

"Yes!" the group said in unison.

"Okay, then. For our next meeting I'll see if I can find a psychologist willing to tell us how to recognize if it's true love or if it's just romance."

Her mother raised her hand.

"Yes, Mom?"

"By saying true love, aren't you playing into the romantic myth that there is only one love out there for us?"

"You're right. Thanks for pointing that out. I need help just as much as everyone else. That's why I started the group. Okay, we won't use the terms 'true love,' 'soul mates,' or anything else that indicates fanciful, romantic thinking. Does anyone else have anything they'd like to contribute?"

No one else offered to speak.

"All right, then, the meeting is adjourned. Same time next week. Remember, if you have the urge to do or believe something romantic, give one of your fellow romanceaholics a call. I have handouts with the list of names and phone numbers. There's coffee and cookies on the table in the back if anyone would like to stay and chat."

As Rachael headed for the coffeepot, feeling as if the first meeting had gone quite well, Rex Brownleigh sauntered over.

"I gotta tell you, Rachael," he said, "I'm really impressed by your initiative. It took guts not only to graffiti the Valentine billboard but to start this group. You're being proactive, taking charge of your life."

"So are you, Rex." She smiled. "By coming here."

"I was wondering..." Rex paused, ducked his head, shuffled his feet.

Omigosh, she thought, *he's going to ask me out*. How was she going to handle it? She should have expected something like this to happen in a group of romanceaholics, but she wasn't prepared.

Gulping, she felt the smile leave her face. "Um...yes?"

He raised her head, met her gaze. "If you'd be interested in getting even with Trace Hoolihan."

That took her by surprise.

"He shouldn't get away with treating you so badly," Rex said.

Revenge, Rachael knew, was never an honorable motive, but it was a very human one. Temptation took hold of her. It wasn't the normal temptation of romance. It was a different kind of thrill. One she'd never experienced before.

Well, she rationalized, if revenge could release her attachment to Trace, ultimately wouldn't that be a good thing, even if her motives were less than pure? He certainly hadn't been thinking pure thoughts when he'd said those unkind things about her on national television.

Politely tell Rex no and walk away, said her principled side, but her all-too-human side won and instead she said, "What do you have in mind?"

Rex grinned. "YouTube."

"Pardon?"

"You know, the Web site on the Internet where people upload videos—"

"I know what YouTube is," she interrupted. "What I don't get is how that's going to help me get even with Trace."

"We show your side of the story."

Rachael shook her head. "I don't really see the point."

"Vindication."

She had to admit, she wanted it.

"And," he said, "it'd be a great forum for Romanceaholics Anonymous. The more people you reach with the message, the more people you help."

She wanted that even more. "What exactly do you have in mind?"

TWO WEEKS HAD passed since the parking meter incident and Amusement Corp's visit to Valentine to see the town and review Kelvin's proposal. Nervously, he waited for a call back. They'd promised to contact him by the end of the previous week. Now it was Wednesday and there was still no word. The time lapse made him realize exactly how much he wanted this deal to go through. Not just for himself, but for the good of his hometown.

"Any messages?" he asked Rex when he returned from lunch, noticing a blob of Higgy's chili pie on his tie.

"Amusement Corp didn't call," Rex said.

He was tired of playing cat and mouse. Tired of being in the "depend" role. He was going to take the bull by the horns. "Get Amusement Corp on the phone for me," he said and stepped over to grab a paper napkin off Rex's desk.

In the process, he dislodged a trifold brochure that fluttered to the floor. Kelvin bent to pick it up, barely glancing at it as he laid it back on Rex's desk. He was halfway to his office door before he did a double take, backpedaled, and snatched up the brochure.

Has Romance Made Your Life Unmanageable? Take Charge of Your Future Today. Join Romanceaholics Anonymous.

"What in the hell is this?" he asked Rex.

Hand poised over the telephone, Rex shrugged as if he had no idea what Kelvin was talking about, but he looked sheepish.

"Romanceaholics Anonymous." Kelvin flipped the brochure over. "They meet at the public library every Tuesday night. Who ever heard of Romanceaholics Anonymous?"

"It's a new twelve-step program."

"I get that," Kelvin snapped. "What I don't get is what this brochure is doing on your desk."

"Um." Rex shifted uncomfortably. "I went to the first meeting last night."

Kelvin narrowed his eyes. "Who's behind this?" His first thought was Giada Vito.

"Rachael Henderson."

"That meddlesome woman? What's her problem?"

"She thinks Valentine pushes an unrealistic view of romance," Rex said. "There's a lot of people in town who agree with her."

Kelvin snorted. "Are you really that clueless?"

"What do you mean?"

"Without that supposedly unrealistic view of romance, this town wouldn't even exist."

The phone picked that moment to ring.

They both jumped. Rex looked grateful as he reached for it. "Mayor's office, Rex Brownleigh speaking."

He pressed the hold button and shot Kelvin a look. "It's Amusement Corp."

Kelvin did a jig all the way into his office. He closed the door, counted to ten, and then picked up the extension. "Mayor Wentworth here."

"Mayor, Jackson Traynor, Amusement Corp."

"Jack. How are things?"

"Just fine. I want to apologize for not getting back to you sooner."

"I've been so busy I hadn't noticed," Kelvin lied smoothly. "I hope you're calling with good news for Valentine."

"Um, that's the reason for my delay."

Jackson Traynor's tone of voice had Kelvin's testicles drawing up tight.

"We ran your proposal past our research team and there were some concerns."

"What kind of concerns?" Kelvin had spent ten years preparing that proposal. It was spotless.

"Are you aware that Valentine's town charter prevents the construction of a project of this size without seventy-five percent approval from the taxpayers?"

"Is that what has you worried?" Relief pushed out his fear.

"Frankly, yes. We loved your proposal, but your remote location is a strike against you and we can't commit to this project until you have a bond election."

"I can guarantee the votes. My family brought tourism to this town. The constituents will do whatever I want."

"We did a straw poll while we were in town and you don't have as much of a lock on the town as you might think you do."

"Meaning?"

"Your approval rating is only forty percent. Apparently a lot of people in Valentine are thinking about voting for your opponent."

Giada Vito. Kelvin narrowed his eyes. "I'll get those votes. I'll get that bond election passed."

"I really hope that you do, Mayor, because we're gung ho on your project. But we're looking at another property site outside Tyler and we can't finance both. You have until November to pass this bond," Traynor said. "Otherwise you lose out."

Kelvin hung up the phone feeling at once elated and belligerent. Between them, Giada Vito and Rachael Henderson were trying to hijack his town and he'd be damned if he was going to let them get away with it.

RACHAEL GOT A copy of her wedding video from Tish, who'd taped the ceremony. In between dishing up meals at the senior citizen center as part of her community service, she spent her spare time at Rex's house creating her YouTube montage.

Making the video was a painful experience, but useful in helping her overcome any lingering attachment she had to Trace—and hopefully to romantic love. Every time she watched the moment where her supposedly idyllic life crumbled, her resolve to forsake romance strengthened.

Idealizing men and marriage was not the road to happiness.

There she was in her wedding dress walking down the aisle on her father's arm. A traditional church wedding with all the trimmings. She'd planned it since she was a child. Making scrapbooks of it and gathering items for her hope chest. Doves and candles. Orchids and white roses. A soprano soloist warbling "A Forever Kind of Love." Six bridesmaids. Her sister Hannah's adorable three-year-old daughter as flower girl. The works.

It was the most perfect of wedding ceremonies.

Until the critical moment when the pastor asked, "Does anyone have any objections to the union of this man to this woman?"

It must have been cosmic timing.

In the hushed momentary silence of the church came the distinctive ringing of a cell phone.

With a clutch in her throat, Rachael recalled the fateful moment. The irritation she'd felt over the sheer rudeness of the guest who hadn't thought to silence their cell phone before entering the chapel.

"Speak now," the pastor said on the video. "Or forever hold your peace."

Rachael remembered beaming up at Trace, wishing the minister would hurry up and get to the good part. The part where he pronounced them husband

and wife and they would walk hand in hand into their happily-ever-after.

But that moment never came.

"Here it comes," Rex said, timing the sequence of events for the video. "Wait for it, wait for it…three…two…one…"

"Since no one has any obj—"

"Stop the wedding," Trace Hoolihan's agent, Bob Boscoe, said, shooting to his feet.

Every single time Rachael saw it, a sick feeling rose inside her. Hand to her stomach, she took a deep breath and forced herself to watch, even though she desperately wanted to close her eyes. Aversion therapy.

The minister looked startled. Every gaze in the place turned to stare at Boscoe.

Except for Rachael's.

As if caught in a surreal dream, the on-camera Rachael just kept smiling—denying reality, determined that she was going to live the dream even if no one else was cooperating.

It was scary sad.

Rachael cringed and squirmed in Rex's rolling swivel chair, parked beside the bank of computers lining his living room wall. Rex was at the keyboard, making adjustments to the color, sounds, dimensions. Enhancing and enlarging. Splicing and merging. He clicked the mouse, zooming in on Boscoe's face.

"What is the nature of your objection?" asked the minister.

"Trace," Boscoe said, pushing aside the guests as he headed toward the altar waving his cell phone. "You've just had an offer from the Chicago Bears. They want you in as first-string wide receiver."

Rachael saw it happen all over again as, deep in her soul, she felt the moment she'd lost him. The pure joy on Trace's face as he let out a whoop, stepped away from Rachael and into Boscoe's embrace.

A heartbeat passed.

She relived the taste of bile spilling into her mouth. Experienced all over again the bone-crunching disbelief of shattered dreams. She smelled the cloying scent of too many flowers. Heard the shocked intake of the spectators' collective breaths.

"Trace?" Rachael's trembling on-camera voice whispered tentatively. Her eyes were wide, the smile on her face slipping. "What's going on?"

She was so pathetic.

Self-loathing took hold of her and she had to close her eyes and breathe deeply to fight off the nausea. She'd seen the video six times since the wedding and every single time it still clipped her hard.

"I'm going to Chicago," Trace crowed.

Not *we're* going to Chicago, but *I'm* going to Chicago.

"But what does this mean?" Her voice rose. On-screen she was blinking rapidly, swallowing repeatedly.

"I'm sorry, Rachael," Trace said, looking contrite. "But this is a once-in-a-lifetime chance to get back into the game. The wedding is off."

The church had erupted. People scrambled to their feet, surging the altar, most of them rushing to congratulate Trace.

And there she stood in the midst of it all, buffeted around like foam on the ocean. She saw Delaney step forward to wrap an arm around her shoulder. On-camera, her face went deathly white and she looked as if she was going to faint.

It wasn't the anger or disappointment or hurt that upset Rachael the most. Rather it was her wimpy reaction that made her want to reach out and slap her own silly face.

How could she have been so gullible, so naive, so trusting?

"Idiot," she muttered.

"Fool for love," Rex said.

"Just plain fool. I can't believe the way I twisted myself around for his affection."

Awkwardly, Rex patted her shoulder. "It's okay. This is therapeutic. You've got the proof of your mistake right in front of you and we can all learn something from it."

He was right.

"Hey," Rex said. "Look what I did since the last time you were here. This ought to make you feel better."

With a few finger strokes to the keyboard, Trace's head morphed into that of a jackass. He turned to the camera and brayed.

Rachael burst out laughing.

"Thatta girl." Rex chuckled along with her. "It gets better. Watch this."

He changed computer monitors and switched from her actual wedding video to the one he'd created for YouTube. The music began. It wasn't the music from her wedding, but rather "Love Stinks" by the J. Geils Band.

"Once upon a time," came Rex's deep-throated voice-over, "there was a beautiful young girl from Valentine, Texas, born on Valentine's Day, who'd been taught to believe truly, madly, deeply in the romantic myth of finding her Prince Charming and living happily ever after."

On-screen, Rachael appeared on her father's arm walking through the door of the chapel, looking radiant

in her wedding gown, beaming brightly, the beautiful floral bouquet clutched in her hand. The picture of dreams
come true.

"She thought she'd found the perfect man."

The shot cut to Trace standing at the altar looking
ultracool and impossibly gorgeous with his thick mane of
blond hair swept back off his forehead and his lantern jaw
thrust forward. The traditional black tuxedo fit him like a
fantasy, the pink rosebud boutonniere at his lapel a promise of everlasting love.

"Ha!" came Rex's voice-over.

"Love stinks!" shouted the J. Geils Band.

A camera shot showed the packed church. On the front
pew Rachael's mother sat beside her father, both looking
grim-faced, just moments before Rachael's entire world fell
in. She should have seen the signs that her parents' marriage was on rocky ground. Why hadn't she seen the signs?

"Rose-colored glasses hide a lot of flaws," Rex's voice-
over said.

The camera swung back to Rachael coming up the
aisle, her gaze fixed on Trace's face. A rose-colored lens
covered everything with a soft, dreamy filter. The shot
dissolved with clueless Rachael stepping up to the altar.

"And then she was betrayed by the thing she held most
dear," Rex's taped voice continued.

"Love stinks."

The sound of a beating heart galloping faster and faster
as she watched the painful scene again of Bob Boscoe
jumping up to announce the deal with the Chicago Bears.

Trace had known all along Boscoe was working on
the deal. He had to have known. She'd been his backup
plan if the Chicago Bears hadn't picked up his contract. It

was only then that it occurred to Rachael that Trace might have been marrying her for her daddy's money.

She didn't know why it hadn't occurred to her before. Maybe because money didn't matter much to her. She'd been born and raised with it and she supposed she took it for granted. What she valued was love and romance.

"Dodged a bullet," Rex said and turned down the volume on the video.

"Huh?" Rachael blinked.

"You've got that 'woe-is-me' look in your eyes," he said. "Just imagine if the Chicago Bears hadn't done you a huge favor and lured Trace away. How long would it have been before you realized what a huge mistake you'd made?"

"Twenty-seven years?" She posed the question thinking of her parents' marriage.

The J. Geils Band kept right on singing.

On-screen, Trace was breaking her heart all over again, and then literally turning into a jackass compliments of Rex's moviemaker program. He'd also spliced in a clip of Trace's *Entertainment Tonight* interview, proving most everything he'd told the reporter about Rachael was a bald-faced lie.

Then came the pitch for Romanceaholics Anonymous.

"Single, lonely, looking for love in all the wrong places?" Rex asked on the audio. "Has an addiction to romance caused your life to spiral out of control? Don't make the same mistakes Rachael did. Keep your heart safe. Stop spending your life on a roller coaster of expectation looking for Mr. or Ms. Right. Stay sane. Get help now. Join Romanceaholics Anonymous. For more information, call..." And then Rachael's cell phone number flashed across the screen.

Rex pushed back in his chair and slid her a look. "What do you think? You ready to upload it to YouTube?"

He was right. It was the perfect revenge.

"Upload it," she said.

"There's no going back."

"I know. That's the point. I need to seal the deal, because even after all he's put me through, if Trace were to call up, apologize, and beg me to take him back, I can't promise that I wouldn't."

"Stay strong," Rex said. He did his magic with the keyboard and the next thing Rachael knew, it was too late to turn back. There her video was on the YouTube queue. *Trace Hoolihan Ditches Bride at the Altar.*

"Wanna watch it again?"

"Sure."

Rex clicked the button straight from YouTube.

As the video clip played out, and Rachael realized that hundreds, possibly thousands of people would see this and know the truth, something strange happened to her. She didn't feel scared or nervous or as if she wanted to take it all back. Gone were any doubts or uncertainties she might have had about her inner motives.

She felt empowered. She felt as if she was finally taking charge of her life. She felt as if she owned the world.

Chapter Nine

July melted into the dog days of August. With the increased heat came an increase in crime. The fistfights at Leroy's grew more frequent. Brody's dinner was interrupted twice to mediate domestic disputes at the Love Line trailer court. And three times, Enid and Astrid Pope had called him over to their house the next block over because someone kept peeling the red glitter hearts off their white picket fence.

Brody had to consider whether it was the same culprit who'd vandalized the parking meters, but then he found Maisy playing with the glitter hearts in question and he made her take them back to the elderly ladies and apologize.

The rise in crime was a yearly pattern, but even so, the normally quiet town had seemed edgier and more restless since Rachael had come home to Valentine and started Romanceaholics Anonymous. From the patrons at Higgy's Diner to the customers at Audie's Hardware to the old men who played checkers in Bristo Park, the town was buzzing with both gossip and opinions.

Kelvin's "decision" to remove the parking meters around the courthouse went over big with his constituents, just as Brody had predicted. Brody had analyzed the tool markings and he'd been correct: A pipe cutter the same diameter as the one stolen from Audie's Hardware had been used to behead the meters, but he wasn't any closer to discovering who'd done the deed than he had been the day it happened. He was hoping the vandal was satisfied with beheading the parking meters and he or she was done with their crime spree.

Brody was sitting in his office ordering supplies when Jamie called to him from the dispatch desk.

"Sheriff, come here. You gotta see this."

He got up and sauntered into the next room to find Jamie's eyes glued to the computer screen, listening to the sound of the J. Geils Band singing "Love Stinks."

"What are you looking at?"

Jamie crooked a finger at him. "YouTube."

Curious, he moved behind the dispatcher to see what had so captivated her attention. What he saw simultaneously stirred his sympathy, amused him, and concerned him. There was Rachael getting dumped on her wedding day,

Damn it, Rachael, what are you thinking?

Here she was stirring up trouble again. While he couldn't blame her for wanting to get even with the jerk who'd dumped her at the altar, she didn't seem to realize the problems she was making for herself. *Put the woman in a cage with a sleeping lion and she'd poke it with a stick.*

"I love it," Jamie said. "Down with romance. I think I'm going to attend the next meeting of Romanceaholics Anonymous and show her my support."

Brody groaned. Things were getting way out of hand. He had to go talk to her, ask her to take the video off

YouTube before lookie-loos and reporters started showing up in Valentine.

He was halfway to the front door when the call came through.

"Sheriff's office," Jamie answered over the speaker phone. "How may I direct your call?"

"It's Selina Henderson. Tell Sheriff Carlton someone's vandalized my daughter's car right in our driveway."

Brody's eyes met Jamie's. "Tell her I'm on my way."

Five minutes later, he pulled onto Market Street and caught sight of Rachael's jaunty pink VW Bug, now savagely graffitied with militant slogans in angry black paint. VALENTINE — LOVE IT OR LEAVE IT. ROMANCE ISN'T THE PROBLEM, YOU ARE. But the one that chilled his blood was GET OUT OF TOWN, BITCH, OR SUFFER THE CONSEQUENCES.

Rachael stood there, arms wrapped around her chest, cradling herself. She looked so damned vulnerable. A feeling he'd never felt before and couldn't identify pressed down on him. A strange sensation tingled his upper lip and a sudden heaviness pulled at the back of his spine.

He got out of the car, his hand riding near the gun at his hip. He realized with a start he'd willingly shoot anyone who tried to hurt her.

She took one look at him and relief flooded her face. "Brody," she said simply, and the sound of his name on her tongue unraveled something inside him.

"Are you all right?" he asked, resisting the urge to reach out and touch her. He was here on official business. His inappropriate impulses had no place in this conversation.

"I'm fine," she whispered.

He fisted his hands to keep from touching her. God, how he wanted to touch her.

"Do you have any idea when this could have happened?" he asked.

She shook her head. "I came outside to get the newspaper and saw it. I suppose I should have expected something like this. A lot of people don't want to see Valentine change. The nail that sticks up is the one that gets hit."

Selina came over to wrap her arm around Rachael's shoulders. "It's okay, sweetheart. You have as many supporters as you do detractors. We're not going to let some small-minded individual terrorize us. Brody will find out who did this."

In order to hold his emotions in check, Brody kept his expression neutral and his mind on the job. He stepped closer to examine the VW Bug. He could have the paint analyzed to see if it matched the paint stolen from Audie's Hardware. But it would take time and funds to confirm what he suspected. That the person or persons who had stolen the paint and the pipe cutter had cut the heads off the parking meters and graffitied Rachael's car.

Except his theory didn't parse. The person who'd beheaded the parking meters appeared to be sending an anti-romance message. Whoever had graffitied Rachael's car seemed pro-romance.

Unless...

The intention wasn't to take a stand on either side of the issue, but rather to pit the townsfolk against one another.

But who? And why?

It was something to consider. He had more investigating to do. And that included interviewing Kelvin again.

Brody turned, not realizing Rachael had come to stand

directly behind him, and his arm collided with her shoulder. The protective instinct rushed over him again.

"Sorry," she mumbled and stepped back.

"Hold still."

"What for?"

"I said hold still," he said more gruffly than he intended. He was still upset over the crude messages on her car. "You've got black paint on your cheek."

She seemed so tiny next to his bulk and he could feel heat emanating off her compact body. She stood stock-still, staring at the buttons of his uniform as if she were afraid to meet his gaze. He reached over with a thumb and tried to smear the paint away but it wouldn't budge. Just as he suspected. Oil-based.

Then he had an arresting thought. Rachael had bought black oil-based paint to use on the billboard. How did he know she hadn't vandalized her own car to stir up sympathy?

He hated that his cop's mind even went there. Hated to think she would do such a thing and the minute the thought was in his head he knew it couldn't be true. She was trembling, for Pete's sake. She was truly scared.

"Are they…do you think they'll…" She swallowed. "Could this turn violent?"

"Don't worry," he promised, knowing he was starting down a slippery slope but sliding headfirst anyway. "I won't let anyone hurt you."

BY THE FOURTH meeting of Rachael's Romanceaholics Anonymous group, Selina was surprised to find attendance had quadrupled. And even more surprised to find many had driven in from neighboring counties. Word had gotten out.

The pleased expression on her daughter's face did Selina a world of good. She'd been down in the dumps ever since she'd wrecked the Caddy.

And she was tired of being idealistic. She needed an intervention herself.

Selina was here to support Rachael's cause, but deep inside she feared she would never stop loving Michael, no matter how hard she tried.

And he'd been making her life miserable by sending flowers and chocolates over every day, along with cute little cards declaring his abiding love for her. The delivery boy seemed to enjoy it when she thrust the roses and Godiva truffles at him and said, "Give them to your girlfriend."

Then she would methodically shred the cards, gritting her teeth against the tears. She stuck the pieces in an envelope and mailed them back to him.

He wrote her more love letters, begging her forgiveness.

She sent him the bill for the Caddy's repair.

He paid it.

She ran up his charge card, buying hip, stylish clothes for her slender new figure. She'd dropped twelve pounds since she'd left him. Misery had some small benefits.

Without a whimper, he'd paid that, too.

Who was she kidding? Selina wasn't just there for Rachael. She was here for moral support. She needed help to keep from forgiving Michael, packing her bags, and moving back home.

Because she missed him something terrible. Twenty-seven years she'd lain next to him, bore his children, cooked his meals, been his constant companion.

And all this time, he'd carried a torch for Vivian Cole.

Pain and resentment crowded out nostalgia and longing. She deserved better than finishing second place in her husband's heart. Knotting her hands into fists, Selina determinedly held on tightly to her resolve.

People kept piling into the room, looking for places to sit. Her face flushed with pride, Rachael had the librarian bring in more chairs. The sound of metal folding chairs being dragged across the linoleum floor mingled with the buzz of voices as they made room for the newcomers. The air smelled of books and strong coffee.

Audie Gaston winked at Selina. "You can scoot over next to me."

She knew Audie was halfway sweet on her. He gave her a ten percent discount at his hardware store. His wife had died years earlier and he'd grieved for a long time. He wasn't a particularly good-looking man, but neither was he ugly. He was tall, thin, balding, and wore owlish Harry Potter glasses. But he had a nice smile.

And a nice butt.

Selina smiled back and scooted her chair closer to him.

Take that, Michael.

Rachael was at the podium. She looked so brave, standing up there in her simple floral-print sleeveless cotton blouse, wheat-colored Capri slacks, and beaded summer sandals. Her daughter hadn't worn a hint of her signature pink since she'd come back home. Pink, she'd told Selina, was for romantic fools and little girls and she was no longer either one. While Selina was proud of her for facing her character flaw and putting a plan into action for overcoming it, she couldn't help feeling a little sad that she was giving up on romance entirely. Selina couldn't help wishing something would develop between her eldest daughter and Sheriff Brody. Hypocritical, maybe, but ultimately all she wanted was for Rachael to be happy.

Brody was the kind of man Rachael needed. Strong, capable, empathetic, but not a pushover. Unfortunately, he hadn't been back across the street since the day Rachael's car had been vandalized.

It was probably for the best, she told herself. Any romance Rachael entered into now was bound to flop. Her eldest daughter was on the rebound. She simply wasn't ready, and the last thing Selina wanted was to see her get hurt again.

The meeting continued as person after person got up and told stories of woe brought on by romance. They were heartbreaking. Then a third of the way through the meeting, the door opened, creaking loudly on its hinges. Everyone turned to stare.

Michael lumbered in.

Selina's heart did the crazy swoon it always did whenever she unexpectedly caught sight of him in a crowd. But then it slid uneasily into the pit of her stomach.

His hair was rumpled, his eyes bloodshot, his gait unsteady. He'd been drinking.

Selina was shocked. Michael rarely drank. A New Year's toast, an occasional beer with a business associate to be social, but that was it. In fact, she'd only seen him completely drunk once, on the night before their wedding. The night he'd been with Vivian.

From her place at the podium, Rachael stopped speaking. Every eye in the place swung toward the doorway. "Daddy?"

In that moment, she sounded ten years old and it broke Selina's heart. What in the hell was wrong with Michael?

"Hey, sweetheart," he slurred and wriggled his fingers at Rachael. "Looks like you've attracted a nice-sized crowd."

Rachael cringed as if she wanted to crawl underneath the podium and cower there until everyone went away. Selina's heart wrenched. Her daughter was trying so hard, not only to hold it together after everything that had happened, but to recover and ultimately thrive.

"What are you doing here?" Rachael asked her father.

"I'm here for the meeting." He swayed.

"Hey, Michael," someone in the audience called out. "AA is meeting across town at Riverside Baptist church."

The comment drew a nervous laugh from the crowd. Anyone in the room who was from Valentine knew what was going on with the Hendersons. It was a small town and along with Kelvin, the Hendersons were the biggest fish in it.

Selina wanted to grab Michael by the throat with both hands and throttle him. How dare he spoil what Rachael was trying to do here just to get even with her?

"If you're going to stay, Daddy, then please take a seat," Rachael said.

"Rightee-o," he said, sounding like some misplaced Brit. Selina used to think his little catchphrase was cute. Now it sounded utterly ridiculous. Michael nodded and swung his gaze around the room looking for an empty chair.

But there wasn't one.

His gaze lit on Selina sitting next to Audie.

"I'll have someone get you a chair," Rachael said.

"I've got it," Michael said, making his way toward Selina. "I'll just have a seat right here." He plopped down on the floor between her and Audie and drew his knees to his chest to keep his feet from colliding with the chain of a lady sitting in the row in front of them.

Rachael hesitated. Clearly, she didn't know what to do. Selina watched the emotions war on her daughter's face—uncertainty, embarrassment, nervousness, self-doubt, all mixed with a tinge of anger. The audience watched her with interest, trying to anticipate how she would handle this turn of events. It was a lot of pressure and Selina's urge to throttle her husband escalated. She could smell the beer on his breath and it was all she could do to keep from kicking him.

It was much easier feeling angry at him for hurting their daughter than for hurting her.

Selina studied the top of his head and for the first time noticed a spot that was starting to thin. *What happened to the guy I married? Where is the kind and considerate man who'd got down on one knee and excitedly proposed the minute I'd told him I was pregnant?*

Honestly, though, wasn't that when all the trouble had started? The doubts and fears she'd had thinking he was marrying her simply because of the baby? Why else would a handsome, wealthy man like him marry the daughter of simple restaurant owners?

Rachael was talking again, inviting people to come up to the podium and share their stories of romance gone wrong.

Selina dipped her head and leaned over to whisper, "You shouldn't have come here."

Michael swung his gaze up to meet hers. He was clothed

in white dress slacks and an oversized Hawaiian shirt, looking like the privileged son he was on vacation in the tropics. But his gaze was sharp in spite of the alcohol.

"Maybe if you'd answered my phone calls I wouldn't have had to resort to this."

"You could have come by the house," she said as sternly as she could at whisper pitch.

"I tried. You didn't answer the door."

"That's because I didn't want to see you. I still don't want to see you." Selina glared.

Who was this man? After twenty-seven years he remained a mystery to her. Shouldn't she know him inside and out by now? But she did not. Maybe that was the problem. On the surface, Michael was an affable, charming guy. But underneath it all ran a current of something deeper, darker. There was a part of him that he'd never revealed to her and his secrecy hurt as much as his betrayal with Vivian.

Blinking back the tears she was terrified were going to fall and give her away, Selina bit down hard on her bottom lip.

"I'd like to speak," Michael said and got to his feet.

Every eye in the place was back on him again.

"Sit down," Selina hissed.

"Since this is your first meeting, maybe you'd prefer to just listen tonight, Daddy," Rachael offered, a hint of panic in her voice.

"Nope. I wanna talk."

Rachael's gaze met Selina's. She looked as desperate as Selina felt. Michael started toward the podium. How tempting to stick out her foot and trip him.

"Let him go," Audie whispered to her. "Let him make a fool of himself."

And of me.

Miraculously, Michael reached the podium without stumbling. Rachael stepped aside with another *Help me!* glance at Selina. But her soon-to-be ex-husband already had the microphone in his hand.

"My name is Michael Henderson," he said, "and I'm a romanceaholic."

"Hello, Michael," chimed the crowd.

"Just look at what romance has reduced me to," he said. "A public drunk."

A ripple of sympathy went through the crowd as they made noises of condolence.

Irritation grated Selina. They were feeling sorry for him? He was the jerk who had broken her heart. He was the one who'd made a mockery of their marriage, not her. Why were they on his side?

"Most of you here know me. Nearly all of my entire adult life I've been a faithful husband—"

"Ha!" Selina interjected.

"To one woman," he continued as if she hadn't said a word. "I could have cheated. Right, Evangeline?" He winked at the flirty, curvaceous Rite Aid clerk sitting in the front row who blushed a blistering shade of crimson. "But I did not."

Michael looked out at the audience, but his eyes were focused on Selina and she knew he was speaking only to her. "What can I say? I'm a romantic guy. I showered my wife with gifts and trips. I put in a pool so she wouldn't swelter away in the Valentine summers. For her forty-second birthday I sent her to Tuscany so she could take gourmet cooking lessons from a famed Italian chef—and by the way, how do I know she didn't have an affair while she was there?"

The crowd was watching the action as if it were a prime-time soap opera, raptly shifting their gazes from Selina to Michael and back again.

Selina couldn't take anymore. She shot to her feet. "That was uncalled for. Francesco was nothing more than my teacher."

"Ah," Michael said, green eyes that same color as Rachael's snapping in anger. "But what exactly was he teaching you?"

The sound of the door opening and then quietly closing ratcheted the emotional tension in the room. Selina, along with everyone else, looked to see who'd come inside.

It was Brody Carlton. In uniform.

He surveyed the crowd, taking it all in, and seemed to size up the situation almost instantly. He doffed his Stetson and moved to stand with his back against the wall.

"How do I know what Selina was doing at the country club when she was supposed to be taking tennis lessons from Gunther?" Michael continued. "I never accused her of an affair. I never entertained the idea. I trusted her. I loved her that much. But you can sure as hell believe I'm entertaining the idea now."

Selina's heart pounded and her ears rang and her breath left her body in one whoosh of pent-up air. She jumped to her feet, chest heaving. "Not once in twenty-seven years did I even glance at another man because I was so stupidly in love with you, but I'm beginning to think I should have had flings all over town. No one would blame me. You're always waving money in my face, bragging about how well you provided for me, expecting a pat on the back. Give him a hand, folks." Selina clapped. "Third-generation oil money who never had to work a day in his privileged life buys his poor little Mexican wife expensive baubles and expects to be lauded for lifting her out of poverty."

"So that's what this is all about," Michael said. "You're the one who feels inferior about your heritage, not me. I didn't marry you for your tamale-making abilities."

"Then why the hell did you marry me, when you were still in love with your high school sweetheart?"

"You're forcing me to say it?"

Selina sank her hands onto her hips, thrust out her jaw. "Go on, I dare you."

"You want me to say? I'll say it."

She'd never seen him looking so angry, but she was determined not to flinch. She grit her teeth, knotted her fists.

"I married you because you were knocked up."

A collective gasp went up from the crowd at Michael's confession and then everyone fell completely silent, waiting to see what would happen next.

Selina felt as if she'd been kicked in the gut. This was it. He'd finally admitted it. Finally voiced her greatest fear. In a weird way, she felt strangely exhilarated. Finally, they were communicating.

She heard Rachael make a soft noise of distress, and from the corner of her eye she saw Brody step forward. "Mr. Henderson," he said firmly, his hand hovering above the gun holstered at his hip, looking like Wyatt Earp swooping in to save the day. "Your Porsche is hanging out in the middle of the road and blocking traffic. It needs to be moved."

Michael's jaw set in the resolute line Selina knew too well. He realized Brody was taller, bigger, and had the weight of the badge behind him, but he was Valentine's favored son. He was accustomed to getting his way, even with law enforcement officers.

Brody took his handcuffs from his pocket and started for the podium, looking equally resolute.

"That's enough!" Rachael exploded. "I've had enough of this from all of you."

Everyone's attention volleyed to Rachael.

Selina had never heard her sweet-natured, accommodating daughter sound so authoritative. It both shocked and pleased her.

"Brody," she said to the sheriff, "back off. Someone will move my father's car in just a minute. Dad, have a seat on the stage." She pointed to the chair she'd just vacated. "Mom, come up here."

To Selina's surprise they all obeyed her. Brody stepped out of the aisle. Michael sank down in the chair and Selina went to the front of the room.

Once she and Michael were on the stage together, Rachael paced in front of them, hands clasped behind her back, a frown of supreme disappointment on her face. She looked like a harried mom with two squabbling toddlers and she wasn't quite sure how to discipline them. Selina squirmed.

"For twenty-seven years," she said at last, "you two have allowed a pie-in-the-sky fantasy of what you think marriage is supposed to be rule your lives."

"Your mother certainly has," Michael said at the same moment Selina said, "Your father is the unrealistic one."

"Excuse me, but I'm talking here."

They shut up.

"Do you two want to stop romanticizing marriage and

love?" she asked, looking so serious it was all Selina could do not to laugh. As if Rachael had any clue what marriage was really like.

"I don't romanticize—"

Rachael cut her off with a raised palm and a shushing noise. "You do. Most of the citizens of Valentine do. People," she said, shifting her gaze to the audience, "we've bought into the hype we've been promoting to lure tourists to our town. Marriage is not a piece of cake. It does not solve all our problems. If it did, would my parents be up here acting like spoiled brats?"

Spoiled brats?

Selina had gone to work in her family's Mexican food restaurant when she was nine years old. The middle child of seven, she'd grown up never having owned a new pair of shoes. Until she'd met Michael her life had been about hard work and sacrifice. No one had ever accused her of being a spoiled brat.

Michael, on the other hand, was the epitome of a spoiled brat. The only child of the town's second-most-prominent family, he'd had every possible advantage. Tennis lessons, swim coaches, golf clubs. He'd been the high school quarterback, the prom king, the class president. His first car had been a Mustang Cobra. He'd even gotten into Harvard, although he hadn't gone. All because she'd gotten pregnant.

His family had never let her hear the end of it.

"It's time to stop acting like spoiled brats and figure out what you really want for the rest of your lives. It's time to split the sheets, go your own way, and once and for all stop pretending you're Cinderella and Prince Charming."

Rachael's words carved an empty hole inside Selina.

It was true. For twenty-seven years she'd pretended she was living a fairy tale but deep inside, she'd secretly been waiting for the castle walls to come crashing down.

The fairy tale was over.

The realization made her want to cry. She didn't want to let it go.

"It's tough, I know," Rachael said, her voice heavy with sympathy. "For all of you. But it's time to stop the hurt. It is possible to have a normal, healthy, loving relationship without all the game playing and the drama and the fantasy."

"Yeah," someone called out, "but where's the fun in that?"

"The fun," she said, glowering at the group, "is freeing yourself from a toxic pleasure-pain cycle. Peace is what you're really looking for. You're using excitement to fill the void. Real love isn't loud or flashy or grand or hurtful. It's calm and quiet and tender and honest. Until you can be honest with yourselves, you'll never find the happiness that keeps eluding you."

Selina blinked, amazed by her daughter's strength, courage, and perceptiveness. Rachael was going to be okay. She wasn't going to end up like her mother and her father — married twenty-seven years without ever really knowing each other.

"Dad," Rachael said. "Go home. Leave Mom alone. She's done with the marriage."

Michael blinked as if he'd been poleaxed.

"And Mom, let go of your anger. There's no point in staying mad at him. You can't move on as long as you keep holding on to your anger."

Selina's heart sank and she recognized something

important. She'd kept fanning the flame of her anger, because she knew if she let it go out, the last shred of her love for Michael would go with it.

BRODY WAITED FOR Rachael as the romanceaholics filed out of the library. The flinty gleam in her green eyes was at odds with the soft roundness of her rosy cheeks. She looked like a kitten that had just unleashed her tiny but exceedingly sharp claws.

Brody suppressed a grin. Normally, he wasn't attracted to cute, cuddly women but from the first moment he'd spied her dangling from the Valentine lips, nothing about his feelings for her had been normal.

Or for that matter even rational.

His gaze drifted over the lush curves of her breasts sexily sheathed in a blue floral blouse. What was it about her that had so captivated him? How did she manage to wield such power with those startling green eyes?

No matter how much he tried to deny the attraction, every evening when he came home from work, he found himself gazing out the living room window hoping for a glimpse of her sitting out on the porch swing in the gathering dusk. Or watering Mrs. Potter's flower garden.

"Great meeting," Brody said when the last person had left the room.

Rachael cut him a razor-sharp glance. "I could do without the sarcasm, Carlton."

"I'm not being sarcastic," he said. "You did a great job."

She slumped down into a chair. That's when he realized her legs were trembling. "It was a nightmare."

"You didn't pull any punches. You told your parents exactly what they needed to hear."

"I wasn't thinking of them," she confessed. "I was hurt and mad and lashing out."

"It didn't come across that way at all."

"Really?"

"You sounded calm and sensible and full of wisdom far beyond your years."

"*Real*-ly?" Rachael asked, putting extra emphasis on the first syllable.

"Really."

"I was just fed up." She glowered and crossed her arms over her chest, ruining his view of her terrific cleavage.

"Remind me never to make you mad," Brody said, resisting the urge to lean over and kiss her frown away. "I loved the way you busted the whole Cinderella, Prince Charming thing."

"You don't think I'm turning into one of those bitter, men-hating women, do you?" she asked pensively. "I want to give up my romantic notions, but I don't want to give up on the opposite sex."

"Neither do I," he murmured, his gaze glued to the flutter of pulse at the blue vein in the hollow of her throat.

"You think I was out of line, don't you? Butting into my parents' marriage and offering them advice like I knew what I was talking about," she said.

"You're projecting your self-doubts onto me," he said, fascinated by her neck. God, she was gorgeous.

And passionate.

"Be honest. You think I'm an emotional mess."

"I never said that."

He didn't really think she was an emotional mess. A

little overly focused on her emotions, but that was part of her charm and he was jealous of her ability to express her feelings. Brody had spent so many years holding himself in check he hadn't even been able to work up a good head of steam over Belinda. He'd just let her go. No fear of fairy tales in that relationship.

Or of real love, either.

"I know I'm an emotional mess, that's why I'm here. Doing this." She swept her hand at the empty room.

"You're not a mess," he said, wishing he'd led with that. Compelled by a force he couldn't explain, Brody stepped closer. "You're hurting and looking for a way to salve the pain. There's nothing wrong with that. You're human."

"It was crazy," she said. "The way I grew up."

"Uh-huh." He made sympathy noises, but his nose was filled with the smell of her watermelon-scented shampoo.

"It was like living in a fantasy land."

"That's a bad thing?"

"Yes," she said adamantly. "It doesn't prepare you for the real world. There's nothing quite as shocking as when happily-ever-after goes kaput."

"You're confusing shattered illusions with real tragedy," he said, hating that she'd made him think of Iraq. He'd been enjoying the fantasies dancing around in his head, fantasies of Rachael naked in his bed. Now he was thinking of war.

"Why do people do it?" she asked. "Why do they get married? Why do they make promises they have no intention of keeping?"

He thought of his own marriage and winced inwardly. He'd made a mistake with Belinda and he was leery of making another one. "Most people don't intend to break their promise when they get married. Most people don't count on divorce."

"You're talking about your own marriage."

"I guess."

"So what went wrong?"

"My wife said I wasn't romantic enough. Plus there was the whole cheating on me thing."

"There you go," Rachael said.

"There I go where?" He didn't know if it was her screwy logic confusing him or the sight of her sweet peach-colored lips. Peach lips, watermelon-scented hair, grape green eyes. The woman was a virtual fruit salad and suddenly he wanted a taste of her.

"Romance, messing up a perfectly good relationship."

"It wasn't a perfectly good relationship," he said.

"No?"

"No."

"Then why'd you marry her?"

Brody shifted. He didn't like talking about his biggest failure. "She thought she was pregnant."

"You slept with her, even though you didn't love her?"

"Yeah," he admitted. "Not particularly admirable, but there you go."

"So you know how to separate sex from love."

He shrugged. "Biology is biology. Love is..."

"What?"

He swallowed, feeling the heat of her inquisitive gaze on his face. "I don't know what love is."

She tilted her head. Her gaze warmed his face. "How do you do it?"

"Do what?"

"That separating sex from love thingy." She wriggled

two fingers. "I can't do it. I fall in love with every guy I sleep with."

The thought of Rachael sleeping with other guys poked a fist through his gut. "It's because you romanticize them."

"Exactly."

"Maybe next time instead of focusing on their good qualities you should focus on their flaws."

"There's not going to be a next time," she said, a staunch expression on her face.

"You're going to stay celibate for the rest of your life? You're only what? Twenty-five?"

"I'm twenty-six." Rachael nibbled her bottom lip and looked hesitant. "Okay, clearly I haven't thought this thing through."

"You're the founder of Romanceaholics Anonymous. Maybe it's something you should think through." Although, he quite liked the idea that if she wasn't going to be sleeping with him, at least she wouldn't be sleeping with anyone else.

What is wrong with you, Carlton? The woman is in emotional upheaval. A smart man would stay as far away from her as possible.

Sound advice, but somehow, he couldn't seem to take it.

"What I need," Rachael mused, "is hot sex with no strings attached."

Sex.

The word was a lightning rod, attracting sparks, zapping their gazes together.

"I need," she said, the gloss of her lips glistening in the glow from the overhead lamp, "mind-blowing sex."

Me, too.

She was calling to him with her eyes and with her

mouth, but her body stayed rooted to the spot, and she had her arms folded tightly underneath her chest. She wanted him in theory, but in reality she still clung to her dreams of happily-ever-after. Tigers couldn't change their stripes. And no matter how much she might fight it, Rachael was a dyed-in-the-wool romantic.

Her lips parted, inviting him to kiss her. But she tightened her arms, hugging herself.

He leaned closer.

Her eyes widened.

He gave her his most formidable law enforcement stare, just to see how easily he could scare her off.

Rachael did not drop her gaze. She tilted her chin upward, hardening it stubbornly.

Surprising him.

Brody had expected her to turn and run for the door. He took a step forward, closing the short gap between them. Desire pulsed in his loins. He couldn't be around her and not want her. But even stronger than the desire was the need to hold her, comfort her, protect her.

She didn't move. Didn't flinch.

Not even when he raised his hand and reached out to trace her jaw with his thumb. The smell of books hung in the air, along with her fruit salad fragrance and the aroma of something more—something darker, muskier. It was the intense scent of sexual yearning.

He felt the tremor run through her body, but she held her ground. A corresponding shiver ran through him, down his spine, lodged in his groin.

What in the hell are you doing?

Why was he encroaching on her space? Was he trying to make her run or...*or what?* Take a stand?

The intelligent spark in her fascinating green eyes told him she just might be onto him.

He cupped her chin with his palm, tilted her face up even higher. Held her gaze with the power of superglue. He rested his other hand on her waist. Her flesh felt so soft underneath the thin material of her blouse.

She sucked in air at his touch, but she did not back up or look away. She just kept staring up at him, waiting.

The tension built.

Brody grew harder. There was no hiding his desire now. He flicked his gaze down the length of her throat, to her bodice. Her arms were still folded underneath her breasts, accentuating her cleavage. Her nipples were knotted so taut they pointed through the fabric of her bra.

"Rachael," he murmured and looked back at her face.

Her eyelashes fluttered. Her teeth parted. She wanted this kiss as much as he did.

He was barely breathing.

She swayed closer. "Brody."

His gaze fixed on her lush little mouth and he wondered what she was going to taste like. The fruit salad? Or the lust? Or a heady, wild combination of both?

Sweat pooled along his collarbone and his groin weighed thick and heavy.

Rachael pressed the tip of her tongue to her upper lip and Brody just about came undone.

The verdant spring in her eyes darkened to deep summer moss. He pushed his palm up the length of her jaw, splaying his fingers until they caught in the tangle of curls at the nape of her neck.

He dipped his head.

She made a hungry noise of approval.

His lips closed softly over hers.

She tasted a hundred times more delicious than he'd imagined. He savored the full flush of fruit salad—raspberries and melon and pineapple and peaches—mingled with the earthiness of longing need. And underneath all those layers of flavors, he tasted a heady dose of bravery and a yearning for experimentation.

A primitive, wholly masculine urge overtook him. He wanted to take her right there on the small stage in the back room of the Valentine Public Library among the smell of binding glue and inked pages and knowledge.

Carnal knowledge.

He wanted to undress her with leisurely fingers, and press burning kisses along the smooth creamy curve of her throat, to partake of her body and give her as much pleasure as he intended on taking.

Rachael molded her body to him. Lifting her arms up, wrapping them around his shoulders, pulling him closer. He cradled the back of her head in his palm and made a low, feral noise of need.

Brody deepened the kiss, slipping his tongue between her parted lips. He'd been aching to do this for weeks.

Chapter Ten

Rachael gasped with pleasure, the strength of her need taking her by surprise.

She drank from Brody's lips, not caring that they were in a back room of the public library and anyone could walk in on them at any minute. She was as moist for him as a woman could get and growing damper by the minute. Her pulse rate spiked like a motorcycle kick-starting on high throttle and it sent a rush of hot, restless blood spilling into her heated pelvis.

Any doubts she might have had about what they were doing vanished in the hazy magic of his mouth. She forgot that she'd sworn off romance. Forgot that Brody was the very first man to ever break her schoolgirl heart. Forgot everything except the exquisite feel of his tongue against hers.

Rachael was devoured by a need so essential it surpassed everything else. She felt it to her very core, this crippling want. She'd never experienced any kiss quite like this and she'd experienced a lot of kisses.

Uh-oh, watch out, romantic fantasy alert, whispered the voice at the back of her mind, but his kiss drowned out the sound.

He made her feel so womanly, so desired.

Don't they all?

Actually, no, they did not. She'd just thought they did. This thing. This was different.

Yeah, right. Have many times have you told yourself that?

A dozen? More?

"Rachael," he murmured into her mouth. "You taste so damned good."

Could he be feeling it, too? she wondered hopefully.

Stop it, stop it, you're falling for a fantasy. Haven't you learned one damned thing?

Maybe, she told herself, maybe this could be just sex.

It was a lovely thought, but she had no idea how to create those boundaries. How to separate and compartmentalize love and sex. If she did, she wouldn't be here.

Could she learn? Could Brody be her teacher?

She'd been so gullible for so long, she wasn't sure she had the strength to overcome it. Especially with the man she'd had her first crush on. Her heart was so ready to get involved. She was a powder keg and he was a lit match. It was a stupid, stupid notion.

But here she was, seriously entertaining it.

Because who could resist lips like these? Her body burned wherever his mouth touched—her cheek, her chin, her forehead, her eyelids.

Unable to resist him, she just shut down her mind and let herself feel.

Blindly, without purposeful thought, Rachael lightly ran her tongue along the pounding pulse at the juncture of his throat and collarbone. He tasted salty. His rugged skin tightened beneath her mouth and a masculine groan escaped his lips.

Her mouth crept from his neck to his chest, her fingers

working the buttons of his uniform, escalating the intimacy between them and sending her libido reeling into the stratosphere.

The air smelled of charged electrical ions rampant with sexual need.

She was acutely aware of something important shifting between them. But she didn't know if the shift was a good thing or a bad thing. The question was, did she really want to find out?

He stared deeply into her eyes, with something akin to desperation on his face. Brody took her by the shoulders, pulled her back. "Don't," he said, closing his hand around the fingers working at his buttons. "Not here, not now, not like this."

"Why not?"

"You deserve so much more. You deserve the true love you've spent your life looking for." He looked her in the eyes, desperation etched on his face.

She felt it all at once.

Passion was like a tornado destroying everything in its path. Yearning hormones. Whirling desire. Neediness and loneliness. Appetites and melancholia and hope. Always, ridiculous hope. The emotions collapsed in on her, heavy and warm and overwhelming.

Here we go again.

His gaze was a maelstrom. An obliterating cyclone.

They both stood motionless, his shirt half-undone, her lips puffy from his kiss, hair tousled, heart thumping.

He traced a finger over her cheek, his eyes lasering into hers.

Rachael's body stiffened. Wanting him, but terrified of where it would lead.

Heartbreak.

Brody dropped his hand, took two steps away from her.

Don't go, her treacherous heart whimpered.

Obliged by the same force that had caused her to make one romantic mistake after another, Rachael went after him.

"Your shirt," she said by way of an excuse, and reached up with shaky fingers to twist closed the buttons that she'd undone.

He stood stony as a statue, unmoving, unblinking.

What did she want from him? Rachael swallowed, moistened her lips.

Please?

His eyes darkened, lips tightened. He was fighting his impulses. It was like watching an epic battle unfold. She could see the interplay between common sense and temptation in the way his expression changed. Full of desire one minute, closed off the next. Behind it all she spied something startling.

He was afraid of the way she made him feel.

Her blood surged, thick as the mounting tension stretching from him to her and back again.

The second kiss was wilder than she had ever dreamed it would be, hot and hard, a restless driving force to taste and smell and feel. To consume. An opportunity to conquer, to plunder, to possess. The demanding flick of his tongue against hers brought a famished response so intense, she felt weak, as if all her energy had been drained.

Brody groaned and locked his fingers in her hair. Kissed her harder, deeper, and wilder still.

The taste of him!

He tasted like power and peppermint and Valentine's Day all rolled into one. Fanciful, romantic, idiotic.

But she could not stop. She inhaled him.

While the world shrank down into the minute width of mouths, she opened herself up to possibilities as yet undreamed. She was completely disarmed. With any other man the quick intimacy and astonishing sensuality would have appalled her, but with Brody everything was different.

Was it a difference she could trust? Or was it all an illusion of her own making?

Her lips shuddered against his mouth and her body molded to his. In Brody's arms, she felt cherished.

The sensation scared her.

She could not let this happen. Not again. She could have sex with him, but not until she learned how to stop spinning these silly romantic fantasies.

But she wanted so badly to believe in the dream.

Rachael vacillated, ensnared between who she was and who she really wanted to be. She did not appreciate this emotional tug-of-war. For years, she'd been living in a daydream, buying into a fairy tale that did not exist, pretending that someday some man would sweep her off her feet and make her life perfect.

That was never going to happen. She'd learned that only she was in charge of her life. Only she could change the future. Only she could alter her world.

"I'm sorry. This was wrong. I shouldn't have done that." She splayed a hand against his chest and pushed him away.

"Me, either," he said. "This was a bad idea."

"Awful."

"Terrible."

"Illogical."

"Irrational."

"Insane."

They stared at each other, both breathing hard.

One minute she was staring deep into his whirlpool brown eyes and the next second she was pressed against his chest again. His mouth closed in for a third kiss.

Third time charmed.

His tongue delivered thrills so hot Rachael feared she'd burst into flames. He sucked the oxygen right out of her lungs. Her head spun, the back of her knees wavered. If she died now, she'd have nothing to complain about.

Then he just let her go and stepped back.

Rachael stumbled against the podium.

"Good night, Rachael," he murmured and walked out the door.

What was going on here? Was he taking himself out of the running for her heart because he was a nice guy?

KELVIN STOOD IN his underwear eating cold fried chicken over the sink. He'd just gotten back from his Elks Lodge meeting and he couldn't stop thinking about what he'd seen when he'd driven past the library.

Vehicles.

Lots of vehicles. So many cars and pickup trucks and SUVs that they couldn't all fit in the parking lot. They were parked in the vacant lot next door and overfilled even that. They were parked along both sides of the street. Michael Henderson's Porsche had been blocking the driveway, his fender sticking out into the road. And Brody Carlton's Crown Vic had squatted up on the curb.

Among the conglomeration of vehicles, Kelvin had spotted Rex's red Ford quarter-ton. What was up? If there had been a place to park, Kelvin would have gone in to see for himself.

He'd had dinner at the Elks Lodge, but curiosity dug into his belly like hunger pains and leftover Colonel Sanders made for a nice snack. But after he finished the chicken, he was still famished for information.

Kelvin tossed the thigh bone to Marianne, wiped the grease from his fingers on a paper towel, and picked the cordless phone from its base on the counter beside the microwave. Plopping down at the kitchen table, he propped his feet on the seat of the chair opposite him and punched in Rex's number.

"Brownleigh," he barked when Rex answered. "What the hell's going on at the library?"

"Um...I don't know what you mean," Rex hedged.

"Don't give me that crap. I saw your pickup in the parking lot."

Rex cleared his throat. "It was a Romanceaholics Anonymous meeting."

Kelvin was floored. How had the Henderson girl attracted a crowd that size? "That many people?"

"Standing room only. Over half the attendees came from another county."

"No shit?"

"None, sir."

"But how did people find out about it?"

"Viral video."

"Viral video?" Kelvin repeated and pressed a palm to the back of his neck. "What's that?"

"Rachael put a clip of her wedding video on the Web.

Within two days it was the twentieth-most-downloaded video clip on YouTube."

"YouTube?"

"Dude, seriously, you gotta get on your computer more."

"I'm going to right now and you're going to talk me through this thing." Kelvin got up and headed for his study. Marianne plodded behind him.

"I'm in the middle of an IM session with a girl."

"I don't know what that is," Kelvin said, turning on his computer. "If you're trying to stop being romantic, should you be doing anything with a girl?"

"No." Rex sounded sheepish.

"Then consider yourself saved. Hang up with her or do whatever you have to do to get out of an IM session and talk me through this. I'm getting on AOL right now." He thought about bitching the boy out for being a traitor to his town and everything Valentine stood for by attending Rachael Henderson's anti-romance twelve-step program, but for now, it suited his purpose to have Rex fixed on Kelvin's needs.

Under Rex's tutelage, he went to YouTube, found Rachael's video, and watched it. The second it ended his stomach soured and his mouth went dry. "How many people do you think have seen this?"

"Oh, hundreds of thousands all over the world."

"What!" Kelvin jumped up from his chair and almost dropped the phone. "That many people know about her and this romanceaholics mess?"

"She's been bombarded with phone calls and e-mails. It's amazing how many people out there are victims of romance."

"Victims...victims..." Kelvin sputtered. "I'm the victim here. Valentine is the victim. The Henderson girl is going to quash the Amusement Corp deal and Tyler is going to end up with my theme park. I have to shut her down."

"What do you mean?" Rex asked.

"Never mind," Kelvin said and hung up.

He tossed the cordless phone on the leather couch and paced the study. The pictures of his ancestors looked down on him. The replica of Valentine Land mocked him.

You just thought you had the town in a lock.

Rachael Henderson was on a campaign to stomp out romance. He had to find a way to stop her before she ruined everything.

BY THE TIME she'd come home from the Romanceaholics meeting, her mother was already in bed.

Rachael had decided to take a calming hot bath but it wasn't working. She sat slumped in Mrs. Potter's claw-footed bathtub with pineapple-and-coconut-scented bath bead bubbles foaming up to her chin. Her stomach was in turmoil, still trying to digest what had happened at the library tonight.

Brody Carlton had kissed her.

Closing her eyes, Rachael leaned her head against the inflatable bath pillow and pulled in a slow, deep breath, trying to calm her racing mind.

She turned on the faucet with her foot, displacing the cooling waters with a fresh blast of hot liquid. She caught sight of her reflection in the shiny chrome fixtures. Her hair was disheveled, her mouth swollen from Brody's kisses, her eyes murky with concern.

Who was she?

Rachael no longer recognized herself.

Who was she becoming?

On the outside, Rachael was putting on a good front, acting as if she'd conquered her belief in happily-ever-after, but inside, she was still a mess. Distorted by her long-held values and beliefs that resisted change, distorted by the filters life in Valentine had placed on her sense of identity.

What was she if she wasn't part of a couple?

Where did she fit?

Who was she deep down inside?

Unable to answer these disturbing questions, Rachael blocked them out and submersed her head under water, trying to drown out the annoying voice in the back of her brain.

She held her breath as long as she could, listening to the sound of her own blood pounding against her eardrums, beating out a tune of deafening underwater silence. But no amount of breath holding could drown her disappointment. Finally, stripped of oxygen, she surfaced, gasping.

Demoralized, she climbed from the tub, wrapped her robe around her, blew her hair dry, and then climbed into bed. But her thoughts kept returning to Brody and what had happened at the library.

Impulsively, she picked up the cordless phone from its docking station, dialed information, got Brody's number, and called him before she realized it was almost midnight.

"Hello?" His dusky voice, which held the same smooth bite as one-hundred-year-old scotch, filled her ear.

Rachael swallowed hard. If she weren't fairly certain he had caller ID, she would have hung up.

"Hello?" he repeated, demanding that she respond.

Why had she called him?

Oh yeah, to tell him that his kiss had meant absolutely nothing to her. That she was totally immune to his charms. That she had no intention of falling off the wagon and into his arms.

"Rachael?"

Clearly, he did have caller ID.

"Um, yes."

"What's wrong? Why are you calling so late? Has something happened?"

She could just see him, immediately on alert, reaching for his gun, ready to do battle with bad guys.

"No, no, nothing's wrong. I'm sorry to call so late. I just couldn't sleep without clearing the air. Can you talk?"

"Hang on," he said. "I left the bathwater running."

"You take baths?" she asked. She'd never known a man who took baths.

"Helps me think. Hang on."

What did he need to think about? Had their kiss impacted him as strongly as it had impacted her?

She heard him settle the phone against what sounded like a hard surface. His dresser maybe? She could imagine him standing in his bedroom. Was he dressed? In his underwear? Or maybe even naked? Her pulse rate stoked as her mind's eye imprinted a daring picture of him. Bare-chested and bare-assed.

In a second, he was back. "What's up?"

Besides her core body temperature? "I thought...I couldn't sleep..." She heard him take a deep breath and the rough masculine sound sent a shiver through her. "We need to talk."

"What about?" he asked.

She heard the creak of bedsprings. Rachael closed her eyes and licked her lips. She could see his chest, ripped with muscles, minimal chest hair. His washboard stomach was flat and his...

Stop imagining him naked, dammit.

But she couldn't stop.

Oh, this was horrible, awful. She wanted him the way a child wanted a slice of birthday cake. A child didn't care if she gained weight or ruined her dinner or rotted her teeth. A kid spied a piece of cake and she just went for it, full out, no hesitation.

Exactly the same way Rachael had been going after men her entire life — grasping, needy, without discernment.

Except that she'd never before felt cravings this intense.

She ached to consume him in one greedy bite and lick the frosting from her fingers afterward. She hungered for him without any consideration for the consequences. She wanted to inhale his scent, taste his flavor, hear his voice as he groaned her name in the throes of passion.

To heck with one slice, she wanted the whole cake.

Did she have the strength to fight for what she needed? Or was she going to give in to the pull of romance as she'd done countless times before?

Just hang up!

"Rachael? You still there?"

"Uh-huh." She felt dazed, like she'd been in the dentist's chair breathing nitrous oxide.

"Are you all right? You sound...odd."

Not odd, horny.

"Um, fine, just fine," she lied, struggling to keep her mind on the reason she'd called him. She settled back against the headboard and drew her knees to her chest.

"Where are you?" he asked.

"At my mother's house."

"I know that," he said. "Whereabouts in the house are you?"

"In bed."

"Hmm." His voice cracked.

It suddenly occurred to Rachael that he might be having a few late-night fantasies of his own. Stunned, she sucked in her breath as chill bumps spread over her arms.

"So what are you wearing?" he asked in a deep, throaty voice.

Omigod, clearly he had mistaken the meaning of her call. Time to slice things off before they went too far.

"Or are you wearing anything at all?" he asked.

Rachael's cheeks blazed hot. She glanced down at her white cotton T-shirt with the faded Hard Rock Café logo. Sexy as granny pj's.

I am not playing this game, she told herself, but said, "A Victoria's Secret negligee."

From the other end of the phone line, she heard an audible gulp. She pulled a pillow over her head as her face flamed hotter.

"What color?" he asked.

"Black," she improvised, pressing a palm to her feverish neck. "With red satin ribbons."

He hissed in his breath as if he'd walked across hot coals.

She could see him in her mind, his big hand clasping tight to the receiver, his long muscular body stretched across his bed, naked as the day he came into the world.

"And black fishnet stockings," she added, feeling devilishly out of control.

He growled.

"Scarlet stilettos," she went on, enjoying his reaction.

"Stop!" he commanded in his law enforcement voice.

Her fingertips, which had somehow walked from the nape of her neck to the waistband of her panties, froze.

"And tasseled pasties." She kept going, unable to resist.

"Uncle," he croaked. "I give. You win."

Remorse fisted inside her. "I'm sorry," she apologized. "Phone sex was *not* the reason I called."

Brody chuckled, a rough, regretful sound that sent fresh chills slipping down her spine. "Listen..."

Rachael sat up straight. "Yes?"

"I'm actually glad you called."

"You are?"

"I wanted to talk to you about what happened at the library tonight."

"You mean between my parents?"

"I mean between us."

"Um, there is no us. You're you and I'm me and we're separate as separate can be. Separate and single and..." she chattered inanely. *Good Lord, woman, shut up.*

"Rachael," he said.

"Uh-huh?"

"Hush a minute and let me get a word in edgewise."

"Okay." Rachael held her breath.

"I'm not going to pretend I don't feel something for you," Brody said, "because I do."

"You do?" she squeaked.

"Yes, but I'm not the kind of guy who beats around the bush. The timing is off for us. You're in a bad place emotionally."

My sentiments exactly.

"And I'm just now getting over what happened in Iraq and my wife leaving me for another man. Trust isn't my strong suit and you can't build a relationship without trust."

"Okay." Where was he headed with this?

"You've got this whole anti-romance thing going on."

"Yes?"

"I know you feel the chemistry, too. Your kiss said it all. But you also told me you had trouble separating love from sex, so sex is out of the question, because the last thing I want is for you to get hurt again."

"Excuse me?" Was he putting out feelers in a round-about way to see if she could handle a casual fling?

"Isn't that why you called?" He sounded confused.

So why had she called him? "No!"

"Okay, but you were the one who mentioned Victoria's Secret and tasseled pasties."

Guilty as charged. And she was regretting her faux pas more with each passing second. "You thought I called to proposition you?"

"Did you?"

"No.... No... absolutely not," Rachael sputtered. "And I can't believe your arrogance. Why on earth would you think I would have an affair with you?"

"You said you wanted to learn how to separate love from sex. I thought—"

"Think again, Sheriff Egotistical."

He laughed.

Laughed!

Rachael's blood boiled. "I wouldn't have an affair with you if you were the last man on earth."

"That's too bad," he said, "because I think we could have great sex together."

AFTER HER ILL-FATED midnight phone call to Brody, Rachael's life went from bad to worse.

Her cell phone kept ringing with inquiries from people wanting to know how to join Romanceaholics Anonymous and/or praising her for the YouTube video. Rex called, all excited, to tell her that *Trace Hoolihan Ditches Bride* was officially the twentieth most internationally downloaded video of the day, but then he couldn't understand why the news did not make her happy.

"Great," Rachael muttered darkly. "Now I'm an *international* laughingstock."

"You're an international celebrity is what you are," Rex said.

Rachael snorted. She didn't want to be a star. She just wanted to stop falling blindly in love. And she wanted to go back to Houston and get on with her life. She had a week left on her community service sentence and then she was headed home. School restarted in two weeks and she'd have to start searching for a new apartment since she'd given hers up when she and Trace got engaged. Jillian had already told Rachael she could come and stay with her until she found somewhere suitable to live.

By the end of her day delivering meals on wheels she pulled her VW Bug—which she'd had repainted after the graffiti incident—into Mrs. Potter's driveway, and told herself she was not going to look across the street to see if Brody was home.

She looked.

And there he was.

Outside. Shirtless. Pushing his lawn mower across the plush Saint Augustine.

Their eyes met.

Brody raised a hand.

Rachael ducked her head and raced inside the house. *I told you not to look*, she scolded herself, but that didn't stop her heart from beating too fast. Good thing she was leaving town soon.

She found Selina in the kitchen making enchiladas. That was a positive sign. Her mother hadn't been eating.

"Smells good," she said, coming over to drop a kiss on her mother's cheek.

"Someone from Country Day called while you were out," Selina said. "I wrote the contact information on the notepad." She pointed with the tip of her paring knife to the message center by the phone.

Rachael bustled over to look at the note. *Mr. Sears called, he'd like a call back ASAP.* A cell phone number followed. Mr. Sears was the principal of Country Day where Rachael was employed as a kindergarten teacher.

"Must be something about the upcoming school year," Rachael said, picking up the phone and simultaneously kicking off her sandals.

She punched in the numbers, listened to it ring.

"Hello, Mr. Sears?" she said when the man answered. "This is Rachael Henderson."

"Rachael," Mr. Sears said, his voice sounding clipped and serious. "We need to talk."

Something about the principal's tone sent up warning flags. "Yes, sir."

"There was an emergency meeting of the school board last night," he said.

"Emergency meeting?"

"It's come to our attention that you've encountered a bit of controversy over the summer."

"Controversy?" she echoed, feeling blindsided. "The emergency school board meeting was about me?"

"Well, more specifically, about that video you posted on YouTube," Mr. Sears said.

"Yes?"

"The board feels that it's not only inappropriate for one of our faculty members to produce such content, but we're afraid the attention will be detrimental to Country Day."

"Are you asking me to pull the video from YouTube?" Honestly, after all the crank phone calls she kept getting, she was ready to have Rex yank it off the Internet.

"I'm afraid it's gone beyond that. Someone from your hometown notified us that you'd been arrested for vandalism."

Rachael felt a harsh stab of betrayal. Could it have been Brody? But why would he do that? Why would anyone? "Someone from Valentine called you?"

"Yes. Is it true?"

"The charges were a misdemeanor, and I—"

"Nevertheless, in light of your behavior," Mr. Sears

interrupted, "the school board has decided to cancel your contract for the upcoming school year."

She felt at once both furious and terrified. A trickle of sweat ran down Rachael's neck and dropped cold into her cleavage. She'd just lost her job because someone in her hometown didn't like what she was doing. "You have no legal right to cancel my contract."

"Read your contract, Miss Henderson. We have every right to protect the students from a teacher with a criminal record."

Criminal record! All she'd done was paint a sign black.

"Mr. Sears, surely there's something I can do to change the school board's mind. You simply can't fire me. I love those kids, I love my job, I love —"

"You should have thought about that before you vandalized a billboard," the principal said, cutting her off. "I'm sorry, Rachael, but the decision is irrevocable."

ACROSS TOWN, KELVIN Wentworth received a phone call.

"It's done," said the voice on the other end of the line. "She's been fired from her job."

Kelvin smiled. "Good work."

"Are you sure it was such a smart move? I mean, now that she's out of a job, she's free to stay in town and devote all her time to stirring up anti-Valentine sentiment. And causing problems for your reelection campaign."

Kelvin snorted.

"Don't underestimate her. She's already done a lot of damage."

"You've knocked the pins out from under her with this

one," Kelvin assured the man he'd coerced into doing his dirty work. "She'll have to concentrate on finding a job. In the meantime, I'll be winning the election."

Plus sealing the deal with Amusement Corp.

Kelvin smiled. At last everything was falling into place, and he wasn't about to let some snippet of a girl with starry-eyed dreams stand in his way.

MICHAEL HENDERSON HUNG up the phone feeling dirtier than he'd ever felt in his life. He'd just betrayed his daughter to his lifelong rival. He was a complete and utter bastard. No wonder Selina had left him.

"But it's for the best," he told himself. Sometimes a father had to hurt his children in order to ultimately save them. He had to do this for Rachael's sake. He'd had no other choice.

Remorse ate him. *Did you have any other choice?*

No, he didn't. Agreeing to help Kelvin was the only way he could get Rachael to stop her anti-romance campaign. And dropping the romance campaign was the only way she was ever going to find the love she truly deserved. And it was the only way he could win his wife back. Besides, Country Day would have found out about her arrest for vandalism sooner or later and it was better that Rachael lose her job before school started rather than after.

You did the right thing.

Still, he couldn't help feeling devious and underhanded. He was so terribly, terribly ashamed of what he'd done but his motivation came from the heart. This was what he must do to help her. It was a father's cross to bear. Like when he'd had to hold her down for an injection when she was a screaming four-year-old with an appendix that had burst and she needed emergency surgery. Watching her suffer had been like cutting off his right arm. He felt exactly the same way now.

What's Selina going to think when she finds out you got Rachael fired?

"She's not going to find out," he muttered under his breath. "And neither is Rachael."

Because if Selina found out what he'd done, he knew she wouldn't understand. And she wouldn't forgive.

Before he had time to brood over that, the doorbell rang.

Michael frowned. He wasn't expecting anyone.

He walked to the front door, his footsteps echoing loudly in the house, which now felt so empty without Selina in it. He squinted through the peephole and saw Vivian standing on the doorstep in a raincoat.

Immediately, he knew what was beneath that raincoat.

Absolutely nothing.

It was a game they'd played when they were in high school. She'd wait until his parents were gone and come to this very door in her raincoat. She'd ring the bell and say—

"Girl Scout cookies. Get your sweet treats here," Vivian called out.

Michael gulped, closed his eyes, and shrank back from the door. What had he done?

She rang the bell again.

Go away.

The bell chimed a third time.

What the hell, Henderson, are you a man or a mouse? Open the door and tell her you're not interested.

But what if Selina didn't take him back? What if there really was no hope of repairing his ripped marriage? Didn't he deserve something good in his life?

Vivian is not good and you know it. You've been down this road with her before. Sure, she's sexy as hell, but she's nothing but trouble.

He had to take a stand. He'd cruised by for so many years on his money and his looks. He'd taken Selina for granted and he'd hurt her, and instead of being contrite about answering Vivian's e-mail, he'd been defensive. He'd accused her of being jealous and petty. He'd been in the wrong. And he'd wanted her back more than he wanted to breathe. That was the only reason he'd done what he'd done to Rachael. To repair his damaged family.

Michael took a deep breath, opened his eyes, and went for the door. Then quietly, emotionlessly, he told Vivian what he should have told her when she'd sent him that e-mail three months ago: "The only sweet treats I'm interested in belong to my wife."

Chapter Eleven

Faced with no job and an uncertain future, Rachael spent the rest of the next month trying to decide what she was going to do with her life. The heat of August ebbed into the slightly less-scorching heat of September. Football season started and along with it, a constant reminder of how well Trace was doing with the Chicago Bears while she was languishing jobless in Valentine.

Rachael had completed her court-ordered community service shortly after losing her job. She'd done her best to avoid Brody, and for the most part she'd succeeded. He'd raise a hand in greeting now and then if he spied her from across the street, or when he saw her in town. And she would wave back, but that was as far as things went.

The one area of her life where things were going well was with Romanceaholics Anonymous. Due to the popular demand generated by the YouTube video, Rex had helped her start her own Web site, and she'd created a blog devoted to debunking romantic myths. She'd also started several Romanceaholics chapters in surrounding towns.

But while it was emotionally satisfying, her anti-romance crusade wasn't generating any income. Selina had told her not to worry about money, that she'd take care of Rachael's expenses while she went through her metamorphosis, but the truth was she needed something to bolster her self-esteem.

Then one bright afternoon in late September, she came home from setting up a new chapter of Romanceaholics Anonymous in a neighboring town to find a black Lincoln Town Car parked outside Mrs. Potter's house.

Something bad has happened.

The thought seized hold of her and wouldn't let go. Her legs felt leaden as she trod up the sidewalk to the front door. Her heart flipped up into her throat. What else could go wrong?

She found her mother in the living room having coffee with a sharply dressed woman in her late thirties. The visitor wore a tailored suit that hadn't come off any department store rack, drop-dead stilettos, and an expensive, big-city coif. She looked decidedly out of place perched on an aged sofa with a hand-crocheted afghan stretched across the back.

"Here she is," her mother said brightly. It looked as if she'd been having trouble holding up her end of the conversation with the sleek creature on the sofa.

The woman settled her cup and saucer onto the scarred coffee table and rose to her feet, her right hand extended. "Hello, I'm Maggie Lawford. The entertainment editor for *Texas Monthly*."

"Rachael Henderson," she said.

"I know." Maggie Lawford's eyes sparkled.

"What are you doing in Valentine?"

"I'm here to see you. You're the talk of the Internet. My guess is that you're averaging ten thousand blog hits a day. Is that number in the ballpark?"

"I don't know. I'd have to ask my Web guy." Rachael

tucked her bottom lip up between her front teeth. "Really? I'm actually on your radar?"

"Not just on my radar, but in my magazine."

"Excuse me?"

Maggie smiled. "I'm here to offer you a job."

"You drove all the way from Austin to offer me a job?"

"That," Maggie said, "and to see Valentine for myself. It's everything you describe in your blog and more."

Rachael's trepidation vanished and she felt a sense of anticipation that equaled the thrill she experienced whenever she encountered a potential love interest. She hadn't known that anything other than romance could make her feel this way — giddy, breathless, hopeful.

"It's so exciting," Selina said.

Rachael agreed with her mother, but facing her romanceaholism had taught her a few things. Just as she shouldn't romanticize a man, she had no business romanticizing a job, either. "Exactly what would the position entail?"

"Why don't we have a seat?" Maggie invited, settling onto the sofa again and crossing her chic legs. She patted the cushion. "Relax."

Rachael eased down beside the other woman and tried to restrain the surge of enthusiasm pushing against her chest. *Don't look too eager.* "What kind of job?"

"We'd like for you to write a monthly column."

It took everything she had inside her not to squeal out loud. She wanted to say, *Yes, yes, a thousand times yes.* But those were the words she'd used when Trace asked her to marry him. She was done impulsively riding the wave of excitement. She amazed herself by saying, "A monthly column is quite a commitment."

Brody, she thought, would be so proud of her. Immediately, she wondered why she was thinking about him.

"You'd be well compensated," Maggie said smoothly. She named a figure that was almost twice Rachael's salary at Country Day.

It was all she could do to keep from breaking out in a grin. "I'd have to relocate to Austin?"

"Actually, we want you to stay right here in Valentine. Keep your finger on the pulse of America's heartbeat. We can do everything through e-mail."

Hmm, something to think about. She wasn't sure she wanted to stay in Valentine. "What would the column be about?"

"Same thing you're doing on your blog. Raising questions about love and romance. Debunking romantic myths. Highlighting examples of what real love is. Show how movies, music, and the media create false illusions when it comes to courtship and marriage. Draw on stories from Romanceaholics Anonymous."

"Those stories are confidential," Rachael said.

"Fictionalize them," Maggie said smoothly. "Or convince people to go on the record."

Rachael frowned. "Wouldn't that be taking advantage of people's foibles and vulnerabilities?"

"Aren't you already doing that with your Web site?"

"Not specifically. So far, I've only skewered myself and my ex-fiancé."

"Ah, yes." Maggie smiled. "Trace Hoolihan."

Something unpleasant occurred to her. "That's why you're offering me this job, isn't it? Not because of my Web site, but because Trace is high-profile and that will bring readers to my column."

"That's part of the reason, I won't deny it. But you underestimate yourself, Rachael. You're quite the writer. We admire your creativity and your spunk. You didn't take rejection lying down. You fought back. Painted that billboard. Posted that video on YouTube. Plus you know how to hit right at the center of your readers' emotions."

Stroke to the old ego. She had to hand it to Maggie Lawford. The woman was a good persuader.

"I do?"

"Come on. You know you're special."

It was flattery, but she fell for it, hook, line, and sinker. "If I decide to do this, I won't use stories from the people in my Romanceaholics meetings. Even fictionalized. It's unethical. They've put their trust in me and I won't betray them."

"That's fine," Maggie said without missing a beat. "Do the stories of the people whose names are on the Walk of Flames sidewalk on Main Street. Not all of them could have had a happily-ever-after ending."

Rachael looked to Selina to get her take on this. Her mother lifted her shoulders, held up her hands in a whatever-you-think-is-best gesture. "You only want to tell the stories of romances that have gone bad?"

"Conflict sells," Maggie said. "Happily-ever-after might be sweet to live, but romance without any bumps in the road is boring to read. Start with the love-gone-wrong tales. When you run out of those, we'll reevaluate."

Rachael considered it. "What are you thinking of calling the column?"

"We've been tossing around a couple of titles. 'Don't Let the Stars Get in Your Eyes' got the most votes."

Not bad. She liked it.

"Although 'Happily Never After' is still in the running."

Rachael didn't like that one so much. It was too negative. As if romantic love wasn't possible at all.

Maybe it's not.

"So may I call my editor-in-chief and give him the good news that you'll be writing for us?" Maggie asked, drawing her cell phone from her purse.

Rachael paused, knowing she was on the verge of a monumental opportunity. Her mouth was dry, her stomach in knots. Writing for such an acclaimed regional magazine would stretch her creative skills beyond anything she'd ever dared. It was a dream she'd never even thought to dream.

But this wasn't strictly about her. There was something else to think about. What would the column do to her hometown?

It could put it on the map, but it could also hurt a lot of people. Good, decent people who were just trying to make their way in life. Did she have any right to shine a floodlight on her community without the permission of its citizens?

On the other hand, she couldn't be held responsible for the way some people might react to her column. She'd spent her life as a people pleaser. It was time for her to do what she thought best.

Chin up, she met Maggie Lawford's eye. "Tell your editor I'm on board."

"That's wonderful." Maggie smiled. "Now, there's just one more thing."

What now? Rachael's muscles tensed. "Yes?"

"We're planning a big romance exposé edition for Valentine's Day and we want you to lead the charge. To quickly build you a following, we want to get your column started as soon as possible. The November issue will be going to press in three weeks and we want 'Don't Let the Stars Get in Your Eyes' to be in it. With that deadline in mind, we'll need your first column by the end of the week. Can you handle it?"

It didn't give her much time to take a breath, much less think this through. She'd already gone this far out on the limb. What was a couple more feet? "I can handle it."

"Excellent." Maggie Lawford got to her feet and extended her hand to Rachael again. "It's great to have you on board."

It felt great, too.

Except for the sinking feeling deep in the pit of her stomach that she had no idea what to write about that wasn't going to step on a lot of toes in Valentine.

THE PRESSURE WAS ON.

An hour after she'd accepted Maggie Lawford's offer, Rachael sat in Bristo Park across from the courthouse, laptop resting on her thighs, the cursor blinking accusatorily at her from the blank Word document. She hadn't a single idea in her head.

What was she going to write about?

Think, think.

Nothing.

She shifted on the park bench, ran her tongue around the inside of her mouth, twisted a curl of hair around her index finger. Hmm. What could she say that she hadn't already said on her Web site?

The emptiness inside her brain was excruciating. She

wasn't a writer. She was a kindergarten teacher. Why had she agreed to write that column? It had been a momentary lapse of sanity.

Pursing her lips, she gazed out across the clipped green lawn for inspiration and saw nothing the least bit inspiring. A flush of red chrysanthemums encircled the tree. Maybe she could rant about the practice of romanticizing football homecoming games with high school football mums.

It was something.

She typed "Mums." Then paused to nibble her bottom lip. She thought about her own high school football mums and her heart went all melty remembering the boys who'd given them to her.

Snap out of it!

But the mums brought back such happy memories. Why would she want to bash the practice? Why deny other young girls the fun simply because she'd had rotten luck with romance? It felt like sour grapes.

Come on, come on, you're getting soft on me. You're in danger of falling off the wagon. Remember why you painted that billboard in the first place. You said you wanted to get your message out about the folly of buying into the myth of romance. Here's your chance.

Except she just couldn't seem to work up the requisite anger. At least not in reference to homecoming mums.

She backspaced, erasing "Mums."

Great. Blowing out her breath, she cruised her gaze around the courthouse square.

And spied Mayor Wentworth hustling down the steps of City Hall, his white Stetson jammed down on his head. Where was he off to in such a hurry?

Rachael narrowed her eyes. Probably heading out to cook up some new way to bolster his standing in the polls. She thought about the way he'd acted toward her ever since she'd begun her anti-romance campaign and suddenly an idea came to her.

It was perfect in its simplicity.

Lay the blame on Valentine's obsession with romance squarely where it belonged. On the shoulders of the man perpetuating the myth in order to hold on to his job.

And the sweet thing was, she was in tight with the mayor's assistant.

Smiling, Rachael stowed her laptop in its carrying case, then got up and walked across the park to interview Rex for her scathing exposé on Kelvin Wentworth.

RACHAEL PACED MRS. POTTER'S living room. Two days had passed since she'd e-mailed Maggie Lawford her column. Maggie had sent a terse reply, saying she'd call her today. Rachael had been waiting by the phone since eight a.m.

"Honey," Selina said. "You're getting yourself all worked up over this. Come on, what's the worst that can happen?"

"Maggie could pull the plug on the column."

"And you wouldn't be any worse off than before."

Good point, but Rachael wasn't in the mood to listen to common sense. She couldn't explain it, but it felt as if her entire future lay in Maggie Lawford's manicured hands. She'd given up being a starry-eyed romantic to become an eagle-eyed journalist. She was ready to fully embrace this identity and her newfound philosophy on love. The column was a validation of her progress.

Selina looked at her watch. "It's almost six o'clock. She's probably left for the day. I imagine she hasn't even had a chance to read your article, much less—"

The ringing phone cut off her mother's words. "Texas Monthly" scrolled across the caller ID screen.

Palms sweating, Rachael snatched up the cordless phone. "Hello?"

"Rachael," the editor said in her cool, clipped tones. "Maggie Lawford here. Your article..."

"Yes," she whispered and held her breath. In the space of time it took Maggie to answer, Rachael's heart skipped two beats.

"Brilliant. Absolutely brilliant. This is exactly what we were looking for from you."

Relief turned her knees to rubber and she dropped down on the sofa beside her mother. Selina raised a quizzical eyebrow. Rachael covered the mouthpiece with a hand and murmured, "She loves it."

"Yes!" Selina mouthed silently and showed her support by raising her fisted hands over her head in a triumphant gesture.

"I've got to warn you about something, however," Maggie said.

The mindless fear was back, grabbing at her belly and squeezing hard. "What is it?"

"There's going to be fallout from this column when it hits the newsstands next month."

"What do you mean...fallout?"

"The Wentworth name carries a lot of clout. Are you sure of your facts?"

"Absolutely. I have a source inside the mayor's office."

"Okay, then," Maggie said. "But I want you to be prepared."

Rachael ran a hand through her hair. "Prepared for what?"

"This little story is going to set off one hell of a firestorm."

"You're serious? The one article?"

"Rachael, don't you realize what you've done?"

Apprehension tickled her bones. "Um, no."

"Why, honey, you've fired the opening salvo in what I predict will become a protracted civil war between cynics and romantics. And not just in your hometown, but all across Texas."

"WHAT ARE YOU going to do about this business?" Kelvin demanded, slapping a slick new copy of *Texas Monthly* on Brody's desk.

It was more than three weeks until Halloween, but Kelvin looked like he was already gearing up to attend the annual harvest bash as the Incredible Hulk. His blue eyes flashed fire, twin veins at his temples bulged, and his big neck was overflowing the top of his starched white collar.

Brody cocked back on the legs of his chair, interlaced his fingers, cradled his head in his palms, and leveled the mayor with a steady gaze. "Do about what?"

"You haven't seen this?" Kelvin thumped the magazine with a meaty thumb. "Your little girlfriend is making a mockery of our entire town."

"First off, Rachael is not my girlfriend," Brody said

evenly. "Second, it seems to me she's making a mockery of you and your ancestors, not Valentine."

"It's the same damn thing," Kelvin roared.

"Ah, but you see, it's not. That's where I think the problem lies, and actually it's what Rachael's article is all about."

"She's going to cause me to lose the election."

"*You're* going to cause you to lose the election. Not Rachael, not Giada Vito. Your own behavior."

"Listen to this." Kelvin grabbed up the magazine and flipped the pages until he found what he was searching for. "The Wentworth family has molded the town of Valentine into an image that benefits them financially. Since the nineteen fifties, they've perpetuated harmful romantic myths, not out of any real belief in the lasting power of love, but simply to make their fortunes. Valentine isn't so much a town as it is a tourist trap, with its romantic novelties and a man-made, heart-shaped lake. And Mayor Wentworth, who, by the way, has never been married, is the ringmaster of this romantic circus."

Kelvin flung the magazine across the room.

"Any part of that untrue?" Brody asked.

"She makes it sound like I don't care about this town and the people in it. She's unpatriotic, un-American, un-Valentinian. What's the matter with her? Everyone believes in true love."

"Even you?"

Kelvin snorted. "Of course I do."

"Then why haven't you ever been married?"

"Because I never found the right woman. You have any idea what it's like to live in a town saturated with romance? To grow up indoctrinated in the family business of making

Valentine's Day novelties, while all around you people are falling in love, but you never find that special someone?"

"Wow," Brody said. "You're sounding dangerously close to believing what you're saying."

Kelvin's eyes flashed in anger. "I have supporters. People in this town loved my father, my family. They love me and everything I've done for Valentine. This is going to cause a heap of trouble. Are you prepared for an uprising?"

"There you go being all dramatic again."

"And there you go, not taking this seriously."

Truth was, Brody was struggling not to smirk. "I can't arrest her for having an opinion, Kelvin."

"It's Mayor Wentworth," Kelvin said, pulling rank.

Brody couldn't resist. A smiled curled his lips. "Enjoy the title while it lasts... *Mayor*."

Kelvin whipped his head around to drill Brody with a glare. "What does that mean?"

"Rachael's got her supporters, too. And I happen to be one of them. I think the Wentworths have made this town look foolish for too long."

Kelvin stared at Brody as if he'd kicked him in the family jewels. A pained expression pulled his mouth downward. "I supported you for sheriff."

"You did."

"And this is the thanks I get?"

Brody spread his hands. "It's just an article. It'll blow over if you don't make a big deal of it. Show the town you have a sense of humor. Show them that—"

But he didn't get any farther. Kelvin stormed out the door, flipping Brody the bird as he went.

Brody shook his head and let out a breath of air. From

the way things were stacking up, it was going to be a long few weeks until the election.

RACHAEL WASN'T HAVING any better a day than Mayor Wentworth. The phone had been ringing off the wall with citizens calling to read her the riot act over her column in *Texas Monthly.*

She'd been called a traitor, a communist, a bitter jilted old maid, and much worse. People she'd known her entire life snubbed her on the streets. Her hairdresser canceled her appointment, saying that under the circumstances she felt it would be hypocritical of her to cut Rachael's hair when Rachael hated the town so much.

That one really stung.

Maggie had warned her, but she still hadn't been prepared for the vitriol.

Sure, she had her supporters—the folks from her romanceaholics group, her mother, her father, and her sister, Hannah. Even Delaney, Tish, and Jillian had called to offer moral support. But she really hadn't expected the onslaught of hatred. Perhaps she was naive, but she'd thought people would appreciate her shedding light on Valentine's flaws. She'd mistakenly believed they would want to change the things holding the town back.

What had happened to her life?

Unbidden, her gaze slid over to Brody's house. She saw the patrol car parked in the driveway. He was home. Deana's car was gone, however.

He was home alone.

Rachael remembered the last time she'd been alone with him and her heart knocked. She saw his gate was open. She could hear the faint sounds of music coming from his backyard. It was a Chris Isaak tune about not wanting to fall in love.

The haunting melody drew her across the street.

Before she could stop herself, her hand was pushing his honeysuckle-covered gate open wider and she was walking into his backyard.

She rounded the corner of the house, his name on her lips, but the word died on her tongue when she saw him standing beside the patio table in his swim trunks, his tanned body glistening wet from a dip in the hot tub.

His back was to her and he was drying off his shoulders with a fluffy white bath towel. Her gaze slid down the well-defined muscles of his shoulder blades to the waistband of his shorts. Her mouth went dry. She could smell the scent of chlorine and redwood decking mingled with the fragrance of honeysuckle flourishing all along the fence, blocking the neighbors' view of his backyard. She heard the sound of the hot tub jets churning, Chris Isaak's mournful lyrics, and the soft, brisk, whisking noise of the towel rubbing vigorously against his skin.

He ducked his head, toweled his hair.

Then her gaze dropped from the view of his wet swimsuit cupping his firm butt to his thigh.

Her breath left her body in an exclamation of air as she saw the rounded stump below his knee where his right leg had been. The stab of hurt and sadness that she felt inside her heart for him was so powerful, she took a step backward.

And she bumped into a metal patio chair.

It screeched across the cement.

Brody lifted his head, looked toward her.

Rachael froze, her gaze riveted on his damaged leg.

"What are you doing here," he demanded, his voice harsh. He dropped the end of the towel to hide his leg. "Get out of here."

"Brody...I...I..."

"Go on." His face was a mask. She couldn't tell what he was thinking.

"I'm sorry," she said, feeling compelled to hold her ground. If she ran away now, he would think it was because the sight of his leg disgusted her. It did not, but she realized he was prepared to believe that.

For the first time, she spied the prosthetic leg propped against the hot tub decking. It looked bionic. Futuristic. Fascinating.

She took a step forward.

"Get out," he said harshly.

"I'm not afraid of you."

He was throwing daggers at her with his eyes. "You damn well should be."

"Why?" She raised her chin.

He hardened his jaw, pointed a finger in the direction of her house. "Go."

"There's nothing to be ashamed of."

"You're trespassing."

"Your gate was open."

"Maisy must have forgotten to close it." His dark, damp hair fell across his forehead. He looked so vulnerable standing there trying hard not to look vulnerable. He was embarrassed that she'd caught him in a moment of weakness. Her heartstrings tugged.

"Brody." Her voice came out lower and softer than she'd intended. The sound of his name hovered between them like the wings of a butterfly, soft and fluttery.

His jaw clenched tighter, as if he were holding back words or emotions he didn't dare let escape.

"Brody," she whispered again and crossed the patio between them, until she was directly in front of him, the thin towel the only barrier separating him from her.

Rachael shouldn't have done what she did next. She knew it as she was doing it, but she couldn't stop herself, didn't want to stop. Brody needed to know that he wasn't repulsive or disgusting or half a man. He needed to know that she found him sexy and virile and very attractive.

Her eyes didn't leave his face. She stared at him, stared into him, telegraphing with her eyes how much she admired and respected and desired him.

God, how she desired him.

He dropped the towel. She didn't see it fall because her gaze was transfixed on his, but she felt the terry cloth brush against her ankles as it landed on the cement. She didn't look down. For her there was nothing to see but his beautiful face.

"Rachael," he murmured.

His hand—fingertips, actually—brushed her hair from her forehead, then dropped down to feather her cheekbone, his calloused palm curving against her soft skin. She stared into chocolate brown eyes glittering with an emotion she couldn't decipher. Sexual hunger? Yes, lust was certainly a component, but there was much more lurking in the shadowy depths of his gaze. She saw tenderness and concern and worry and apprehension as well.

You're romanticizing him. Stop romanticizing him.

But damn her, she could not stop.

Inside his manly features she could still see the boy next door who'd been her childhood crush. Older, damaged to be sure, life settled hard onto his broad shoulders. He was tough and scarred and changed, but some small part of him was still the same. The small-town boy who believed in the goodness of humankind, in spite of all the atrocious things he'd experienced. He was a ruggedly handsome man in green-and-orange Hawaiian-print swim trunks, the lingering smell of chlorine clinging to his bare, hard-muscled chest.

Her stomach contracted. She looked at him and she was seven years old again, besotted, silly with adoration.

"Rachael," he said her name again. It sounded half like a prayer, half like a curse of defeat.

He dipped his head.

She met him halfway, going up on tiptoe, leaning into him.

He cupped her face in his hands.

She slipped her hands around his waist, pressed her body against his. She'd wanted to do this from the moment they'd tumbled from the ladder underneath the Valentine billboard.

His erection was hard and unmistakable beneath his thin, wet swim trunks. He wanted her as much as she wanted him.

Joyous blood strummed through her veins as Brody's lips closed over hers and she felt his power drill straight into her bones.

Her ears sang with the sound of the humming hot tub and murmuring music. Her nose twitched with the sharp, chlorine-tinged smell of his skin. Her arms tingled against the tight skin of his taut muscles. She closed her eyes to deepen the minty taste of him against her tongue.

It was as if an invisible fist reached into her body,

curled strong fingers around her heart, and squeezed. Emotions spattered inside her like shed blood. Desire and attraction. Hope and craving. Fear and thrill and nervous energy. Feelings toppled in on her, hard and sudden and scary as hell.

She was doing it again. Falling for the wrong man at the wrong time in the wrong place. Following her reckless, unrestrained heart when she should be listening to her head. She knew the dangers of this headlong feeling. She'd been here before. Many times. And each and every time, she'd come away singed.

Pull away, run, get out of here while you still can.

But romance addict that she was, Rachael could not obey her own admonition.

His kiss was hot. A searing brand.

His lips made her body quiver.

She made a soft mewling sound. He pushed his inquisitive tongue past her teeth, wrapped his arms around her, and drew her up tight against the expanse of his chest.

Rachael was surprised by his equilibrium, but she shouldn't have been. She already knew he was a steady, sturdy man. Built for endurance. Strong and reliable. Centered. Objective. Balanced.

In the past she'd been drawn to showy, charming men with unusual careers and big personalities. She'd been dazzled by flash and brash when what she'd really needed was substance. She'd never been with a man like him.

You're not with him now. He's not your boyfriend or your lover. He's just the guy who lives across the street.

A guy who took her home with him so she wouldn't have to spend the night in jail. A guy who brought her peaches when she was feeling down. A guy who seemed to understand her sometimes crazy, illogical behavior without judging her.

He threaded both hands through her hair, cradled her head in his palms. Holding her in place while he explored her mouth as if he was determined to unearth every secret she'd ever kept.

She melted. Just turned to butter right there in his back-yard, beside the churning whirlpool. Melted and morphed and melded into him.

"Aw," he murmured against her lips, "you taste like peaches."

"Your peaches," she whispered right back.

That made him chuckle as his mouth took possession of hers all over again.

Her pulse swirled. Light, airy, floaty. Swept away.

This second kiss was fiercer than the first. Demanding, urgent, skipping beyond subtleties to unveil the hungry animal lurking inside the controlled man. A beast yanking at its chain. This kiss told her Brody Carlton was not as restrained as he seemed.

The thought scared her.

And excited her even more.

The insistent probing of his tongue against hers conveyed an urgency she'd never guessed prowled inside him. The commanding pressure of his lips induced a helpless response from her so intense it felt as if time and space vanished and she was left dangling over a bottomless abyss by a thread as thin as a spider's web.

He sucked the breath right out of her body, leaving her weak-kneed and giddy. Her mind spun ridiculous fantasies. She saw them standing at a wedding chapel, a preacher pronouncing them man and wife. She saw herself giving birth to his babies, watched him smile at her as if she'd given him the most prized gift in the world. She envisioned them growing old together, holding hands as they strolled along Valentine Lake every evening at sunset.

Brody kissed her harder and deeper, holding on to her as if he couldn't get enough. He made her feel powerful and cherished and terrified.

Rachael teetered. Caught on the twin horns of hope and fear. Oh, this was crazy. Wishing for something that did not exist. Unable to separate fantasy from reality. Seeking, always seeking the refuge of romance when it had done nothing but rob her of her vision to see life clearly. To see men clearly.

Brody was not some brave, stalwart knight who could slay all her dragons. He had no magical powers to wipe away her troubles. She would not find the answers she needed in his kisses. Falling in love with him would not solve all her problems. He was just a decent guy, with his flaws and fears like anybody else.

She had to stop this and she had to stop it now. Rachael jerked back. Ending the kiss. Ending the daydream.

Immediately, he let her go. He did not try to hang on. He did not cling.

She spun away and, head down, ran for the back gate. She never looked behind her. She couldn't bear looking behind her because she knew what she would see.

Dear, battle-scarred Brody, standing there on his one strong leg, looking hurt and confused and angry and sad and vulnerable. She couldn't bear knowing that she had led him on, made reckless promises with her lips.

Promises she dared not keep.

Chapter Twelve

Across town, Giada Vito sat in her office reading the *Texas Monthly* article. A huge smile broke across her face and she realized she had an important ally she'd been overlooking.

With the article, Rachael Henderson had given her a helpful gift, considering that Kelvin's recent standing in the polls had spiked with the addition of the bond election for Valentine Land.

Giada gritted her teeth.

Theme parks. Fantasy lands. Artifice. Bah!

A theme park might bring in jobs, but at what cost to the town? The last thing Giada wanted was to see her adopted hamlet turned into another Anaheim or Kissimmee with tons of traffic and congestion as tourism crowded out what was real and true and honest about Valentine.

According to *Texas Monthly,* Rachael wasn't the only one who disdained misguided romanticism and oversold commercialism.

She had to talk to Rachael and convince her to join her campaign. It was going to take a lot of scraping to win against the man whose thumb was pressed firmly on the town's jugular. And Rachael—with her contingency of recovering romanceaholics—could be her ace in the hole.

Deciding to skip her late-afternoon walk around Valentine Lake, Giada hopped into her Fiat, left the schoolgrounds, and headed for Rachael's house. Five minutes later, she turned down the tree-shrouded street at the same time she saw Kelvin Wentworth's Cadillac approaching from the opposite end of the block.

What was the irritating man doing here?

She parked at the curb to the left of Rachael's home at the same time Kelvin pulled up on the right. Simultaneously, they hopped out of their cars. He had a copy of *Texas Monthly* rolled up like he was going to whack something with it. Giada's copy was sticking out of the handbag she had slung across her shoulder.

"Vito," Kelvin said in a tone that was half-sneer, half-amusement. The sneer she understood. The amusement part irritated her.

"Wentworth," she countered, disdain in her voice. She hurried up the sidewalk, trying to get ahead of him, but she was wearing stilettos and Kelvin's long legs ate up the ground until they were rushing shoulder to shoulder onto the front porch.

She rang the bell. Kelvin hammered on the wooden door.

"You oaf," she said. "You'll scare the poor woman to death with your clumsy pumping."

"No one's ever complained about my pumping before," Kelvin said, a wolfish gleam in his eyes.

Giada frowned, and then she caught the sexual innuendo. She'd meant to say pounding, not pumping. Although she'd been raised from childhood with English as her second language, it was still a complicated and confusing tongue. And she'd left herself wide open to Wentworth's smirk. She made a face at him and rang the bell again.

She tried not to notice how good he smelled. He wore a spicy-scented cologne that enticed her nose. Kelvin laughed; the sound was rich and deep. It sent strange prickles up her spine. Prickles she did not enjoy.

"You're here to join forces with her," Kelvin said flatly.

Giada didn't answer. She didn't owe him an explanation. The air was thick and laced with the fragrance of the rust-colored chrysanthemums flourishing in the flower box underneath the window. She poked the doorbell again. In spite of the pink Volkswagen sitting in the driveway, she was beginning to suspect Rachael wasn't home.

Kelvin stepped closer, crowding her space.

The tiny hairs at the nape of her neck lifted. *Step aside. Move back.*

And let him win?

No way.

She didn't have to dither long. Kelvin was the first to move. He took her elbow, spun her around to face him.

A thrill of alarm buzzed through her. Her heart reeled recklessly against her rib cage. She turned her head, unable to meet his gaze, reaching for the doorbell again. *Please be home, Rachael. Answer the door.*

But there was no salvation. No rescue.

Kelvin dropped the magazine he'd been holding. It hit the welcome mat with a soft plop and his arms went around her waist. Her breath left her body in one abrupt whoosh. Her knees turned to noodles as his big hands settled on her hips.

His body heat seeped through the fabric of her silk skirt, past the lace of her thong panties, and into her quivering flesh. Liquid heat rolled through her, licking like flames. He splayed his hands, covering her buttocks with his big fingers. The sensation spreading out through her nerve endings was more provocative than if he'd actually stroked her bare flesh.

He bent his head.

Giada's heart lodged in her throat. *He's going to kiss me.*

What scared her most was that she didn't even try to get away. Her mace lay forgotten in the bottom of her purse. Her good sense was addled by the fragrance of his cologne mingled with the scent of fall flowers. His warm breath feathered the fine hairs at her forehead. His hands were still splayed across her buttocks. He pulled her up flush against him.

What was she doing? This was a small town and she had no doubt that at least one nosy neighbor was peeping from behind mini-blind slats.

His mouth covered hers and the first thing she thought was, *He tastes just like licorice.*

Licorice had been her father's favorite flavor of chewing gum. He'd always carried a pack in his front pocket. When she was particularly successful—bringing home good grades, coming in first at dance recital, winning first place in the science fair—he'd reward her with a stick of gum. Giada associated licorice with reward.

Kelvin's kiss sucked all the air from her body. Sucked common sense right out of her head. She would never have guessed a man like Kelvin Wentworth—born and reared in a small town that he'd never left—could kiss like this!

He kissed as if the sun rose and fell on her lips. As if the earth spun on its axis because of her. His kiss was dizzying and demented and utterly unforgettable.

What shocked Giada most of all was her uninhibited response.

She'd often thought he was egotistical and opinionated and thickheaded. A Neanderthal who'd once ran a football so fast and far that he'd bamboozled the town for all eternity.

But she wasn't thinking those things now.

What she thought now was a lyrical throwback to her Italian girlhood. She remembered a story her grandmother had told her about the magic of a kiss and the power of true love. Her father had pooh-poohed the stories from her mother's side of the family. Romance, he'd taught her, would lead her down the wrong path. If she wanted to make it in the world, she needed a solid grounding in math and science and a firm, sensible head on her shoulders.

Instinct urged her to wrap her arms around Kelvin's neck, pull his head down closer, deepen their connection, extend the kiss.

And if Rachael Henderson hadn't chosen exactly that moment to come barreling up the sidewalk, Giada had little doubt that's exactly what she would have done.

Kelvin broke the kiss, stepped away from her. In unison, they turned to see Rachael standing on the bottom step, eyes wide, breathing heavy. Her lips looked swollen. Giada pressed the back of her hand against her own mouth, still moist from Kelvin's.

"What do you want?" Rachael cried, the panicky note in her voice out of step with any misgivings she might have felt by finding the mayor kissing the high school principal on her doorstep. Something else was going on with her. "Why are you here?"

She and Kelvin both spoke at once, drowning each other out.

Rachael raised a hand, climbed up the steps. "Please," she said. "Get out of my way. I have no desire to speak to either one of you." Shouldering them aside, she pushed into the house and slammed the door behind her.

Kelvin turned to Giada. He gave a shrug. "I guess we caught her at a bad time."

"It appears that is the case."

"I'll just come back later," he said.

"Me also."

Neither one of them made a move to leave.

"What you're doing is a mistake," he said.

"What is? Trying to stop you from turning this town into a theme park?" Giada asked.

"It's the only thing that's going to save Valentine."

"Says you."

"Yeah," he said, narrowing his eyes. "Says me."

"The town should be allowed to hear both sides, to make an informed decision. It's time you stopped treating Valentine as if it's your child and you're Big Daddy who knows best."

He arched an eyebrow. "Spoken like a foreigner who came strolling into town without any sense of history, determined to muck things up and ruin our traditions with dangerous ideas."

Giada sank her hands onto her hips, her mouth burning with regret. She'd been an idiot to let him kiss her. If she'd had some Scope, she'd gargle and spit right here. "I am a United States citizen. I have lived in this town for fifteen years and in this country for twenty. I belong in Valentine just as much as you do."

Kelvin snorted.

Giada's blood boiled.

She spun on her heels and scurried down the stairs, her knees stiff with anger, her movements jerky. Egotistical bastard.

It wasn't until she was speeding away in her Fiat that she realized he'd won. He'd chased her off.

She stopped at the red light in front of the Dairy Queen and slapped the steering wheel with both hands, imagining just how pumped up and pleased with himself he was feeling right now. Giada glowered at her reflection in the rearview mirror. Kelvin might have won that little skirmish, but she was determined to win the war.

LEG QUIVERING, BRODY plopped down into the lawn chair, his skin suddenly slick with sweat. He saw the hem of Rachael's skirt swish as she jerked the tall wooden gate closed behind her. He heard the latch click firmly in the lock.

His stomach churned. His lips burned. His heart knocked like a jalopy. He needed much more than a kiss. Wanted much more than just her body. The depth of his desire rippled wide as shock waves.

Rattled, he shoved his hands through his hair and stared at the beach towel lying on the ground to one side of his Power Knee.

She'd seen him without his leg. And she hadn't turned away in disgust. In fact, she'd made the first move, covering the ground between them, her eyes daring him to kiss her.

He'd never been able to resist a dare.

What if she was only doing it because she feels sorry for you?

He hated the thought of it. Clenching his jaw, he tried to harden his heart against soft emotions. Tried not to feel the things he was feeling.

But what if it wasn't just pity? What if she'd honestly wanted him as much as he'd wanted her?

Brody grunted. What was this strange hold she seemed to have over him? She made him think stupid, romantic thoughts. Thoughts he knew better than to entertain. He'd witnessed firsthand just how much damage romantic love could do to a man, to a woman, to a family. He didn't want any part of it.

Love?

Come on, he wasn't falling in love with her. He liked her spunk. He admired her courage. He thought she was gorgeous as all get out and that body of hers...

Recalling the way her hot, curvy body had felt pressed against his, he hissed in a breath and his own body responded to the remembered stimulus. His fingers tingled from the feel of her silky hair. His ears pricked at the echo of her soft sighs. His mouth watered at the ghost of her taste, so sweet and rich and feminine.

All he could think about was getting his hands up underneath her skirt and pulling off her panties, then laying her down in the grass beneath the pergola and making love to her.

His erection stiffened.

It had been so damned long since he'd been with a woman and he wanted her so badly it made him ache all over.

But Rachael wasn't just any woman. She was special.

Thinking about her made him smile. A crystal clear picture of her rose in his mind—that cascade of wavy blonde hair tumbling helter-skelter over her slender shoulders, the excited light in her almond-shaped green eyes, the sweet, honeyed flavor of her lips.

Truth was, she'd gotten to him. Slipped past his guard with her earnest beliefs and heartfelt desire to reinvent their hometown. He'd spent so many years on alert, in tight control of his emotions, holding himself back, keeping his feelings in check. He was stunned to discover how little self-control he really possessed when it came to Rachael.

Lose control. It's okay. Just let go.

Easy to think, much harder to do. She wanted him as much as he wanted her. He'd tasted it on her. Her need. His hunger.

So go after her. Seduce her.

Brody fisted his hands. He couldn't, he wouldn't. But his dick was so hard he could barely draw in air. Dammit, how he wanted her.

She'd done this to him. Made him desire her in a way he'd never desired another. Miserable. He felt mindlessly miserable.

He tried to think of his ex-wife, tried to remember if she'd ever affected him like this. But for one blind moment, he couldn't even remember her name. All he could think about was Rachael.

Sassy, delightful Rachael, who'd turned both him and his hometown inside out.

His hand strayed to the laces of his swim trunks, his fingers fumbled as his breath came hard and fast. He imagined it was Rachael provoking him, stroking him.

Her fantasy touch caused every nerve ending in his

body to jolt with electrical awareness as he recalled the feel of her soft arms entwining around his waist. He visualized her long silken curls tickling his bare skin. He saw her full, peach-colored lips tip up in a beatific smile.

Daydream mingled with memory as his imagination escalated the scenario playing out in his head. His cock throbbed. His pulse raced. His brain hung on one thought and one thought only.

Rachael.

Stop, stop. You've got to stop this.

But it was too late for that. His self-control was shot to shit. He was lost. Overcome by lust and need and too much deprivation.

He stripped off his swim trunks and palmed his penis. His rhythm was frantic, desperate. He felt in equal parts embarrassment and inevitability and determination. He had to do something to alleviate the weighted need that had settled in him like granite from the moment he'd first spied her dangling from the Valentine sign.

Just get it over with. Quick. Empty out the testosterone. Get your brain back.

He closed his eyes, took in a deep breath, did what he had to do to reclaim his sanity.

Rachael.

A groan, half-pleasure, half-despair, slipped past his lips. How he wished she were here with him. Doing this to him.

The lawn chair screeched against the cement, but he didn't care. There was no stopping now. He was caught. God, what had she reduced him to?

And then the orgasm was upon him.

Rachael.

Clenching his jaw, he shuddered as hot ribbons of milky white ejaculate shot up and spilled over his fist.

In that moment of weakness, Brody realized something deadly profound. No matter how much he wanted to deny the dangerous pull, he *was* falling in love with her and he had absolutely no idea how to stop himself.

"Rachael," Brody muttered, feeling more confused than ever. "Dammit, woman, you've ruined me for good."

KELVIN SCOOPED UP his copy of *Texas Monthly* from Rachael's porch. He thought about ringing the doorbell to see if she'd open up, but his heart wasn't in it. What he needed was someone to talk to. His gaze swung across the street to Brody Carlton's house.

He walked over and knocked on Brody's door.

It took a while for the sheriff to answer. He was wearing swim trunks and nothing else. It wasn't often he had his prosthesis on display and it was something of a shock to see the bionic leg. Brody hid his injury so well, three-fourths of the time Kelvin forgot he was an amputee. The sheriff looked both breathless and irritated.

"Can I come in?" Kelvin asked.

"Can I say no?"

Kelvin didn't bother to reply, he just stepped over the threshold. "You alone?"

"Yes."

"Where's your sister? She coming home soon?"

"She's taken Maisy to see our aunt in Del Rio. They won't be home until Sunday night."

"Good." Kelvin sank down on Brody's couch. He picked up the remote control and flicked on the TV to ESPN.

"Come right in, make yourself at home."

"Thanks."

Brody sat down in the chair across from him. "What's the matter, Mayor? You look like you've been sacked in the end zone. Did you just find out Giada's kicking your ass in the polls?"

Kelvin tensed. "What did you hear?"

"Nothing." Brody frowned. "Seriously, Kelvin, are you okay?"

"Women. They screw with your head."

"Not going to argue with you there. Any woman in particular got you twisted up inside?"

"I'm forty-seven years old, Carlton. Forty-seven and I've never felt like this." Kelvin sprawled his arms across the back of the couch.

"Are you saying you're in love?"

"No." Kelvin rasped in a breath, but that was exactly what he was afraid of. "Not love, but something..."

"So who's the woman?"

Kelvin scowled. "You promise you won't laugh."

"I won't laugh."

"It's Vito."

Brody laughed.

Kelvin slapped a palm against his forehead. "I know; it's fucking hysterical."

"Hey," Brody said. "I've got problems of my own."

"She's going to win this election," Kelvin said gloomily, "and I'm going to be left with nothing."

"Maybe not. I mean, come on, the Wentworth name founded this town."

"That doesn't seem to matter much anymore. People want a change. There's a restlessness going around.

Nobody wants to believe in love anymore, or traditional hometown values."

"Do you really think a theme park reflects hometown values?"

Kelvin shrugged. He didn't know what he believed. "I can't even think straight anymore."

"If Giada ever figures out that she's got you running scared, you're seriously screwed."

"Tell me about it. Thing is, I can't stop thinking about her. A smart politician would drag her through the muck, doing whatever it took to win, but…hell, I just can't. There's something about her that's dug into me itchy as a chigger. It's weird. I feel as if it's more important for her to win this election than for me. I don't want to fight her anymore." Kelvin leaned forward and propped both elbows on his thighs, wishing he hadn't said all this to Brody.

"Okay." Brody raised his palms and gave Kelvin a shaky grin. "You've officially got me scared. You want me to make an appointment with Doc Edison for you?"

"Hey, look," Kelvin said, turning off the mute button on the television. "Roy Firestone is interviewing Trace Hoolihan."

Quickly, Brody turned his attention to the TV.

Kelvin sank back against the couch again and tossed the remote onto the coffee table. His gaze was fixed on the screen, but his mind was hanging on to Giada. Initially, he'd been attracted to her smoking-hot body, then her square-shouldered moxie. The woman possessed more passion and determination than most men he knew and Kelvin respected her for those qualities.

Except that when he'd kissed her, he'd discovered

something else beneath that tough, competitive outer shell. He'd found a rival who could just as easily become a friend. There was a tender, generous woman hidden underneath those layers and he couldn't help wondering just what he would find if he could peel them all away to expose the real Giada Vito.

Was he kidding himself? Was it possible to fall in love at forty-seven? Was he falling prey to his own PR hype? Or deep down inside was this really his last chance at finding true happiness?

BY THE TIME the doorbell rang two hours later, Rachael had managed to pull herself together after what had happened in Brody's backyard. Her mother had gone quilting with a group of friends and Rachael was alone in the house, the remains of a Lean Cuisine chicken scaloppini frozen dinner still resting on the TV tray in front of her.

The doorbell rang.

Brody.

She hopped up off the couch, ran to the door, and peeked through the peephole.

Giada Vito stood on her front porch. Her head was held high, her shoulders ruler straight. She looked determined.

Disappointment pushed air from Rachael's lungs on a long sigh. Reluctantly, she opened the door. "What do you want?"

"May I come in?" Giada asked in impeccable English. Except for the faint hint of an Italian accent, no one would ever guess she hadn't been born and raised in Valentine.

Rachael stood aside.

Giada swept into the room.

"Have a seat." Rachael waved at the couch.

Giada perched on the edge of the cushion. She wore a silky peach-colored blouse cut in an Empire style, slim-legged black slacks, black-and-peach sandal stilettos, and pearl earrings. Her hair was pulled back from her face in an elegant twist and anchored to her head with a fat brown barrette. She held her black-and-peach Coach handbag in her lap and crossed her legs at the ankles, the epitome of culture and cool. The woman possessed an efficient kind of beauty that made Rachael feel like a slacker in her gray sweatpants, faded blue cotton T-shirt with the slogan I HEART VALENTINE on it, and slouch socks with a hole in one toe.

"I want you to join my campaign," Giada said.

"That's straight and to the point," Rachael said. "I'm not very political."

"You don't have to be political. You just do what you do."

"Meaning?"

Giada leaned forward, her expression intent. "We've got to shake this town up. They've been putting too much emphasis on romance. Education takes a back burner and that concerns me. When I asked my students about their life goals, fully three-quarters of the high school girls said they want to get married and have babies. Can you imagine? No ambition."

Rachael could imagine. Once upon a time she'd been one of those girls. Could still be one if she let herself give in to temptation. She thought of Brody, then pushed the thought aside. Too much temptation.

"I've already stirred up trouble." Rachael nodded to the

copy of *Texas Monthly* resting on the coffee table beside the Lean Cuisine tray.

"Exactly," Giada said. "That is precisely the reason I want you on my campaign. You have started a passionate dialogue in this town the likes of which has never been seen. For the first time people are examining what this town stands for and they're beginning to realize they've sold out their inner values and beliefs for the sake of tourism."

"Tourism *is* Valentine's economy."

"It doesn't have to be," Giada said. "I know a way we can turn this town around."

"Oh?"

Giada lowered her voice. "I don't want to tip my hand. I have to know if you're a confederate before I let you in on my secret weapon."

Rachael ran her tongue over her lips and shifted uncomfortably. A couple of months ago, caught up in the heat of anger from being jilted, hung up on the fact that her parents were divorcing, she would have jumped at Giada's offer, anxious to get her message out. But now, in the fallout from the article, with her lips still achy from Brody's kisses, she wasn't so sure.

"You're addicted to it," Giada said.

"Addicted?" Rachael asked, trying to play innocent, but she heard the stress in her own voice.

"To romance. It's why you started Romanceaholics Anonymous. Why you wrote the article."

Silently, she nodded.

"This is why it's so important to do something about it before more young girls become addicted to the fairy-tale belief of true love and happily-ever-after."

"I know," Rachael croaked.

Giada reached over and put a hand on hers. "What are you so afraid of? I'm throwing you a life preserver. Grab hold, Rachael. Hold on for dear life. Save yourself."

She thought of Brody. Of how much she wanted to romanticize their relationship. Of how badly she yearned to fall madly in love with him. Already she imagined herself moving into his house, wearing his ring, having his babies. Making the same old mistakes. Leaving her heart open for more pain and disappointment. She had to nip these feelings in the bud.

Thoughts whirling, she met Giada's eyes. "Okay," she said. "I'll do it. I'll join your campaign."

FOR DAYS RACHAEL'S article in *Texas Monthly* and speculation over the upcoming political debate between Giada and Kelvin buzzed through the Valentine grapevine like wildfire through a timber drought. The restless edginess over romance that had started the day Rachael desecrated the billboard escalated as the town took sides. Divisions split friendships and families and love relationships.

Brody's wariness grew. With everyone stirred up, something unpleasant was bound to happen. The vandal hadn't struck again—not since graffitiing Rachael's car, but Brody hadn't stopped investigating. He had the field narrowed to a handful of suspects—most of them mischievous high school boys—but he had no proof. All he could do was wait for the vandal or vandals to strike again.

And Rachael was a prime target.

He kept a close eye on her house, watching her comings and goings across the street with a pair of high-powered field binoculars. He told himself it was protective surveillance, but more than once his gaze had lingered inappropriately on the sensuous curves of her fine body and his mind would wander to that day in his backyard.

As he watched her, Brody was sorry that his family had moved away when he was twelve. That he hadn't lived next door to Rachael during her teenage years. That he hadn't been there to watch her blossom from gangly kid into gorgeous young woman. Why did he feel as if he'd missed out on so much?

The Friday before the political debate, Brody performed his new bedtime ritual. He took the binoculars from the drawer in his bedside table, pushed back the curtains, and trained his sights on Rachael's driveway. It was just after ten, and while the VW Bug sat parked in the driveway, Selina's Cadillac wasn't there.

Rachael was alone.

The realization raised the hairs on the back of his neck as he imagined her all alone in that house, maybe stepping out of the shower naked, toweling herself dry. . . .

That's when he spied a figure dressed in black ducking through the shrubbery surrounding the house.

"Sonofabitch," he said, flinging the binoculars on the bed and reaching for his pants.

Minutes later he was across the street, pulse thumping, gun drawn. A neighborhood dog barked. Crickets chirped. He could hear the gentle whirring of his Power Knee as he crouched and scanned the darkness.

He spied movement at the back of the house. Was it a tree in the breeze or something far more sinister?

And then Rachael screamed.

Chapter Thirteen

Brody's appearance at her back door was almost as startling as the face she'd seen — distorted by a stocking — peeking in her kitchen window.

She caught her breath at the sight of the sheriff. An angry frown furrowed his brow and he held a gun clutched in both hands. "What is it? What's happened?"

Stunned, she waved at the window and managed to squeak out, "Peeping Tom."

"I'll be right back," he said. "Lock the door behind me."

He disappeared as quickly as he'd come, leaving Rachael feeling shaky and unsettled. She locked the door, then sank down at the kitchen table, the glass of milk she'd come downstairs for completely forgotten.

She'd managed to drag in a couple of deep calming breaths by the time Brody tapped on the back glass. She got up to let him in. He closed and locked the kitchen door behind him and laid his gun down on the counter.

"Whoever it was got away. But there's footprints in the dirt underneath your window. I'll make an imprint. See if I can discover what kind of shoes the Peeping Tom was wearing. Was it a man?"

"I think so." His eyes met hers and Rachael realized she was trembling.

"Peaches," he said, calling her by the sweet little nick-name. "Are you all right?"

Helplessly, inexplicably, she burst into tears.

"Aw, hell, Peaches." He reached for her, pulling her into his arms.

It felt so good here in the circle of his embrace. So safe.

"Don't cry." His voice was raw and scratchy and he smelled of minty toothpaste and cotton pajamas. He was wearing his pajamas.

"You were in bed," she said.

"On my way there."

"How did you get over here so quickly? I barely had time to scream and there you were."

"I saw someone creeping around your house."

"You were watching my house?"

"I was."

"Watching over me?"

"You've stirred up a lot of trouble in town. I wanted to make sure you were all right."

"Thank you," she whispered.

Brody squeezed her tight. More tightly than he should. She felt so familiar in his arms. As if she'd always belonged there. It was a dangerous feeling but he could not shake it. Her body was so soft and warm and supple pressed against his. The scents of roses and lavender emanated from her smooth, creamy skin. Tears clung to her eyelashes and he had an irresistible urge to kiss them away.

This was what he'd been so afraid of, from the very moment he'd fetched her down off the billboard. That she would somehow worm her way into his heart. And now he was holding her as if both their lives depended on this hug and his heart was pounding so hard he feared it might explode.

At some point Brody realized he was rocking her like a child and smoothing her hair with his palm. And he had another flash of memory from their childhood. She'd gotten skates for Christmas one year and she'd fallen in her driveway and skinned her knee. He'd been out shooting hoops and had seen her fall. He'd gone over and scooped her up, holding her then much as he was holding her now. Seeking to comfort her. Make everything okay in her world.

He hadn't recalled any of this stuff in well over a decade, but now his head was flooded with memories of her: Rachael coming over to show him the blue ribbon she'd won in the second-grade spelling bee; Rachael, pigtails flying, running down the street to catch up with him as they walked home from school; Rachael, dressed as Cinderella, trick-or-treating on his front door step.

The treasure trove of memories tucked away in the far recesses of his mind amazed him. But he shouldn't have been surprised. How could he forget anything about Rachael?

With a quiet sniff, she pushed from his arms. "Sorry I wussed out on you. I don't know why I started crying."

"You've been under a lot of stress and it's damned scary to look out your window and see a face staring back in the middle of the night. And then I barged in here waving a gun around."

She smiled bravely. "You're just being kind. You don't have to keep propping me up."

"Listen," he said, "I'm right across the street. If you need anything—"

"I appreciate the offer," she interrupted, "but I can't go

around depending on you. I created this monster. I have to learn how to deal with it."

"I'm afraid things are going to get worse before they get better. Tempers are running high."

"It's all my fault," she said.

He hadn't intended to make her feel responsible for what was happening. "You might have stirred up some controversy, but you do not deserve having your car vandalized or your privacy violated. I'm going to find out who's doing this and hold them accountable."

"Do you think it could be the same person who graffitied my car?"

"Maybe. But that was several weeks ago, so maybe not."

"I have unwittingly made a lot of enemies."

"Hopefully," he said, "that'll all be settled after the election is over."

"A lot can happen between now and then."

He nodded. "I'm worried about the debate. I wish you wouldn't speak."

"I have to."

He stroked her cheek with the back of his index finger. "I know."

"Thank you for understanding." She looked at him with such admiration it stole the air right out of his lungs. The urge to make love to her was so strong that if Selina hadn't picked that moment to arive home, Brody might have done just that.

In Brody's two years as sheriff of Valentine, a need for crowd control had never arisen. Until the bond election debate.

The political rally was scheduled for noon, but by ten-thirty Main Street was already jammed with people coming out for the free hot dogs, soft drinks, and ideology the politicians were giving away. One look at the throng of people headed toward Bristo Park, where the grandstand had been constructed, and the steady stream of cars rolling in off the highway, and Brody could smell trouble in the air.

That many out-of-towners could mean only one thing. Word about the town's conflict had gotten out in a big way. And people wanted front-row seating for the fireworks.

He spied a white van wrapped with the logo of the Del Rio television station. The media were here. Not good. He pushed his Stetson down on his head and adjusted his firearm at his hip.

The crowd was moody. People carried signs and banners declaring which side of the fence they were on. ROMANCE IS A LOAD OF HOOEY versus ALL YOU NEED IS LOVE. They toted camp chairs and Igloo coolers as if they were heading for a tailgate party.

He heard grumbling in the crowd, caught snatches of conversations as people walked by.

"—trying to ruin our community."

"Giada's right, we don't have our priorities straight."

"Why don't she just go back to Italy where she came from? We don't need no foreigners telling us how to run our town."

"Unrealistic expectations about love wrecked my marriage."

"I'm telling you, the real culprit is that Rachael Henderson. Just because she can't hold on to a man she thinks everyone else has a problem with romance."

At the mention of Rachael's name, Brody's gut tensed. He whipped his head around to see who was running her down and spotted the dour-faced woman who owned the local bridal shop. She was carrying a sign that read: KEEP VALENTINE IN LOVE WITH LOVE. VOTE WENTWORTH FOR MAYOR.

Brody unclipped the two-way radio from his belt. "Zeke," he said, depressing the button on the handset as he spoke into it. "Get the crowd-control barricades over to the park ASAP."

"Um, Chief..." Zeke came back. "Do we even *have* crowd-control barriers?"

Good question. He had no idea.

"Go down to Audie's, get a dozen sawhorses and a couple of cans of Day-Glo orange spray paint. And hurry."

"How am I supposed to pay for it?"

"Tell Audie to put it on my account."

"You really think there's going to be a riot?" Zeke sounded both apprehensive and excited.

"I hope not, but I intend to be prepared. Now go."

"Will do."

By ten minutes to noon the crowd had swelled so large the park could barely contain them. The sawhorses, now spray-painted bright orange, were arranged in a circle around the grandstand.

Zeke was positioned at the entrance to the parking lot to escort Giada in when she arrived. Brody had called in his two part-time deputies to help with crowd control, but he couldn't help thinking they were seriously undermanned. If things turned unpleasant...

Think positive. This is Valentine, hometown of eternal love. How bad could it get?

A good fifty percent of the crowd booed as Zeke

escorted Giada and Rachael up the steps of the grand-stand, while the remaining fifty percent cheered, clapped, and glared at the other half.

Brody moved toward the grandstand and his eyes met Rachael's. He inclined his head toward the crowd. She smiled and winked.

At him.

Brody experienced a strange tickling sensation deep in the center of his chest and the air seemed suddenly thin. She was so damned kissable in the black silk dress she wore, thick with a pattern of red roses. With her hair tumbling down her shoulders, she looked as if she'd stepped from the pages of one of the fairy-tale stories his mother used to read to him and Deana when they were kids, stories about stalwart knights slaying dragons to rescue beautiful damsels in distress. Brody pictured himself as one of those brave knights. Scaling steep tower walls to claim a kiss. Driven by chivalry and a desire to be near such a compelling woman.

He was tempted to go up onstage and tell her to get out while the getting was good. He was worried for her safety. But another part of him was proud of her for taking a stand. She was fighting for what she believed in, even if it meant being a lightning rod for the town's anger.

Resisting the urge to go onstage, he curled his hands into fists and surveyed the crowd. Not all of the faces were friendly and his concern escalated.

A few minutes after Giada and Rachael arrived, Kelvin appeared, looking like the Fourth of July in a navy blue suit with a red-and-white-striped shirt and red and white boutonnieres in his lapel. The guy knew how to put on a show; Brody would give him that.

Kelvin received the same fifty-fifty mixed greeting Giada and Rachael had collected.

The debate began with Judge Pruitt acting as moderator. As the incumbent, Kelvin went first, grandstanding as usual. He had Purdy Maculroy set up the small-scale mock-up of Valentine Land on the table beside the stage. He invited people up to have a look. Brody cringed as the crowd pushed forward, oohing and aahing.

"Valentine Land will change lives," Kelvin waxed. "And in a big way. Today, young people leave Valentine because they don't have any opportunities for a vibrant future. Valentine Land will bring jobs to our community and stop the exodus of our youth."

"Yeah," someone in the crowd shouted. "But they'll be minimum-wage jobs."

Kelvin ignored the salvo, instead bragging about his accomplishments as mayor. Since the town hadn't changed much in fifty years, he took credit for the things his ancestors had done, especially emphasizing how the Wentworths had saved Valentine after the oil had dried up.

"Somehow, Kelvin, I don't see you as much of a knight in shining armor," another voice from the crowd catcalled. "We're not your kids and you're not our savior."

Kelvin's face darkened, but he let that comment slide as well. "I have with me Jackson Traynor from Amusement Corp. If you'll just give him a listen, I think you'll see why voting yes in the bond election will spell more money in your pockets."

While some of the citizens of Valentine felt free to razz Kelvin, they were considerate when it came to visitors and they heard Jackson Traynor out when he took the microphone and painted a prosperous picture of how Amusement Corp could put their town on the map in a big way. The man was good at his job. By the time he was done, Brody was halfway convinced Valentine Land was a good thing.

"Now," Judge Pruitt said after Jackson Traynor had finished his pitch, "it's Giada's turn for rebuttal."

Giada tossed her sleek auburn hair as she stepped up to the microphone and sent Kelvin a dirty look. The mayor grinned at her. Giada glared at him fiercely. "Mayor Wentworth and Mr. Traynor would have you believe that Valentine Land is going to put money in your pockets. Yes, maybe the theme park would generate additional tourist dollars, but at what cost?" Giada fixed the crowd with a steady gaze. "As a wise person in the audience already pointed out, most of these will be minimum-wage jobs."

"Any job is better than no job," called out a man whom Brody recognized as an unemployed regular at Leroy's.

"But a bond election is going to cost you money long before you ever see a return," Giada pointed out. "And the person who's really going to be getting rich is sitting right here." She pointed at Kelvin. "I say Mayor Wentworth is wealthy enough."

"Yeah!" shouted a small collective near the stage.

"Here's something else to consider," she continued. "Valentine Land is going to change the whole flavor of our community. The small-town atmosphere will be gone forever."

"You can't stand in the way of progress," Enid Pope yelled.

"Don't listen to my sister," Astrid Pope chimed in. "Enid's always gone for newfangled ways and look what happened to her when she got a computer. Fell for one of those Internet spam scams and lost twenty grand of our savings to some Nigerian scoundrel."

"You weren't supposed to tell anyone about that," Enid huffed at her sister.

"Yes, well, I told you to buy those cute little Rath sausages for the sauerkraut at the church potluck, but oh, no, you had to go buy those big old thick Polish kielbasas they inject with red dye. No one likes a giant red wiener in their sauerkraut."

"Speak for yourself," Enid retorted hotly. "Personally I love big red wieners. With or without sauerkraut."

Brody edged through the crowd, determined to get to the two elderly sisters before they started pushing and shoving. *It's come to this. Two old-maid sisters going at it over sausages.*

"Thank you, ladies, for your input," Giada said, "but let's get back on track. I believe if good-paying jobs are an issue for our town, there's another, less-destructive industry we can woo to Valentine."

"What's that?" someone asked.

"The goat weed that grows wild around Valentine is used in a popular herbal remedy. I've already been in talks with companies that manufacture them. We could start farming goat weed and everyone who had a chunk of land could have a piece of the pie, not just Mayor Wentworth and his Amusement Corp cronies."

That caused a ripple of conversation to run through the group.

"And," Giada added, pacing back and forth onstage, "my third objection to Valentine Land is just as important as low-paying jobs and changing the complexion of the place we love so much. Rachael Henderson has been instrumental in calling our attention to it. I'm going to let Rachael speak to you about it."

Giada handed the microphone to Rachael. Brody watched her square her shoulders and take center stage.

"As most of you know," Rachael said, "I started Romanceaholics Anonymous to counter the unrealistic romantic expectations living in this town engenders. Valentine Land will only serve to perpetuate these dangerous values and misguided beliefs."

"Oh, can it, Rachael. You're just pissy because you got left at the altar," a man at the back of the crowd shouted.

"Yeah," said a woman near the front. "It's just sour grapes on your part because you can't hold on to a man."

Rachael's face paled and she clenched her jaw.

Anger, unexpected and hot, blasted through Brody. He had an overwhelming urge to track down the hecklers and either punch them or arrest them. Or maybe both.

Whoa. What the hell was wrong with him?

Rachael.

That was what.

Rachael of the wheat-blonde hair and exotic green eyes that caused his heart to skip beats. Rachael of the fruit-flavored lips that made a man ache to sin. Rachael of the tight, compact body that stirred his flesh.

She wasn't letting the detractors affect her. She was still talking about how Valentine had impacted her life in a negative way. How she'd made repeated mistakes in love because of the screwy values the town had instilled in her. She talked about how she'd spent her life chasing rainbows and unicorns and the myth of happily-ever-after that promised all would be well if she just found that one right guy, that perfect mate.

As he listened, Brody found his muscles tensing, his mind growing restless. He hated that she'd been hurt, but what he hated even more was that she'd lost her faith in love.

Why should that bother you? You don't have faith in love.

The thought struck him from out of the blue. While he might not have faith, some small part of him secretly had hoped that he was wrong, that you could find and hold on to great love without it destroying you.

The realization was a total surprise. How long had he been holding on to hope?

And then he realized something else.

He wanted to believe. In her. In love. In happily-ever-after. How ridiculous was that?

Brody was so distracted by his thoughts that it took him a split second longer than it should have to recognize something was going on in the crowd. A ripple in the sea of bodies. A hum that told him the mood was changing. He didn't know if the change was for Rachael or against her. He just sensed something was about to happen.

Instinctively, his hand went to the gun at his hip. He did not draw it, but his gaze was beaded on the thick of the crowd. Tensed and on alert, he waited.

Just as Rachael was talking about being left at the altar by Trace Hoolihan, a man from the opposite side of the grandstand rushed the stage. He was dressed all in black and held something clutched tightly in his hand.

Was it a weapon? Not a gun. It was too big for that.

However, Brody wasn't taking any chances. Not when it came to Rachael's safety. He was on the move, headed for the podium, his pistol drawn.

The crowd gasped, parted.

"Rachael, get down!" he shouted. "Duck!"

But his warning came too late.

"DUCK!"

Rachael turned toward the sound of Brody's voice just in time to see a pie sail through the air.

It caught her full in the face.

The shock of it left her gasping—and tasting rich, chocolaty French Silk.

Her vision was gone, obscured by pudding and Cool Whip and graham cracker crust, but she heard the crowd erupt in a chaos of concerned exclamations, stunned murmurs, and nervous laughter. She reached up with the fingers of both hands, scooped globs of pie filling from her eyes and blinked, but still she could not see. She tried to take a deep breath, but pie went up her nose.

Sputtering, she shook her head. Panic gripped her. She couldn't breathe. And then she felt strong, calming arms go around her.

"It's okay, I've got you. You're safe."

Brody.

Immediately, the panic subsided.

He lifted her up, carrying her in his arms, walking down the steps of the grandstand. Barking out orders. Telling Mayor Wentworth to get back up to the microphone and end the rally. Directing Zeke to disperse the crowd. Instructing one of his other deputies to find out who'd thrown the pie.

Rachael wrapped her arms around his neck, holding on for dear life.

My hero.

No, no, that was dangerous thinking. She didn't need a hero. She was perfectly capable of saving herself.

But as she looked up at him, past the blur of French Silk clinging to her eyelashes, she couldn't deny the crazy emotions squeezing her heart. Safe, protected, cared for. But that wasn't all. She also felt nervous, giddy, surprised, curious, and underneath it all, a not-so-small dollop of fear.

She was scared, and not because someone had smacked her in the face with a pie. She was terrified, yet secretly thrilled. Where was he taking her? What was going to happen next?

Still cradling her in his arms, he marched across the town square toward the sheriff's office. And darn her, she didn't resist. Didn't tell him to put her down. Didn't even try to wriggle out of his embrace. Rachael felt rather than saw the crowd jumping aside to let him pass.

Without putting her down, Brody pushed through the door into his office. He didn't let her go until he'd deposited her in the rolling swivel chair.

"Sit," he commanded, and she didn't dare move.

He stepped into the bathroom that adjoined his office and came back with a stack of paper towels. "Are you all right? Are you hurt? Injured?"

She shook her head and a blob of pie filling fell from her chin. It hit the floor with a soft plop. Suddenly, unexpectedly, she felt like crying, but she had no idea why.

Brody knelt beside her and tenderly wiped pie goop from her eyes with the wet paper towel. It was barely discernible, but she realized his hand was shaking.

Reaching out, she grabbed onto his wrist and stared him in the eyes. "Brody, are *you* all right?"

"Hell, Rachael, I thought…" He paused, swallowed.

"Yes?"

"I thought the pie-throwing guy had a weapon. I thought…"

He didn't finish the thought. He was breathing hard and staring at her.

"It was just a pie," she said.

"But it could have easily been a weapon. You could have been killed."

She laughed. "Over my anti-romance politics?"

"It's not a laughing matter. I've seen people killed over a lot less. I've seen…"

He had been in the Twin Towers on 9/11 and lost his best friend there. He'd been a soldier in Iraq. She could not even begin to imagine what he'd seen. Her stomach knotted up. "Brody," she whispered.

"Rachael."

Their gazes fused.

She let go of his wrist.

He dropped the damp paper towels, doffed his Stetson and sailed it across the room.

They both moved at once. Her arms went around his neck. His hand slipped around her waist. Neither of them cared that pie smeared her face.

He didn't hesitate. His mouth crushed hers.

Rachael tasted chocolate and whipped cream and graham crackers and delicious, delectable Brody.

The sensible, liberated part of her that had learned the dangers of falling in love indiscriminately wanted to struggle, to resist. But the part of her that was addicted to romance, the weakness that seemed inborn in her, totally capitulated.

He moved his hands up to cradle her head in both his palms, pinning her in place while he ravaged her lips, sweet with pie.

A searing blast of heat burned through her. Blistering her tongue, her throat, her chest and beyond until she was sizzling from the inside out with the power of his kiss.

She'd been kissed a lot in her pursuit of romance. She'd had her fair share of boyfriends. But nothing, no one, compared to this.

Brody was raw and real. He was both primal and patient. An odd combination that escalated her desire. They meshed liked peaches and cream. But what was happening here was far more serious than any sweet indulgence. Uh-oh, she was getting herself in deep all over again.

I should call someone. Mom, Jillian, Delaney, Tish, Deana, Rex, someone, anyone from Romanceaholics.

But his tongue stole all rational thought.

God help her, she was lost.

She whimpered.

He groaned.

The next thing Rachael knew Brody had pulled her out of the chair, rolling her atop him as he curled his back against the floor. Pie filling was between them, on them, everywhere—sweet and sticky and glorious.

She was astride him, legs anchored on either side of his waist, the tile cool against her knees.

He pulled her down to him and planted a series of hot, openmouthed kisses from her cheeks to her chin to her jaw to the vulnerable hollow of her throat.

Heaven.

While she'd always been a romantic, had loved kissing

and holding hands and gentle cuddling, Rachael had never considered herself particularly passionate in bed. She liked sex well enough, and always tried to keep her man's needs in mind, but when it came to orgasms — well, hers were few and far between and generated mostly by battery-operated sex toys. Really, all she'd ever wanted was emotional intimacy. The physical part she could take or leave.

Until now.

Until Brody.

A couple of well-executed kisses from him and she blazed with a craving so hot it hurt. In his arms, she felt so alive. Fluid and free.

This man would never leave her at the altar. Never intentionally break her heart. She knew this about him, even though she could not say why or how. She just knew it as surely as she knew he'd willingly take a bullet for her. And her certainty pushed her headlong into perilous territory.

Greedily, she worked the buttons of his uniform shirt, frantic to get at him, desperate to expose his muscular chest, hungry to lick the salt from his bare skin.

Her breathing came hard and fast as she finally got the last button undone and recklessly stripped his shirttail from the waistband of his pants. She could feel his erection through his trousers. She grinned at his burgeoning hardness.

"Rachael." The sound of her name, wrenched from his throat in a harsh exhalation, had her muscles tensing tighter. He was as needy as she! His fingers were doing to her dress what she'd just done to his shirt.

When her blouse was open and he caught sight of the pink bra she wore underneath, he sucked in a fresh breath on a hiss of air. The sound—wholly masculine and appreciative, caused her womb to contract in response.

He reached up to thread his hands through her hair and pulled her head down to his once more. He stared into her eyes, never looking away, letting her see deep inside him.

She thought of how she must look, covered in French Silk pie, and she laughed.

He laughed, too, robust and raw.

And she started giggling and couldn't stop. She tumbled off him, landing on her fanny on the tile. Brody sat up, pushing a strand of hair back off his forehead, grinning broadly.

"This...is...this is..." She was laughing too hard to finish her thought.

"Are you laughing at me?"

For one brief second, he looked so vulnerable it hurt her heart, but just as quickly as it came, the expression vanished from his face. She shook her head. "Not...you..."

"The situation?"

She hiccuped. Nodded. She felt at once silly and giddy and profound. Everything made a weird kind of nonsensical sense. How had she gotten to this point in her life? Kissing the sheriff on the floor of his office, covered in pie, both loving it and fearing it and completely out of control?

And then, without warning, she started to cry. She had no idea why she was crying. One minute she was laughing and the next minute salty tears were streaming down her face, mingling with the sticky chocolate on her cheeks.

Alarm lit Brody's face, but then he pulled her into his lap and pressed her cheek against his chest as he wrapped her tightly in his arms. She could hear the steady strum of his heart, feel the heat of his body radiating through her.

"I...don't...know—" She broke off as a sob escaped her throat. "Why...I'm...crying."

"Shh," he whispered and pressed his lips to the top of her head. "It's too much, too soon. That's all."

She nodded against him, smearing a thin residue of chocolate over his pecs. He didn't seem to mind.

"You must think I'm an emotional mess."

"I think you've been through a lot over the last few months. Getting jilted at the altar. Finding out your parents are getting divorced. Losing your job. Incurring the wrath of fifty percent of your hometown. I'm amazed just how damn well you've held up, Rachael."

"I didn't mean to start this," she said.

"You didn't start it."

"Don't take the blame. I'm the one who started undressing you," she said.

"I kissed you first."

"I didn't stop you."

"I didn't want you to stop me."

She pulled back from his chest because she wanted to see his face. He looked down at her with the gentlest eyes she'd ever seen. How could a soldier have such gentle eyes?

"What are we going to do about this?" she wailed. "I can't get involved with you. I want to and that's the problem. I've never been without a boyfriend in my entire life, until the last couple of months. I don't trust myself. I don't trust these feelings I have for you."

"That's okay," he said. "I understand."

With the saddest look in his eyes, he took her by the shoulders and put her away from him, and then he slowly, tenderly buttoned up her dress.

Leaving Rachael more confused than ever.

*   *   *

Two days after the rally Rachael was at home working on her next article for *Texas Monthly* when Deana knocked on her door.

"I gotta talk to you," Deana said, breezing over the threshold. "I'm in trouble."

"Trouble?" Rachael blinked, her head still in the article. She forced herself to focus on Deana, who plopped down on the couch.

"Big trouble."

"Oh dear." Rachael perched on the arm of the couch beside her. "How can I help?"

"I need an intervention."

Rachael clucked her tongue. "Are you romanticizing a relationship?"

"More than that," Deana moaned. "All this time I've been going to the Romanceaholic meetings, pretending I'm clean and clearheaded, when I've been secretly sneaking around with someone."

Rachael placed a reassuring hand on Deana's shoulder. "It's okay. We all slip up," she said, thinking about Brody. "The main thing is to get back on track."

"How do I do that?"

"You're going to have to back away from this relationship. Give it some time to cool off. Then you can look at it objectively and see if there's a real future for the two of you as a couple or if what you're feeling is all hormones and daydreams."

"I'm afraid it's too late," Deana said. "He's in my blood. I'm addicted."

Rachael blew out her breath. "You've got to stop using

language like that. He's not in your blood, you're not addicted to him. Do you want to end up in another relationship like the one you left?"

Anxiously, Deana rubbed her palms together. "He's nothing like my ex-husband."

"How can you be so sure?"

"He's just not."

"Is he charming?"

Deana laughed. "Not in the least. At least not in the way I used to describe charming. He's something of a dork. He's a computer geek. But I find his dorkiness charmingly refreshing. It makes me want to take care of him, but here's the weird part: he takes care of me. Other than Brody, no man has ever looked after me. He's sweet and smart and Maisy adores him."

Rachael sighed. "You are romanticizing him."

"I know," Deana said. "But how can you tell the difference between romantic notions and real love?"

Rachael had to think about that one. Honestly, she wasn't sure she knew the answer. "Time."

"But if time is the determining factor, how come things fell apart for your parents?"

Good question. She didn't have a ready answer. "I'm not sure what happened with my parents."

"Basically, you're saying we can never be sure about love."

"Yeah," Rachael said. "I guess that is what I'm saying."

"He makes me laugh," Deana said. "And he's got the sexiest voice."

"Where did you meet him?"

Deana looked shamefaced. "At a Romanceaholics meeting."

"Deana!"

"I know." Deana groaned, tilted her head, pressed her knees together and turned her feet inward.

"You simply can't get involved with another romanceaholic. You're both playing into the same addiction. He's romanticizing you. You're romanticizing him. It's a disaster waiting to happen."

"Well," Deana said, "as long as we have the same fantasy, what's the harm?"

"You have a daughter. You have to live in the real world for her. She's your top priority."

It sounded strange hearing that advice come out of her own mouth. When had she become the voice of reason when it came to romantic relationships? Honestly, who was she to tell anyone how to run their romantic life? She'd made a mess of hers from the moment she'd started dating.

"Let's get real for a minute," Rachael said, feeling like Dr. Phil. "Tell me the negatives about this guy. Is he employed?"

"He has a very good job."

"What kind of job?"

"If I tell you, you'll figure out who he is."

"That's a red flag statement. Why don't you want me to know who he is?"

Deana blew out her breath. "I'm afraid you'll think he's too young for me."

"How much younger is he?"

Deana gritted her teeth, then admitted, "Eight years."

Computer geek. Smart. Dorky. Sweet. Romanceaholic. Eight years younger than Deana. Rachael put it all together. "Omigosh, you're seeing Rex Brownleigh."

Chapter Fourteen

Brody was having a crappy week. Ever since the rally, Valentine had become even more divided, with the romantics on one side of the fence and the cynics on the other, arguing the pros and cons of Valentine Land, and Kelvin Wentworth versus Giada Vito.

Brody and Zeke had been called out to break up more than one liquor-soaked debate at Leroy's that had deteriorated into fisticuffs over the difference between sex, romance, and true love. A local B&B on the banks of Valentine Lake, renowned throughout the state for its romantic getaway packages, had all ten of their bicycles-built-for-two vandalized. Someone had cut them completely in half.

With a pipe cutter.

This was the last straw for Brody. He was determined to catch the vandal before the election. For weeks he'd been trying to figure out who was behind these acts with no luck. It was time to set a trap. What he needed was something tempting the vandal couldn't resist vandalizing. But what?

At the request of its listeners, Valentine's radio station KVAL—which had once played only upbeat romantic tunes—had taken to giving equal airtime to anti-love songs like "Love Stinks," "Heartbreak Hotel," and "Fifty Ways to Leave Your Lover."

But the greatest cause for concern was the number of couples who'd filed for separation or divorce. At just fifteen percent, the divorce rate in Valentine had been far below the national average. This past week, the rate had jumped to forty-five percent.

Added to the chaos were his chairman duties on the Fish-A-Thon for Love committee. The fishing tournament was a charity event held the last Saturday in October. The money raised from entry fees went to supply the coffers of the local food bank and to buy Christmas gifts and clothing for the needy children of Jeff Davis County. For years, Judge Pruitt had hosted the event Kelvin's father had created. All the town's prominent citizens and business leaders were expected to attend.

At least the tournament was a way to bring the town together for a day at an event that had nothing to do with romance.

Brody hadn't spoken to Rachael since that day in his office. Mainly because he knew if he got around her he was going to have to touch her and he wasn't real sure how to deal with that. The Friday afternoon before Saturday's fishing tournament, he walked into Higgy's Diner for a late lunch. The blue plate special was chicken and dumplings.

The restaurant was practically empty, save for a couple of the waitresses taking their lunch break. At the table in the corner a foursome of old-timers played dominoes. The hearty smell of roasted chicken and yeast bread filled the air.

And there, underneath the *Dirty Dancing* poster, sat the woman he'd been fantasizing about.

Rachael's laptop was open on the pink Formica tabletop and she had an empty bowl of what had once held chicken and dumplings sitting off to one side. She was busily tapping away at her keyboard with her back to him. Her hair was pulled back in a ponytail and she wasn't wearing any makeup, other than a shine of peach-colored lip gloss. He thought she was the most gorgeous thing he had ever seen.

Brody plunked down across from her. "You've caused me a lot of trouble this week," he said.

"How so?"

It wasn't his imagination. She was as excited to see him as he was to see her. The sparkle in her green eyes was a dead giveaway. She had on a pumpkin-colored turtleneck sweater that hugged her curves in all the right places.

"Half the town wants to canonize you, the other half wants to lynch you."

"So I see your week has been going pretty much like mine," she said. She reached up a hand to pull the elastic band holding her hair back. A cascade of long blonde curls fell to her shoulders. She tousled the silky strands in a casual gesture.

"I'm worried about your safety."

"I'm okay."

Brody nodded at the laptop. "You working on another inflammatory article?"

"I guess it all depends on your point of view."

"What can I get for you, Brody?" asked April Tritt, who'd strolled over to the table, smoothing out the creases in her apron. She batted her eyelashes at him and leaned over to give him a good view of her ample cleavage.

"I'll have what she had." He inclined his head toward Rachael's bowl.

"Chicken and dumplings, gotcha. Black coffee?"

"That'll be fine."

April sauntered off and he turned his attention back to Rachael only to find her closing the lid on her laptop and winding up the cord on the power pack. "You leaving already?"

"Yep."

"You're going to make me eat alone?" he protested.

"You've got plenty of company." Rachael indicated April, ogling him from across the room.

"Jealous?"

"No." She made a derisive noise that told him she was jealous indeed.

"Stay here and make April jealous of you," he said.

She got to her feet, stowed her laptop in her computer bag. A long curl of hair fell softly against her breast. "Sorry, Sheriff. You're just going to have to entertain yourself."

"Why're you running out on me, Rachael? Afraid of what will happen if you stay and chat?" He certainly was, and he had no idea why he was taunting her. Maybe to ease his own anxiety.

"Nothing's going to happen between us."

"How do you know?"

"Because I'm not going to let it," she said, steely determination in her voice.

"Did something else happen?" His body tensed. If someone had done anything to her, he'd murder them.

"No . . . no, nothing like that." Concern knit her brow.

"But something happened."

She shrugged. "Let's just say I've had to do a lot of hard thinking about my mission."

Me, too.

"The whole love-versus-romance thing?"

"I realize I've been a poor example. Those kisses we

shared..." She swallowed. He could see the longing on her face because he felt a corresponding longing deep inside him. "Let's just say I have to keep myself on a tighter leash. If I can't control my urges, how can I expect my Romanceaholics Anonymous members to control theirs?"

"You do realize you just issued me a challenge."

"I didn't."

"You did."

They stared at each other.

"Brody Carlton, I swear, if you try to kiss me again, I'll—" She broke off the sentiment.

"You'll what?" he dared.

"I'll...I'll move away from Valentine," she said, and with that, turned and flounced out the door.

Brody's chicken and dumplings arrived but he couldn't eat. His hunger for food had been replaced by a different kind of hunger: He had to have her and that's all there was to it. He'd told himself he wouldn't ever get involved in a grand love affair because great love destroyed lives, but he knew down deep in his soul she was the love of his life. And he had to convince her that she could have her happily-ever-after. The first step was to get her into his bed. He'd worry about the happily-ever-after part later.

It was time to take action.

Determinedly, he took out his cell phone and put a call in to Judge Pruitt.

"Hello, Brody," Abigail Pruitt said when her secretary had routed him through to her. "Is everything in order for the tournament tomorrow?"

"It is."

"I heard there's been a lot of trouble lately over this anti-romance nonsense stirred up by Rachael Henderson."

"Rachael's entitled to her opinion."

"True, true." The judge must have realized she was rubbing him the wrong way because she injected a soothing lilt into her voice. "But she's misguided. Getting dumped at the altar, along with the situation with her parents, has unfavorably changed her views."

"I think it's other people's reactions to her opinion that's the issue here."

"We can't have any problems. This charity is important. Not only to me, but to the underprivileged children of Jeff Davis County. And it's not just the tournament that concerns me. I'm tired of seeing my hometown divided into two opposing camps."

"My thoughts exactly," he said. "That is in fact the reason I'm calling."

"I'm listening."

"Although you and I might not see eye-to-eye on this matter, I think we both want what's best for the town."

"Agreed."

"I want to mend the rift."

"How?"

"By making the key players in this rift kiss and make up," Brody said.

"Excuse me?"

"I have a plan, Judge, but I need your help."

SELINA DIDN'T WANT to go to the fishing tournament. As Michael's wife, she'd been obligated to attend the event for the past twenty-seven years. Now that she was free, she'd planned on spending the last Saturday in October curled up in bed reading the latest Karen Rose thriller.

But Giada had ruined all that by insisting all the teachers enroll in the tournament.

So here she was standing around the marina with the rest of the town, wearing layered flannel shirts, wool pants, wading boots, and a water-resistant peacoat. The air smelled of fish, fog, and wood smoke. She thought of the warm, cozy bed she'd left, sighed, and looked over at her daughter.

Rachael was busy scribbling in a composition book, jotting down notes on the tournament for her next *Texas Monthly* article. She looked serious, dedicated. Selina had to admit writing the column had done her a world of good.

Pride lumped in her chest. Her daughter had gone from a starry-eyed romantic who always had to have a man in her life to a clear-sighted, strong, independent woman who was making her own way in the world. Selina wished she'd had such bravery at Rachael's age. If she had, maybe she could have confronted Michael before it was too late.

Michael.

Involuntarily, she swung her gaze through the crowd, searching for him, and found him clustered with his cronies at the end of the dock, surveying the row of fishing boats.

Michael must have sensed her stare, because he glanced up. In that moment he looked as handsome as on their wedding day, a dimpled grin carved into his right cheek, his dark eyes sparkling, his hair ruffled by the breeze.

Selina's heart squeezed and her pulse galloped. No matter what had happened between them, the mere sight of him still weakened her knees. Stupid, foolish, yes, but how did you stop yourself from loving someone?

He caught her gaze and his smile disappeared.

Quickly, she ducked her head, studied the tips of her bright yellow wading boots.

"Mom?" Rachael said. "Are you okay?"

She met her daughter's eyes, forced a smile. "Fine. I just wish they'd get this show on the road."

"They should be drawing the names any minute." Rachael pointed to the redwood gazebo positioned at the head of the dock where the scales were located, alongside a microphone stand and a large circular lottery cage on a spindle filled with numbered ping-pong balls. It was the same equipment St. Jerome's Church used to call bingo every Friday night. "Here comes Judge Pruitt."

Selina noticed her daughter didn't comment on the fact Brody Carlton was escorting the judge to the gazebo. To be perfectly honest, it looked as if Rachael was struggling hard to avoid catching his eye. Just as Selina was avoiding Michael's.

Was her daughter falling for the sheriff?

Before Selina had time to consider this further, Judge Pruitt stepped up to the microphone. Posted on the wall behind her was a grease board grafted with the names of the contestants. After a microphone check, she began her welcome speech. She talked about the importance of the charity and then explained the rules. It was hardly necessary. Each year it was the same collection of faces who showed up.

The fishing boats went out in teams and the teams were selected by lottery—hence the caged ping-pong balls. You had no say in the matching process. You were stuck with whomever the lottery dealt.

The team who bagged the most fish during the course of the day won a trophy, Angler of the Year bragging rights, and the honor of being the largest contributor to the local food bank's freezers for the coming year. Michael was the reigning champion, having won it the last five years in a row. Her husband would probably win it this year as well.

Correction. Her soon-to-be ex-husband.

She felt suddenly hollow inside. The divorce papers had arrived in the mail last week and they were still sitting unsigned on Selina's bedroom dresser. All she had to do was write her name down and mail the papers back to the court and it would all be over.

Twenty-seven years down the drain. Kaput.

But she hadn't been able to bring herself to sign them.

Helplessly, she looked back toward Michael as Judge Pruitt picked a ping-pong ball from the hopper. "Michael Henderson," she called out.

"Yo!" Michael raised his hand.

"You're in boat #1 and your teammate will be…" Brody spun the cage. When it came to a stop Judge Pruitt stuck her hand in and came up with another ball. "Contestant #13." The judge turned to look at the board behind her. "That would be your wife, Selina."

"WHAT ARE THE ODDS?" Kelvin asked, whacking Michael on the back. "Getting teamed up in the tournament with your ex-wife."

"We're not divorced," Michael murmured. "Not yet."

"You could try asking Judge Pruitt for another teammate," Kelvin suggested.

"I don't want another teammate. She's the only teammate I've ever wanted."

Kelvin studied Michael. "You're still in love with her."

"I am."

"After all she's put you through?"

Michael nodded. "Especially after all she's put me through."

That made no sense to Kelvin. "I don't get it."

Michael made an odd noise. "Maybe someday, if you're lucky, you'll understand what real love is all about."

"If your love is so damned real," Kelvin said, feeling irritated, "how come you're getting a divorce?"

"Because I've been a blind, ignorant ass. Now if you'll excuse me, here comes my teammate." Michael turned away and headed for Selina, who was coming down the dock toward him.

Kelvin stood watching them, feeling half-jealous, half-smug that he'd never fallen in love.

"Kelvin Wentworth," Judge Pruitt's microphoned voice rang out across the water.

"Yes?"

"You're in boat #2."

He nodded.

The lottery cage spun, spit out another ping-pong ball. "And your partner is contestant #32."

Cupping his hands around his mouth to carry over the buzzing crowd, he called out, "Who's that?"

The judge looked at the board. "Contestant #32 is Giada Vito."

The minute Kelvin heard the woman's name, a spike of anger hammered straight through his temple. He'd rather eat arsenic with a smile than be stuck in a fishing boat with that woman.

"Oh, hell, no," he said, pushing his way through the crowd on the dock, headed for the gazebo. He thundered up to Judge Pruitt. "Get me another teammate. I refuse to fish with that woman."

Unflinchingly, Judge Pruitt pulled herself up to her full five-foot-three-inch height and met his scowl with a judicial icy glare. "I'm running the show, Kelvin. Either accept your teammate and deal with it, or forfeit your entry fee and withdraw from the tournament."

Kelvin fisted his hands. He'd seen that stubborn expression on the judge's face before and he'd never won against it. The notion of just walking away was tempting.

But something kept him from storming off. He didn't know if it was the realization that if he left, Judge Pruitt would win, or if it was Giada, standing off to the side, arms crossed over her chest, with a look on her face that said she was enjoying his misery.

"What's the matter?" Giada taunted. "Chicken?"

"To be with you?" Kelvin snorted, trying to deny the sweat popping out along his shoulders in spite of the chilly morning breeze floating in off the water.

"After all, we're going to be out on the water all day. All alone in that tiny little boat," she goaded.

He knew what she was up to. Vito wanted him to quit and storm off so she could look like the bigger person, but he wasn't about to give her the satisfaction. He might be stuck with her, but she was equally stuck with him and he was determined to make her miserable.

"Fine with me," he said, taking some small measure of pleasure at the startled expression dipping her eyebrows inward. "Get your gear and let's go."

ONE BY ONE, couple by couple, Judge Pruitt executed Brody's scheme. She'd rigged the event, pairing cynics with romantics, forcing ex-lovers together, and teaming up business rivals. Each time the names were drawn, matched emotions ripped through the air—anger, disappointment, frustration, surprise, concern, and hope—until the docks were thick with tension.

"We'll be lucky if someone doesn't end up getting killed by the end of the day," Judge Pruitt muttered to Brody.

"You've gotta trust me on this," he said sagely. "I know what I'm doing."

Judge Pruitt looked at him with new respect. "Why, Brody Carlton," she said. "I think you're finally starting to believe in the magic of true love."

Brody's eyes found Rachael in the crowd. Maybe he was.

On and on she went, pulling names until all the slots were gone, all the ping-pong balls drawn, all the participants off in their boats, except for two—Brody and his teammate.

Rachael. The lone remaining contestant left standing on the dock.

He took one look at her standing there in her wading boots and blue jeans and his gut turned to mush. Judge Pruitt had turned the table on him. "You did this on purpose," he accused.

"But of course. You think I'm blind just because I'm pushing sixty." She winked. "I saved the best for last. Now go fishing. Everyone else has a head start on you."

"Judge . . ."

"Brody . . ." She leveled a stern glance at him.

"This isn't going to work."

"She needs you, and you need her."

"Clumsy attempt at matchmaking."

"Okay, look at it this way. The town needs you to tone her down. Show Rachael that what she knows in her heart is the truth, no matter how much she's been hurt."

"And what is that truth?"

The judge handed him a bucket of minnows. "Get out on that water and find out."

He went because he wanted to be with Rachael. He took the bucket and walked toward her. She waited, her smile growing brighter the closer he got.

"Looks like it's me and you, Peaches," he said, stopping a few feet from her. "Is that a problem?"

"Not for me," she murmured. "You?"

He shrugged, suddenly feeling like he was in fifth grade at his first coed party, his mother nudging, prompting him to ask a girl out onto the dance floor. His heart was thumping and his fingers felt strangely numb curled around the minnow bucket as he led Rachael toward the last remaining boat tied to the pier.

Brody climbed in first, set down the minnow bucket, then turned and offered his hand to help her into the boat.

She placed her palm in his.

And he felt Abigail Pruitt's Valentine magic.

It wrapped around his heart soft and sweet as Rachael's smile. Wrapped and twined and twisted until he was knotted up with it. Knotted up with her. The scent of her perfume curled in his nose. The feel of her skin against his ignited a fire deep inside him. The sight of her hair falling from the loose ponytail at the back of her neck had him itching to plunge his fingers through the silky strands.

He shook his head, trying to gain some measure of control over his senses. She sat down in the front of the boat with graceful movements. He focused his attention on starting the outboard motor and guiding the dinghy toward open waters.

Neither of them spoke. They passed several of the other fishing boats bobbing on the water. Brody was encouraged to see most people appeared to be getting along, casting lines in the water, pulling up bass and perch, crappie and catfish.

But his mind wasn't on his constituents or fishing. Only one thing held his interest and that was the woman beside him.

Rachael had her back to him, and she was gazing out over the water as he zipped along, headed for his secret fishing spot. Anxious to anchor so he could tell her all the things he'd wanted to tell her for the past month.

At last they arrived in the narrow slough hidden from the main branch of the lake by a copse of oak trees and surrounded by cattails and water lilies. He cut the engine and let the boat drift for a bit before he dropped anchor.

"You want this?" he asked, bending to pick up a rod and reel. "Or do you prefer a cane pole?"

He raised his head, saw she'd turned around and was now facing him. "I'd prefer it," she said saucily, "if you kissed me."

"What?" he asked, unsure if he'd heard her correctly.

She repeated herself.

He needed no more encouragement and he wasn't asking any questions. He dropped the fishing pole and reached for her.

She was in his arms before he could even kick the minnow bucket aside.

Needfully, he trailed his fingertips over the nape of her neck and leaned to kiss the throbbing pulse at the hollow of her throat. Her silky skin softened beneath his mouth and a tight little moan escaped her lips.

His hand crept from her neck and down the hollow of her throat to her breast, heaving with each inhalation of air—a simple but lingering touch that escalated the intimacy between them and felt extremely erotic.

The air smelled rich and earthy. The boat rocked on the water. Time hung suspended, their mouths fused in an endless forever. Brody did not completely understand the spell Rachael had woven over him. He could think of nothing but melding with her.

She wriggled in his lap, her fanny grinding against his thighs. Her quick intake of breath, low and excited in the vast openness of sky and water, detonated his own need, volleying him higher and higher.

She nibbled his chin. The rasp of her teeth against his beard stubble rocketed a searing blast through his nerve endings and he groaned. What a woman!

Brody's lips found hers again and as they kissed, he raised a hand to touch her breast.

Her nipple poked against the material of both her silky lace bra and her flannel top.

His thumb brushed against her hard little button and she responding by wrapping her legs around his and sliding her bottom against his upper thigh. When he bent his head to gently suckle at her nipple through the material of her clothes, she gasped and clutched his head to her.

No, no, it wasn't good enough. He had to touch her bare skin or go mad.

Sliding his hand up underneath her shirt, he unhooked her bra from behind and set her breasts free. She moved against him, mewling softly.

Any hesitation she might have been feeling was gone, replaced by a stark hunger that shoved his libido into overdrive. No way could he resist the mounting pleasure, nor the sweet little sound slipping past her lips.

"We've got to stop," he gasped, wrenching his mouth from hers. "Or we won't catch a single fish."

"Who cares," she panted.

"We can't show up empty-handed," he said. "This is for charity."

"Then Judge Pruitt shouldn't have paired us together."

"How do you know she paired us up on purpose?"

"For heaven's sake, Brody, I might be a blonde, but I'm not dumb. Statistically it would be extremely rare for Giada to end up paired with Kelvin and my mom paired with my dad at the same time you and I got put together. She's playing matchmaker."

"Actually," he said, "she was shooting for peacemaker. The theory was that if everyone who'd been feuding ended up in a small confined space for several hours, they'd work things out."

"Or kill each other."

He shrugged. "We considered that possibility. Judge Abigail felt like love would win out."

"So you were in on this all along?" She pushed her hair from her forehead and shot him an assessing gaze.

He just smiled.

"That's collusion."

"I knew about the others, but I didn't know she was going to pair us together."

"Um," Rachael said, wriggling away from him. Suddenly his lap felt very empty without her in it. "You can tell your buddy the judge I'm not dropping my anti-romance campaign just because she paired me with a pretty face. Seriously, does she think I'm that easy? Throw romance at Rachael and she'll cave?"

He feigned shock. "That's all I am? A pretty face?"

Grinning, she raked her gaze over him and said slyly, "Well, there is the hot body."

"I'm just a sex object to you." He shook his head and pretended to pout. He was teasing, but the joke didn't feel so funny. The idea that she wanted him strictly for sex bothered Brody more than he was willing to let on.

"All that kissing made me thirsty," she said. "You want some water?"

"Yeah," he said, his gaze tracking her body as she leaned over to open the Igloo cooler.

Her shirt rode up in the process, giving him a tantalizing glimpse of her bare waist. Straightening, she handed him a water bottle and twisted the lid off one of her own.

"As I was saying," she continued after taking a long swallow of water. Brody couldn't help watching. God, she even swallowed sexily. "I've been giving it a lot of thought. I'm ready to learn how to separate sex from love and I want you to teach me how to do it."

He stared at her. "What?"

"You. Me. Sex. No strings."

Brody was not prepared for the invisible blow that suddenly slammed in the general region of his heart. He'd never felt a pain quite like this one, because he'd always been able to detach from his feelings when the situation called for it.

But not now, not with Rachael.

It was as if the regulator valve on his emotions had broken off at the hilt and his feelings were spewing out full throttle.

"You game for a good time?" She slanted him a sexy glance with those exotic green eyes of hers.

His gut torqued tight. *Say yes,* prodded his penis.

He lowered his eyelids, crossed his arms over his chest, and leaned back in the boat. He sent her a pensive stare while his mind scrambled around trying to find just the right thing to say. "Keep talking," he said. "I'm listening."

"You're considering it?"

"Peaches," he rasped, "what man wouldn't consider taking you to bed?"

Her cheeks pinked at his comment and she looked flustered. "If we're going to have a fling, there's got to be ground rules."

"Such as?"

"No compliments."

"Come on, no compliments?"

"Compliments are romantic. I don't do romance. Never forget that." Rachael shook a finger at him.

He made a face, but agreed. "Okay, no compliments."

"And no pet names. You can't call me Peaches."

"But I like calling you Peaches," he protested. "You're so sweet and juicy and..."

"Uh-uh." She held up a hand, shook her head. "That's a compliment. It's not going to fly."

"You're tying me up here."

Her eyes sparkled impishly. "Now that's sexual. That's allowed."

"Oh?" He grinned. "Is this your way of hinting that you're into bondage games?"

"Don't know," she said. "I've never given it a whirl, but I gotta tell you when I see the outline of those handcuffs in your back pocket I heat up inside."

He was heating up just hearing her talk about it. He'd never given it a whirl, either, but it sounded like fun. Anything with her sounded like fun. Even if they kept their clothes on.

"Good to know," he said. "Too bad I'm off duty and my handcuffs are sitting on my bedside table at home."

"If you had them, you wouldn't actually use them on me out here." Her eyes widened. "Would you?"

The game they were playing was making him sweat. "I might," he said, keeping his tone low, suggestive.

"On the water?" She sounded breathless, her voice high and tight. "In a semipublic place?"

His grin widened and he held her gaze. He saw the shiver of excitement shimmy over her body, felt a corresponding shiver run down his own. Slowly, he nodded.

"But..." she said. "You're sworn to uphold the law."

"Law enforcement officers can have a bad boy side, too," he said.

"How bad?" she asked, flicking out her little pink tongue to run it along her full bottom lip.

The look he gave her was all about sex, not a hint of romance in it. "I could show you right now."

She leaned closer. "Yeah?"

"Yeah."

"Brody," she said in a husky voice that turned him inside out.

Not only could cops be bad boys, but they could also be very, very stupid. What he did next was on par with the antics shown on *America's Dumbest Criminals*. He wanted her and not just for sex. He had to have all of her—body, soul, heart, the lot. Because somehow, in some way that he couldn't fully articulate or even understand, she'd become his deliverance.

She was in his arms again and he was kissing her as if the world were about to end. His fingers were at the zipper of her pants and her hands were threading through his hair as he pushed her back onto the floor of the boat.

The minnow bucket was in the way. Blindly, he grabbed the thing and slung it overboard. He didn't care about anything except having her.

Oh yeah, he thought as her zipper sprang open to reveal the swatch of scarlet thong panties hiding underneath.

Helter-skelter, he pressed his lips to her bare skin — her belly, her hand, the inside of her thigh, stripping the pants down over her hips in a frantic free-for-all.

She helped him, kicking the material free until she was naked from the waist down except for her panties, and the boat was bucking crazily on the waves.

"I want you," she said. "Now."

Brody rocked back on his heels. He wanted her, too, but not like this. His daydreams had centered on his bedroom, where she had once spent the night. He'd pictured long, leisurely lovemaking sessions, with music on the stereo and a great meal in their bellies.

But that was a fantasy and this was reality, and he knew the only way he was going to get to her was through sex. Because of her disillusionment with love and romance their relationship would have to go ass backward. He had to make love to her first, charm her later.

He could do that.

Right?

He thought of his leg and his self-confidence vanished.

He remembered why he daydreamed of making love to her in his bed. Why his fantasies hadn't been more creative. In his bed, in his house, he could be in control. Of the lighting, of how he positioned himself, of how he'd camouflage his damaged leg.

Out here, in the open, in a dinghy, in the harsh light of day, he had no control.

But looking down at her, seeing the desire for him reflected in her eyes, he decided that control was decidedly overrated and impossible to achieve anyway.

Go with the flow.

She made a soft noise of encouragement, egging him on, pleading with her eyes.

Forget about your damned leg. Think only of pleasing her.

His trembling fingers tugged at the thin scrap of dark red lace, but his eyes were on hers, deeply searching her face.

"Kiss me," she whispered.

He did. Capturing her mouth, spearing his tongue past her parted lips.

Her breathing grew choppy, urgent, and she fisted her fingers into his chest, balling the material of his shirt in her palms, pulled him down flush against her.

The boat bobbed violently.

Rolling on the water, eyes closed as he kissed her, gave Brody the sensation of falling.

Falling, hell. He'd already fallen and there was nothing he could do about it except find a way to convince Rachael this thing between them was worth taking a chance on.

God, he needed her in the worst way.

He braced his upper body, his forearms pressed on

either side of her, holding up his own weight as he stared down at her. He could feel her bare legs against the material of his jeans. The hard metal of his bionic prosthesis rested between her knees.

That realization unnerved him and he moved his leg, repositioning himself. Dragging his mouth from her lips, scooting down, pushing up her shirt as he went, planting kisses down her soft abdomen until he reached those panties barely covering the curl of beautiful blonde hair at the apex of her lush thighs.

When he slid his calloused fingers under her lacy panties, she hissed in an edgy breath.

"Spread your legs," he murmured and she obeyed, sweetly parting her tender flesh for him.

He slid her panties down her thighs. She shuddered when he trailed his fingers over her silky curves and his breathing went perfectly still. "Ah, you're so wet…" He almost called her Peaches, but he bit back the word.

"You're the cause," she said in a strangled voice. "It's all your fault."

"I'll gladly take that blame."

"I want you, Brody."

He raised his head and met her eyes. "But just for sex."

"Yes."

That's what you think.

He bent his head, kissed her down there, where she was wet and soft and smelled so womanly. His fingers played with her slippery heat. She moaned softly and arched her pelvis against his mouth, showing him her rhythm.

But somehow, miraculously, he already knew it. It was as if he'd always known her and what she needed—how hard, how soft, when to use a light touch, when to be firm.

Her hungry, gasping cries grew noisier as Brody wound her body tighter and tighter until she was begging for release.

Except he wasn't letting her off the hook that easily. He kept teasing her, increasing the pressure and pace but each time she was on the verge of coming, he'd back off, let the lull pull her back down. Up and down he went, his mouth learning the landscape of her most intimate terrain.

Finally, she splayed a palm against the back of his head, holding him in place, making him finish what he had started. Brody made a noise of approval low in his throat and in response, she fisted her fingers in his hair.

He licked and suckled, cajoled and kissed. And then all at once, she burst apart.

He felt the tremor roll through her as she exploded for him, over him, because of him.

Her breathing slowed and she lay limp on the bottom of the boat. He was slow to move his mouth from her and slower still to wipe away her moistness with his palm. The glorious taste of her stayed on his tongue. He felt more whole than he'd felt before he'd gone to Iraq.

She'd brought him back to himself again. To the man he'd once been.

A hard man, still horny for her. But his release could wait. They had time. This moment had been all about her. Gently he redressed her as she looked at him through sated, dozy eyes. He pulled up the scarlet panties, worked her legs into her wool pants. He smelled her in his nose, on his skin, all over—the imprint of her indelible.

Chapter Fifteen

While Brody and Rachael were blissfully drifting with the current, Giada and Kelvin were out in the big middle of the lake, surrounded by fishermen. Kelvin was still pissed off about being paired with her. He had a sneaking suspicion Brody and Judge Pruitt had rigged the drawing simply to get under his skin.

If they were trying to rattle his cage, he had to admit their scheme had the desired effect. No one could irritate him faster or more completely than his fishing partner.

Judge Pruitt and the sheriff, he decided, could just look somewhere else for campaign donations the next time they came up for reelection.

Kelvin looked over at Giada. She looked so self-assured sitting there on her little folding camp chair in her tight jeans and snug red sweater, with that smug canary-swallowing grin on her feline face — because she did look like a cat with her mysterious watchful eyes and her lithe, controlled movements. And like a cat, it was impossible to knock her off balance. She landed on her feet every time.

She was facing away from him, knees crossed, swinging one leg as rhythmically as a calico swishing her tail. She held the rod and reel loosely in her hands — casual, relaxed, a woman who had the world by the balls.

Who was he kidding? She had *him* by the balls.

Kelvin wished a big fish would swim along, take the bait, and snatch the pole right out of her hands.

"We could be friends, you know," she said, completely out of the blue.

"Huh?"

"There's no reason we have to be enemies."

"The fact you're gunning for my job is reason enough for me." He didn't like talking to the back of her head.

"Don't pout."

"I'm not pouting."

"Yes? So why's your bottom lip protruding?"

Kelvin sucked his bottom lip up against his teeth. She was looking out over the bow of the boat. He was behind her. How the hell could she tell he'd had his lip poked out?

Giada pulled back lightly on the pole and turned the reel half a turn, softly murmuring something in Italian. The seductive sound of her native tongue spoken on the crisp late-autumn air sent a spike of hot desire straight through his gut.

She uncrossed her legs and leaned forward on her camp chair, closely watching the ripples on the water. "That's it, my sweet, take the bait."

"You gotta nibble?"

"Shhtt." She held up a hand, silencing him.

Her abrupt gesture irritated him. Everything about the woman irritated him, while at the very same time she turned him on in a way he'd never been turned on before.

He hated it. He loved it. Confused by his feelings, he plowed a palm down the length of his face.

"Gotcha," she whispered in urgent victory, setting the hook and tugging back on her pole as she dialed in the line on the reel.

Eyes narrowed, Kelvin watched her haul in what had to be a fifteen-pound catfish. He snorted.

She tossed him a saucy look over her shoulder. "Jealous?"

He scowled.

"You know," she said, expertly taking the catfish off the hook and slipping it onto a stringer, "you can sit there and be miserable, feeling sorry for yourself all day, or decide to get over your foul mood and make a competition of this."

That piqued his interest. Kelvin was nothing if not competitive. "A competition?"

"Whoever catches the most fish today cooks dinner for the other," she said, and the lilting sound of her voice raised hairs on his forearms.

"I have an even better idea."

"Yes?" She swung around to meet his gaze.

"If I catch more fish, you drop out of the election."

Giada's hearty laughter carried across the water. "I don't give up that easy."

"Stubborn woman."

"Pigheaded man," she tossed back.

He studied her for a long moment. "How about this. If I catch more fish than you, you'll give me a chance to prove to you that Valentine Land would be good for this town."

Giada paused, considering his proposal. "I suppose that wouldn't hurt. I am open-minded."

"Fair enough."

"And what do I get?" she asked, eyebrows cocked on her forehead. "If I win."

"That, Ms. Vito," Kelvin said with the confidence of a man who'd never lost a competition in his life, "ain't gonna happen."

"Don't be so sure of that," Giada said, and held up the stringer with the flopping catfish. "I've already got a leg up."

ON THE OPPOSITE end of Lake Valentine, at the very apex of the heart, things were shaky for Selina and Michael.

Selina had told herself she would be the bigger person. That she could get through this day and come out on the other side exorcised from the ghost of her marriage. *Face your fears and all that jazz*, she told herself.

But that's not what happened.

She sat rigid, arms crossed over her chest, looking in the opposite direction as Michael guided the boat through the water. At this point, she was seriously regretting not kicking up more of a fuss on the dock, even getting into the boat with him. What had she been thinking?

Honestly, she'd been thinking this was her very last chance to work things out, to save her marriage. It seemed a foolish notion now. Michael hadn't even looked at her since they'd cast off.

He found a secluded spot near the shore, cut the engine, and dropped anchor. Without a word, he went about baiting the hooks of both fishing poles.

"You don't have to do that," she said. "I can take care of my own pole."

Michael raised his head to look at her. His face was cool, expressionless. "I never said you couldn't."

"You've always treated me as if I were helpless."

"Huh?" Now he looked genuinely confused.

"You never let me run my own household," she said. "You hired nannies and housekeepers and gardeners."

"Most women would appreciate those things."

"I know how to perform manual labor, Michael."

"I know you do."

"I'm not some hothouse orchid."

He shook his head. "Am I thick as a brick or is this some woman thing that I'm not getting?"

Her cheeks burned as hot as if he'd boxed them. "It's not a woman thing. It's a human being, self-worth thing," she snapped. "And yes, sometimes you're as thick as marble."

"What did I do?" he cried. "Just tell me what I did!"

"The fact that you don't know," she said, "is indictment enough."

"Selina." He put out a hand to touch her, but she drew back, raised her arms defensively.

"Don't," she said. "Just don't."

She turned her head, peered down at the water.

"Are you crying?"

"No." She sniffled.

"Honey," he whispered. "Are you all right?"

She raised her head, drilled him with her eyes. "Fine, I'm perfectly fine."

"You don't look fine."

"Well, I am."

She jerked her gaze away again, busied herself with casting her fishing pole.

"You're driving me crazy." He shoved a hand through his hair. "If you hate me so much, why don't you just sign the damn divorce papers and be done with it?"

"Is that what you really want?" she asked quietly.

"No, it's not. It was never what I wanted!" he shouted, the temple at his vein throbbing.

"Then why did you have an affair with Vivian?"

"How many times do I have to tell you? We didn't have

an affair. Okay, I admit, I flirted with her through e-mail. Big deal. It was harmless. It meant nothing until you made something out of it."

His words stabbed her heart. The man truly did not get it. "I wasn't talking about now," she said quietly.

He blinked at her. The anger came out of him in one loud whoosh of air like an inflated balloon let go without being tied off. "Selina . . . it wasn't what you think."

"Please," she said, raising her palms to ward off his excuses. "Don't insult my intelligence by lying to me again. For once, stop denying the truth. Once and for all, come clean so I can forgive you."

Their eyes met and what she saw reflected there both surprised and puzzled her. Michael looked as if he was hurting more than she was. "Okay," he said and gulped. "You want to hear me say it?"

"I've been waiting twenty-seven years."

"You sure?"

"I already know the truth. You reeked of her perfume when you came stumbling in from your bachelor party that night."

His face contorted with pain and shame. "Okay, yes, yes. I had sex with Vivian on the night before our wedding."

The words fell like bricks, hard and rough. They echoed off the water, sending ripples of sorrow throughout Selina's body, even though she'd braced herself to hear them.

"Say it again," she said, keeping her face as emotionless as she could.

"Sel . . ." His eyes begged her forgiveness.

"Say it again."

"I had sex with Vivian on the night before our wedding," he repeated, his voice filled with contrition.

"I already knew."

"How did you know?" He looked haunted.

"I know you better than you know yourself. What I want to know is why," Selina said, sounding as clinical as a psychologist even to her own ears. "If you loved me the way you said you did, why did you have sex with the one woman who could kill my soul?"

"Because I was scared out of my skull, Selina. I was nineteen years old. I wasn't ready to be a husband and a father."

"You think I was ready? You think I wanted to give up *my* dreams of college?"

He looked stunned. "I thought…I thought being a mother was the most important thing in the world to you."

"It was. Is. But if I could have chosen, I would have waited ten years to have babies. But I loved you and—" She broke off that train of thought. "What I do want to know is the reason you had the affair. Was it because you thought I trapped you into marriage?"

"It was just one night!"

"One night that changed the whole trajectory of our marriage. All these years, have you been pining for Vivian?"

He reached across the boat and grabbed her wrist. "No! God, no."

The fire in his eyes sent blood rushing to her heart. She clenched her jaw. "It's okay to tell me the truth. I can take it."

"You've got to believe me. From the minute I first saw you, there was never anyone for me but you."

Selina furrowed her brow. "And yet you slept with your ex-girlfriend the night before our wedding."

"I was drunk," he admitted. "But it was no excuse. I was scared and…"

"Looking for a way out."

Michael grabbed her by the shoulders and stared her straight in the eyes. The look she saw there was so passionate a faint flicker of hope flared in her chest. "You were the one I loved," he declared. "The only one I've ever loved. And since we've been married I've never once cheated on you. Not even after you left me."

"You haven't" — Selina paused, appalled by how much hope was surging through her — "slept with Vivian since she came back to town?"

"No."

She knew this man inside and out. Knew when he was telling the honest truth and when he wasn't. His eyes did not lie. She swallowed, splayed a hand against her chest, felt her heart gallop.

They were breathing hard, staring at each other. Feeling things they hadn't felt in years. Anticipation, relief, tentative trust, and a brief, bright flash of joy.

For one lovely moment, she thought he might kiss her. He leaned in closer. She tilted up her chin, her mouth suddenly dry.

If he kissed her, she was gone.

Please let him kiss me. Please let everything be all right. Please let the last twenty-seven years of my life have meant something.

A noise from the shore disturbed the moment. It was the sound of an expensive sports car engine.

Selina looked from Michael to the bank. They were near a picnic area. Cement tables and chairs. Shade trees. A parking lot. The scarlet red Jaguar pulling up was impossible to miss.

And so was the sophisticated woman slipping from

behind the wheel, dragging a wooden picnic basket done up with a red-and-white gingham bow along with her.

Vivian.

She walked to the water's edge, swinging the basket. She waved at the boat. "Yoo-hoo, Michael, I brought your lunch."

Disbelief squeezed out the hope. Suspicion squashed the relief. Betrayal stomped the tentative trust.

"What's she doing here?" Selina asked, hearing the ice in her voice. *I won't shout. I won't do it. I won't give that bitch the satisfaction of seeing me lose it.*

"Honestly, I don't know." Michael stood, the boat rocking beneath them. Selina stood up, too.

Michael had to have set up a rendezvous in this spot. He had to have known Vivian was coming. The woman was cunning, but there was no way she could have known where they'd be fishing if Michael hadn't already told her.

Selina crossed her arms over her chest. "Don't lie."

"Okay, okay." He raised his hands. "I might have told her where my favorite fishing spot was, but you have to believe me. I did not invite her out here."

"Really, Michael," she said. "I don't give a damn. You want to be with Vivian. Go be with Vivian."

Then Selina placed two palms against his chest and shoved him headlong into the chilly October waters of Lake Valentine.

JUST BEFORE DUSK, Rachael and Brody returned to the marina empty-handed. After Brody had done what he'd done to her, they'd spent the rest of the day kissing and canoodling and enjoying each other's company.

While other Fish-A-Thon entrants unloaded their

catches, she and Brody sat in the boat grinning at each other, waiting their turn to tie up at the docks. His gaze was on her. His eyes alight with a spark of sexual hunger so hot it caused a trickle of sweat to roll down her breast-bone in spite of the cooling air.

The wake of arriving boats rocked their little craft like a cradle. Water splashed against fiberglass in rhyth-mic, soothing sound. The remaining rays of late-after-noon sunshine dappled off the lake in a glistening golden glow.

The combination of Brody's hungry gaze mixed with the pastoral tempo of the lake ignited a deep yearning inside her. It was all she could do not to reach across the boat and kiss him again, in a dizzying lullaby of love.

No, no, not love.

Lust.

She had to stop confusing the two. Would she ever learn to stop confusing the two? She was a terrible Romanceaholics sponsor, unable to control herself when faced with tempta-tion. The embarrassing thing was, she wanted more.

Lots more.

As long as you acknowledge what you're feeling is lust instead of love, it's okay to want him. Just don't romanti-cize him and you're hunky-dory.

But if she slept with him, really slept with him, all night, in a bed, with full-on sexual contact, did she have a prayer of keeping her heart out of the fray?

There was the rub.

Her fingers itched to pull his shirt over his head and run her fingers across his bare chest. Her mouth—which was already achy from so much kissing—tingled to taste him again. Her ears pricked up, desperate to hear him murmur her name in the throes of the most intimate of embraces.

Anticipation tightened her spine. Sexual hunger narrowed her eyes. Tension curled her toes inside her wading boots. Would these stupid boats ever move along so they could get out of here?

By five o'clock, all the contestants had returned except for her parents' boat. Because they hadn't made it back in time, they were disqualified. If Rachael hadn't been so wrapped up in Brody, she might have wondered where her parents were. She might have spun fantasies about them getting back together. Instead, all she could think about was what Brody looked like naked.

Finally, it was their turn to dock and climb ashore.

Judge Pruitt was in the gazebo, weighing fish and tallying up the scores. Rachael was surprised to discover that not only did Kelvin Wentworth and Giada Vito win the competition, but they were eyeing each other like lovers instead of enemies—an odd turn of events that would have aroused her curiosity if she had not been so preoccupied with Brody.

"Well," Brody said, walking her to her car as the crowd dispersed into the gathering twilight.

Rachael pulled out her car keys. "Well," she echoed.

They both laughed, staring at each other as if no one else existed. It was a scary realization. Knowing they both wanted the same thing. Knowing how dangerous this step was.

Lust, lust, lust, Rachael told herself. *Just lust.*

"You wanna grab a bite to eat?" he asked.

She sniffed at her shoulder. "I smell like fish."

"You could come over to my house," he invited. "I whip up a mean omelet."

"Are Maisy and Deana there?"

"Yes. You'll be safe."

"What if safety was the farthest thing from my mind?"

He arched an eyebrow and his smile turned wolfish. "How about your place?"

"Mom's there." She frowned, wondering where her mother had gotten off to. "Or if she's not there she could walk in at any moment."

He leaned in closer, lifted a finger to trace a strand of hair curling against her chin. "We can't have that."

Her heart was a caged tiger clawing at the prison of her breastbone.

He stepped toward her until there was barely room between them and lowered his voice. "We could sneak off somewhere. Finish what we started in that fishing boat. Maybe drive over to the state park and rent a cabin for the night, out of sight of the Valentine gossipmongers. We could pick up some groceries along the way."

Watch it. Slow down. Think things through. Are you sure you really want to take this step?

His body radiated heat. His gaze burned.

Her stomach quivered.

Please don't let him ruin it by saying something romantic. Please, please, please let this be strictly about sex.

"I want you," he said, "in my bed."

"Oh, Brody," she murmured and sank against him. "I thought you'd never ask."

AFTER SHE'D PUSHED Michael overboard, Selina went to Audie's hardware store and rented an electric jackhammer from the teenage clerk behind the counter. With most everyone in town out on the lake for the Fish-A-Thon, she didn't meet with any resistance as she dragged the heavy equipment out onto Main Street and borrowed an electrical outlet from Higgy's Diner to plug in the thick orange extension cord.

She counted off the concrete sidewalk tiles hand-carved with hearts and flowers and entwined doves. One, two, three, four steps away from Higgy's front door she found it.

Their square.

Michael Henderson loves Selina Hernandez forever and always, June 21st, 1981.

Tears clumped in her throat as she remembered the day he'd carved it for her. It was the same day she'd told him she was pregnant with Rachael. They'd been pouring the new sidewalk down Main Street and everyone who was in love had been rushing to grab the prime spots. He'd bribed Kelvin to guard a section in front of Higgy's until he could get over there to make his mark.

Selina's heart clutched as she recalled the way Michael had looked, on his knees, a Phillips-head screwdriver in his hand as he used a heart to dot the 'i' in her name. When he'd finished, he'd thrown her a boyish grin over his shoulder, his face flush with the excitement of young love. It made her heart clutch just thinking about it.

They'd both had such high expectations.

What had gone so wrong?

Her insecurities? His wealthy family? The kids? Vivian Cole? All of the above?

Or was it simply that those same high expectations that had initially sustained them, in the end became their downfall? No marriage could live up to the romantic fantasies they'd spun in their heads. Life just didn't work that way.

A tear trickled down her cheek, but she brutally swiped it away with the back of her hand. The romance was over. The ride at an end. It was time to move on. With this symbolic gesture, she was setting herself free.

Sucking in a deep breath, Selina positioned the jackhammer's chisel tip at the apex of the heart. Forever and always was such a short time.

Bracing herself for the impact of the vibrating jackhammer, Selina flicked the switch.

Nothing happened.

She flicked it again. Off, on, off, on, off.

Dismay, as sudden as it was overwhelming, washed over her. She'd worked up the courage to eradicate her past and fate was conspiring against her.

She laid down the jackhammer and stalked over to the electrical outlet set into Higgy's outside wall. Maybe she'd tripped the ground fault breaker. She switched outlets and punched the reset button, then resolutely walked back to take up the jackhammer again.

You chisel this up, you can't get it back.

That was the point. She needed to do something irrevocable to show her commitment to her new path. To prove to herself she was over Michael.

Ha! You'll never be over him. You can't even carve up the sidewalk with his name on it.

The hell she couldn't. Grimly, Selina grasped hold of the jackhammer and flicked the switch again.

It jumped to life in her hands.

The power of the jackhammer was unexpected. It jerked her around like a rag doll. Her top teeth slammed against her bottom teeth, rattling her head. Her boobs jiggled. Her entire body vibrated. She felt as if she were inside a food processor.

The force was so strong she couldn't hold it in place.

On the sidewalk, the chisel tip bounced across the surface of the cement, hopping adroitly over the letters she was trying to destroy, doing little more than kicking up dust. Purposefully, she gripped the jackhammer tighter. The tip made a loud *rat-tat-tat* noise as it bit shallowly into the cement. Yes, yes, it was working. She could do this.

But her triumph was short-lived when she realized the tip had moved so much she was no longer even on the same square. She was chiseling up someone else's heartfelt declaration of love.

Crap!

She tried to drag the jackhammer back to the right square but her arms felt like they'd been jerked from their sockets. Dirt flew into her mouth and she spat, only to taste a fresh round of grit. Her hair swung, slapped across her face. Her eyes watered. Her ears rang. She trembled from head to toe. Maybe she should have spent a few weeks pumping iron at the gym before tackling this project.

To hell with it.

Selina dropped the jackhammer. It snaked across the ground, vibrating impotently. Angered by her lack of results, she grabbed hold of the extension cord and tugged it out of the wall.

The jackhammer fell silent. Cement dust motes swirled in the suddenly still air, but her ears kept ringing.

She looked up. A small knot of old-timers had appeared in the doorway of Higgy's Diner. They stared owlishly at her. Nodding curtly, she picked up the jackhammer, ignored her throbbing arms, and dragged the damn thing the four blocks back to the hardware store.

"You gotta clean it if you want your deposit back," said the kid behind the counter. He had a stainless-steel spike in his chin and a tattoo of a snake trailing up one arm.

"Keep the deposit," she snarled.

"Dude," the kid said, raising his arms defensively. "I just work here."

Selina narrowed her eyes at the teen, who could have stepped right out of a *Beavis and Butt-Head* cartoon. "You ever been in love?"

"No," he said.

"You're smart." She pointed at him. "Stay away from love. Have sex if you want, but stay away from love. And for God's sake, use a condom. You're certainly in no position to care for a wife and children."

The kid looked stunned by her frankness for a fraction of a second, then he snorted a laugh as Selina turned and walked out of the store, feeling hurt and angry and defeated. She couldn't even do a simple thing like break up a chunk of concrete.

But there was something far more irrevocable than jackhammering up Main Street that she could do.

Selina went home and climbed the stairs to her bedroom. She plucked the divorce papers off the bureau, sat down at her desk, and signed them. Then she stuck the papers in an envelope, sealed the flap shut, and took it to the post office.

Chapter Sixteen

It was pitch dark by the time they arrived at the rustic cabin deep in the heart of the state park. Brody's pickup truck was laden with supplies for their sexual tryst and Rachael's body was tense with anticipation. She'd been waiting for this from the moment he'd dragged her down off the billboard.

Brody had called Zeke and told him not to contact him for the remainder of the weekend unless it was for an extreme emergency. Rachael tried to phone her mother to tell her that she wouldn't be home until Monday morning, but Selina wasn't picking up, so she'd just left a voice mail. Deep inside she was hoping that her parents had mended fences and at this very moment were together rekindling old sparks. The thought made her happy.

And so did the fact that she was here with Brody.

A comfortable silence had descended over them and they didn't speak as they unloaded the truck and settled into the cabin. Brody started a fire while Rachael took a shower. Neither of them had wanted to go home for clean clothes or toothbrushes, so when they'd stopped off at Wal-Mart for the food, they'd each bought toiletries, a change of clothes, and a big box of condoms. They didn't want anything to mar the delicious momentum that had them traveling headlong into wilderness lust.

Lust, Rachael kept reminding herself, was all this was.

Rachael emerged from the shower feeling fresh and clean. She pulled on the sage green long-sleeved cotton top she'd bought and paired it with black Lycra lounge pants and fluffy avocado-colored socks. She brushed her hair until it shone and when she was finally ready, she took a deep breath and slipped into the main room of the cabin.

A crackling fire in the fireplace greeted her along with the aroma of grilling meat.

"Mmm," she said, coming up behind Brody, who was standing beside the indoor grill, tongs in hand. She slipped her arms around his waist. "He can start a fire and cook, too. What more could a girl ask for?"

"If you don't know," he said, reaching out to wrap his arm around her shoulder and draw her closer to his side, "I've got a lot to teach you."

Grinning, she went up on tiptoes to nibble his earlobe.

Immediately, his body tightened. "Woman," he said, "you're playing with fire."

"Nothing wrong with that."

"There is if you don't want your steak singed." He dipped his head and gave her a quick kiss. "Now behave and toss the salad. We have the rest of the night for dessert."

"Okay," she said. "I'll toss the salad and keep an eye on those T-bones while you grab a quick shower."

"Are you suggesting I stink?" He laughed.

"Hey, if the wading boot fits..." She grinned, feeling lighter-hearted than she'd felt in a very long time.

While Brody showered, Rachael tore romaine lettuce

with her fingers and grated fresh Parmesan cheese for Caesar salad. She popped a loaf of French bread into the oven to heat and flipped the steaks over.

A few minutes later, Brody came back into the room toweling his wet hair, wearing pajama bottoms and a University of Texas T-shirt. Her gaze tracked the length of his body. Broad shoulders, flat abs, lean hips. When she reached his feet, her heart clutched.

He was barefooted and her eyes lingered on his artificial leg. Looking at it made her stomach hurt for him and all that he'd suffered. She quickly looked up to see that he'd followed her gaze and a somber expression had darkened his eyes.

"Scary, huh?" he said.

"No, no," she murmured. "Not scary. Not scary at all. It's a symbol of your honor and bravery. The leg doesn't bother me."

"Don't feel obligated to patronize me."

Her heart clutched for everything he'd lost. The skeptical expression on his face was just so darned vulnerable she couldn't stand it. Anxious to make it clear that his handicap didn't matter to her in the least, she crossed the room, reached up to wrap her arms around his neck, and pulled his head down for a long, heartfelt kiss.

"Hmm," he said, when they came up for air. "We better check those steaks."

"Pull them off the grill. I'll set the table."

She set the table and took the bread from the oven. He plated the steaks and opened a bottle of pinot noir. They sat across from each other at the redwood table. The cozy atmosphere, the smell of great food, the company of the ruggedly handsome man stirred romantic feelings and her mind immediately started to spin "what if?" scenarios, but she realized what she was doing and stopped herself before her fantasies spun completely out of control.

Live in the moment. Forget about tomorrow. Forget about everything except now.

The thought freed her and she settled down at the table across from Brody with an uncluttered mind.

"A toast." Brody held up his wine glass.

Rachael raised hers. "What are we toasting?"

"To living in the moment."

The hairs on her forearms stood at attention. He'd read her mind. How eerie was that?

"To the moment," Rachael echoed and she clinked the lip of her glass against his.

They ate without speaking. The silence was comfortable, anticipatory. She watched him watching her enjoy the meal. The steak was cooked perfectly, the salad crisp and fresh, the bread warm and hearty, the soothing wine washed it all down. The fire crackled. The smell of pine wood wafted on the air. She allowed herself to fully experience the moment without wondering what was going to happen next.

Following the meal, they cleared off the table and washed the dishes together. Brody poured them both a second glass of wine, then took her by the hand and led her gently to the sofa in front of the crackling fire.

He took her hands in his. Rachael realized she was trembling.

"You're chilled," he said and she didn't contradict him even though she wasn't cold. She was trembling in anticipation.

"Brody," she murmured. "Brody."

He dipped his head until his mouth was almost touching hers. "Yes, Rachael?"

Time hung suspended as they stared deeply into each other's eyes, his lips so close she could already taste the pinot noir on him, his fingers kneading her knuckles. Her speeding pulse raced blood through her body.

"Rachael," he whispered, his breath warm against her skin.

"Brody."

Lightly, he squeezed her fingers, the pressure sweet and reassuring. But she wasn't looking for sweet. She wanted sex. Good, hard sex. No romantic trappings. No idealizing something that didn't need idealizing.

Brody was so different from any other man she'd ever known. He had a calm, unflappable exterior but inside he seethed with a smoldering intensity. He was brave, but vulnerable. Honorable, but wary of people. The contradictions in him were exciting. A complicated man full of surprises.

And carnal delights.

His tongue was doing crazy, thrilling things while at the same time his calloused palm was pushing up under the hem of her T-shirt, to discover she was not wearing a bra. He made an appreciative noise as his hot fingers gently grazed her bare breasts.

In the past, she'd always closed her eyes when being kissed. It helped her to romanticize the moment. Carried her away to some sweet dreamland. But she no longer wanted anything to do with fantasy. She wanted the real man. She wanted to experience every sensation now.

His eyes were open as well and he was looking into her as deeply as she was looking into him. His tongue dueled with hers and his fingers stroked her breasts. His gaze was a vortex, drawing her into him, holding her pinned gloriously to the spot, his body doing wild things to hers. His palms planed her skin, thumb and index fingers of both hands nimbly squeezing her nipples.

Rachael moaned and arched into him.

"I've gotta have you now," he said. "I've been wanting you for three months. I can't wait any longer."

He stood up then, holding his hands out to her. She got to her feet and he led her to the bed in the opposite corner of the room. Her heart fluttered as fast as hummingbird wings.

He tugged her shirt off and then she pulled his over his head. Their gazes fixed on each other as they simultaneously tossed the garments onto the floor.

"Aw, Peaches," he said when he saw her breasts. "Your breasts are even prettier than I imagined they were."

"Don't call me Peaches," she whispered.

"Oh, right," he said. "No romance. Just sex."

"That's right."

Sexual tension pulsed between them, an alluring, blistering force. At the look of red-hot desire in his eyes, Rachael felt her cheeks burn.

He went down on his left leg in front of her, splayed a hand at the small of her back and pulled her to him. His mouth was level with her lust-swollen breasts. And when his tongue flicked out to gently suckle one protruding nipple, she hissed in a sharp breath and planted both her palms on his head.

While his tongue slowly licked her heated flesh, his hand strayed to untie the drawstring of her pants. He edged them down her legs, fingers skimming her thighs as he went. The center of her throbbed at the memory of his lips, of what he'd done to her in the boat. Instantly, she felt herself grow wet for him all over again.

She was acutely aware of everything. His touch. His scent. The sound of his breathing. The taste of her own desire burning on her tongue hot as cinnamon.

He inched her panties down as well until her clothes pooled at her feet. He buried his face in the triangle of hair between her thighs and breathed deep. "God, you smell great."

Feeling slightly embarrassed, she stepped away from him and out of her clothing. It wasn't fair. She was undressed and he still had his pants on.

She held out her hands to him. "On your feet, Carlton."

Brody glanced up at her and she could see the hesitation etched on his face. He'd been dragging this out, trying to avoid the moment when he had to get completely naked in front of her.

He was a little off-balance and he had to take hold of her hand to keep from falling over when he pushed up off the floor. When he was standing again, she reached for the waistband of his pajama bottoms that barely contained his erection.

Her eyes latched onto his.

He looked a bit panicky. The pulse at his throat jumped and he had his jaw clenched tight.

"I…" Brody cleared his throat. "Rachael…there's something you've got to know before we take this any farther."

"Shhh, there's nothing to tell," she said, running her hands underneath his waistband. His bare skin was so warm to her touch, his body so responsive.

"Listen to me." He grasped her by the shoulders, cupped her chin in his palm, and forced her to look him. The expression on his face was somber.

She straightened. "I'm listening."

"I haven't…" He hesitated, his dark eyes growing darker still. He heaved in a deep breath. "I haven't been with a woman since…"

She waited. Didn't prompt him. Let him go at his own pace.

"Since I lost my leg."

At once she understood his fear. He was afraid of disappointing her in bed, worried that he couldn't measure up to a man with two good legs. Rachael laced her fingers together around his waist and didn't break his gaze.

"It's okay," she murmured. "It's all right. Everything is going to be just fine."

"What if I…" He swallowed. "Can't live up to my end of the bargain?"

"Brody," she said. "Being here with you is the bargain. Anything else that happens is just cream on the peaches."

The look of gratitude that came into his eyes humbled her. To think he held her in such high regard!

She kissed him then, like she'd never kissed him before. Poured her heart and soul into it. Showing him without having to tell him how special this moment was to her, what a unique man he was. She rained kisses on his mouth, his chin, his jaw, and down his throat.

It seemed as if he was the first man who'd ever really seen her. It was as if he saw straight to the essence of who she really was. Neither a romantic nor a cynic. Neither a kindergarten teacher nor a columnist for *Texas Monthly*. Neither a starry-eyed bride-to-be nor someone's jilted fiancée.

She was simply Rachael.

In that moment she experienced total serenity. As if the world had finally clicked into place and nothing could disturb her equanimity. All these years she'd been chasing happily-ever-after. Holding on to and intensifying romantic feelings through her active imagination. Tying herself up, holding herself down with unrealistic expectations.

But through Brody's eyes she glimpsed her authentic self.

It wasn't some romantic notion. It wasn't a flight of fancy. It had nothing to do with elaborate emotions or tender feelings or the intensity of intimate dreams. It was a tangible, unshakable knowledge. A deep-down abiding faith in him.

And it confused her deeply.

Slowly, he took off his pants and sank down on the bed. He gave her a wan smile. "This is me baring myself in front of you."

"Thank you," she said. "For trusting me."

Rachael's gaze strayed to his penis and she gulped back her amazement. God might have taken this man's leg, but he'd graced him in other ways.

He followed her gaze and chuckled. "Is that wide-eyed look for me?"

Mutely, she nodded.

"I promise to be gentle with you if you promise to be gentle with me," he teased, and she loved that he could joke about this. "Unless, of course, you're not into gentle."

"Gentle is good." Okay, so maybe earlier she'd wanted hard, pumping sex, but now that had given way to this perfect-pitch moment and she was going with the flow. Gentle sounded fabulous.

Brody lay back against the pillows without taking off his Power Knee. He reached for her and pulled her down beside him. Cradling her in the crook of his arm, he smiled into her eyes.

Feeling utterly treasured, she curled against him.

He kissed her with exquisite tenderness, while he stroked her skin with the back of his hand. Slowly, leisurely, they explored each other with all five of their senses. Massaging, caressing, licking, tasting, finding the spots that made each other sigh, moan, and whisper.

"Give me your hand," he said.

She placed her hand in his and he guided her palm to his chest. She felt his heart thundering underneath his breastbone as if he'd just completed a triathlon. Curiosity fused her hand to his skin. She couldn't pull away.

Mesmerized. They stared into each other.

Magic. It felt like total magic.

It hit her then, what she was doing. Going down the wrong path, romanticizing this moment. Romanticizing him. She knew better, but the slow tempo he'd set had drawn her into the magic of the moment. She had to break the spell.

Live in the moment. Stop thinking. Just be.

Good advice, but how could she do that when he was looking at her as if she was the most precious thing he'd ever seen? Only one way. Sex. Not love. Not tenderness. Not emotional intimacy. Just sex. Hard and hot and real. Powerful, orgasmic sex to blow away the mist of fantasy.

She removed her hand from his chest and pushed him back against the pillow with both hands. She captured his mouth with hers, pulled his bottom lip up between her teeth, and bit down lightly.

He groaned.

Yeah, this was the ticket.

She pulled away to slide her mouth down his neck one hot kiss at a time. She tracked a path from his throat down the middle of his chest—with a quick detour to his nipples—before resuming her trek over his muscled abdomen, past his navel, to his pelvis, and finally ending up at his most impressive erection.

He shuddered when her lips touched his hot moist tip.

"Mmm," she murmured. "You taste delicious."

"Hang on," he said. "Two can play at this game."

"What . . . ?" she asked, pushing her hair back from her face.

But he already had his hands around her waist, maneuvering them around so that while she was licking him like a lollipop, he was angling his head toward her most sensitive spot.

She sucked in her breath as his tongue flicked at her inner cleft. To counter his surprise, she stretched her lips over the expansive width of his penis.

His tongue was hot and wet and so was hers.

She swirled. He licked.

Up and down, around and around until they were both moaning and writhing, consumed by mutual pleasure.

On and on they played. He on her, she on him. Licking, sucking, tasting. Glorious sensations rippled through her body, turning her inside out. They increased the tempo as the pressure built, rising to the inevitable crescendo.

Rachael mewled softly whenever he did something right, grunted when he made a wrong move. It didn't take him long to pick up her rhythms, learn what she liked and give her more of it.

She took him deeper until she felt him pressing against the back of her throat, juicy and slick. She rolled her lips back, stretching wider to accommodate his bigness. She wanted to swallow all of him.

Finally Brody broke away, pulling his mouth from her throbbing anxious clit. "I can't stand it anymore. I have to be inside you."

"Condoms," she gasped, so addled by passion she was impressed that she had remembered. Thank heavens she'd remembered.

"I'm on it," Brody said, stumbling from the bed. He returned in a matter of seconds, but she was already drifting down from the pinnacle.

"Hang on," he panted, ripping open the box with his teeth and sending packets of condoms flying around the room. One smacked Rachael on her belly.

"Let me." She laughed and peeled open the foil wrapping. He was already in bed again. The leg didn't slow him down one bit. Rachael popped the condom between her teeth and proceeded to roll it onto him.

He groaned, took her by the shoulders, and flipped her onto her back. He was trembling so hard he could barely mount her.

And then he was inside.

She'd never had a man so thick, filling her up until she feared she might not be able to take any more.

"Peaches, you're dripping wet for me."

"I am, Brody, I am."

He was so damned beautiful. Hard, lean, a fine spray of dark hair between his nipples. Her hips twitched against his, the muscles between her thighs clenching.

Their breathing changed, getting hoarser, raspier. Their

coupling was primal now. Fierce and hungry. He plunged heedlessly into her, driving them closer and closer to the edge.

They were almost there. Both of them. Ready to come together. As one.

"Ah-ah-ah." Rachael made a noise, desperate, hungry.

He must have misinterpreted her sound of encouragement and thought she wanted him to hurry when she wanted the exact opposite. He began to pump faster, sliding in and out of her, quickening his rhythm.

Why was he speeding up when they'd been so in sync before? If he kept this up, he was going to go off without her. Half-cocked.

It had been too long for him. She feared he wasn't going to last.

And then Brody just stopped.

Rachael felt as if she'd been left hanging headfirst off a cliff. Bizarre sensation. Then she realized her shoulders and head had slipped off the bed and she was indeed dangling.

"You're falling off the bed." Brody slipped out of her and gently moved her back onto the pillows.

They looked at each other.

"I was going too fast," he said.

She nodded.

"Tell me these things. Don't let me be a bad lover," he pleaded and his vulnerability hit her straight in the heart.

She stroked him, but kept talking, low and soothing. "You're not a bad lover, not at all. You're just a surprise. It's okay if our first time together feels a little strange."

In the past, she would have taken any glitch in love-making as a sign they weren't meant to be. Now, that seemed incredibly shortsighted. They were just getting to know each other's bodies.

"I surprise you?" he asked.

"Sheriff," she said huskily, "you have no idea."

"How do we overcome this strangeness?"

"No way through it..." she started to say.

"Except to do it," he finished for her.

They smiled at each other.

And began anew.

He kept up the steady rocking, driving her deeper and deeper into the savage wanting that was changing everything she had ever known about herself and what she was capable of.

Brody thrust into her again and again. His entire being seemed to slide deeper and deeper into hers until she could not differentiate where her body stopped and his began.

Something earth-shattering happened. Something she'd never experienced before. It was as if his soul had leaped from his body and shot straight into hers along with his orgasm.

He cried out as his essence poured out of him, imbuing her with streaming currents of his masculine energy.

Together, they melted.

Nothing else existed.

Even the cabin was gone, disappearing in the laser-beam moment of blissful orgasmic feeling.

He cried out one last time and shoved himself as deep as he could go into her warmth.

The walls of her sucked at him, gripping, kneading, pulling this man into the very core of her.

Mystical, magical sparks of flesh and fire melded

together. Shattering, scattering, torturing. Melting her heart from the inside out.

A second orgasm sprang up from inside her groin, flooded her body, drowning her brain. She was numb, wrung, spent.

Brody's body shuddered, then went limp.

They clung to each other, helpless, as wave after wave of energy rippled through them. Gasping, he rolled over, sinking onto his back and taking her with him. He held her close as her chest heaved and quivered.

She slipped her arms around his powerful neck, squeezing him tight as tears flowed warm and free down her cheeks. His strength pinched her chest and stole her breath.

And she had the most terrifying feeling that he had given her his heart for safekeeping and she had tucked it irrevocably inside her soul.

RACHAEL WOKE IN the night to find Brody snuggled up behind her. His thick forearm was thrown around her waist, her butt tucked against his pelvis. In that brief moment of hazy half-sleep, Rachael allowed herself to dream.

Mine.

Joy flooded her heart. Weightlessness lifted her mind. Her toes curled inside her socks and a grin spread across her face. But just as quickly as her joy came, it was immediately replaced with crippling fear.

Her smiled vanished. Her toes straightened. Reality stomped around inside her head like a stevedore in hobnailed boots. The joy drained from her heart, swirled away into the darkness of the quiet cabin.

She'd been here before. Thought the same romantic thoughts. Found out later she was wrong. She'd promised herself she wasn't going to romanticize any man ever again and she'd gone and done that very thing with Brody.

Sadly, the poor guy had no clue what he'd let himself in for and she had a horrible feeling he was falling in love with her.

Hope flickered again, a desperate flame struggling to take hold. Ruthlessly, Rachael snubbed it out. No. She was not doing this again.

He stirred in his sleep, pulling her tighter against him.

Panic flapped inside her rib cage. She wriggled out from under his arm and sat up. She had to distance herself.

"Rachael?" he mumbled drowsily. "Are you okay?"

"Fine, go back to sleep, just heading for the bathroom."

"Hurry back," he said and patted the spot beside him. "It's lonesome without you."

Lonesome without you.

Oh! She so wanted to rhapsodize that comment. Instead, she dug her fingernails into her palms and padded to the bathroom.

She stayed in the bathroom for at least fifteen minutes, giving him time to fall back asleep. Finally, after her butt grew numb from sitting so long on the toilet, she headed back to bed.

And the minute she sank down onto the mattress, his arm was around her again, drawing her flush against him as if they were spoons in a drawer.

Wistfulness mingled with regret inside her. Why couldn't she have met him before Trace and Robert and all the others?

Wait. She had met him first. He was her first unrequited love. He'd had his chance and he blew it.

Come on. You were seven. He was twelve. It was a childhood crush. What did you expect from him?

The heat from his body warmed her. The reassuring sound of his steady breathing made her feel safe. The smell of him was in her nose, rich and masculine and so utterly...Brody.

"What's the matter, Peaches?"

Peaches. His pet name for her. Oh gosh, she was going to have to hurt him.

"Nothing," she mumbled.

"Can't sleep?"

She didn't answer.

"Would you like to talk about it?" he asked.

Now was as good a time as any, she supposed, to get it over with.

"I..." she started. "I have a feeling you want more than I can give you."

He responded by pushing her hair aside and kissing the nape of her neck. "I have no expectations."

"Honestly?" She turned, faced him.

"Honestly."

"Um...why not?"

"Why not what?"

"Why are you satisfied with what you can get? Don't you want the fairy tale? Great love, kids, happily-ever-after."

"The fairy tale is a myth," he said. "You know that."

"What about great love?"

"Great love scares the hell out of me."

"Really? How come? I was under the impression nothing scared you."

He didn't say anything for the longest time and she figured he wasn't going to tell her, then he said, "I saw great love destroy my parents."

She rested her chin on his chest and looked into his eyes. It was too dark to see any more than a glimmer. His body was a rock-solid layer of muscle beneath his skin, hard and warm.

"Love destroyed them? How?"

He shifted. She felt his breathing quicken.

"My parents were always that couple you see holding hands at the shopping mall. The couple who give each other knowing looks across a crowded room, even after they've been married for years. You never saw one without the other. They were always together."

"That's how my parents were. It was nice," Rachael whispered.

"Mom got sick," Brody continued. "She needed an operation but we didn't have any insurance because my dad was self-employed. Her surgery was going to cost double my dad's annual salary. This was during the first Gulf War and oil companies were paying huge amounts of money for people to rebuild Kuwait. My dad signed up to go in order to earn money for my mother's surgery. That's why we left Valentine when I was twelve. To go live with my mother's parents in Midland while my dad was away."

He told the story matter-of-factly, but Rachael heard the underlying pain in his voice.

"Six months later, my dad died in an oil-rig accident in Kuwait." Brody loosened his grip on her. "My mother was devastated."

Silence filled the cabin. An ember from the fireplace glowed dark red.

"The company had taken out life insurance on him, but by the time all the legal rigmarole was over and the money arrived, my mother was dead."

"Oh no." Rachael hissed in a breath.

"Not from her illness. If she'd held on, the operation would have had a good chance of curing her, but out of grief over losing my father. Without him, she didn't want to live. Not even for Deana and me."

"I'm so sorry, Brody."

He grunted. "So was I. But losing my parents at such a young age taught me a lot. It taught me how to stand on my own two feet and not depend on anyone to rescue me. It taught me life was damned hard. And, it taught me to stay away from great love."

"So," she said. "You've spent your life avoiding great love. That's why you married a woman you didn't really love. Because it was safe."

"Something along those lines."

Tears for everything he had suffered welled up inside her. She wanted to tell him great love was worth taking a chance on, but she didn't know that. She'd taken chance after chance and she'd never found the kind of great love his parents had shared.

"You see, Peaches, you've got nothing to be scared of where I'm concerned. So you can relax. The last thing I'm looking for is a great love."

Chapter Seventeen

Long after Rachael had gone back to sleep, Brody lay in bed listening to the gentle sounds of her soft breathing and thinking about how he'd lied to her.

He'd told her he wasn't looking for a great love. The truth was, he'd already found it.

In her.

But he knew if he'd said that, if he'd given her the slightest inkling that he was stone-cold in love with her, she would run for the hills, afraid of her own feelings, afraid to take one last gamble on love.

He realized the only way to convince her was to not convince her. He couldn't romance her, no badly how he might want to. Romantic gestures would make her skeptical. She'd learned to see right through flowers and candy and long moonlit walks. The woman needed substance. A man she could believe in.

And he was determined to be that man. No matter how hard it was to keep his distance.

She was staunch in her anti-romance stance and he applauded her for her convictions. She'd grown a great deal in the past few months. She had gone from starry-eyed innocent, ready to believe any man who murmured the words "I love you," to a self-confident woman who refused to let anyone define who and what she was capable of becoming. He admired her for that, even though it made things harder for him.

He also had to admit he liked the challenge. And when he won her, it would be for all the marbles — a ring, marriage, commitment, kids, happily-ever-after, a forever kind of love.

Because Rachael wasn't the only one who had changed, and he hadn't fully realized it until tonight, until he'd been inside her, made love to her, fused with her.

He'd been wrong about his parents, about great love. He understood now that he was experiencing it. Great love didn't destroy. It made you whole in a way nothing else ever could. Rachael made him feel that way. Whole again.

And for a man who'd lost his leg, feeling whole again had seemed impossible.

He loved her not just for what she was — which in itself was significant with her beauty, her spontaneity, and her profound passion for life — but for what he was when he was with her.

Rachael's honesty about her emotions and inner struggles helped him face his own feelings. Feelings he'd kept buried for a long time, feelings that needed to be examined and then released. Her playful charm made him feel like a kid again, unburdened and free. And her supportive compassion had him trying his best to live up to the ideal of the man he saw in her eyes.

He loved her not for what she had made of herself — turning from a jilted bride dependent on a man for her self-worth into a sharp woman in charge of her own life — but for what she was turning him into, a man who was no longer afraid to put his heart on the line.

And that was the thing, wasn't it? He was no longer afraid, but she was. Ironic, really.

Brody smiled into the darkness, smiled and smiled and smiled because he knew she didn't have a chance. One way or the other, he was going to have her heart. And he could wait until she was ready because Rachael was worth waiting for.

BRODY HAD A plan for trapping the vandal. His time with Rachael had unleashed his creativity and he realized what he could do to put a stop to the shenanigans that had been disrupting his town.

The Monday after the fishing tournament and his rendezvous with Rachael, he strode into Kelvin's office. "I want to borrow your mock-up replica of Valentine Land and put it on display in the town square."

Kelvin leaned back in his chair, feet propped on his desk. "Now why in the hell do you think I would agree to that? The model was ten years in the making."

"To catch the vandal and up your chances of getting the bond election passed."

That got the mayor's attention. He sat up straight, dropped his feet to the floor and leaned forward, fingers steepled. "I'm listening."

MICHAEL HAD SPENT the weekend trying to get hold of Selina but she didn't answer her phone or come to the door. They'd been close to something out there on the lake before Vivian had shown up and ruined it all.

He hung around Higgy's Diner hoping Selina would

show up in town. Audie Gaston took great delight in telling the story of how Selina had rented a jackhammer to break up their heart on the Walk of Flames. Michael's heart had slid uneasily in his chest. He'd gone right out and counted out the squares. One, two, three, four. There it was, scuffed but still intact. He'd inhaled a hungry lungful of air and it was only then that he realized he'd been holding his breath.

On the following Monday Michael walked the quarter mile down their driveway to the heart-shaped mailbox in his boxer shorts and bathrobe. On the stroll, he'd been thinking about ways to win Selina back. Romantic gestures hadn't worked. Neither had Rachael's advice to leave her alone. He knew there had to be some way to get through to her; he just didn't know what that was.

He popped open the mailbox lid, took out the bills and circulars and the ubiquitous credit card applications, and then he saw it.

The yellow envelope from Purdy Maculroy.

Michael's heart pinched painfully. He slipped a finger underneath the flap and got a nasty paper cut, but he barely felt it. His heart was what hurt as he took out the divorce papers, flipped to the back, and saw Selina's signature.

The pain in his chest intensified, shot up his shoulder, down his back, through his arm. The cut on his index finger was leaving dabs of blood on the divorce papers. His vision blurred. Sweat popped out on his forehead. He sat down hard on the ground, clutching his left arm. His mouth went dry. His body shook.

His heart!

He'd never felt such pain.

Later the doctors told him that if Brody Carlton hadn't

driven by when he did, Michael wouldn't have survived the heart attack.

SELINA AND RACHAEL arrived at the hospital together and raced to Michael's bedside. The minute Selina saw her husband lying in the hospital bed hooked up to tubes and machinery she wanted to burst into tears. She was heartsick for the man she'd loved for as long as she could remember.

She expected Michael to say something to her but he did not. Instead he looked at Rachael. "Sweetheart, tell your mother to sit down. She looks like she's about to faint."

What? He wasn't even going to speak to her directly? Selina swayed on her feet. If Michael wouldn't talk to her after a heart attack it truly meant things were over for them. The thought hit her in the belly like a solid punch. She'd lost him forever.

"Mom?"

Rachael's voice sounded far away. She felt her daughter's hand on her shoulder, pushing her down onto the plastic chair at Michael's bedside. Selina swallowed back the tears. Even when she'd been so angry over Vivian she'd never stopped loving him. She'd simply been hoping against hope that he would prove to her she truly was the one he loved. That she hadn't made a mistake all those years ago.

Now those hopes were shattered.

But he was still the father of her children and she cared about him, even if he didn't care about her.

Michael didn't meet her gaze. "Rachael, could you run

down to the cafeteria and get me a soda from the Coke machine?"

"You're not supposed to have…" Selina started, then bit down on her bottom lip.

"Sure, Daddy." Rachael headed for the door.

"Why don't you go ahead and have breakfast while you're down there," he said. "The nurse told me they have an omelet station until ten."

Was he sending Rachael away on purpose? Hope lifted her heart.

"You want to be alone with Mom?"

A muscle ticked at her husband's eye. He nodded, but did not smile. An ominous feeling twisted inside Selina and her hopes nosedived.

"She looks stretched thin," he commented as the door shut behind their daughter.

"Rachael's got a lot on her mind. She's divided the town and it's eating her alive. She wants what she wants but she doesn't want anyone else to get hurt in the process."

"I know how she feels," Michael murmured.

He looked so pale beneath his tan. Selina knotted her fingers together, dropped her hands into her lap, and stared down at her interlaced digits as if they belonged to someone else.

Then he reached out and placed a hand on her arm. She lifted her head.

He gazed at her and the steady light in his eyes stirred up memories of how gentle he'd been with her on the first night they'd slept together. The night she'd given him her virginity on a pallet under a carpet of stars at Lake Valentine. She thought about how his eyes had sparked with happiness when she'd told him she was pregnant with Rachael.

She hadn't imagined it. He *had* wanted that child. What she'd never been certain of was if he'd really wanted her.

As he squeezed her elbow and his eyes darkened with sadness, Selina realized how quick she'd been to assume the worst, to doubt his love. She'd needed far too much proof. Why had she been so insecure? Could her insecurity be the very thing that had pushed him away?

He took her hand in his, raised it to his lips, and gently kissed her knuckles. His lips were cool against her skin. His expression was serious.

"I'm so glad you came, Selina."

"You're my husband," she said. "You had a heart attack. Why wouldn't I come?"

"Because you won't speak to me. Because you signed the divorce papers. Because...I hurt you."

"No more than I hurt you," she admitted.

He looked at her and the expression in his eyes was so intensely remorseful she felt as if she'd been struck across the face. "I want..." He swallowed.

"Yes?" She leaned in close, breath bated. The hope was back, stronger than ever.

He frowned, but didn't continue.

Her heart skipped a beat. "Michael," she said at the same time he said, "Selina."

Her name on his lips sounded like a prayer. A shiver went through her, stark and anxious.

"Don't die on me," she whispered. "We need to get this worked out. Need to get beyond this."

"I'm not going to die."

"You promise?" She could no longer contain the tears pressing against the back of her eyes. They seeped out, rolling down her cheeks.

"Aw, sweetheart." He reached up to flick away her tears with his thumbs. "Don't cry."

"I've been so stupid."

"No," he said. "I was the stupid one. Looking back to the past, trying to recapture my youth."

"You don't"—Selina hesitated, gulped back the tears—"want Vivian?"

Michael's harsh laugh sounded hollow inside the room. "I never wanted Vivian. It was foolish. I just wanted the way she made me feel. Like a young, virile stud."

"And I don't make you feel like that," she said flatly. "Marriage ruins the fantasy."

"It's a ridiculous fantasy," he said. "And I was looking like exactly what I was, a silly old fart trying to hang on to his youth. What I didn't realize was how selfish I'd been. All these years I kept holding on to the thought of what I might have been if you hadn't gotten pregnant. If I'd married Vivian. If I'd gone to Harvard."

Selina sucked in her breath, knotted her hands into fists. She'd known it. For twenty-seven years Michael had wondered what it would have been like to have a different life, a different wife. All the time he was sending her flowers and cards and showering her with gifts, he'd just been trying to convince himself he'd done the right thing. Married the right woman.

"You're free to go to her now," Selina said. "I won't hold you back. I'm sorry you've felt chained to me for so long." She tried to pull away from his grasp but Michael wouldn't let go.

"No, no; you made me see the light. It wasn't until you left me that I finally understood. I belong here in Valentine. I would never have been happy on the East Coast.

Texas is in my blood. And I'm sure if I'd married Vivian we wouldn't have lasted a year."

The depth of emotion in his voice touched Selina profoundly. Finally, he was letting go of the past and getting in touch with the part of himself he'd let get pushed aside while he chased a fantasy.

"I'm sorry for the hurt I put you through."

"It's okay. It's all right."

"It's not. I'm to blame for what went wrong between us."

"No one is one hundred percent wrong," she said, finally realizing she had been laying one hundred percent of the blame on him. "I was too ready to imagine the worst of you."

Was it her imagination? Was it his near death experience? Or was that a deeply compassionate look in his eyes she'd never seen before?

"Why was that, Selina?" He stroked the back of her knuckles with his thumb. "Why couldn't you believe I really loved you?"

Selina swallowed. "I never felt good enough for you. A Mexican girl whose family owned the local taco restaurant. You a hilltop Henderson. Everyone knew you were marrying me because I was pregnant."

"That's not true," he said. "I'd been carrying your engagement ring around in my pocket for weeks before you told me about the baby, trying to work up the courage to ask you to be my wife. Ask Kelvin. He knew how nervous I was that you'd turn me down flat."

Selina sat up straight. "How come you never told me that?"

A sheepish expression crossed his face, making him appear incredibly boyish for his forty-six years. "I was afraid you wouldn't believe me."

She opened her mouth to protest, but then shut it. He was right. She wouldn't have believed him.

For a long moment, she just sat there studying him, thinking about the past and all they'd been through together. The ups and the downs. The highs and the lows. How far they'd come together. How much farther they had to go.

Michael toyed with her engagement ring and wedding band. "You're still wearing my rings."

She met his gaze. "Yes."

"I'm sorry, Selina," he said, his voice choked with husky emotion. "It was never my intention to hurt you. Since you've been gone I've realized how much I need you. How much a part of my life you are. Ever since you walked out, it's like my right arm has been amputated. Selina, I love you more now than the day we got married. I've never stopped loving you in spite of having acted like a damned fool. Please come home. I..."

His words trailed off. She was shocked to see a mist of tears in his eyes. She'd never seen her husband cry. Not even when he lost his parents. Not even when their children were born.

He held his arms out to her and she came to him, gingerly resting her head on his chest as he held her. Emotions fluttered inside her. Such a mix of feelings, misting her own eyes, filling her heart. He wrapped both arms around her and kissed the top of her head.

"Selina," he murmured. "My sweet, sweet Selina."

She tilted her face up to look at him. He brushed his lips against hers. "I wish," he said, "I wasn't hooked up to all this tomfoolery. I'd show you exactly how happy I am to have you in my arms again."

"Shh." She placed an index finger against his lips. "There will be time enough for that as soon as you get well."

"Sexual healing is the best medicine," he said.

"That's all going to have to wait until I get you home."

Home.

It sounded so good.

IN THE DAYS leading up to the election, Brody tried his best to stick to his plan of not romancing Rachael, no matter how much he longed to do exactly that. Instead, he treated her like his oldest and dearest friend, and when he thought about it, that was precisely what she was.

They'd been kids in the sandbox together, living side by side until his family had moved away when he was twelve. He went through old scrapbooks and family photo albums and found pictures of them at backyard barbecues, swimming pool get-togethers, and neighborhood block parties. When he'd first started the project, he wasn't sure what he was looking for. Maybe some inkling of a spark between them, even back then.

What he discovered was the magical childhood they'd both had until life had intervened and taken him from the gentle cocoon of Valentine, Texas.

And then he found it.

What he hadn't really known he was looking for.

A Valentine card. Dulled with age, but made by hand from construction paper and dime-store lace. Intended for the girl next door, whose birthday just happened to fall on Valentine's Day. The edges had curled, the lace yellowed, the block-letter printing faded, but the sentiment was still there — young and so heartfelt.

When he lifted the card from the keepsake box he found among his mother's things, his chest tightened and his pulse quickened. Gingerly, he thumbed the card open.

Dear Rachael, I made ya this Valentine card for your birthday. Hope you like it. Your friend, Brody.

He remembered sitting in his room, cutting out the red construction paper, gluing on the lace, setting it aside to dry when his friends had come to the front door bouncing a basketball. He'd been twelve and easily distracted. He'd gone outside to play basketball and that's when Rachael had come over.

He still remembered the stark terror that had gripped him when she'd given him a slick, store-bought card and his friends had starting chanting, "Brody and Rachael sitting in a tree…"

Humiliated in front of the guys, he hadn't even thought of her feelings, he'd just ripped the card up and shoved it back at her. Memories came rushing back as he recalled how her cute little heart-shaped face had instantly dissolved into tears. How he'd hardened his heart, desperate to look tough around his friends.

What a jerk he'd been.

Okay, he'd been an embarrassed teenager, stuck with feelings he hadn't known how to deal with, but he shouldn't have treated her so callously. You'd think his behavior would have been enough to sour her on love right there. But no, Rachael, the eternal optimist, had kept searching and getting hurt until she'd finally had enough of romance, just at the time he was learning to open up his heart and take a chance on love.

Ironic as hell.

Bide your time. Hold out. Give her a chance to break down.

Good advice, but could he do it?

Brody glanced out his bedroom window toward the house across the street. Rachael now lived alone in Mrs. Potter's old house since Selina had moved back in with Michael following his heart attack and their reconciliation.

The jaunty pink VW Bug, repainted after the graffiti incident, had just pulled into the driveway. Rachael got out with a handful of plastic grocery bags and headed toward the front door.

Mesmerized, he watched her hip-swaying walk and his heart reeled drunkenly in his chest.

I love you.

It took every ounce of control he possessed not to streak across the street after her. He stood breathing heavily, curtains parted, eyes fixed on her house long after she went inside. And if Maisy hadn't come upstairs to tell him Zeke was on the phone, Brody couldn't say how long he would have waited there for another fleeting but soul-sustaining glimpse of her.

"Vandal struck last night," Zeke said when Brody picked up the receiver. "Your trap worked. He smashed Kelvin's tiny Valentine Land to smithereens. What now?"

Brody smiled. *Gotcha.* "You and I get busy hooking black lights up to the voting booths."

By ELECTION DAY the black lights had been installed in all the voting booths in town and volunteers had been first tested, then given instructions to call Brody as soon as they'd identified the suspect.

The polls hadn't been open an hour when Enid Pope, who was volunteering at precinct three, located in the First Methodist Church across the street from the courthouse, called Brody. "Omigoodness, Sheriff," Enid said, excitement causing her voice to come out high and reedy. "It's just like you said. Purdy Maculroy is glowing green."

"CARE TO TELL me why you smashed Kelvin's replica to smithereens?" Brody asked Purdy as he led him to the jail cell.

"I have the right to remain silent," Purdy said.

"True, true." Brody nodded.

"These charges aren't going to stick, you know." The lawyer glared. "It's entrapment."

"You wouldn't have gotten phosphorescent paint sprayed all over you if you hadn't been vandalizing mini Valentine Land."

"How'd you know I'd vote?" Purdy asked, as good as admitting he was the culprit.

"I didn't." Brody shrugged. "I just took a chance that whoever was behind the vandalism had a political agenda."

Purdy scowled.

"You went one step too far when you graffitied Rachael's car and peeped in her window. That made it personal for me."

At that moment Kelvin came bursting through the door of the sheriff's office. "I heard you caught the bastard." He skipped to a halt in the hallway outside the jail. "Purdy?"

Kelvin jerked his head toward Brody. "It's Purdy?"

"He's the one glowing green." Brody waved a black light in front of Purdy and he lit up like a Christmas tree.

"I thought we were friends," Kelvin said. "We play golf together."

"And I always have to let you win," Purdy spit out.

"You cut the heads off the parking meters."

Purdy didn't answer.

"You cut those bicycles-built-for-two in two."

Purdy made a face.

"But why?"

"He's not talking," Brody said.

"I know why." Jamie popped out from behind the dispatcher desk. "I just got the rundown on Purdy's finances."

"Hey," Purdy said. "You have no right…"

"You've been charged with felony criminal mischief," Brody said. "Your records are up for grabs. I had Jamie contact the bank."

Jamie passed him the documents she held in her hand.

"What's this?" Brody asked. "Fifty thousand dollars was deposited into your account the morning after Rachael vandalized the billboard. And the deposit came from the town of Tyler."

"Tyler's in the running against us with Amusement Corp. You traitor!" Kelvin lunged at the bars.

Purdy backed up.

"You sold out your hometown for fifty grand." Kelvin raised a fist.

"Calm down." Brody slung an arm around Kelvin's shoulders. "The vandal's behind bars and it's election day. You've got other things to worry about."

IT WAS THE biggest election in the town's history. Main Street was lined with red, white, and blue banners. Voters packed the polling locations, many waiting in line as long as an hour to cast their ballot. A first for Valentine.

The high school gymnasium was Giada's campaign headquarters, while Kelvin's supporters collected at the courthouse. The air hummed with conversation and controversy as people argued, weighing the pros and cons of the theme park bond, the mayoral candidates, and the scandal of Purdy Maculroy.

A festive atmosphere prevailed. Higgy's Diner offered an election day–themed blue plate special menu including Pork Barrel barbecued spare ribs, Hanging Chad coleslaw, Polling Place potato salad, and Ballot baked beans. The high school marching band took several laps around the town square, tooting out a heartfelt rendition of "Stars and Stripes Forever." The two retirement homes in town made a party out of it, bringing in their voter-eligible residents in shuttle vans, most of them hopped up on Geritol, wearing slogan buttons, waving palm-sized Texas flags, and talking about back in the day when Kelvin's grandpappy had been mayor.

By the time the polls closed at seven, Giada was so nervous she briefly considered taking the Xanax that Lila Smerny, the high school librarian and her campaign manager, offered her. In the end, she waved it away. If she lost, she lost. She didn't need pharmaceuticals to cushion the blow.

The first results that came in were mixed. While Giada was excited to learn she was leading Kelvin with a two percent margin, a large majority of the voters were saying yes to the theme park bond.

"They're so misguided," she moaned to Lila. "They have no idea what this thing is going to do to our lovely little town."

"And if you win, you're going to have to handle the fallout."

Giada blew out her breath. "Thanks for reminding me."

By eight o'clock, three-quarters of the votes had been counted. Giada was leading Kelvin 564 votes to 523. There were 854 votes for Valentine Land versus 233 against. Amusement Corp had obtained the seventy-five percent approval they needed to proceed with the project.

A camera crew from Del Rio was there, covering the story on a town divided, rehashing details about Rachael and Romanceaholics Anonymous. The media presence only served to escalate Giada's anxiety.

"The Xanax is in my pocket with your name on it," Lila whispered as the reporter headed Giada's way.

"Thanks, but I can handle it."

"Ms. Vito," the reporter said. "We've just confirmed Mayor Wentworth is throwing in the towel. He's on his way over here to concede the election."

"What?" Giada hadn't expected this. Kelvin was the type to go down swinging.

At that moment, the mayor, surrounded by hangers-on, strode through the door of the gymnasium. A camera crew was trying to get to him, but Brody Carlton and his deputy Zeke were acting as bodyguards.

Giada gulped.

Kelvin stopped in front of her. "Ms. Vito."

"Mayor Wentworth."

"I concede the election." He held out his hand. "You ran a good, clean campaign. Congratulations."

She took his hand and looked into his eyes but she could not read what he was feeling. He wasn't acting like himself. No grandstanding. No "look at me" behavior. He nodded, said a few words to the reporter, and then strode out of the building as quickly as he'd arrived.

Giada stood openmouthed, watching him go, her hand still tingling from his touch. *He's hurting and he's trying to salvage his pride.*

People were coming over, slapping her on the back, pumping her hand. Other supporters were throwing confetti into the air and blowing on celebratory kazoos. Someone wheeled in a big cake that had been waiting in the wings. The red velvet cake with cream cheese icing and neon blue frosting proclaimed: *Congratulations, Mayor Vito.*

She thought about calling her parents but it was the middle of the night in Italy. So she smiled and smiled and smiled and felt empty. Champagne corks popped. Someone pressed a chilled champagne flute in her hand. She had a sip but tasted nothing. Her mouth was dry, her head muddled.

She had won.

Yet she did not feel triumphant. For one thing, she'd lost her fight against the bond election. The Valentine Land proposition had passed.

And all she could think about was the sound of utter decimation in Kelvin's voice when he'd congratulated her.

Cell phones had been ringing nonstop. Everyone wanted to talk to her, but she had nothing to say. Since the day she'd declared her candidacy, she'd thought of nothing else but winning the election, besting Kelvin. Putting the arrogant mayor in his place. But now that she'd achieved her goal, the victory felt surprisingly hollow.

The hubbub in the gym grated on her nerves. She needed to get out of here, needed to isolate and identify the feeling gnawing at her. If she could identify it, she could quell it.

Without telling anyone where she was going, she slipped out the side door, got into her Fiat, and just started driving.

Twenty minutes later, she ended up at Lake Valentine. She parked at Lookout Point and got out of the car. There was a chill in the early November air and she hugged her sweater tighter around her. She could see the lights of Valentine spread out below.

She was the new mayor. This was her town now.

Giada knew she should be feeling overjoyed, but she was not. She leaned against the hood of the Fiat and drew in a deep breath. It hit her all at once.

She was lonely.

It washed over her in a wave as she thought of all she'd sacrificed to be a success. No husband. No kids. Her family still in Italy.

A sound of a snapping twig echoed behind her.

She wasn't alone!

The hairs on her arms rose and she realized she'd left her purse inside the car—her designer handbag with Mace in the side pocket. Heart pounding, Giada whirled around and spied a tall figure lurking in the shadows of the trees.

The world dropped away.

Kelvin stepped into the clearing, his big body clad in a gray wool suit with a jaunty canary yellow shirt and a brown bolo tie. He looked like the king of the jungle and she'd robbed him of his crown.

She had the strangest urge to fling herself into his arms

at the same time she felt a desperate need to jump into the Fiat and peel rubber. She was alone in the dark with her archrival. He could kill her, weigh her down, dump her body in the lake, and no one would be the wiser.

Her knees turned to Jell-O. Her toes went numb. What was he doing here? Had he followed her?

The mossy smell of damp lake breeze made her shiver. His dark, wicked smile sent her pulse thumping. The hairs at the nape of her neck stood up. This wasn't a man who took defeat in stride.

Her head spun.

"Hello, *Mayor*." Kelvin's dark voice slid over her, inky black as the night.

Giada took a step back, teetered on her high heels.

He reached out a hand to steady her. His grip was hot, firm. She felt as if she'd been branded.

She tried to twist away. He didn't let go.

Her head spun. The evening air crowded her lungs, heavy with the noise of croaking frogs and thickening mist.

"I hope you know what you're doing," he said.

"Pardon?" Her voice came out in a whisper.

His hand moved from her elbow to touch her suit jacket, stiff with shoulder pads.

Breathing hard, she wrenched away from him. "You're not going to intimidate me to keep your stranglehold on this town," she said. "You lost the election fair and square, Wentworth. Now step off."

"You don't know what you're getting into—"

"No," she interrupted. "You don't realize how the Wentworth dynasty has been holding this town back."

"I was just thinking about you."

"Ha!" Her short bark of forced laughter echoed eerily out over the water.

"I was hoping," he said quietly, "you'd take a chance on me. On us."

"Bullshit," she said. "You just don't want to relinquish your position. You're thinking if you can date me, you can influence me into doing your bidding. Well, you've met your match, Kelvin Wentworth. You can't manipulate me like everyone else in this town."

"What are you so afraid of?"

You. I'm afraid of you.

He tracked his hand from her shoulder to her cheek and Giada suppressed a shudder. She was determined not to let him know how much he affected her.

She raised her chin, met his eyes with a stony stare. "I'm not afraid of anything."

"Except for not being in control."

"Don't you dare project your fears onto me."

He ran the pad of his thumb over her cheekbone. "Why'd you come after me?"

"I didn't come after you," she cried indignantly.

"You ran for office, you took my job. What was that all about if you weren't trying to get my attention?"

"You egotistical bastard." She shoved his hand away. Fury snapped her jaw closed.

"What drives you, Giada? What is it you really want?"

"I want you to piss off."

He threw back his head and laughed, a big rolling sound that sucked the energy right out of her bones.

"What's so damned funny?" Glowering, she sank her hands onto her hips.

"We're just alike, you and me."

"We are *nothing* alike."

"I know exactly what drives you, woman. You have to be the best at what you do. There's no such thing as second place. You're either a winner or a loser." He paused and she hoped he was finished. She wanted out of here, but he was blocking her way to the driver's-side door. She had a feeling if she tried to go around him that he'd just step into her path. "But sometimes winning isn't everything," he said, lowering his voice. "Sometimes you've just got to know you tried your best and that was enough."

"Oh, that's rich, coming from a scoundrel like you."

"If you're not worried," he said, "then why are you out here by yourself when you should be down at Leroy's Bar celebrating your victory?"

"I don't drink." She sniffed.

"You know what I mean."

"Why are you here?" She turned the tables on him. "Why aren't you down at Leroy's drowning your sorrows?"

"Because I was worried about you."

Giada snorted. "Please, you expect me to believe that? Why should you be worried about me?"

He stepped closer. Giada sucked in her breath. Gently, Kelvin slipped his fingers through her hair and raised her face up to meet his gaze. "Because I know how lonely it is at the top."

Deep inside she felt something splinter, slip.

"I know what it's like to need someone but be too afraid of being vulnerable to ask for what you really need."

It was as if he totally got her. As if he'd peeled off the top of her head and stared straight down into her mind.

He saw past her tough façade to the girl who'd constantly striven to win her father's love and had failed time and again.

"You don't have to be afraid with me," he said. "I know you, Giada Vito, because I'm just like you."

"You're not," she cried, suddenly terrified. "We're not anything alike. You're just saying all this because you can't admit the truth. I won and you lost."

"Are you sure of that?" he asked.

Confused, she blinked at him. What did he mean by his comment? Was he going to challenge her win? Demand a recount? She fully expected it. "I won fair and square."

His eyes darkened in the moonlight. "I guess that all depends on what you mean by winning."

Chapter Eighteen

The Monday after the election, Kelvin Wentworth flew to Austin to meet with Jackson Traynor. He had the speech rehearsed in his head, but he still couldn't believe he was going to deliver it. After all the lobbying he'd done to get them to consider Valentine for a theme park, he was going in there to tell them the deal was off. The whole deal with Amusement Corp had been contingent on his putting in an airport and hotels and restaurants. He was withdrawing his end of the bargain.

What was wrong with him?

Giada Vito. That was what. She had him so tied up in knots Kelvin didn't know who he was anymore.

The knots twisted even tighter when he walked into the conference room and spied Giada sitting there in a gray tweed suit, purple blouse, and a sharp new hairstyle shot through with streaks of auburn. He'd always been a sucker for redheads.

One look into her enigmatic brown eyes kicked his pulse up and he felt strangely breathless.

"What's she doing here?" Kelvin asked Mr. Traynor. He was so unnerved at the sight of Giada he went on the defensive, tightening his shoulders, narrowing his eyes, and curling his hands into fists.

"Mayor-elect Vito is the one who called this meeting," Traynor said.

"Could I see you in the hallway for a moment, Ms. Vito?" Kelvin asked, not sure what he was going to do with her once he got her out there, but his hands were just itching to hold her.

"If you'll excuse us, gentlemen." Giada smiled at the men collected around the conference table. "We'll be right back."

She followed Kelvin into the corridor. Once the door snapped closed behind them, he turned to face her. "What are you doing here?"

"I could ask you the same question."

"I came to tell them to back off Valentine Land," Kelvin said.

"And I came to give them my complete support."

"Why?" they asked each other in unison, and then both said, "Because you were right."

They looked at each other and laughed.

"Are we friends now?" he asked.

"Better than friends," she said, a seductive look coming into her eyes.

Kelvin felt his body respond. He couldn't take not touching her one minute longer. He slung an arm around her waist and tugged her to him, caveman-style.

Giada wrapped herself around him as if she'd been yearning for him to do just that. Her enthusiasm caught him off-balance and he had to tighten his grip on her to keep from stumbling.

He'd heard about hot-blooded Italian women; was he about to get the scoop firsthand?

"I can't believe you traveled here to give up your dream for me," she said.

"Ditto."

Her eyes rounded. "So what does this mean?"

"You tell me."

"I think it means you like me." She lowered her eyelids, sent him a sultry glance. "A lot."

He snorted. " 'Like' isn't the word for it."

"Why, Mayor, what are you saying?"

"I'm not the mayor anymore. You are."

"Not until January." She studied his face. "Is this going to be an issue for us?"

"Us?" he echoed.

"As in you and me. Or is that too forward? Too much of an assumption?"

"I've been a bachelor all my life."

"I know," she said, her gaze never leaving his face. "I've never been married, either."

"Too hard to get along with?" he teased.

"No harder than you."

"I'm pretty hard right now."

"I can tell." Her laugh was throaty.

"I think I just might be falling in love with you."

"You sure of that?"

"Okay, I'll admit it. I'm head over heels," he said, looking at her as intently as she was looking at him. "How do you feel about me?"

"I fell for you hook, line, and sinker."

"So you'd marry me if I asked?"

"Are you asking?"

"Of course not. I'm a die-hard romantic. If I were asking

you to marry me, I would make a Valentine-sized production out of it."

"That's good," she said, "because I've come to expect big productions out of you."

"In case you haven't noticed, I'm not a subtle guy."

"Subtlety is overrated. Besides, you have the ability to change." She reached up to run a finger over his cheek. It was all he could do not to shudder with desire at her light touch. "I still can't believe you came here to turn down Amusement Corp's offer."

"I had a mistake to correct. You were absolutely right. I was letting my ego get in the way of what was best for Valentine. You know I love that town."

"It's one of the things I love most about you," she murmured.

He heard only respect and admiration in her voice and it made him love her all the more.

"You know," she said, "I'm a novice when it comes to public office. I was hoping you might give me some pointers."

"You mean it?"

"I'm not as confident as I appear. In fact"—she lowered her voice—"I'm scared to death. I mean, I'm responsible for running an entire town. A little guidance would be much appreciated."

He narrowed his eyes. "You're not just saying that to stroke my ego."

She shook her head. "I'm being honest here. For the first time in my life I feel like I can admit when I'm overwhelmed and it's all because you make me feel secure enough in my insecurity."

"Woman," he said, "I am so turned on by you right now."

He pulled his car keys from his pocket. "You want to drive to the airport or shall I, after we tell Amusement Corp Tyler can have the theme park? If they want it badly enough to hire Purdy Maculroy to vandalize his hometown, they can have it, problems and all."

"You can drive this time," she said. "I'll drive home from the airport."

"Deal," Kelvin said and then he kissed her, knowing he'd made the best move for Valentine he'd ever made in his life.

RACHAEL WAS KEEPING the faith as best she could. It was hard since she was living at Mrs. Potter's alone now that her mother had moved back home. Her parents were doing well. Her dad was healing and her mother was radiant in a way Rachael had never seen before.

She decorated the house for Christmas and wrote her column for *Texas Monthly*. She'd upped her attendance at Romanceaholics meetings from once a week to twice a week, then to three times a week, until she was attending a meeting somewhere almost every day—often driving as far away as Del Rio to find a session.

But no matter how many meetings she attended, she couldn't get Brody out of her head. He was always there, a constant in the back of her mind. No matter what else she was doing, she thought of him. Attending meetings, running errands, giving speeches, or writing her column. He was with her, his name a silent prayer.

Brody, Brody, Brody.

She kept waiting for him to make a move. To convince her that romance *was* all that it was cracked up to be. She had a speech prepared to shoot down his arguments. She kept it tucked in her purse.

He did not make a move.

That rattled her.

Why didn't he make a move?

You don't want him to make a move. This was supposed to be casual sex, remember. You lived in the moment. The moment is over. Live in this current moment.

But by contrast, this moment without him in it felt lonely and dull.

You're romanticizing him again.

It was harder living here without her mother for distraction. She called her friends several times a day. Delaney and Tish, with their babies to attend to, sounded distracted and rushed. Jillian was the only one who would patiently listen to her talk about Brody and then tell her to stay strong.

It was hard to do when he was quietly, secretly doing nice things for her.

Every morning since that night in the cabin, she found the *Valentine Gazette* sitting on her front welcome mat instead of in the shrubbery where it usually landed. After a cold snap blew through one morning, covering the cars in a sheet of ice, she toddled outside, wearing three layers of clothing and armed with an ice scraper, only to discover that her windshield was already scraped clean.

When the flood lamp over the driveway went out, Rachael arrived home one evening to find the light shining brightly and Brody Carlton standing on his front porch in the dark, watching until she was safely inside.

She'd raised a hand to thank him.

He'd waved back.

That had been the extent of their exchange.

But he was quietly, steadfastly showing her what real love was. She was just so scared to trust. To believe again.

The fact that he wasn't tempting her tempted her all the more. She found excuses to go across the street. Borrow a cup of sugar from Deana. Invite Maisy over to make Christmas cookies. Christmas caroling with her Romanceaholics Anonymous group.

None of those brief encounters satisfied.

Then on Christmas Eve, as she was wrapping presents, the doorbell rang. Her mind leaped to one conclusion.

Brody!

Excited by the notion that the sheriff was on the front porch standing underneath the mistletoe she'd hung up, she raced downstairs and flung the door open without first checking to see who it was.

Trace Hoolihan stood there holding a gigantic bouquet of pink roses.

"What do you want?" she snapped.

"I came to see you," Trace murmured, his voice coming out thick and husky.

"Me?" She narrowed her eyes. "What for?"

Trace took a deep breath. He was just as handsome as ever. Too handsome, actually, with his slicked-back, stylishly long blond hair, perfect nose, tanned skin, and big, white, straight smile. He looked as if he'd stepped off the cover of *GQ* in his tailored suit, cranberry silk tie, expensive Italian shoes, and camel-colored cashmere coat.

She couldn't help comparing him to Brody.

Rugged, good-looking Brody with his dark, precision-cut hair, crooked nose, and lopsided smile. If he were to be on the cover of anything, it would be *Outdoor* magazine or *Texas Highways*, in his Stetson, cowboy boots, and faded blue jeans.

She thought of how easy life had been for Trace, a banker's son, and how hard Brody had had it. Losing both parents by the time he was fifteen, being in the Twin Towers when tragedy struck, leaving behind a piece of himself in Iraq. How had she ever preferred the softness of someone like Trace to the substance of a man like Brody?

"You look so beautiful," Trace said.

She crossed her arms over her chest and glared. "What do you want?"

"I came to tell you how sorry I am for the way I treated you."

Then before Rachael had time to react, Trace tossed the bouquet onto the porch swing, pulled her into his arms, and kissed her underneath the mistletoe.

BRODY WAS CRUISING down the street in his Crown Vic, returning from picking up nutmeg at the grocery store. Deana was whipping up eggnog for Kelvin's annual Christmas party that evening. He'd been wondering if Rachael would be attending when he saw her standing on her front porch kissing some guy. One look at the red Corvette with the Illinois plates in the driveway, the Chicago Bears parking pass sticker on the back windshield, and a huge bouquet of pink roses sitting on the porch swing, and he knew the guy in question was most likely her old flame Trace Hoolihan trying to weasel his way back into her good graces.

The realization hit him like a sledgehammer.

Rachael was getting back together with her ex.

You blew it, buddy-boy. Holding back was not the way to go. As much as Rachael denies she wants romance, that's exactly what she wants.

His gut soured and sweat beaded at his collar. His caveman instincts had him wanting to slam the car in park right there in the middle of the street, get out, and challenge Hoolihan to a good old-fashioned fistfight, winner take Rachael.

But he couldn't give in to his natural inclinations for three reasons. One, he was an officer of the law and he didn't take his duty lightly. Two, after Iraq, he'd sworn off violence. Three, Rachael wasn't a possession men could fight over. She was a human being with a mind of her own. He couldn't treat her like an object. If Trace was the man she wanted, it would do no good to get angry. Never mind that she was tearing him apart inside. That was his cross to bear. He loved her, even if she didn't love him back.

Wincing, he turned into his driveway and got out of the car, just in time to see Rachael let Trace Hoolihan into her house.

And with that, the tender hope for the future Brody had been nurturing for weeks was snuffed right out.

"THE BEARS ARE headed for the play-offs and I'm first-string running back," Trace said. He peeled off his cashmere coat and hung it on the rack by the door while Rachael trailed into the kitchen scouting for a vase for the roses.

She'd let him in only to get him off the porch, and she

prayed none of the neighbors had seen him. She knew how quickly gossip spread through Valentine.

Her lips were still damp from Trace's wet, sloppy kiss. How had she ever convinced herself that she liked his kisses? She wiped her mouth with the back of a hand and finally just stuck the roses in a Mason jar.

"Don't you have a vase for those?" Trace asked, coming into the kitchen behind her.

"This is as sophisticated as it gets," she said, feeling irritated.

"Are you still mad at me?"

"Let's see. You ran out on our wedding to join the Chicago Bears and then you disrespected me on national television. Why on earth would I be mad at you?"

Trace hung his head, looking chagrined. "Not two of my finer moments. I'm truly sorry for that. But you got back at me," he pointed out, "with the whole YouTube thing."

"You saw that?"

"I was the laughingstock of the locker room for weeks."

"You deserved it."

"I did."

Rachael turned to face him. "Why are you here, Trace?"

"I missed you, Rach."

She snorted indelicately. "Come on. You've been the star of the Chicago Bears since September. I know you've got more groupies than you can handle."

"I don't want groupies, I want you. I've come to realize all the groupies in the world can't offer me what you were so willing to give," he said.

"And what's that?"

"Your support, your loyalty, your love."

"You had your chance with me."

"I was a fool."

"Yes," she agreed, "you were." She could forgive him because she'd grown beyond the petty need for revenge.

"I want to spend the rest of my life making it up to you," he said. Then he sank down on one knee and reached for her hand.

Her stomach pitched. Her pulse raced. Panic swept through her. No, no.

He withdrew a small black-velvet box from his pocket. It sprang open with a sharp cracking sound to reveal a three-carat diamond sparkler. "Marry me, Rachael. I really mean it this time. I can't make it without you in my life. I thought fame and fortune were what I wanted but I found out it doesn't mean a damn thing if you don't have anyone to share it with."

Once upon a time, after a speech like that, Rachael would have forgiven him anything. Back before she'd learned all that glitters isn't gold. Once upon a time, she would have been impressed with the appearance of things, with the trappings of romance—the roses, the diamond, the going-down-on-one-knee thing. Once upon a time, she would have accepted his proposal, terrified that she might never get another one. But that was before she'd learned she was worth something in her own right. That she didn't need a man or romance to define her.

Rachael pulled her hand away from him and stepped back. "Get real. I'm not about to marry a man who treats me the way you treated me."

"I won't take no for an answer," he said, rising to his feet. "I'm pursuing you with my last dime. I'll send flowers every day. I'll buy you gifts and spoil you with vacations and spa treatments."

"I don't want those things anymore, Trace. You were the one who helped me realize that I was living a false life. I was happier with fantasies and illusions than I was in the real world. That's no way to live."

"I don't get it." He looked truly puzzled. "You prefer to live alone in a crappy little house in this dried-up town rather than marry me, move to Chicago, and live in the lap of luxury."

"Yep," she said. "I do."

"You're breaking my heart here. What am I going to do without you, Rachael?"

"If you're lucky, you'll do the same thing I did when you broke my heart. You'll find the real Trace hiding inside." Using her knuckles, she tapped his chest at his heart.

Bewildered, he stared at her. "You've changed."

"Thank you." She smiled.

He shook his head. "I don't know how I'm going to get through the Super Bowl without you."

"Face it. That's the real reason you're here," she said.

"Huh?" His look was blank. Trace had no idea what his true motives were, but she understood him better than he understood himself. Somewhere along the way she'd learned to look past outer appearance to the truth that lay beyond.

"You're stressed out about the Super Bowl and you need a woman around that you can trust to prop you up. Groupies can't do that for you, but you knew I could."

He blinked. "I don't get it."

"You don't really love me, Trace. You loved what I did for you. I was there to hold your hand when things got tough. Remember, you proposed to me on the day the

Houston Texans cut you from the team. And the minute things got better you ditched me. I'm nothing more than a security blanket."

"That's not true," he denied, but she saw it in his eyes. It was totally true.

"Trace," she said. "You don't need me. Honestly, you're a big boy. It's time to toss out the security blanket. You can handle this all on your own. You won't choke during the Super Bowl. You're going to be fabulous. Now go back to Chicago where you belong."

KELVIN WENTWORTH'S PARTY was in full swing by the time Rachael arrived. Elvis Presley was on the stereo, dreaming of a "White Christmas." Festive twinkle lights were strung around the room. The Christmas tree was oversized and spinning gently on a rotating stand. Giada was at the refreshment table, ladling up cups of spiced eggnog and gazing adoringly at Kelvin, who was playing Santa to a group of children.

The outgoing mayor's bullmastiff, Marianne, wearing antlers and a crocheted red-and-green doggie sweater, weaved her way through the crowd, picking up dropped tidbits of food like a high-suction Hoover. The incoming mayor's cat, Hercules, curled up on the window ledge, watching the proceedings with yellow-eyed disdain.

Rachael hung up her coat, deposited the presents she'd brought with her on the long table laden with gifts, and slipped away from the main room. She was still a bit off-balance after Trace's visit that morning and his ensuing marriage proposal, but she was feeling liberated in a way that she'd never felt before.

She had closure. She could let go of the remaining vestiges of her past and move on.

That's when she saw Brody, looking dashing in a pair of black Dockers and a red-and-green-striped, button-down Western shirt—a cowboy's version of Christmas attire.

Standing under the mistletoe.

It was all she could do to keep from going over there and kissing him. Just when she'd decided, *Aw, to hell with it, I'm going to kiss him anyway,* April Tritt, dressed as one of Santa's elves in a skirt so short you could practically see Australia, beat her to it.

The kiss April planted on him was not a light peck on the cheek. As the oversexed woman pulled Brody's head down to hers, jealousy chewed off a big chunk of Rachael's heart.

April finally let go of him and stepped back.

Brody raised his head, saw Rachael.

Their eyes met.

Brody stepped past April and came toward her.

Suddenly feeling self-conscious, she ducked her head and turned toward the refreshment table, her green jingle bell earrings jangling merrily. She heard the scrape of Brody's boots on the polished hardwood floor, but she didn't look up.

"Merry Christmas, Peaches," he murmured.

Rachael looked up.

His eyes were dark, enigmatic.

"Brody." His name came out of her like a sigh.

"Rachael."

"You've got lipstick…" She made a motion toward the corner of his mouth.

He swiped it away with the back of his hand. "That business with April—"

"No need to explain." She held up a palm.

He reached for two cups, raised his eyebrow at her. "Eggnog?"

She shrugged. "Sure."

He dipped them both a cup and passed one to her. She curled the cup in her hand.

"How you been?" He was staring straight at her. No, that wasn't right. He was staring *into* her.

"Fine. You?"

"Good."

She blew out her breath.

He shifted his weight. Brought the glass of eggnog to his lips, but she saw that he didn't swallow.

"That bad?"

"What?" He looked startled.

She nodded at his glass. "The eggnog. Is it so bad you're just pretending to drink it?"

"It's spiked with rum and I'm driving."

"So why even take it?"

"Something to do with my hands, I guess."

"Oh." She looked away again, unable to bear the heat of his scrutiny. Unable to say all the things she desperately wanted to tell him.

"I saw you," he said.

"You saw me?"

"This morning. On your front porch. With Trace Hoolihan."

Rachael remembered the kiss Trace had given her. "That's the trouble with mistletoe." She glanced over his shoulder at April, who was glaring at her from across the room. "It can cause a kiss to look like something it's not."

"Hey." He shrugged. "More power to you."

"You don't care that I was kissing Trace?" She could hear the dismay in her voice and she knew he heard it, too.

"We agreed, no strings attached, just sex. Exactly how you wanted it."

"You said you wanted it that way, too, remember? You said great love destroys."

"Maybe I was wrong."

She hissed in a breath through clenched teeth. "Yesss?"

He nodded at Giada and Kelvin, who were gazing into each other's eyes. "What about those two?"

"First blush of romantic love. It'll wear off."

"And then look at your parents. They were able to find their way back to each other."

"After my dad almost died."

"Sometimes it takes the threat of losing the thing you love most to give you a wake-up call." And with that, he turned and walked away, leaving Rachael shaken to her very core.

Chapter Nineteen

On Christmas morning, Rachael awoke alone to a throbbing headache from the three glasses of spiked eggnog she'd downed at Kelvin's party after Brody had run off. She glanced at the clock and shot out of bed. She was due at her parents' house for brunch.

Fifteen minutes later her mother greeted her with a hug. Her father looked fantastic for someone who'd had a heart attack six weeks earlier. Hannah chattered while her daughters played chase around the kitchen table, and her husband carved prime rib for the brunch buffet as the rest of the guests arrived. It seemed almost half the town was at the celebration, including Deana and Maisy and Rex Brownleigh. Deana and Rex kept exchanging moony-eyed glances.

Rachael cornered her mother in the kitchen as she flipped crepes onto a warming plate. "Did you invite Brody?"

"Of course I did. He said he was working so Zeke could have Christmas Day off with his family."

"Oh." Then to show she wasn't asking about him specifically, she added, "Did you invite Kelvin and Giada?"

"They had private plans."

"Sounds like things are heating up between those two."

Selina lowered her voice. "Giada told me they're moving in together."

"No kidding."

"I'm happy for her."

She touched her mother's arm. "How are things with you and Daddy?"

Selina's face dissolved into a beatific smile. "I haven't been this happy in years. Oh, Rachael, I love him so much. I've always loved him, but nothing like this. We finally opened up to each other and talked about things we should have discussed years ago. He's stopped cloaking his true feelings with romantic gestures and we have real intimacy at last."

"I'm so glad." She gave her mother a squeeze.

Selina smiled as tears misted her eyes. "Here." She handed her daughter a jar of peach preserves. "Put these on the table to go with the crepes."

As everyone gathered around the buffet table filling their plates, Rachael opened the peach preserves and spooned a dollop onto her crepes. She found a seat in the corner of the kitchen, out of the general fray, settled in, and took a bite of crepe draped in peach preserves.

It tasted as if summer exploded in her mouth—rich and ripe and full and as juicy as the fresh peaches plucked from Brody's tree. Each bite brought back memories of the day he'd brought that bushel of peaches across the street.

She thought about peaches and romance. She thought about her parents and what they'd been through. She remembered her mother, upset and hurting, smashing the peaches, decrying love and marriage. She thought of Kelvin and Giada, middle-aged and never married and yet still finding each other, willing to risk, to take a chance on love. She thought about Deana and her new romance with Rex.

But most of all she thought about Brody. How steady he was. How honest and straight and true. He hadn't given her flowers. Hadn't wined and dined. No grand romantic gestures from him. But he'd given her something much better. He had given her his summer peaches on the day she'd faced her greatest humiliation. He'd been there for her when her father had had his heart attack. He'd made love to her. And just last night, he'd told her he loved her more than anyone else on earth could ever love her.

Tears tracked down her face as she ate. Her epiphany grew brighter, stronger with each bite of peaches. Yes, the first flush of romantic love was like a beautiful, perfectly ripe peach. And like her mother had said, life could knock you around. Smash the romance right out of you.

But this was what she realized: In order to have these delicious peach preserves in the winter, the peaches had to be smashed up, boiled down, condensed, distilled. That sweet little romance of summer had to disappear in order for the rich, sustaining preserves to exist.

One spoonful of preserves was ten times sweeter than the freshest peach.

Her chest pinched and her breath went shallow. This, then, was the difference between romance and love.

Romance was fun and light and frivolous. You could enjoy it, have a good time with it, but it did not sustain you for long. Only the preserves could do that. Only true love.

With that understanding, Rachael knew what she had to do.

THE LAST THING Brody Carlton expected to find when he wheeled his Crown Vic past the Valentine library was

Rachael's pink VW Bug parked in the middle of the street and the lights on inside the building.

But there weren't any cars in the parking lot.

Was she hosting a Romanceaholics meeting tonight and the members had yet to show up? Had she forgotten to set her VW's parking brake and the car had rolled back into the street?

Brody pulled his cruiser into the parking lot and got out. He heard the sound of music in the air but it wasn't Christmas music. Instead, it was Bonnie Tyler's "Holding Out for a Hero." Every time he heard that song he thought of Maisy's favorite movie, *Shrek*.

Smiling, Brody went up the steps to the side door of the library where the Romanceaholics usually entered. He stepped inside and saw a big banner stretched across the empty room that read: JUST PEACHY? OR DOES YOUR LOVER HAVE WHAT IT TAKES TO BECOME PEACH PRESERVES?

What the hell?

"Rachael?" he called out. "You in here?"

His voice echoed back to him over the sound of Bonnie Tyler emanating from the boom box on the stage.

"Brody?" Rachael's head popped out from the closet behind the stage.

"Yep."

She came out of the closet holding what appeared to be a giant papier-mâché peach.

"What's that?"

"Prop for the Peach Festival," she said, as if that explained everything, and sat it down on the stage next to the podium.

"Oh."

"You're too early. You're not supposed to be here yet."

He cocked his head and grinned. He'd grown accustomed to her seemingly nonsensical conversations. He'd learned how to read and interpret her. "When was I supposed to be here?"

"I'd imagined you coming in during the middle of the meeting while—" She raised a hand to cover her mouth. "I'm doing it, aren't I? Projecting a romantic fantasy. I should just let reality happen the way it's going to happen. You're here now. It'll do."

"Okay," he said, knowing if he waited she'd explain herself.

She wore a green-and-red festive Christmas dress that made her eyes look even greener than usual and her cheeks were flushed. She smelled sweet and fresh, just like summer, even in the dead of winter. She sank her top teeth into her bottom lip and then she told him her theory about peaches, peach preserves, and love.

"What do you think?" she asked and anxiously knotted her fingers together.

"Sounds like a solid hypothesis to me." He went toward her, pulling off his leather jacket and Stetson as he went. When he was close enough, he put them on the lectern. "The peach analogy appeals to me."

Her eyes were wide. They were only a couple of feet apart. He wanted to touch her so badly his hands stung. He wanted to push his fingers through her hair, dip his head, and kiss her with all the passion he'd been holding back.

"It's what I'm going to tell the Romanceaholics."

"Is it, now." He wanted her to come to him, to bury her face against his neck and tell him how much she wanted to be with him. Instead, she swayed there, just staring into his eyes.

"I've come to realize everyone is entitled to a little

romance in their lives, just as long as they don't mistake it
for the real thing."

"What's that?"

"Great love," she said on a whispered sigh.

"Rachael," he replied, and then he couldn't say another
word because his chest was so knotted up.

"Brody, I said you were just casual sex to me, but that
was a lie. From the moment you risked life and limb to
haul me down off that billboard, I knew you were a true
hero. A good man. A man who wouldn't leave me standing at the altar while my bouquet wilted. I knew you were
the kind of man who fought for what you believed in. I
knew you'd never pick a sports team over me."

"What took us so long to get here?"

She moistened her lips. "I was so scared of making
another mistake that I couldn't trust what I knew about
you deep down inside." She knotted a fist and placed it
against her belly. "I was terrified of getting hurt again."

"I was pretty terrified, too," he admitted. "I'd convinced
myself it was better to stay away from great love than to
take a chance on losing it. But ever since I came back to
Valentine I've felt like I've just been waiting for something
big to happen to direct the rest of my life. I think that big
thing was you."

Rachael brought both hands up to cover her mouth.
Her heart was pounding and her eyes burned with unshed
tears of joy.

"Hang on," he said. "I've got something for you. I was
saving it for Valentine's Day but the time feels right."

He left her standing there and sprinted out the door.
She felt off-balance and scared. Did he have a ring? Was
he going to ask her to marry him?

Don't romanticize it. Just let the moment happen the way it's going to happen. Be present. Get out of the castle in your mind.

And there he was, back inside the library, breathless, his hair mussed, his cheeks reddened from the cold night air.

"It's early," Brody said, extending the envelope toward her. She noticed his hand was trembling. "No, it's late. In fact, it's almost twenty years overdue. I know it doesn't make up for not giving it to you all those years ago, but here I am, asking you to be my Valentine."

She took the envelope, yellowed with age, opened the flap, and slipped out the handmade card. It was a red construction-paper heart with lace—faded yellow like the envelope—glued around it. In the handwriting of a twelve-year-old the card read:

Dear Rachael, I made ya this Valentine card for your birthday. Hope you like it. Your friend, Brody.

She jerked her gaze up to his face. "You made me this? When you were a kid?"

He nodded. "I found it in one of my mother's keepsake boxes."

"You saved it. Why would you save it?"

"I'd like to take credit for that, but it was my mother's doing. I'm glad she was a packrat."

"Oh, Brody." She sighed. To think the first boy she'd ever loved had been the right one all along.

"You were my great love even back then," he said. "I just didn't realize it."

"I'm sorry it's taken me so long to understand the difference between show and substance."

"I've missed you," he said, wrapping his big, strong sheriff-y arms around her and lifting her off the ground.

He squeezed her tight and kissed her hard. She could feel the strength of his love, every inch of it, as he let her slide gently back down the length of his hard body until her feet were firmly on the ground.

"Is this the happily-ever-after?" she asked.

"Nope."

"It's not?"

"Nope."

"I dunno," she teased, "it feels dangerously like happily-ever-after to me."

"Can't be," he said.

"Why not?"

"This is the happily-ever-before."

"Before what?"

He put his forehead against hers and she stared deeply into those delicious brown eyes she knew so well. "Before the greatest adventure of our lives. Full of ups and downs. Laughter and tears. Romance and sorrow. Joy and pain. And love. Always, forever, love."

The door opened just then and several of her group members appeared in the room.

"Meeting's canceled, folks," Brody called out to them. "Your fearless leader has learned the true meaning of love. She'll let you in on it at your next meeting."

Then he swept Rachael off her feet, and to the sound of the romanceaholics clapping and cheering, and Bonnie Tyler singing about a hero, he carried her out of the library and into their newfound love.

Epilogue

On Valentine's Day, Brody and Rachael got married where they'd met cute: underneath the Valentine billboard. Yes, it was nostalgic and romantic, but Rachael didn't care. It might not have been the wedding she'd dreamed of since she was six years old, but it was absolutely perfect in spite of the chilly breeze and the big fat rain clouds bunching up overhead.

Brody looked handsome as all get-out in a Texas tuxedo and a black Stetson. The man took her breath away.

Rachael wore a brand-new wedding gown and the magical wedding veil, which in the end had granted the deepest wish of her heart, if not the actual wish she'd made that day on the cement bench in the Valentine jail. She hadn't exactly gotten that love monkey off her back. What she'd gotten instead was a new, liberating view of love, romance, and all the myriad emotions in between.

Judge Pruitt presided over the proceedings and almost the entire population of Valentine was there, including Kelvin and his bride, Giada, who, according to rumors down at Higgy's Diner, was already pregnant. Delaney and Tish and their husbands and babies, along with Jillian, had driven from Houston. Selina served as Rachael's matron of honor, wearing the same silk, peach-colored dress she'd worn when she and Michael had renewed their wedding vows the week before. Her father stood up as Brody's best man in a Texas tuxedo of his own.

"If anyone knows any reason these two should not be wed, speak now or forever hold your peace."

Silence fell over the congregation and then Rex, who was standing with Deana and Maisy, said, "Hell, Judge, marry them already. Everyone in town knows these two were meant for each other."

The crowd laughed.

Rachael passed her bouquet to her mother, then turned back to Brody. He took her hands in his and stared deeply into her eyes with a love so strong and true it took her breath away. This, then, was real love. Friendship, sexual attraction, steadiness, community. Rachael felt herself enveloped in the power of it.

"I now pronounce you man and wife."

And with that, Rachael and Brody were married. The romantic equation was completed. She'd at long last found her hero and he'd found his romantic heart.

And everything, Rachael realized, was just peachy.

For a preview of the next book in the
Wedding Veil Wishes series...

Jillian's Story

Chapter One

Houston Assistant District Attorney Jillian Samuels did not believe in magic.

She had never thrown pennies into a wishing well. Had never plucked a four-leaf clover from a springtime meadow. Never blew out the candles on her birthday cake to make a wish, mainly because as far back as she could remember there'd been no birthday cakes.

For Jillian, the Tooth Fairy and the Easter Bunny had always been myths. As for Santa Claus, even thinking about the jolly fat guy in the red suit knotted her stomach. She'd tried believing in him once and all she had gotten in the pink stocking she'd hung on the mantel were two chunks of Kingsford's charcoal—the kind without lighter fluid. On Christmas morning, while the other kids rode bicycles, tossed footballs, and combed Barbie's hair, Jillian received her message loud and clear.

You're a very bad girl.

No, Jillian didn't believe in magic or fairy tales or happily-ever-after endings, even though her three best friends, Delaney, Tish, and Rachael, had supposedly found their true loves after wishing on what they claimed was a magic wedding veil. Her friends had even dared pass the damnable veil along to her, telling Jillian it would grant her heart's greatest desire. But she wasn't falling for such nonsense. She snorted whenever she thought of the three-hundred-year-old lace wedding veil shoved away in a cedar chest along with her winter cashmere sweaters.

When it came to romance, Jillian was of the same mind as Ernest Hemingway: *When two people love each other there can be no happy ending.* Hemingway had known what he was talking about.

Not that Jillian could claim she'd ever been in love. She had decided a long time ago love was best avoided. She liked her life tidy and from what she'd seen of it, love was sprawling and messy and complicated. Besides, love required trust, and trust wasn't her strong suit.

Jillian did not believe in magic. What she did believe in was hard work, success, productivity, and justice. The closest she ever came to magic was in those glorious courtroom moments when a judge in a black robe read the jury's guilty verdict.

This morning in late September, dressed in a no-nonsense navy blue, pin-striped Ralph Lauren suit, a cream-colored silk blouse, and Jimmy Choo stilettos (to show off the shapely curve of her calves and add three inches to her already imposing five-foot-ten-inch height), Jillian stood at attention waiting for the verdict to be read.

On the outside, she looked like a dream prosecutor—statuesque, gorgeous, young, and smart. But underneath the clothes and the makeup and her cool, unshakable countenance, Jillian Samuels was still that same little girl who'd never rated a Christmas visit from Santa.

"Ladies and gentlemen of the jury, have you reached a verdict in this case?" Judge Atwood asked.

"We have, Your Honor," answered the foreman, a big slab of a guy with carrot-colored hair and freckled skin.

"Please hand your decision to the bailiff," the judge directed.

Jillian drew a breath, curled her fingernails into her palms. She felt slightly sick to her stomach, the way she did before the reading of every verdict.

The bailiff, a gangly, bulldog-faced middle-aged man with a Magnum P.I. mustache, walked the piece of paper across the courtroom to the judge's bench. Judge Atwood opened it, read it, and then glared at the defendant over the top of his reading glasses.

The defendant, twenty-three-year-old Randal Petry, had shot Gladys Webelow, an eighty-two-year-old great-grandmother, in the upper thigh while robbing a Dash and Go last Christmas Eve. Gladys had been buying a bottle of Correctol and a quart of two percent milk. He'd made off with forty-seven dollars from the cash register, a fistful of Slim Jims, and a twenty-four pack of Old Milwaukee.

"Will the defendant please rise?" Atwood handed the verdict back to the bailiff, who gave it to the jury foreman to read aloud.

Head held high, Petry got to his feet. The man was a scumbag, but Jillian had to admire his defiance.

"Randal LeRoy Petry, on the count of armed robbery you are found guilty as charged," the foreman announced.

As the foreman kept reading the verdicts on the other charges leveled against Petry, Jillian waited for the victorious wash of relief she always experienced when the word "guilty" was spoken. Waited for the happy sag to her shoulders, the warm satisfaction in her belly, the skip of victory in her pulse.

But the triumphant sensations did not come.

Instead, she felt numb, lifeless, and very detached, as if she were standing at the far end of some distant tunnel. Waiting...waiting...

For what, she didn't know.

People in the gallery were getting up, heading for the door. The court-appointed defense attorney collected his papers, stuffing them into his scuffed briefcase. The guards were hauling Petry off to jail. Judge Atwood left the bench.

And Jillian just kept standing.

Waiting.

It scared her. This non-feeling. This emptiness. Her fingernails bit into the flesh of her palms, but she couldn't feel that, either.

"You gonna stand there all day, Samuels, or what? You won, go knock back a shot of José Cuervo."

Jillian jerked her head around. Saw Keith Whippet, the prosecutor on the next case, waiting to take his place at her table. Whippet was as lean as his name, with mean eyes and a cheap suit.

"Chop, chop." He slammed his briefcase down on the desk. "I got people to fry."

"Yes," Jillian said, but she could barely hear herself. She was a bright kite that had broken loose from its tether, flying high into a cloudless blue sky. Up, up, and away, higher and higher, smaller and smaller. Soon she would disappear, a speck in the air.

What was happening to her?

She looked at Whippet, a weaselly guy who'd asked her out on numerous occasions. She'd shattered his hopes every single time until he'd finally given up. Now he was just rude. Whippet made shooing motions.

Jillian blinked, grabbed her briefcase, darted from the courtroom.

Blake.

She had to talk to her mentor, District Attorney Blake Townsend. He would know what to do. He'd tell her this feeling was completely normal. That it was okay if the joy was gone. She would survive.

Except it wasn't okay because her job was the only thing that gave her joy. If she'd lost the ability to derive pleasure from putting the bad guys behind bars, what did that leave her?

The thing was, she couldn't feel happy about jailing Petry because she knew there were thousands more like him. Knew the prisons were overcrowded and Petry would be released on good behavior after he'd served only a fraction of his sentence to make room for a new batch of Petrys.

She realized Petry would eventually be back on the streets to start all over again. The realization wasn't new. What was startlingly fresh was the idea that her work didn't matter. She was insignificant. The justice system was a turnstile and her arms were growing weary of holding open the revolving door.

She was so unsettled by the thought she found it difficult to catch her breath.

Blake. She needed to speak to Blake. Other than Delaney, Tish, and Rachael, Blake was the closest thing to family she could claim. He never lied to her, so she desperately needed to hear him say everything was going to be okay.

Anxiety pushing her, she rushed from the courthouse to the district attorney's office across the street, heels clacking a rapid rhythm against the sidewalk.

By the time she stepped into the DA's office, she was breathing hard and sweating. She caught a glimpse of her reflection in a window and saw that her sleek dark hair that she kept pulled back in a loose chignon had slipped from its clasp and was tumbling about her shoulders.

What was happening to her?

The whole room went suddenly silent and everyone stared in her direction.

"Is Blake in his office?" she asked his secretary, Francine Weathers.

Francine blinked. It was only then that Jillian noticed her reddened eyes. The woman had been crying. She stepped closer, the anxiety she'd been feeling morphing into real fear.

She stood there for a moment, panting, terrified, heart rapidly pounding, staring at Francine's round, middle-aged face. She knew something bad had happened before she even asked the question. "What's wrong?"

The secretary dabbed at her eyes with a Kleenex. "You haven't heard?"

A hot rush of apprehension raised the hairs on the nape of her neck. "Heard what? I've been in court. The Petry case."

"I..." Francine sniffed. "He..."

Jillian stepped closer and awkwardly put a hand on the older woman's shoulder. "Are you okay?"

Francine shook her head and burst into a fresh round of tears. Jillian dropped her hand. She'd never been very good at comforting people. She was the pit bull who went after the accused. Gentleness was foreign.

"This morning, Blake...he..." Francine began, hiccuped, sniffled into a tissue, and then finally whispered, "dropped dead in the middle of Starbucks while ordering a grande soy latte."

♥ ♥ ♥ ♥ ♥ ♥ ♥ ♥ ♥ ♥ ♥ ♥ ♥ ♥ ♥

From the desk of Lori Wilde

Dear Reader,

Starry-eyed Rachael Henderson from ADDICTED TO LOVE (on sale now) is mad as heck, and she's not going to take it anymore. After being stood up at the altar—*twice!*—on the very same day, she learns her parents are getting divorced after twenty-seven years, and it's the last straw. Born on Valentine's Day in Valentine, Texas, she's convinced she's been fed a line of bull about love. She's a romanceaholic, but no more! She's drawing a line in the sand. Determined to stomp out unrealistic ideas about love, she starts Romanceaholics Anonymous.

Except she never counted on one very sexy sheriff with a heart as big as Texas.

Take Rachael's test to see if you, too, might be a romanceaholic. And visit Rachael's Web site at www.romanceaholicsanonymous.com.

You might be a romanceaholic if:

- You replace the heroine's name with yours when reading a romance novel;
- You knock down bridesmaids to catch the bouquet;
- You go to the rodeo just to watch the wranglers in their Wranglers;

- You wear nothing but a black silk teddy and stilettos while cooking dinner;
- You have a wedding planner on speed dial;
- Your everyday dishes are Royal Doulton's ALLURE bone china;
- You purchase rose-colored prescription eyeglasses;
- Your voice mail says, "Leave a message, hug, hug, kiss, kiss";
- You've placed your phone number inside fortune cookies and passed them out to handsome single men;
- And, last but not least, you spray lavender on your sheets at night.

Hope you enjoy ADDICTED TO LOVE!

Lori Wilde

www.loriwilde.com